# Friend of China

The Marketeer: Part Three

Adrian Liley

copyright 2008 by Adrian Michael Liley

First published in Great Britain by Lulu Press
This paperback edition first published in 2008
Revised and Edited in 2017

All rights reserved. Adrian Liley asserts the moral right to be the seen as the author of this work

All characters in this publication are fictitious and any resemblance to real persons, living or dead, is purely coincidental... honestly.

All companies, institutions and schools named here are also totally fictitious and resemblance to real companies again is completely coincidental.

Adrian Liley also asserts that he actually really likes living in China quite a bit and that he hopes any Chinese people reading this novel have a broad sense of humour

Front Cover photograph of a window in 'Humble Administrator's Garden' in central Suzhou by Adrian Liley

Typeset in Palatino Lynotype

## The Marketeer Series:

*One: The Man in the Middle*

*Two: The Selling Game*

*Three: Friend of China*

*Four: The Long Road Home*

*Five: School without Scandal*

*Six: The Battle of Plumstead Marshes*

Author' note:
The Marketeer Series consists of: 'The Man in The Middle' and 'The Selling Game' forming one tale; 'Friend of China', 'The Long Road Home' and 'School without Scandal' another and the 'Battle of Plumstead Marshes' is a stand-alone tale.

# Friend of China

(The Marketeer: Part Three)


Acknowledgements

This book would not have been possible without...

Steve Liley, Jennifer Littlejohn, Tom Liley, Tammy and Tubby, Zhou Xing, Sue Coulthard, Steve Blewitt, Yvette Chu, Danny Chang, Frank Yuan, Teresa Lei, Yang Yang's Restaurant, Candi from Suzhou Starbucks, Rock Station DVD Shop, George Tang, William Xi, Bob Burger, Eddie Wu, Steve Brent, Murtagh Forde, Rich and John Smith, Lizzie, Michelle, Vivian and Harriet (Suzhou University teachers), Carl Hiaasen, Tim Dorsey, Dave Barry, Janet Evanovich, Terry Pratchett, Christopher Brookmyre, Bill Fitzhugh, PG Wodehouse, Evelyn Waugh, Old Speckled Hen, Abbott Ale, large currant scones, Friedrich Nietzsche, JRR Tolkien, Dan Simmonds, Starbuck's Grande cappuccino with chocolate sprinkles, Yumway's western breakfasts, taro ice cream, The Pudong Shangri-La Hotel in Shanghai, the ICEF, ALPHE and Study World English language workshops, the Chinese police, Eric Idle, The music of Yes, Pink Floyd, King Crimson, the Chengdu and Wolong Panda Reserves, the people of China

and yet again...

Gisela and Charles Liley (my parents)

Albert and Lizzie Liley (my grandparents)

and Geraldine Carton (my even more long-suffering wife)

And really finally... a very special thank you to: my good friend in London, Jackie Abbott, who was the first person to read Parts One and Two, cover to cover, and then to say nice things about the whole experience!

# A FEW MORE QUOTES

"The death penalty is very good for the environment."
(Chinese student's view on capital punishment)

"It's called the Yellow River, because it's brown."
(Philosophical Chinese taxi driver)

"The most terrible illness on Chinese campuses is cat abuse."
(from a speech on 'College Life' by a university student)

"It's our duty as Chinese citizens to charge foreigners double for their carrots and cabbages."
(Suzhou market trader)

"If you do something a little bad, the police will do a small inconvenience to you."
(Suzhou shopkeeper's view on the police force)

"Americans love peace, but war makes money for them, and they love money more than peace."
(Suzhou University student's view of the superpower)

"Animals have the same rights as humans, but unfortunately they are also very delicious."
(Suzhou University student on vegetarianism)

"The greatest person ever? Forget Shakespeare, Dickens, Confucius, Colonel Sanders or Beckham. It must be Michael Jackson. He has given so much to the children of today."
(Suzhou student's view on the greatest person ever to have lived)

"Confusion will be my epitaph."
(King Crimson – from a song called, unsurprisingly, 'Epitaph')

"I'm sorry to tell you this, but your country belongs to England."
(A Shanghai shopkeeper explaining basic geography to my Irish wife)

"In China there are many accidents where trucks run people over. There's not a lot we can do about that. We can't take the drivers' licences away. It's the only way they can make money."
(A Suzhou traffic policeman's practical view on traffic accidents)

"The tighter the sweater, the looser the girl."
(A fashion statement, courtesy of my mother - Gisela Liley)

"Radioactivity in small doses can be very beneficial to your health and can even cure diseases."
(Advertisement for a newly-opened spa in Suzhou)

"Carpets are very excellent for warmth, health and sound-proofing in your home, but best of all, they are very safe."
(A Suzhou salesman introducing the novel idea of carpeting to the Chinese public)

"I hope you'll forgive me, but when I started reading 'The Marketeer' I wasn't expecting the book of the century."
(Jennifer Littlejohn – a good friend living in Suzhou as well)

## What has gone before...

**"You need chaos in your soul to give birth to a dancing star."**
**Friedrich Nietzsche**

Percy Gabbitt lives in Bromley, South London and expects to lead a life of complete mediocrity as a junior sales executive at a rather doubtful English language school called the Royal English Language Institute (RELI), in Albemarle Street, Central London. That is until one evening, after a trustees dinner in Mayfair, he stumbles across a man in an alley who has been beaten up.

As Gabbitt attempts to help, he is approached by two large and very unsavoury characters, who claim to know the man and say they want to help as well.

In the next frantic few minutes Gabbitt's life is to change forever. The man passes Gabbitt a package and tells him to run...

'**The Man in the Middle**' is the first book of 'The Marketeer' series and tells the story of Percy Gabbitt's attempts to escape the clutches of a gangland mob run by a mysterious figure known only as 'The Voice; a multi-national Japanese conglomerate; American gangsters and the police led by the rather ineffective Inspector Pringle.

Gabbitt is sent on a marketing trip by his odious boss, Nero Nassington Handsworth, to the Far East and 'The Man in the Middle' ends after an unsuccessful attempt on his life by persons unknown in a Taipei hotel. A totally confused Gabbitt leaves Taipei for Seoul and the second leg of his Far East marketing trip.

The second book in he series, '**The Selling Game**' continues where The Man in the Middle left off. Gabbitt is in denial in Seoul. He can't still believe that there are people out there intent on causing him all manner of harm. So, he does what any sane Englishman would in the circumstances. He ignores the bullets and threats and… carries on doing his job, selling English language courses to a variety of bizarre Korean agents. He also meets a shady figure who sells suits, called Pep Musket.

On another level, Gabbitt is a member of the Bromley Gaming Society (BGS), which meets intermittently to play fantasy role-playing games on the living room carpets of its various strange, middle-aged members.

It is after one of these evenings that the characters of the latest quest take on a life of their own. Roger the Norse Fighter and Tammy the Goblin echo Gabbitt's traumas in the real world with their epic fights against the forces of evil in dungeons, caverns and orc-infested cave-systems.

Incidentally, for those of you not ued to the antics of Roger and Tammy, they are back again in "Friend of China', but have upraded themselves into the cyber world.

'The Selling Game' ends with a massive and confusing battle on Box Hill, south of London, which involves all the main protagonists along with an irate bull, a homicidal geriatric survivor of the last war, several Americans with enormous guns, an escaped panda and a clutch of people all dressed up as magicians and beastmen out for a day of fantasy in the hills around Reigate. The police are there in force as well and the story concludes with mayhem at the old signal fort at the hill's apex.

When the dust has settled, The Voice is unmasked as none other than Nero Handsworth, Gabbitt's boss. He suffers a mild heart attack on the hill while being arrested by Inspector Pringle. Gabbitt walks away, relieved that it is all over and he can return to a life of mediocrity.

Two years pass…

# PROLOGUE

*"When I woke up, it was tomorrow morning."*
**From a Suzhou University student's examination paper**

...Five, six, seven, eight....

I'm still counting.

And the slop bucket needs emptying again.

But they won't come for another three hours or so.

I'm still in the city of Suzhou in deepest China, residing in a small cell in the local prison in the centre of the city, which is why I have a slop bucket next to my bed. I think I'm the only foreigner in the place, but don't really know for sure. Actually, I haven't met any other inmates, Chinese or whatever... although I've heard them. Well, I've heard one, anyway.

As for me? All I've done is a bit of sales and marketing – hardly a crime, even in China. But then again...

I push the slop bucket to the door and sit down on my narrow bunk bed. It creaks rustily.

I know it is three hours before a guard will appear even though I don't have a watch. I have what I call a spit clock. It's all I have. Oh, it's not my spit, by the way.

Actually, I've been rather clever. Let me explain. There's a primary school next door to Suzhou's prison and I know that every day they do their eye exercises at exactly eleven o'clock. Eye exercises? Well, all children below the age of ten have five minutes massaging their own eyes to music under draconian teacher supervision in their classrooms. The idea is keep their eyes strong and healthy, while still soft and young.

But what's all that got to do with me in here and my spit clock? Well, every day at eleven sharp the music begins. So... I have a start point. My days begin at eleven with the children's eyes.

Now, how do I work out the time for rest of the day? This is the tricky part. This is where my neighbour comes in. My very unhealthy neighbour. Put simply, he spits extremely regularly.

So, I count to sixty as carefully as I can, noting that he coughs up twice during this period. I then repeat the experiment again and again to make sure. Interestingly, it is always two times. I like counting, as you may recall – I think it keeps my brain occupied and relatively sane.

Anyway… I think you can work out where I am going with this. My spit clock is in place. Rather crude, I know, but effective. Something like a sundial without the sun… or the dial. More like a metronome where the tick-tock pointer is actually the insides of my neighbour's lungs.

All I have to do is make a mark in pencil on the wall every time he does two spits. I then have my minute marker!

The great thing about it is that he never stops – he's as regular as clockwork. Never a frantic spitting attack to make the time race in my cell, or never a healthy moment to make time drag over here. No, it's spit and spit again – twice a minute.

So, it's three hours or three hundred and sixty spits until the slop bucket gets emptied.

Tick-tock, tick-tock, cough, splutter, hawk…

I run a grubby hand through my long lank hair and stare at the ceiling. Cough… spit.

A guard arrives. I can hear him shuffling down the corridor. Cough… spit. The door opens two feet and a voice speaks from the corridor.

"Paper," he says as he eases a few sheets into my cell under the door with his boot. Cough…spit.

"Why?" I try. I am genuinely interested to know why my guardians keep giving me so much of the stuff. Cough… spit.

"Yes," comes an enthusiastic reply through the door.

"Paper? Why?" I cry out in vain. Cough… spit. There are not many more ways that you can ask the same thing in a different and more understandable way when you can't even see your fellow conversationist, who clearly cannot speak English. Cough… spit.

"Much paper you like - no problem," is the frustrating response.

"What you want me write?" I ask, resorting to Yoda English. Cough… spit.

"Good," comes the muffled reply. "Tell things good now. He wants good. And many paper here," concludes the guard and walks away from my cell door laughing deliriously. Cough… spit.

Ah, a confession.

The swines expect me to write a confession.

"Why are you doing this to me?" I croak at the closed door. Cough… spit.

The guard is long gone and total silence engulfs the cell.

I run a hand through my hair again and feel like weeping. Cough… spit.

Solitary confinement. I thought that that sort of thing was reserved for the really violent or totally undesirable in society – the mass murderers, the psychopaths and other perverted deviants. Not marketing people. Or maybe the Chinese just lump us in with the worst of them. After all, marketing and sales are the foundation pillars of a capitalist economy.

But there's been a slight change in my conditions recently. About forty thousand spits ago. I'm not locked up in here all the time. I get an hour a day to walk outside in a yard between high walls. It usually snows or rains when I'm allowed this privilege, while it's blazing sunshine when I'm locked up here in my own personal urinal. But that's China for you. Even the weather disapproves of foreigners who have transgressed.

And I have my paper and a pen. Freedom of sorts, I suppose. Freedom of the mind. I can travel anywhere I like as long as it's in my head. Great.

I'm in my mid-twenties, have brown hair which always needs washing, I like inoffensive rock music like Snow Patrol, Coldplay, early Yes, Pink Floyd and Genesis, lower division football and taking photographs. I don't say photography because this implies that I'm quite good at it. OK, so you've taken a mild dislike to me already, but at least I'm man enough to admit these faults.

I also have had a variety of jobs in a small career, which has included language teaching and sales and marketing. You probably really are beginning to hate me now, but just a minute... I actually am not that fond of the sales and marketing thing either, so give me a break. There may be the odd redeeming feature tucked away in the next page or so.

And I'm in prison in China, so some might say that I've got what I deserved.

Anyway, the marketing bit was the lowest point of my life, until I was put behind bars here. It introduced me to a certain Nero Handsworth, probably the most odious man on the planet and someone who nearly got me killed on more than one occasion. I'm safe from him now since he's locked away in a tiny cell somewhere in London, while I'm incarcerated in a cell of similar dimensions on the other side of the planet. Nice irony that. The most despicable man alive is locked up in a cosy British gaol, while I'm in solitary in a Chinese slammer. Very ironical, that.

Still, I should thank my lucky stars that the chances of our paths crossing in the near future are distinctly remote. This is one of the positive sides to my current predicament.

I smile.

All that was two and a half years ago, I think. A lifetime. And long forgotten by nearly everybody.

But not by me.

Box Hill.

Ah yes, Box Hill. That dreadful place somewhere south of the M25 covered in those repulsive, gnarled box trees, which reek of cat urine when rained on…

I don't remember very much of that at all. Well I do actually, but mostly at about three in the morning just before I wake up screaming and in a pool of sweat. My brain tends to shut down on Box Hill related topics even when I'm fast asleep.

Box Hill.

My brain jumps a few points and is in a siding… thinking different thoughts.

Totally unrelated thoughts.

Memories of Caroline Williams telling a riddle bobs to the surface of my mind. A neat little thought amid the untidy flotsam and jetsam. Pinch don't rub, she said.

Now she's telling a riddle involving an arm in a box in a desert.

Any takers on that one?

No, I didn't think so.

Box Hill.

England.

What I like to recall mostly as I lie in this hot and stuffy hell-hole is the smell of an autumn in England even if it was on Box Hill, or Box Hell as I now call it. The mown grass, the leaves turning red and yellow, icy ditches, a raw wind… anything that gets me away from thinking of a Chinese prison cell with the heaters on maximum, day and night, while outside it's snowing. Perhaps this is just another example of oriental torture. Boil the inmates, while people are dropping from hypothermia in the streets just a few feet away.

Box Hill. No, not Box Hill.

Let's think about red and yellow leaves. England in the autumn - the musty aroma of damp trees, the earthiness of frosty ditches and that crispy tingle to everything as night falls.

Box Hill.

The bull – I never did find out how that got loose up there, the maniacs with the rocket launcher, the Americans, the Japanese, the tank. The bloody tank. And lots of beastmen, goblins and magicians. Not forgetting the panda. Panda? I'm starting to sweat again.

I sigh.

Get a grip.

Best forgotten.

Postmodernism gets a passing nod as well. Not sure why. Selling stuff in a principled way. I frown. Bastard idea. That's what got me in here.

The end of my story…

…Well, not quite.

There's still the small matter of how I wound up here.

I'll tell all in a minute.

Another good question - how long have I been in here?

Three months? Six?

Or is it still just a few weeks?

Or days?

Who knows?

I only started the spit clock about a hundred and twenty thousand spits ago.

What must that man's lungs look like? Worse still, what must his spit bucket look like?

Who cares how long?

Well, I do… but probably no one else does. Still no visit from the British Consul or even a Chinese policeman with enough English to explain the situation. And still not officially charged… I think. Although they might have done all this in Chinese – I wouldn't have known.

But I'm talking to myself now and asking lots of stupid questions which I know I can't answer.

And sometimes I'm shouting them worryingly loudly in this little cell.

That can't be good either.

Insanity beckons.

It's probably doing a lot more than beckoning actually. Pushing me with both hands into the back of the little green van and tying me down, more like…

I lie back on my bed and dream of crispy tingles, damp trees. Cough… spit.

…a dark chocolate digestive biscuit pops into my mind.

I sigh again.

Insanity beckons with a nasty smile.

I can't get Box Hell out of my mind for some reason. Cough… spit.

It's like a Wombles pop song.

Once there, it goes round and round and round in my skull, until I think I'm Uncle Bulgaria. Cough… spit.

Box Hell.

Underground, over-ground, Wombling free. Cough… spit.

I sit up and stare at the mashed potato clouds far beyond my window. Oh, I have a window. My link with the madness out there. It's very high on the wall opposite my bed. And quite small and grubby. Cough… spit.

Uncle Bulgaria...

Box Hell.

So, you want to know how I got in here? Well, even if you don't, I'm going to tell you, so tough.

I pick up the slightly crumpled piece of paper and reach for a pencil.

I scribble just five words on the sheet.

**The End**
**Well... not quite**

Cough… spit.

# ONE

*"Most criminals are unconscious at the moment they pull the trigger."*

**(Suzhou University student's degree research paper on 'Capital Punishment')**

## Six Months Previously, somewhere in London

Summer in London. It was raining hard. Chucking, bucketing and stair-rodding it down so that drops bounced a full six inches up off the pavement. Everything wet, cool, windy and very unpleasant.

Leaden clouds scudded across the sky to make room for the next storm centre to move in.

And that's mid-August in London.

Down on the streets of London in an area called Holborn, a man was walking purposefully towards a squat building, which could have been a Victorian workhouse in another age. He smiled and looked up at the red brick edifice and a broken piece of guttering six floors up, which was allowing a small waterfall to cascade down the building and onto a row of parked bicycles below.

He walked in through the main entrance and grinned winningly at the Reception desk. He then strode for the elevators. No one said anything or shouted a challenge of any sort. No, that would not happen. That never happened. No one ever stopped fat men in a hurry. It was just not done.

He chuckled to himself as an argument broke out behind him. Someone was shouting in a very bad Russian accent that he wanted his money back or he would call the police and the army.

It was turning out to be rather too easy.

The elevator doors hummed open. He walked in and spotted a man in smart suit running for the lift as well. He pressed the 'Hold' button to keep the doors from closing. No sense in being unnecessarily nasty, he thought.

"Thanks a million," said the man as he tumbled into the lift. The doors clicked shut.

"Uno, dos, tres, er, four, five, sex?" asked the fat man in a bad Peruvian accent.

"Tres," said the man in the suit, after a brief pause as he tried to think in limited Spanish. The man then adjusted his tie, wiped a layer of sweat from a glistening brow and looked at his Spanish-speaking companion. "Nice day," he said in a way that implied that it clearly was not.

"Si senor," said the fat man with rather too much of a Mexican inflection.

"Where-do-you-come-from?" asked the man in the smart suit as they reached the first floor. Clearly this was a man who found silences unbearable in enclosed spaces.

"Keelburn," was the reply, now in Colombian Spanish.

"Argentina?" queried the man in the suit.

"Si," came the response in broad Catalan, after a thoughtful pause.

"Thought so. I've been there," said the man, extending a hand. "Conference a few years back. Nice women there, if you know what I mean." He gave the man a wink.

"Si," was the predictable response, now in 'haut' Spanish.

"Are-you-learning-English-here?"

"Si."

"How-long-you stay-here. amigo?"

"Si."

There was another short silence and then the doors opened on 'Tres'.

The man in the suit hit the 'Keep Door Open' button. He clearly had not finished. "Me Director," he said in pidgin English. "Any-problem-speak-to-my-secretary. Her-door-always-open. Have-a-nice-day… senor."

The doors hummed shut and the man smiled.

"Prat," said the fat man to the closed door. Kilburn in Argentina. Maybe there was a Willesden in Uruguay as well. Prat. Speak to my secretary. Lazy bastard. He slowly shook his head and then closed his eyes in preparation.

The doors opened to the fifth floor and he strode into a large open-plan area filled with computer stations and the typical detritus of an office. Cuddly toys under table lamps, executive stress balls on mouse mats and the usual array of family and pet photographs looked up at him as he made his way through the office.

He eventually found a workstation in a nicely-secluded corner and sat down. It was clearly a marketing or sales desk. Two stuffed bears sat squatly under the screen. They had silk sashes across their furry tummies proclaiming to the world - *'English for the World with LICE'*. He frowned and suddenly felt a pang of sorrow for the little creatures.

Next to them was a Star Trek badge (circa Next Generation) perched on top of a Perspex cube containing a glutinous blue liquid with a small plastic surfer riding any wave that came along when the cube was picked up and vigorously shaken. Definitely a sales person, he thought.

He looked at his watch. Perfect timing. Nearly everyone was at lunch or away from their desks. It could not have been easier.

He tapped away at the computer keyboard and accessed a system called ELOISE. The computer had a long think about allowing him in, but then started flashing up a menu of rather nice possibilities. No password protection. Unbelievable.

Two blond secretaries walked into the office chatting squeakily about the new range of fat-free food on offer at the sandwich shop down the road. He sank down in his chair and hid behind the large screen.

The mailing base popped up and he quickly highlighted the top thousand email addresses and copied them into an email address box. This was going to be the biggest email message of the week, he thought slyly.

A moment later and he was tapping away furiously. The message began:

**URGENT NEW INFORMATION FROM THE DIRECTOR OF THE LONDON INTERNATIONAL COLLEGE OF EDUCATION (LICE)**

**I am sorry to have to inform you that we will be closing operations at the school for the autumn months of October and November due to an unforeseen outbreak of Green Monkey Disease.**

**I should hasten to add that this unfortunate situation was not caused by any employees or teachers at LICE in any way at all, but was the introduced into the school by several members of a Korean group recently staying here.**

**Naturally, we understand that this will be very inconvenient for you, but suggest that you divert all future bookings to our neighbouring school – Languages Are Us, which will provide an excellent service for these two months, while we fumigate our school completely...**

He wrote two more shorter paragraphs which described a novel refund policy, which he had thought up in the taxi on the way to the school, and a special offer to all agents consisting of forty per cent commission for the remainder of the year as recompense for the inconvenience caused.

Very nice, he thought. A disease blamed on the Koreans and all business diverted to a competitor, not to mention a commission increase and the refunds. Very nice indeed. He hit the Send button and accessed the next thousand addresses. Five minutes later and ten thousand emails had been shot out from his terminal to places as far afield as Fukuoka in Japan to Recife in Brazil. A good day's work, he thought and sat back in his chair.

And now the 'coup de grace'.

He pulled a CD from his pocket and slid it into the computer tower. A few moments passed and the system was impregnated with something called the 'Synergy' virus - a rather vicious little thing which kicked into action whenever the user wrote any of the following key words: 'total commitment', 'fact-finding', 'benchmarking', 'pro-active', 'cutting-edge', 'highly-motivated', 'full-immersion' and 'synergy' of course.

He was rather proud of these trigger words. – the detritus of a society which made the greasy art of selling into a grubby science.

He reckoned that it should take all of about one minute after lunch for the user of this machine to tap at least one of these phrases.

It was a very simple virus too - a virus which immediately expunged all instances of the letters 't', 'r', 'u' and 'h' from the computer's hard drive.

He had wanted to spell the word 'truth' out for all to see when the system was eventually restored, but unfortunately, there had to be two letter t's in the damn word. They would have to settle for 'truh' and worry about that little cryptic message instead. Knowing this lot, they would probably miss the point entirely and re-arrange the letters to form the word 'hurt'. He sighed. Marketing and sales had a lot to answer for in the modern world.

The real beauty of the virus was that when typed and thoroughly infiltrated into the computer system, it then hopped to other computers on the same network if the key words 'No Refund' were ever typed. Again, he reckoned this would take about ten minutes of the user's typing time after lunch. It was that sort of school.

And now for the cherry on the cake, he thought happily. He pulled a pair of yellow plastic washing-up gloves from a jacket pocket, slipped them on and then proceeded to press his fingers on as many parts of the computer as he could. He even did a small finger waltz across the screen.

"And Mr Percy Gabbitt does it again," he whispered to himself and then pulled the gloves off and put them away in his jacket pocket.

Finally, he trousered the disk from the computer tower and popped the two sad-looking bears into his jacket pocket. No sense in leaving them in such a miserable place, he thought rather kindly, proving that even bastards like him had a heart of sorts.

He turned the computer off and slipped out of his seat. A job well done, he thought and walked to the lift and a pint at the pub opposite where he would meet Jack, given that he had finished his diversionary argument with the good people at Reception.

## Meanwhile... somewhere on the other side of the planet

Summer in China. It was shimmeringly hot and humid. Not that you could see the sun or blue skies up above. The thick yellow dusty pollution prevented that little pleasure. But the heat got through, no problem.

But that's mid-August in China... or more precisely, the small city of Suzhou, which lies just up the line from downtown Shanghai.

The temperature had just topped thirty-six degrees, the humidity was about three hundred per cent and it was dull-ochre, grittily-sandy, sickly-puce and dingily-yellow overhead. The chemical factories down the road were to blame for that.

Far down below and plodding along a crowded street, a very sweaty Englishman was not thinking about the weather. He had other problems on his mind. Problems of a very different nature.

He had just been asked the unanswerable question.

"Do you think I pretty?"

Percy Gabbitt looked down at a small Chinese woman. She had shortish black hair cut in a traditional Chinese bob. She also had very red lipstick, thick blue eye shadow and was wearing one of those slinky satin Chinese jackets, which were usually covered in angry red and gold dragons. But hers was not - it was a rather tasteful violet and had gold trimmings. There weren't any dragons either – not even on her back. Her skirt was slinky too and short. Very short. Breathtakingly short.

Gabbitt looked up and down the street. A small crowd had begun to gather. It was not often that they got a bit of street theatre involving a foreigner. Something clearly not to be missed.

"I think you think I pretty," said the girl, with a massive smile.

"Is that what you think?" muttered Gabbitt, worriedly. He did not like it when people started thinking for him. It generally meant several steps in a direction he would never dream of taking.

"I think so," came the artful reply. The lipstick parted slightly to reveal a row of snow-white teeth.

"Maybe you are," said Gabbitt, guardedly. "But I think I go now," he tried and attempted to walk off slowly but decisively, as any Englishman would.

"I think you buy me small drink maybe now. I think you think you be crazy man to walk away from pretty girl like me."

"Well, I..." responded Gabbitt, as he gamely wrestled with who was thinking about what.

He was interrupted by an arm being placed around his waist and then a gentle pull being exerted towards the entrance of 'Big Boy Bar' which gleamed in purple neon splendour just ten feet away from where Gabbitt stood with his new girlfriend.

"No, I don't think..." squawked Gabbitt.

"Yes, I think you think I think same as you think..." trilled pageboy-bob.

"No, I really must..."

The doors to Big Boy Bar suddenly flew open and three large women bundled into the street. They all headed for Gabbitt and took up strategic positions to prevent a rapid getaway. One had very long black hair and a face like a small badly-nourished and deranged pony. Another had bright orange hair permed into an electric fuzz like an afro-cut done by someone who hated Jamaicans. The third had blond hair and a face shaped like a massive white moon... with pimples. All three had dark, hypnotic eyes and wore similar shimmering Chinese satin dresses which had deep slashes on either side which ended about half a mile above the knee.

The one with the orange afro-cut had dragons on her back. Gabbitt instinctively moved a step away from her.

There was flurry of Chinese and then a lot of laughter.

Gabbitt relaxed. Perhaps they had just realised that all this was just a misunderstanding and now he could go on his way.

He was still thinking this a few minutes later as he sat down on a green velvet stool near a plate glass window which looked out onto the street crucially from within Big Boy Bar.

Pageboy, Afro-Cut, Pimply-Moon and Deranged-Pony were all gathered around him. A barman appeared out of nowhere and suddenly four large Tsingtao beers were being emptied into tall glasses before Gabbitt.

"But I..."

"Thank you," squeaked the girls in unison.

The barman, a sleek creature in a tuxedo with lizard eyes, immediately reached for a bottle of vodka on a back shelf and glugged the contents into four large tumblers. He then added one small ice cube to each and winked at Deranged-Pony. She pretended not to notice and turned her full attention to Gabbitt, who was quickly measuring the distance between his seat and the door.

"I like American," crooned Afro-Cut happily.

"Much money," chipped in Pimply-Moon.

"I think I like too," said Pageboy.

"You pretty boy," laughed Deranged-Pony, sipping at her vodka.

"I think I..." began Gabbitt and started to climb off the stool.

"You from New York?" queried Pimply-Moon seriously. It was said like it was the most important question she had ever asked in her life.

"No," replied Gabbitt. "Northampton."

"Ah, North - Hamp - Ton," they all said, like they knew their Northamptons just as well as their Shanghais and Nanjings.

"In England," continued Gabbitt, impatiently.

"Ah," they said again.

"I'm English... not American," he said, a little limply.

"Ah."

They all reached for their glasses and supped quietly for a few moments. Deranged-Pony looked a little crest-fallen, if truth be told. She stared up at Gabbitt and whispered slowly:

"So, you have no money?"

"Ah," said Gabbitt quietly.

Clearly, they did know their Northamptons.

There was a long and very thoughtful pause. Gabbitt sighed loudly and stood up. Time to go, he thought.

"Evening Mr Northampton," said a very un-Chinese voice from within a shady alcove to one side of the bar.

Gabbitt started. It was not every day in China that you hear a distinctly western voice cutting through the tortured Chinglish.

"Hello," said Gabbitt, still very much on his guard.

A figure emerged from the darkness. It was squat, blond-haired and was wearing a garish Hawaiian shirt, khaki shorts, white socks and black shoes. It also clutched a bottle of imported lager.

An Australian, thought Gabbitt, as he surveyed the fashion-wreck, slightly nervously.

The man growled a few words in what sounded like Chinese and the girls melted away into the background of Big Boy Bar.

"Time to pay up and leave, I think," said the Aussie and pulled out a wad of red notes which he then placed onto the bar.

"How much do I..." began Gabbitt reaching for some hundred yuan notes from an inside pocket.

"Keep the good Chairman in your pocket, mate. This one's on me."

"Are you sure?" mumbled Gabbitt, as he made for the door.

"Best you keep your money nicely tucked away or you'll find that it's suddenly all disappeared. A drink in here can cost a year's salary if they think you're both an American and a bit... green."

"Green?"

"Well, new to China?"

"I've been here two weeks."

"And not lost all your money yet?"

"No," said Gabbitt sulkily.

They were out on the street again and walking away from Big Boy Bar towards the bright lights of a crossroads.

"Lucky then," sniffed the Australian Hawaiian. "Just remember the golden rule here. Never go anywhere called a bar, especially if the place is filled with pretty girls and is virtually pitch black inside or, worse still, red or pink."

"I'll remember that," said Gabbitt.

"The name's Bob. Bob Irwin. We should have a proper drink sometime. Here's my card. See you around."

And with that, Bob Irwin suddenly bobbed across the street deftly avoiding a cyclo-taxi driver, an electric bike and a taxi. They all hooted at him angrily, but Bob just waved happily back at them and disappeared into the steaming mass of humanity on the other side of the street.

Gabbitt frowned. Strange man, he thought. Rescues me from a fate worse than death, then pays for my drink and finally gives me a lot of rather patronizing advice about what not to do in China.

He had never understood Australians. Perhaps no one ever did - even fellow Australians. He stared for a moment or two at the business card that Irwin had given him. Bob's job seemed ominously innocuous.

*Bob Irwin – Marketing Manager*
*Arapacana Associates*

Strange name for a company, thought Gabbitt - probably the name of a dwarf crocodile, down-under. He stuffed the card into a back pocket.

He reached the crossroads and walked over a small bridge before ducking down a side alley and in through a small glass door above which was written:

## Ock Stat on

Gabbitt had only been in Suzhou ten days, but even he had worked out that the shop had lost it's 'R' and 'i' and was in fact called either 'Rock Station'... or 'iock StatRon' depending on how bloody-minded you were feeling.

This was the usual haven for foreigners out for a stroll and with nothing really to do on a Friday evening.

Gabbitt nodded to the old lady at a counter by the door and made for a rack opposite her. He then pulled out a small vinyl folder upon which was written *'Hairy Botter and the Filofaxical Stain'*. He smirked and pulled another out. *'The Load ov the Rungs: Pert Too. The Tow Towels'*.

Percy Gabbitt was standing in that emporium of culture; that purveyor of gems from the silver screen; that seller of dreams... the rip-off, bootleg DVD store.

Every movie ever made and available for just fifty pence a throw. And not just Hollywood movies either. On the top shelves were rank upon rank of small cardboard boxes all stuffed with the latest Stir Trick series, CSE capers... even Dictor Why. And you could get the whole 'Fiends' omnibus (series one to ten thousand) for just about twenty quid, should you be so inclined.

The quality might not be A1, but well, what did you expect for fifty pence? To be honest, this sometimes leant to the appeal of the whole bootleg DVD thing. It was amusing to realise that the film just purchased was recorded by some poor soul on a hand-held camcorder somewhere in a Hong Kong movie theatre.

It added to the mood of the occasion when King Bong was about to lay waste to New York and you suddenly spotted a shadow to the bottom right of your screen standing up to leave the movie theatre. Priceless stuff. Unintended Woody Allen. Accidental David Lynch.

Gabbitt pulled out the four *'Hay Lion'* films. He rather fancied watching Cigar-Knee Weavil doing her stuff again against the most vindictive creatures in the galaxy. All four films for two quid. Not bad at all. Would she manage to defeat the vicious stellar hay lion again? He smiled. The evening was looking up. He read the back cover. Apparently, a Loss Angina movie reviewer had given the series: 'Two thumbs all the way up!'

"You want new release?" enquired a heavily-garlicked voice from about three millimetres from his left ear.

Gabbitt started and dropped: *'Stir Whores II: Attack of the Cloves'* onto the floor.

"Back room," continued the voice. "Door in my backside."

Gabbitt frowned. To be ushered into any kind of back rooms by a whispering Chinaman with bad breath and a door in his backside was not really very high on his list of priorities that evening. He had already had one questionable experience and was feeling a bit obstinate and considerably wary. He continued flicking through another row of DVDs, feeling slightly intruded upon.

"Best quality for valued customers. Special DVDs," hissed the voice again. "DVD9," it finished, as if this was the argument-winner.

Percy Gabbitt slowly turned round and stared at the clandestine whisperer. He was a shortish man with a full head of hair, a pale complexion, a large grin and a dangling cigarette. He must have been about twenty-five years old and probably had lived in the DVD shop his entire life. The smile grew broader.

"No problem to have a just-looking," he said with a gleam in his eye.

Gabbitt sighed and looked at the shop's backside. Sure enough, there was a door which led to another room. A door which promised a mountain of special DVDs – even DVD9s. It was covered in posters depicting a bald Brute Willie shooting men with moustaches and wielding guns the size of mini metros.

"DVD9?" queried Gabbitt as if he knew what he was talking about.

"DVD9," came the emphatic response.

Well, thought Gabbitt, there can't be any harm in a 'just-looking', can there? And anyway, he would probably find out what a DVD9 was and why it was better than a DVD7 or an 8.

"OK," he shrugged as confidently and non-committedly as he could and wandered slowly to the door.

In hindsight, Gabbitt would ruminate that this was probably the worst decision he had made in a long time. A decision which began the ball of destiny rolling again. A decision which dusted Damocles' sword down and repositioned it, dangling from a thin cord, a millimetre from the top of Gabbitt's head. It was, quite simply, a dreadful decision.

*Roger the Norse Fighter sighed deeply. He was not at all happy about sitting behind a desk wearing a tartan jacket and a dark blue silk tie. It did not really fit with the image of being a heroic warrior. He too was thinking about dreadful decisions.*

*"Very nice," said a small figure in a maroon dressing gown beside him. It clapped its hands and grinned maniacally. "We'll make a gentleman of you yet."*

*"A gentleman Norse Fighter," said Roger as sarcastically as a heroic warrior could and sighed again.*

*"Yes, a gentleman barbarian!" exclaimed Tammy the Goblin dramatically. "You'll be a barbaric oxymoron," he said and laughed loudly.*

*"I don't think I like your tone," muttered Roger dangerously, as he wondered what sort of moron could be considered as an oxy. He then wondered what an oxy was and realised he did not have the faintest idea. He did know what a moron was though and had killed people for less.*

*He sighed a third time and looked hard at the smiling goblin standing within slicing range of the heavy broadsword which should have been swinging from his waist. How he longed for his loincloth, a leather belt and… his sword.*

*"It's just a figure of speech," said Tammy. "You're a walking contradiction. A sum of complete opp…"*

*"Well, I've had enough," interrupted Roger, standing up and taking his tie off. "It's time to draw a line in the sand. I will not start wearing these ridiculous clothes and carrying a small case around filled with worthless paper."*

*Tammy sighed deeply. It was not easy civilising a beast more used to filleting Minotaurs in deep necropolises.*

*"Well, all right," he said quietly. "The tie can go, but please keep the jacket. It makes you look... managerial."*

*"I don't want to look managerial," said Roger tersely. "I want to look frightening."*

*"You look frightening in that tartan jacket," said Tammy, truthfully.*

*"I will not..." began Roger angrily.*

*He was interrupted by a door opening and the sleek form of a violet coloured banshee gliding soundlessly into the room. It paused expectantly, as it reached Roger's desk.*

*"What is it, Susie?" asked Tammy impatiently. "Can't you see we are in an executive meeting?"*

*"Nice jacket," she whispered as she eyed Roger not a little lasciviously.*

*Roger sighed again and slumped down into a deep velvet armchair.*

*"Bad news!" said the banshee, suddenly rather seriously. Banshees were like that. Every sentence contained a different mood.*

*"What?" murmured Roger sulkily. "The beastmen want a bigger cafeteria? The place has been invaded by goblin oxy-mormen? You have tonsillitis?" Roger was feeling slightly sarcastic in his tartan jacket.*

*"Oh no," replied Susie, eyebrows raised. "The beastmen are delighted with their new dining facilities, especially with the fast food hatch. Don't know about goblin Mormen, but I can assure you that banshees never catch tonsil..."*

*"What is your news?" asked Tammy impatiently.*

*The banshee shifted noiselessly from side to side looking slightly uncomfortable.*

*"It's your sister, Bunty," she whispered, as tears began to well. "She's disappeared."*

Caroline Williams sat down at her desk and turned her computer on. While it warmed up she went to her kitchen, made herself a weak cup of Twining's Earl Grey tea and took two McVitie's dark chocolate digestive biscuits from a tin on a low shelf. She then returned to her living room.

The computer was ready and waiting.

Caroline had a small sip and began tapping. After a moment, it beeped authoritatively and Caroline was deep into cyberspace.

<Hi Percy? R U there?>

She smirked and raised an eyebrow at her usage of the R and U. Maybe if Gabbitt upset her enough, she would be able to throw in 'asi9'. She rather hoped so. She stared at the screen for a few moments.

Nothing. There was a long pause. Then more nothing. Caroline continued to stare at the screen as she nibbled the chocolate off one of her biscuits. Still lots of nothing. She frowned a little. Clearly Percy was not there despite their regular daily arrangement. Perhaps he had been delayed? Maybe his computer had crashed. Or the Chinese police had closed him down? A visitor at his door could be distracting him?

Or...he had forgotten.

Caroline frowned very hard indeed and then typed the same line again, only this time inserting a small yellow Smiley which was doing the opposite to smiling. Still nothing. She closed down her Messenger box in a fit of pique.

She sighed, folded her arms, pushed her long chestnut her behind an ear and looked at the empty screen. She was not happy. And when she was not happy there was only one answer.

She ran her cursor down her Favourites Menu and tapped onto a button entitled: 'Mega Games Supremo'. A moment later a multi-coloured mountain range appeared on her screen covered in complex written instructions. She pressed 'Enter' and stepped into the world of 'Supremo', ready to do battle with glyphs from Brazil to Burma, America to Angola and Chile to China. A menu bar appeared at the side of her screen and she scrolled down to her chosen game. Two sips and one crunch later and she was ready for an evening's combat in the fantasy world of Dark Dawn Three.

Caroline looked hard at the screen, frowned again and thought bad thoughts of Percy Raymond Gabbitt. So, he really had forgotten their arrangement.

She sipped again at her tea, shrugged Gabbitt out of her mind and typed in her code name.

The Snark Maiden picked up her elf's bow and marched into action.

"The police are entering me now," whispered a voice urgently.

Gabbitt started and look up from the collected works of Alfred Hatchback.

A small shop assistant was looking round the door with eyes like a hungry goldfish. "Best you find back door as quick as fox in henhouse and leave through my back passage," it continued worriedly. The face then disappeared and the door clicked shut.

Gabbitt gulped. He stared at a picture of James Sewage running from a low-flying plane on the front cover of the DVD9 version of *'Snore by Snore-Vest'*, and knew how Mr Sewage felt. Quickly, he made his way to the door which led back into the shop and opened it slowly, just a fraction of an inch. He looked through the small crack. What he saw made him swallow hard again and then close the door immediately.

Three large Chinese policemen in dark blue uniforms with matching peaked hats were manhandling the assistant out of the door and towards the back of a white police van. Meanwhile, another two Chinese constables were packing DVDs into a large cardboard box by the entrance door.

Percy Gabbitt moved around a stack of distinctly adult movies and made for the door to the back passage. As he reached the door his arm brushed the pile of DVDs and down they went. The noise was like someone dropping a pile of plates onto a hard, concrete floor. DVDs with blurred images of naked people with too many legs and impossible breasts thrashing about on fluffy orange rugs, spilled in all directions.

He dived into the alley outside, tripped on an uneven flagstone and fell against a damp wall, bruising a shoulder and dropping his bag. As he recovered his balance and as his eyes became accustomed to the darkness all about, he heard shouts from the interior of the DVD shop. This was clearly not a moment to be caught by the police in a back room surrounded by a million copies of 'Donkey Man meets the Pussycat'. Not for the first time in his life Percy Gabbitt sprinted as fast as could down an alley towards a dim light in the distance.

What he had not realised as he sped the scene were two things. First, he had not been able to retrieve his multi-purpose daypack by the back door of the shop and second, and more importantly, was that the light which seem to signify freedom came from a rather bulky torch held by an equally bulky Chinese policeman, who had been stationed there by the inspector who was carrying out the raid.

# TWO

*"We Chinese say that Suzhou is Paradise on Earth. It is also famous for having the prettiest girls in China, because it rains so much."*

**(Suzhou greengrocer waxing lyrically over his watermelons)**

Suzhou was a very pretty city.

Many thousands of years ago it gleamed out as a watery jewel on the way from Nanjing to Shanghai. Some called it Paradise of Earth, others said it was the Venice of China. That was then.

In the twenty-first century beauty is interpreted in a completely different way. It's not enough to have a hundred ancient, narrow canals criss-crossing the city, all nicely connected by those rather dinky stone bridges the Chinese are so fond of. It's also not enough to have quite a few pretty gardens – pretty that is if you are into bizarre rock formations, winding concrete paths and dark ponds stocked with millions of laconic goldfish. Quite frankly, it's just not enough to be pretty and old. The twenty-first century tourist needs more.

And this is what the city's elders have realised and have set about correcting. So, the city centre looks a bit like a brickie's backyard, at the moment, after a particularly large delivery of sand and breezeblocks.

Suzhou will probably be a beautiful city again but, it is in a state of flux as it struggles to modernise ancient canals and gardens in a tasteful but ultimately tourist-driven, modern marketing way.

After all, what good are ten delightful gardens with names like Tiger Hill, The Humble Administrator's Garden and the Master of the Nets Garden when there aren't a few KFCs or Starbucks nearby to slake the thirst of the leg-weary and tuckered-out Alabaman.

It's all very well to have long and incredibly photogenic streets from the coach park to the entrance kiosk, but nowadays you need to cater for the modern tourist in more ways than just offering the family from Düsseldorf a carton of the local fizzy drink and a sausage on a stick from a barrow on the pavement.

So, the Suzhou city elders have set about modernising the city with astonishing gusto. Two thousand year old streets have been torn up to make way for a better-designed and newer set of old streets - old streets which have been created to cater directly for the needs of the modern visitor. Modern western-style boutiques, shops and stalls have been built with air-conditioning and toilet facilities beside the new old streets. They all sell quilted 'paintings' of Labrador dogs, Hello Kitty silk pyjamas and paper kites sporting the Nike logo. And there are Rolex watches everywhere, of course. The refrigerators are stocked to the gunnels with Coke, Pepsi, Seven Up and Sprite and there is a Starbucks at every junction.

The modern age is definitely coming to Suzhou and the service industry is determined not to miss out. Suzhou will be dragged into the twenty-first century, kicking and screaming if necessary.

Percy Gabbitt lived on the top floor of a five-storey apartment block a stone's throw away from the Twin Pagodas and a fruit market, smack-bang in the centre of the city in an area still with some semblance of being really old and passably Chinese.

Here you could just about imagine that you really were in China. Old men in powder blue Chairman Mao jackets sit on benches by the canal and talk of better times, while children play in the streets without a care in the world.

There is even no sewer system to speak of unless you count having a plastic bucket, a pair of rubber gloves and access to the canal as an adequate sanitary solution.

Gabbitt's block was hastily erected about five years previously when cheap accommodation was desperately needed as Suzhou became the place to emigrate to if you wanted a half decent job.

The building had no lift. To be honest, it looked like a tenement block in Thamesmead on a rainy day in November. Graffiti adorned every public wall and there were always squadrons of venomous mosquitoes hiding in the shadows of every stair landing.

Each suite of rooms did boast a nice porcelained toilet room, usually next to the kitchen, with a hole in the floor leading to a long drop and a wide gutter at ground level which led directly into the nearest canal - all reasonably hygienic and certainly no chance of blockages.

Tourists with a sense of adventure and looking for ancient Chinese charm, relished a walk passed this building, Sony Digicam at the ready for that moment when a peasant clutching a screaming baby would appear in a shabby doorway or when a toilet was expansively used.

Gabbitt was not thinking of the charm of the area or the toilet facilities, as he sat on a deeply uncomfortable wooden chair at a table with four legs of differing lengths.

His living room was a perfect cube with two doors, one leading into short corridor and then to a kitchen, toilet and a small bedroom. The other door opened onto the communal stairwell and the outside world.

The cube was Gabbitt's sitting room and, besides being furnished with this multi-purpose Tate Modern table, it also had an 'L'-shaped imitation leather sofa, which was just about impossible to sit upon without badly slipping a disc. Gabbitt had wisely given up using it and tended to stack books, groceries and DVDs there instead.

The only other significant piece of furniture in the room was a narrow wooden table propped against a wall, propped being the all-important word, since it only had two worryingly-thin legs. On it sat a gleaming Fujitsu 2000 laptop which looked alarmingly out of place.

Gabbitt held a cup of jasmine tea in one hand and stared blankly at a wall which was showing the first green specks of mould near the ceiling. His thoughts were not on the mould either.

Actually, Gabbitt's mind was a world away. He was thinking deeply about Mayfair alleys and running from people who wished to do him harm.

He frowned and took a sip of his tea. He winced. He had never really liked the bitter taste of Chinese tea. He smacked his lips and thought longingly of a cup of Twining's Earl Grey.

He put the cup down on the table and it promptly toppled over and spilled its contents over his trousers and then rolled onto the floor where it shattered into five pieces.

Gabbitt swore loudly. He had never managed to get to grips with the idiosyncrasies of rocky Chinese tables or delicately-made Chinese tea-cups. He swore again and kicked the table into the corner of the lounge area where it lay on its side like a shot wildebeest.

There was a sound from the downstairs apartment - a sound which indicated irritation. It was only a slight sound – probably a chair being pushed back or something like that. But it was definitely in response to Gabbitt's clumsiness. Then there was silence.

Gabbitt's thoughts drifted back a few hours. It was Mayfair alleys all over again, but with a slight difference. To be caught red-handed sprinting away from the shop by an equally-startled Chinese policeman with a large torch was bad enough, but then to be manhandled into a white van and taken to the local 'nick' along with the three shop assistants from the DVD shop, was really the cherry on the cake. This time he had not got away. This time he had been caught.

The fact that they had let him go, after two hours of form-filling, without any sort of recrimination only served to increase Gabbitt's misery. Not a single word of English had been spoken, just a lot of Chinese shouted mostly at the bowed heads of the DVD shop assistants. Gabbitt had no idea what had happened, only that he had been released.

He stood up and walked over to the small computer desk, crunching the remnants of the teacup under his slippers. He then sat down on a three-legged, blue-plastic stool, which was placed in front of the desk. It creaked ominously before deciding not to give up the challenge of supporting a slightly overweight westerner.

He opened the lid of his laptop and hit the Start button.

*"Excellent!" exclaimed Roger, clapping his hands and standing up.*

*"What do you mean? That's my sister we're talking about," squawked Tammy unhappily.*

*"A rescue quest," said Roger with a gleam in his eye. "Perfect. Just what I need."*

*"Listen you," remonstrated Tammy. "Bunty's not just a sack of jewels in a cave five levels down, you know."*

*"But she needs rescuing, doesn't she?"*

*"Yes, but…"*

*"And that's what I do. Right?"*

*"Well, yes, but…"*

*"So, if you're coming, strap on your dagger and get ready for some real action," said Roger and made for the door.*

*"But we don't know who's taken her, where they've gone and why they've done such a thing. We should have a meeting to discuss… options," squeaked Tammy.*

*"A meeting?" spat Roger contemptuously. "No time for that sort of thing. We need to get going fast or the trail will go cold," he said professionally. "Tell Susie to show us where Bunty was last seen. Then leave the rest to me. No one's going to harm that little goblinesse. She gave me a poetry book, which I nearly started reading last month!" he added and then roared loudly: "Back in business again!"*

The Snark Maiden was not a very happy elfette at all. She had just stepped into the virtual world of Dark Dawn Three and had immediately been set upon by a motley group of barbarians who were demanding that she take all her armour off.

This did not seem fair at all. After all, weren't barbarians supposed to be the good guys? And that rather natty chainmail suit had cost a lot of gold coins at the weapons market just down the road.

The Snark Maiden attempted reason and logical argument. The exchange went something like this:

<Give us your fings>

<Why?>

<Coz we want 'em>

<Can't you spell?>

<Get stuffed and start handin' 'em over>

<Robbing a fellow hero is not fair, you know. We should be fighting demons and orcs together >

<Need better stuff to do that. This best way to equip>

<And if I say no>

<You're toast. 4 of us against little U>

Caroline Williams looked at her screen. She had managed to survive all of ten minutes in Level One and had walked about ten feet from the Village exit before being set upon by these ruffians. She frowned at the screen and wondered how to get out of this predicament in one piece and without losing all her belongings. She hadn't realised that taking part in one of these massive online role-playing games was such a dog-eat-dog thing. Real-time, action fantasy role-playing games were not quite what they were cracked up to be.

She had imagined wandering through green meadows and gradually building up her strength points by battling small spiders, cowardly rats and the odd fox. And when she bumped into other heroes on forest paths she thought they would have a few pleasant exchanges and swap hints and advice. Then she would return to the village, upgrade to better stuff from the Weapons Shop and begin the quest in earnest.

But to be immediately faced by three fully-armoured barbarians with long pointy swords and bad grammar was all a bit dispiriting. Caroline sighed and began typing again.

<My stuff's not worth much>

<It'll fetch a few coins though. Pickings are lean. We have to take wot we can get>

Caroline was about to surrender when a very odd thing happened.

<Defend yourself, craven varlets!>

Another character strode onto the screen all dressed in red and gold. He cut a rather dashing figure as he made his way to the centre of the screen.

<Attack a defenceless maiden, would you?>

<Who the fuck RU?>

<Your death>

And with that the multi-coloured hero began setting about the ruffians with a savagery, which both appalled and delighted Caroline. In just ten seconds the life points of two of the bandits were down to zero and the third was attempting to scamper back to the sanctuary of the village. A well-placed trillium arrow put paid to that though.

Caroline frowned. There was only one hero who used brute force and manic hacking to win all his duels. She began typing.

<So, where've you been?>

<Having problems with the local police>

<You forgot our arrangement>

<Just couldn't get to the computer till now>

<The police?>

<Yes. Usual stuff. Being chased down streets for no particular reason and then getting arrested again for no particular reason>

<You're joking,>

<No... pick up all their armour so we can re-equip ourselves before any friends of theirs come along and have another go at us>

<You OK?>

<Sort of. Anyway, thought you would be at work now>

<Day off. Sick>

<Really?>

<No, a sickie>

<You ready yet? I got told by the wizard down the road that there's a rescue quest in the offing>

<Never mind that. The police?>

<All OK now. Just a case of mistaken identity. Thought I was selling porno DVDs>

<Pardon?>

<Just in the wrong place at the wrong time>

<Where have I heard that before?>

<Anyway, they let me go after they realised what a nice foreigner I am>

<Hmmmmm. You really bringing that goblin with you?>

<He's my familiar>

<So long as he doesn't get familiar with me. Looks like he needs a bath>

<He always looks like that. A lean and hungry look>

<Just watch my back when he's around. Anyway, Dave might be logging on too. Said he'd be by the Trolls' Gate about now if he could make it. Busy in town apparently>

<And Joe?>

<Teaching I suppose>

<Haven't heard from him for weeks. Things still working out in my house?>

<Loves it there. Really done the place up a lot and Nixon likes him too.>

<That's the important thing.>

<Neighbours haven't taken a shine to him though. Not after that incident with the chain saw and their eucalyptus tree>

The conversation might have continued bobbing along in cosy domesticity had not two arrows thrummed past their noses and sailed into a nearby oak tree.

<Oops. Better stop. Business calls>

<Can I use the goblin as a shield?>

*Two arrows buried themselves into a nearby oak tree. Roger turned to meet the foe with a big manic smile on his face. He had not been so happy more months.*

*"This time try to take some prisoners," wailed Tammy, as the Norse Fighter waded into action again. "We need information, remember."*

*A fireball then whistled rather too close for comfort over the goblin's head and incinerated a ruffian with a bow ready and drawn by a small rock.*

*"And you can behave yourself as well," squeaked Tammy at the elfette warrior with the fireballs, who Roger had just saved a few minutes before.*

*"Just keep your head down and we won't have any unfortunate accidents," said the elfette with eyebrows raised, innocently.*

*Roger made short work of three more of the scoundrels and then managed to capture a heavily-wounded fourth.*

*"This just might be your lucky day," he said to the prone figure.*

*"Oh fuck!" came the not-unexpected reply.*

Bob Irwin took out a thick wad of red one hundred yuan notes and passed the sizeable brick over to a policeman in an official flat white hat. The money was carefully counted and then placed in a leather case. Cigarettes were passed round. A few pleasantries were then exchanged and Bob then picked up a large cardboard box and put it rather precariously onto the back off his electric bike.

The police ambled back to two black and white cars and motored off into the heart of Suzhou, lights flashing and sirens wailing.

Bob rode off in the opposite direction and was soon picking his way through the usual mayhem of a crossroads. This one was just a hundred metres further down the road and near a small bridge which led to the popular Shiquan Jie, the street of a thousand bars and restaurants.

He threaded his way through three traffic accidents and a shouting match between two angry motorists eager not to lose face now that they had lost their bikes as moveable vehicles. Thirty metres later he turned off down a side alley which led to a cramped market packed with live chickens, ducks, crabs, geese and various other creatures awaiting slaughter.

He rode down the alley and eventually turned into a parking area, above which shone a brightly-lit neon sign. It read '**Arapacana Asses**'. A garage door hummed open and Bob disappeared into the darkness within.

Percy Gabbitt had four jobs.

His initial intention of just teaching at a Primary School as his main and only job had quickly been forgotten after just three days in Suzhou. People had approached him wherever he went and had boldly demanded English lessons. Rather unwisely, he had not yet learnt how to say 'no' to a Chinese smile and several well-placed 'pretty-pleases'.

He now taught from morning to dusk six days a week and spent most of his free moments in taxies haring across the city to his next class.

His main and 'visa-giving' job was English at a primary school in the west of Suzhou – at a place called 'Suzhou Experimental Primary School Number Nine'. Classes consisted of about fifty six-year olds all rather too eager to sing about Old MacDonald or get scared by The Big Bad Wolf.

The second was as a business tutor at the Sino-Canadian Institute actually located in the heart of the Suzhou University campus. Gabbitt's speciality was macro-economics and he taught mainly Taiwanese and Malaysian students intent on getting a Canadian degree at the lowest price possible, which meant that they did not have to work very hard and, more importantly, did not have to set foot in Canada. Gabbitt had no real idea what macro-economics was and hoped that someone would tell him quite soon.

The third job was at a language school in the centre of the city where he taught conversational English to any of the Suzhou populace who had wandered in off the street. This usually meant students who were failing badly at the nearby university, or bar girls like Deranged Pony and Pageboy, who had no real intention of learning the language at all. They just wanted to bag a foreign boyfriend as fast as possible.

The final job was at a large company in the Singapore Industrial Zone to the east of the city and consisted of teaching business English conversation to three bovine employees, who needed to answer international phone calls from Germany and Ireland.

It was Sunday morning and Gabbitt's day off. He was having a lie-in. This was not that easy given the constant honking of car horns from the road outside, the cloying aroma of fried onions coming from the next apartment and mobile phone users shouting into their devices as loudly as possible in the street two floors below. There was also the spitting, of course.

Percy Gabbitt had just about managed to get used to the general background noise of a Chinese city, but had still to assimilate the spitting. Lying in bed and staring at the paint peeling off his ceiling he listened intently to someone percolate phlegm from the depths of his boots until it had risen the length of his body and was ready for ejection at maximum velocity into a roadside shrub. The whole process took about five seconds and was quite impressive, if you were into that sort of thing.

It reminded Gabbitt of Nigel Firkin - the king of the long-distance spit. Nigel was a boy from his primary school back in England who could arc a gob over the wall into the girls' toilets with Olympic dexterity. Gabbitt wondered what Nigel was doing now. Probably a merchant banker in the City and still gobbing metaphorically over everyone.

Gabbitt frowned deeply and beeped the air-conditioning unit on. It was about ten o'clock in the morning and things were starting to heat up.

There was a knock at his door and then three policemen walked in. Apparently, locked doors in China somehow magically opened to the forces of law.

"This yours?" asked a large officer in an impressive and neatly-ironed blue suit. He waved a DVD of 'Donkeyman meets the Pussycat' at Gabbitt, who was now on his feet and trying to get a t-shirt on.

"Absolutely not," said Gabbitt hotly.

The policeman looked a little confused.

"No," said Gabbitt loudly.

"Ah," said the policeman. "In your bag." He then waved a small daypack at Gabbitt and produced a British passport from the front pouch.

"Ah," said Gabbitt. "I see what you mean."

"So, bag yours, but DVD not?" asked the policeman with all the incisiveness of an oriental Poirot.

"Yes, well no," squawked Gabbitt worriedly. Sudden visions of police frame-ups swam across his mind and he felt he had to quash any 'misunderstandings' immediately.

"This your bag?" tried the policeman again, as he placed it on Gabbitt's dining table, which creaked omiously.

"Yes," replied Gabbitt, feeling that such an admittance might be an argument-loser on several fronts.

His bag. His damn day pack. Why had he dropped the thing? He sighed in a defeated sort of way.

"And this your passport?" persisted the Chinese Poirot cruelly.

"Yes," said Gabbitt.

"But not your DVD," said the officer, unsmilingly.

"No," said Gabbitt still speaking in monosyllables.

"OK," said the policeman slowly. "Have a nice day. Can we borrow DVD?"

Gabbitt's eyes narrowed. This was like the nasty question: 'When did you stop beating your wife?' Any answer would condemn you.

"Yes," said Gabbitt measuredly. "Help yourself." he said, waving a hand at a pile of DVDs in a distant corner. "Take anything you like."

"No," said the officer. "This," and waved the Donkeyman in Gabbitt's face.

"Not mine," repeated Gabbitt innocently.

The officer smiled thickly and thrust the DVD into a case he was carrying.

"Many thank yous," he said after another broad smile. "You nice man, I think."

There was then a flurry of Chinese spoken at lightning speed, after which the three officers stepped out of the apartment and closed the door behind them.

A long silence followed as Gabbitt thought about everything. Ten minutes later and he was strolling unhappily down the Shiquan Jie heading towards a bar called Pulp Fiction. He needed to get out of his apartment and get a drink as fast as possible.

The street was crowded with the usual cross-section of Chinese society. Girls in high black boots with luminous green tights and bright yellow coats swam passed Gabbitt's line of sight. He stared fixedly at the paving slabs which glided beneath him. He tended to work from ground level up nowadays. It was less confrontational and got him into fewer scrapes.

A pair of dirty cream running shoes overtook him, followed by a pair of carpet slippers with fluffy bobbles on the toe areas. Gabbitt frowned. Who on earth would go out on a late summer morning wearing carpet slippers? He risked a look up and was vaguely surprised by the sight of a middle-aged Chinese woman, who was also wearing a pair of Mickey Mouse pyjamas.

A woman then cycled past wearing a fake fur coat and a hard, black felt riding hat normally worn by huntsmen in Leicestershire. Gabbitt quickened his pace towards the sanity of a Taihu beer and a dark corner of the bar. China was beginning to get him down.

He pushed through the door and entered Pulp Fiction just as an Australian at the far end of the bar shouted something very unkind about English cricketers. Gabbitt sat down at a high seat and gestured to the barman for a beer. An joke involving Prince Charles and a corgi sang out across the bar.

It was good to be back in western civilisation again. An oasis from the madness outside. Someone said a string of four-letter words about French people and Gabbitt relaxed completely. A moment later and he had sunk his first beer of the day and life did not seem so bad. He looked at a large sign hanging above the bar. It read

```
Aussie Day!!
Every fifth tinny free for Australians
today!!  Good on yer!
(bring your passport or ID, or you pay the
same as the rest of the bastards)
```

And in even small type underneath:

(valid only between 5.00pm and 6.00pm on Tuesdays)

"You again," said a familiar voice at his elbow.

Gabbitt turned to face the owner of the voice.

"This is a much better place," the voice said. "Owned by an Aussie."

"Is it?" mumbled Gabbitt.

"Better than that place over the road where you nearly got hustled."

The penny dropped. It was that Australian man from the company with the daft name. Bob Irwin from Arapa something. Gabbitt risked a smile and offered him a drink. It seemed like the thing to do after his recent rescue from the clutches of Deranged Pony and Pimply Moon.

"So, you've survived another day in this bastard place, have you?" asked the Australian, as he took a builder's swig at his beer.

"Nearly," was Gabbitt's measured reply.

*"The lair of the dragon king," said Roger the Norse Fighter in a hushed tone. "The big one," he murmured the way bank robbers do when looking at a picture of Fort Knox or the Bank of England.*

*"A dragon king," spluttered Tammy.*

*"THE dragon king," whispered Roger, reverently.*

*"Looks like a big quest," said the Snark Maiden, eyebrows rising professionally.*

*"Are you sure it was THE dragon king?" asked Tammy, very worriedly.*

*"That's what he said," whispered Roger, who was still in awe.*

*"And protected by an army of undead warriors and dragon worshippers?" squeaked Tammy, extremely worriedly.*

*"That's what he also said," said Roger, with a slight tremble in his voice.*

*"Do you believe him?" asked Tammy.*

*The three heroes were sitting on a small patch of grass beside a rather nice looking stream by a forest.*

*"I think I'd have told the truth if someone had prodded a broad sword against my…"*

*"Right," interrupted Tammy. "So, we believe him."*

*"He was telling the truth," said the Snark Maiden quietly. I am certain of it."*

*There was a pause as the three thought long, serious thoughts.*

*"What shall we do for dinner?" sniffed Roger, and lay on his back.*

*"So, my Bunty is somewhere in the middle of a deep catacomb entertaining this Dragon King," mumbled Tammy, sadly.*

*"Indeed," muttered Roger. "I fancy fish cakes and some chips."*

*"An impossible quest," squeaked Tammy, ignoring the Norse Fighter. "She's lost. We'll never get her out alive."*

*"Indeed," said Roger.*

*"What I want to know is why this swine has kidnapped her. She's only a goblinette who writes poems. Why would he want her?"*

*"Well, we're not going to find out sitting here," said Roger, standing up.*

*"Where do you thing you're going?" asked Tammy.*

*"To do the impossible, of course, after I've had something to eat" replied Roger and marched down the forest path.*

*"All right, all right," said Tammy, struggling to keep up with the hero. The Snark Maiden was already thirty yards away, scouting the path ahead for danger.*

*"I really appreciate your enthusiasm," said Tammy. "It's very touching that you want to save my sister, but…"*

*"We shall overcome, whatever the odds."*

*"Oh god," mumbled Tammy. "If we really are going to give this a go, we shall need an elf or a magician."*

*"Fate will take care of all that, my little friend," came Roger's confident reply. "Anyway, we already have the Snark Maiden on board."*

*"But shouldn't we return to the village and recruit properly or something?" tried Tammy.*

*"I have a plan," said Roger.*

*"Oh dear," muttered Tammy.*

*"The Snark Maiden can return to the village and recruit a couple of adventurers who are talented in cavern fighting, while we shall hurry ahead to the Troll's Gate."*

*"Roger that," said the Snark Maiden, who had just returned to report that everything was safe up ahead. She was then off again in the direction of the village.*

*"Shouldn't we wait for them to return?" squeaked Tammy, who was a firm believer in safety in numbers.*

*"No time for that," said Roger, as he increased his pace. "We have to get to the Troll's Gate before sunset."*

*"And why do we have to do that?"*

*"Trolls are not that keen on night-time visitors. Like to shut up shop and disappear underground when the sun goes down. Not happy at all about being roused in the dead of night."*

Percy Gabbitt had finished his third bottle of Taihu Beer and life was looking a little brighter. Bob Irwin had just completed his fourth. They were discussing the Donkeyman.

"It's not such a bad movie," said Irwin, as he stared seriously at his bottle. "Probably would have won an award if movies like that were taken more seriously."

"'Donkeyman meets the Pussycat'?" queried Gabbitt. He was not so sure if Irwin was pulling his leg or not.

"It's postmodernist video art, you see," said Irwin, slowly. "Great use of the camera and pretty good special effects for an amateur movie company. How the cameraman got those angles, I'll never know."

Gabbitt took a hard look at his new friend. Yes, he really was quite serious. Gabbitt sighed. Everything he had heard about Australian men seemed to be true after all. And now postmodernism was intruding onto his world again.

"Have you seen it?" asked Bob.

"No."

"Come round to my place this evening and we'll have a viewing. Donkeyman meets the Gabbitt," said Irwin amicably and patted him in a matey Aussie way.

"Not sure it's my type of film."

"But don't you want to see what happens when the Donkeyman confronts the Pussycat? It's one of those meetings you never forget," said Irwin, rolling his eyes. "Like when Darth Vader meet Luke for the first time or when..."

"I get the picture."

"That's settled then," said Irwin.

Dave Springett, in the guise of a human magician, was getting impatient. He had been waiting at the Troll's Gate for over an hour and still no-one had turned up. True, there had been a centaur and a small furtive-looking ratman, but nothing really out of the ordinary. He had hidden behind a tree and let them pass. No sense in provoking a centaur needlessly. Their kick certainly was worse than their bite.

Springett thought hard. The agreement had been to meet Percy and Caroline and then to discuss 'options'. That is what Caroline had said. She loved using words like that. And she was never late for appointments. She was like that too.

He moved his mouse slightly so that his character could have a good look at the gate again. Nothing. Springett pressed a button and a Menu Bar popped up. He surveyed a long line of colourful potion bottles which spread out along the bottom of the screen. Four healing ones, three fireballs and two for invisibility. He smiled. It was going to be a lot more fun being a magician this time round. The prospects of wreaking mayhem with all this firepower seemed endless.

He also had a staff – a gnarled, wooden one like Gandalf's. OK, it was just a Level Two one, but it did pack a pretty mean fireball.

He tapped another button and the Menu Bar disappeared. Still no sign of anything. A squirrel hopped innocently across the screen. The things the makers of these games did to make it all more realistic, he thought as he levelled his staff at the little creature.

Percy Gabbitt's house in Bromley had been completely redecorated. Gone were the rather dowdy peachy walls in the downstairs rooms and the vast magnolia expanse leading up the stairs to the bedrooms. Joe Slimm was in residence and had made Gabbitt's home his own. In a flurry of activity one weekend just a month after moving in, he had laid waste to the ground floor armed only with a thick horsehair paintbrush and a can of paint, optimistically labelled 'Bokhara Sand Dune'.

The lower floor had been transformed into a golden-brown den. Unfortunately, Bokhara SD also had the rather unpleasant side-effect of smelling like rancid cabbages – a smell which refused to go away whatever measures were taken.

The wall leading upstairs had succumbed to a similar frenzy of painting, only this time it was the turn of a can labelled 'Peppermint Surprise'. This smelt as if someone had squeezed menthol toothpaste all over the wall long after it had dried.

True, both colours were rather nice in their own way, but put together and the wandering eye could not help wincing when sandy brown turned bright green as it rounded a quiet corner at the bottom of the staircase. Slimm quite liked it though and felt that he had given the place a new look. A modern look. A cross between Hockney and Warhol, he liked to think. A look of the twenty-first century.

The front door had also been replaced. Alfred Fennell's tenacious 'spragging' had splintered the door into four different pieces, the only thing holding it together being twenty six-inch nails. Slimm had had the door completely replaced and now a stout, heavily-varnished oak door stood heavily in its new frame. It might have cost an arm and a leg, but Slimm had thought it worth it. Anyway, he was tired of all the groin-high squirming every time he tried to get in or out of the house though the bay window at the front of the house.

Joe Slimm had reached middle age. He was quite thin, had greying hair, wire-rimmed glasses, bushy eyebrows and a permanently sad expression on his oddly square face. A cruel person would have said that he resembled one of those marionettes in Thunderbirds - not one of the main characters, but one of the expendable victims at the start of the programme when the tanker bursts into flames or the car plummets from a high bridge.

As he trudged upstairs, after another totally dispiriting day teaching mathematics at Turpington Comprehensive, he found himself warming to the ever-present odour of minty, rotting cabbages.

Joe Slimm smiled. It was time for a bit of escape. Time for a 'Mercedes' moment. Time for a little controlled madness before bedtime. Time to get away from the pile of yellow exercise books which lay sulkily on his dining room table downstairs. This was not a moment to get involved with the depressing state of 5B's homework on tangents and arcs.

He padded down the corridor to a small box room which looked out onto the main road. In it there was just one long table and a quilted office chair. On the table stood a large and impressive-looking desktop computer. Slimm slid into the seat and pressed the 'On' button.

# THREE

*"I love China, but not when cold. I hate it then. I hate it when hot too. And I hate it during rainy season and when weather changes in spring and autumn. I also hate having big wind. I love China very much all other times."*
**(Chinese shop assistant talking about her love for the mother country)**

Percy Gabbitt stared up at the sign which glowed in neon red above a wide shadowy doorway. It read 'Arapacana Asses'.

There was a loud click followed by a humming sound and the door started to scroll upwards.

"Won't take a second, mate," said Bob Irwin happily. "Just wanted to show you something before we I introduce you to the Pussycat and have a few more beers, of course."

Gabbitt grimaced in the half-light. It was getting late and he wanted to get back to the apartment which he was beginning somewhat reluctantly to call home. He had drunk rather too much and been subjected to Australian philosophy for a dangerously long time. He had only intended to have an hour at Pulp Fiction before starting his lesson preparation for another week's teaching.

However, the hours had drifted by and suddenly he was staring at his watch which brutally told him that it had already gone ten. A whole day spent in a bar drinking beer, eating nuts and Chinese crisps and talking nonsense. It was time to step back, take a deep breath and go to bed.

"Should be a bit of fun," said Irwin and stepped under the retracting garage door and into the gloom within. Gabbitt followed a little uncertainly.

A light was flickered on and Gabbitt found himself staring at a rather battered white Volkswagen Polo and a flight of concrete stairs. Bob Irwin was already on the fourth step and climbing to the first floor, two at a time.

<I wish you wouldn't do that>
<What?>
<Murder squirrels>
<Don't be daft. Just a bit of fun to stave off chronic boredom>
<I don't like it>
<They're only glyphs>
<Well I don't like it, so please stop>
<I'm bored>
<We just have to wait that's all>
<He didn't sign on at all yesterday and I wasted half a day hanging around this gate for him to turn up. I reckon we should go on without him. Blaze a trail>
<U crazy?>
<A magician and an elf could do some serious damage U know>
<Before getting wiped out in the second serious fight. I think not, Dave>
<We've got Joe as well, don't forget>
<I haven't forgotten. Where is he?>
<He's also not signed on, but he's on his way>
<What is he this time?>
<He said he wanted to be a halfling or a dwarf. Something vertically-challenge. Cannon fodder, I reckon>
<As long as he's got good thieving skills, I don't care. U need a light-fingered character for dungeons nowadays. A trap disarmer is vital>

<Rubbish. All U still need is a big chopper and lots of fireballs. U can prat around with dinky thieves and girly elves, but they always get scraped off the walls by Level Four. It's the bloke with the biggest axe, Percy's Roger, who gets through to the final encounter. Hopefully, with a magician, me, in tow. Certainly not an elf… or a halfling>

<That's why U have to protect us Dave… with your fireballs and scrolls - and I intend to be there at the end too, despite being a delicate elfette>

<Well I'm going to have a go at that troll in exactly ten minutes even if Percy bloody Norse Fighter hasn't turned up>

<That's asi9 and you know it>

<How long have U been waiting to say that?>

<U don't want to know>

*Roger the Norse Fighter was having a frustrating time. He knew he had to be at the Troll's Gate by sunset and yet several wrong turns had led him seriously off course and he was embarrassingly lost. Tammy the Goblin was not much help either. He trotted along in Roger's wake with head bowed low and muttering quietly to himself. He was clearly one depressed goblin. Roger crested a small hill and stopped. He looked down at his companion and sighed. "We'll find her. Don't worry."*

*"As long as it's not too late," mumbled Tammy unhappily.*

*"We won't be too late. I've told you before that this is what heroing is all about. You get there in the nick of time, just as the bad guy is about to have his wicked way with the maiden."*

*"I wish you wouldn't say that."*

*"Don't worry, my little friend. The Dragon King's days are numbered."*

*"Just hope that Bunty's aren't as well."*

*"I told you, it doesn't work like that."*

*"I wish we could help her a little more quickly, that's all."*

*"Well, if you want us to be quicker, you could start by looking at the map and finding out why we don't appear to have arrived at the Troll's Gate yet."*

*Tammy stared at the creased parchment in Roger's hands and sighed sadly.*

*"It's upside down," he said and took it off Roger.*

<Hello everybody>

<Where've U been?>

<Staff meeting till late and then a detention for 5C. Bastards defaced the Art Room door. Someone drew a rude picture of the French assistante doing something anatomically challenging with a towel gourd. All a bit puerile. Wish they'd stick to drugs and fags behind the bike sheds, then we could all go home early>

<So, a normal day at Turpington Comp then?>

<Yep. What's happening here? Any interesting fights or treasure yet? >

< That's a joke. Were bored sick waiting for Percy and his goblin friend>

<Not signed in?>

<No. I've told the elf here that I'm going to tackle that troll on my own if he's not here in... three minutes>

<Do U think that's wise>

<Of course it's not. But got to do something. Ran out of squirrels an hour ago. Thought Percy would have been here ages ago. Should have been. He only had to stroll a mile or two down that path>

<Squirrels?>

<We wait and that's that. Maybe he had a few problems with bandits on the way here>

<Hi Caroline>

<Hi Joe. As I was saying…we have to wait until the party is at full strength and then we go in or it'll be curtains for all of us>

<I bet I can hit that deer from here>

<Will U stop slaughtering every non-threatening creature in this land, Dave?>

<I told U before, they're only glyphs. And can we all stop using that daft 'U' thing? What's wrong with 'you'? It's beginning to irritate me! It's just two more taps on the keyboard. Hardly a massive extra effort. More importantly, what's a towel gourd?>

<A towel gourd? Does it really matter? It'll just clutter up Ur already cluttered mind>

<U never know. Knowing what it is just might save our lives one day>

<Yr?>

<Your>

<Sigh>

Bob Irwin snapped on the lights and Percy Gabbitt blinked. He then frowned and blinked again. It was one of those moments when it takes several seconds for the brain to catch up with what the eyes are telling it.

"Thought this would surprise you, mate," said Irwin

Surprise was a slight understatement. Percy Gabbitt stared out at the long hangar type room which stretched away from him. He blinked again.

"This is it," said Irwin a little obviously. "Our headquarters. The place where we plan it all."

"Really?" mumbled Gabbitt, not entirely understanding what he was looking at or what was planned there.

"Welcome to Arapacana Associates," said another voice. A very English voice. Gabbitt jumped.

A man stepped forward. He was tall, dark-haired and wore a dark green shirt and beige trousers. He was casually fashionable in that way which makes most men extremely envious. He looked like the sort of man who had a wardrobe packed with TS Lewin shirts, of all shades. "Mr Percy Gabbitt, I presume," he said, with a large and winning smile.

"Yes," responded Gabbitt a little thickly.

Suddenly, he was aware of more people in the room. Men and women were standing up from behind banks of computers and staring at him. He frowned again, not at all sure what to make of things. One moment he was expecting to be ushered to a back room to watch a film about the Donkeyman, and the next he was standing in a large western-style office with a lot of people staring at him. It was a bit disconcerting.

"The famous Mr Percy Gabbitt," said the fashionable man. And with that, everyone started clapping their hands and whistling as loudly as they could.

It took a good five minutes for the adulation to subside. By then Gabbitt was seated in a chair at a polished wood table and staring at a flute of champagne. He wondered if he had finally gone completely stark, staring mad. He picked up the champagne glass and threw back the contents in one. The bubbles went straight to his nose and he choked. Now everyone was laughing One second famous and the next a clown.

"As you can see, you're quite a popular figure here," said the fashionable man, still smiling rather too widely.

"Hmm," murmured Gabbitt through the bubbles.

"I should introduce myself," said the smiling manikin. "Bob Burley, managing director of Arapacana Asses."

Again, more laughter from everyone. Clearly this was one happy office or maybe they had all been on the champagne long before Gabbitt had arrived.

"Another Bob," was all Gabbitt could manage.

"Yes, there are actually three of us," said Burley gleefully, though Bob Brand could not be here today. He's got a bit of business in London to attend to, you see. You'll meet him soon enough."

"Has he? Will I?" asked Gabbitt, as he watched his flute get a third refill.

"Indeed you will, Mr Gabbitt. You see, Mr Brand is probably your biggest fan. He's been following your work for quite a long time now. In fact, it was he who first came up with the idea of Arapacana. Very keen is Bob the Third. Likes to do everything himself. Still gets a lot of pride from getting his hands dirty, though."

Percy Gabbitt stared at Bob Burley and tried to put a few coherent thoughts together. This was not easy given the pickled state of his mind and that everything he appeared to be hearing was bordering on the plain ridiculous. What made it worse was that every time he tried to speak, everyone started laughing. He frowned deeply. He glanced around for possible exits and suddenly noticed a massive whiteboard on a wall behind one side of the table they were all sitting at. All thoughts of escape evaporated in a second as he read just three words:

Nassington 'Nero' Handsworth

Gabbitt took a deep breath and stared at the name on the board. Memories began flooding back. Very unpleasant memories. He shifted in his seat and began to feel extremely worried.

"Mr Gabbitt, or may I call you Percy?" asked Burley, suddenly.

"You can call me anything you like. People generally do," he mumbled quietly.

"I think we all owe you an explanation and... an invitation," continued Burley.

"I think you do," said Gabbitt, draining his fourth glass. It was immediately filled again by a rather nice looking young woman with extremely blonde hair and green eyes.

"Box Hill!" exclaimed Burley loudly and Gabbitt spilled his fifth glass all over the nice wooden table.

"The pinnacle of your triumph, Percy - your victory over the evil that was ruining the lives of so many people. The place where you finally vanquished the forces of darkness," said Burley, rather melodramatically.

Everyone started clapping and making whooping noises like happy Americans.

"Good on yer, mate," said Bob Irwin, as he gulped down his eighth glass of champagne.

"Arapacana Associates salutes you, Mr Percy Gabbitt. You are our inspiration."

<I told you it would be a mistake>

<I know>

<But you still you had to have a go at that enormous troll>

<Great, wasn't it>

<No, you lost. And you do realise I'm down to my last healing potion, don't you? You never listen to me, do you?>

<I do sometimes. What next? You see, I'm listening now>

<A strategic retreat?>

<I think we should just run like hell. A million miles in any direction away from that f**king troll, which is still running after us, by the way>

<I had noticed >

Everybody needed Percy Gabbitt at that exact moment in time, but the irony was that the man himself was too far gone to savour the wonderful feeling of being wanted.

He sat at the long, highly-polished table and stared wide-eyed at the massive smile that Bob Burley still had on his achingly happy face. Comparisons between cobras and mongooses or mesmerized rabbits in headlights did not really describe how he was feeling.

Bob Burley moved to the back of the room and flicked the ceiling neon lights off and then began tapping at a computer keyboard. A moment later and a large part of the white wall behind him became illuminated.

"Our Power Point presentation!" he exclaimed to the world in general.

"Oh sod," mumbled Gabbitt under his breath. Could it get any worse? A Power-Point presentation – the ultimate horror for any marketing man. Gabbitt sighed as he looked at the screen. Just go with the flow, he thought a little desperately. Just go with the flow, he thought desperately and don't forget to keep drinking.

Burley started clicking and words began appearing on the screen.

**WELCOME TO ARAPACANA ASSOCIATES**

**WHAT YOU ARE ABOUT TO SEE WILL REVOLUTIONISE YOUR WAY OF THINKING AND CHANGE YOUR LIFE FOREVER.**

**PREPARE FOR THE TOTALLY UNBELIEVABLE.**

**PREPARE TO WIDEN YOUR MIND.**

**ARAPACANA – THE REASON FOR A NEW TOMORROW!**

"God," squirmed Gabbitt. What had he stumbled across in this insane Chinese city? A secret religious enclave, a terrorist sleeper cell, a Chinese pyramid-selling company, an overseas branch of New Labour?

There was a pause as the computer seemed to be having a problem loading the next set of graphics. Gabbitt implored the Almighty once again under his breath. He reached for his topped-up champagne flute and was dimly aware that Bob Irwin, slumped next to him, was doing the same.

The screen crackled back to life and Gabbitt found himself watching that bit in 'High Noon' when the hero is walking around the town and looking for help, but no one has the guts to stand next to him. He is alone and the bad guys are minutes away from riding into town to gun him down.

**IT IS TIME FOR THE LITTLE GUY TO STAND HIS GROUND.**

**THE LITTLE MAN IS STANDING UP...AND IS BEING VOUNTED!**

Gabbitt frowned. Vounted?

"Sorry about that," said Burley. "One or two typos still to iron out, but the message is pretty understandable."

"Ah," said Gabbitt, and reached for his flute. The screen then changed again.

**THE WORLD TODAY**

**DOMINATED BY THE EVIL, DECEITFUL AND THE UNSCRUPULOUS**

**A PLACE WHERE MONEY RULES EVERYTHING**

**A PLACE WHERE SIMPLE MORALITY AND HONESTY ARE ALWAYS PUT TO THE SWORD**

**A PLACE WHICH IS RULED BY THE GUYS IN THE BLACK CATS**

"Shit," said Burley.

**AND THE WORST OF THE WORST IN THIS EVER-DARKENING WORLD...**

**THE WHITE SLAVE TRADE**

**NO, IT DIDN'T DIE AT THE BEGINNING OF THE 20TH CENTURY. IT SIMPLY WENT AWAY FOR A FEW YEARS BEFORE RETURNING IN FORCE.**

**THE WORST TYPE OF DECEPTION IN THE MODERN AGE**

**THE ILL TREATMENT OF OUR CHILDREN.**

**WHITE CHILDREN**

**YELLOW CHILDREN**

**BLACK CHILDREN**

**BROWN CHILDREN**

**CHILDREN OF ALL COLOURS**

**OUR CHILDREN – THEIR CRIME**

A picture flashed up of a group of teenagers all holding tennis rackets and smiling

**OUR STUDY ABROAD INDUSTRY**

**AN INDUSTRY WORTH MILLIONS EVERY YEAR TO FAT HAT OWNERS**

"Shit," said Burley, again.

**AN INDUSTRY RUN BY EVIL AND AVARICIOUS JACKALS.**

There was a pause as the screen went white. Then...

**OUR MISSION**

**TO SEEK OUT AND ERADICATE THIS EVIL WHEREVER IT SHOWS ITSELF.**

The lights came on again and Gabbitt found himself squinting through the sudden brightness. The presentation was obviously over and he was none the wiser. Actually, he was even more confused than before.

"That is our mission," said Bob Burley, with an alarmingly-serious expression. "And we can thank you for the inspiration - for the first push which set the ball of retribution into motion."

"Me?" queried a very anxious Gabbitt.

"You and Nassington Nero Handsworth of the Royal English Language Institute," replied Burley, as if such a comment would explain all.

"What?" squeaked Gabbitt.

"You destroyed the evil that was ruining so many lives. You, Mr Percy Gabbitt are the man on the white horse. In the white hat. You are a new hero for our age! Legend!"

There was a loud cheer and lots of clapping from everyone in the office. Gabbitt frowned once again and reached for flute number fifteen. Bob Irwin groaned next to him.

"What?" croaked Gabbitt. "Legend?"

"And we are the new Percys," said Burley, gesturing to his confederates. "You see, what you are looking at here are twenty-three Percy Gabbitts." He stopped for a dramatic moment.

"What?" squawked Gabbitt again, really worriedly. In his world, one was more than enough.

"Take Pamela, for instance," Said Burley, looking at the woman with green eyes, who kept topping Gabbitt's glass up. "She worked at the Exeter Language Academy for three years as a business teacher until one day her boss fired her. Kicked onto the street without even enough money to buy a veggie burger. No reason given. No warning. Disgraceful.

"Or there's Adam over there by the water cooler. He was a marketing man for Total English Forever until the day it was suggested he lie to fifty schoolchildren from Catania in Sicily. He was ordered to tell them that Clacton–on-Sea was, in fact, another name for Cambridge. They then spent two miserable weeks on a rainy promenade by the North Sea and left thinking that Cambridge was a god-forsaken and windswept seaside resort. Adam carried the can and still thinks there's a Mafia hitman after him.

"Then there's Ron and Steve, who are standing by the door in the corner. Summer school teachers who worked an entire summer in the wilds of Scotland virtually twenty-four hours a day... and were then locked out of their school on the last day, because the owner had disappeared with the contents of the company bank account and was last seen in the boarding a plane to the Maldives. One hundred worried Spanish and Brazilian under-eights all left high and dry and wondering what to do next.

"Just a few examples," said Burley. "Everyone here has a story – and not a very nice one, I hasten to add."

"I think..." started Gabbitt uncertainly, not really knowing what he was thinking.

"Arapacana Associates was formed in your wake, even if you didn't know it," interrupted Burley, with an insane gleam in his eye. "Certain people sat up and had a long and serious think after all the fun and games on Box Hill, Mr Gabbitt. Certain people with a conscience and a sense of the moral order of things. Certain people who suddenly realised that they too could be Percy Gabbitts. You are looking at these people, Percy."

"But what do you do?" asked Gabbitt, knowing that he did not really want to hear the reply.

"We police the study abroad world, Percy," replied Burley grandly. "We are the friend of the good and the enemy of the bad."

"Police the study abroad world?" squeaked Gabbitt, as his eighteenth flute went down without touching the sides.

"We do what has never been done before. We protect those Italian and Spanish children. We make sure that they are not exploited. We take up Pamela's cause and pursue her aggressor relentlessly. We look after Adam, Ron, Steve and all the Spanish, Vietnamese, Peruvian and Mongolian children travelling abroad to learn our language."

"But what exactly do you do?" persisted Gabbitt.

"We whack the bastards," said Bob Irwin. "We ruin the buggers, then we burn their places down and pass what's left over to the police."

"You do what?" Gabbitt was goggle-eyed.

"Arapacana exists to destroy evil, to weed out the bad guys and make sure they… disappear forever. People like your Mr Handsworth."

"But I didn't mean…" began Gabbitt again.

"It doesn't matter what you meant, Percy," interrupted Burley again. "The important thing is that you started a fire - a fire which begins in the souls of every mismanaged and aggrieved teacher, employee and student the world over. A fire which cannot be put out until the last evil money-grubbing school owner has been put totally out of business forever. You see, what you don't realise, Percy, is that out there in the study abroad world there are hundreds of Nero Handsworths, who steal from their own companies, mistreat employees, teachers and students, because they think they can get away with it."

"Think…" said Bob Irwin.

"But they're only language schools," attempted Gabbitt. "It's not like it's important like the oil or arms industries. Language schools are pretty small fry in the grand scheme of things."

"Not so, Percy," said Burley quietly. "The study abroad industry is worth billions worldwide. And as English increases its hold, it will eventually become the world's only language. Never has there been a better and more lucrative time for every language school in dark, back alleys in London, New York or Clacton-on-Sea.

"The whole world will all be speaking English in twenty years time and there are billions of euros, dollars and pounds waiting to be extorted from the gullible and naïve by the many Neros out there. Arapacana is the protector of the good guys and will continue to be so until all malpractice and exploitation have been eradicated. It's as simple as that, Percy."

"Talking of money, how can you fund all this?" asked Gabbitt, gesturing to the large number of computers in the room. The British Council don't have the resources or the gall to do anything like this. Do they?"

Burley chuckled and patted him on the back. "Ever wondered where the five million from Box Hill ended up?"

"Ah," sighed Gabbitt. He had wondered.

" Oh, and I nearly forgot - we want you to join us," added Burley, and topped Gabbitt's glass up again.

# FOUR

*"Madness is a three-wheeled bicycle with two wheels missing, but you keep pedalling, just the same."*
**(Suzhou student's metaphor on insanity at a public speaking contest)**

Percy Gabbitt was in Starbucks just by the main moat near the Renmin Bridge. It was the southern most point of the central part of the old city, where property prices soared. This was the expensive bit of the old town where judges and members of the party lived. This was the area where Gucci, Louis Vuitton and Pizza Hut had outlets among expensive residential blocks and leafy streets.

Percy Gabbitt sat in a window seat, nursing a heavily sprinkled Grande cappuccino and looking across the wide moat which separated the rich from the poor. Just a hundred yards of bridge and yet a million miles in lifestyle.

Over on the other side were a jumble of broken-down brick dwellings with corrugated rooves and three-legged dogs standing in puddles at most intersections. Fruit shops selling brown bananas and watermelons stood sentry round cut-price supermarkets, whilst, in the distance, a large chemical plant puffed and wheezed twenty-four hours a day.

Geographically, Suzhou is an odd little place. The emperor, who designed about ten thousand years ago, decided was clearly a mediaeval modernist, with cubist pretensions. You see, the cold city is a perfect rectangle with a wide moat of dirty water highlighting the geometric exactitude. Inside the moat is where rich people lived and where the tourists gravitated, since it was here that most of the city's signature gardens were situated. Outside the moat is where the normal people live and where the main business of the city is conducted in vast industrial areas to the east and west of the central rectangle.

It was Wednesday morning, over two days after Gabbitt's experience with the Bobs at Arapacana Associates. He took a swig at the coffee and sucked bubbles for a few seconds. He stared vacantly at the world outside. A man passed by, took a long look at the foreigner inside and then spat oceanically onto the fake leopard skin saddle of a parked bike.

Gabbitt looked back at his coffee and frowned deeply. His mind wandered back to things past. Visions of London on a grey day swam into focus. Walking up Piccadilly to The Screaming Egg for a late breakfast or down to Green Park and a sandwich on a bench with Caroline. Spilling mayonnaise onto his trousers and having her pinch not rub the stain away. He smiled. The smell of the Bakerloo Line, the station announcer's daily apologies for late and cancelled trains and the rain. Always the rain.

Gabbitt stared at his cappuccino. He had left all that behind. No more London, no more Bromley and no more Nixon. Ah yes, no more Nixon. That had been the hardest past. Leaving his cat behind - the cat with the unkillable fleas, or bugs. Nixon.

Gabbitt sighed and suddenly felt very far from home. He sighed again and shrugged. It wasn't that bad.

He had needed a change of scenery after Box Hill and to get away from a place which only seemed to hold traumatic memories. Gabbitt needed time to heal - time to forget the madness.

So now he was in the middle of the People's Republic of China - in a city far from the police, gangsters and people who wanted him dead. A place famous for its placid, contemplative history and lots of gardens and canals.

He would never have imagined that the headquarters of Insanity Incorporated had decided to move in next door and then invite him to be their new leader.

Gabbitt attempted to drink the inch of coffee through the impenetrable layers of froth in his cup.

Arapacana Associates? Even the name had a touch of silliness about it. It was just plain awful. One of those infernal Bobs had even mentioned Project Fifteen too. How did they know he was here and why had they come to make his life a misery again?

He supped hard at more bubbles and froth and then picked up a chemical-looking orange muffin and took a bite. Crumbs flew everywhere and the thing disintegrated in his hands and tumbled to the floor. Gabbitt brushed the remains off his hands. He reached for more froth and stared out of the window again.

A man on a bicycle trundled past with a thirty-foot high pile of collapsed cardboard boxes strapped to the back of the bike. The load lurched by, momentarily eclipsing the early afternoon sun.

Gabbitt put down his cup and stood up. It was not all bad, he thought. He had just safely negotiated a morning of wading through the swampy area inhabited by Present and Past Perfect tenses and now he had to catch a taxi to the new area to the west of the city and his afternoon of Business English with a group of Chinamen who thought that being successful in the commercial world required excellent telephone English and the ability to give a faultless eight-minute presentation on stainless steel wingnuts.

"We meet again," said a familiar voice from about two inches away.

Gabbitt jumped sideways and upset a wicker basket containing a small cohort of Starbuck's teddy bears all dressed up as rabbits for some worrying reason. Bear bunnies skittered across the floor and attempted to hop under armchairs and coffee tables.

*"So, that's what we're going to do," said Roger and stood up.*

*They had just had a dinner of vegetarian oatcakes and vegetables gleaned from the surrounding countryside, courtesy of Tammy's gastronomic skills. Roger was feeling belligerent. Despite being a vegetarian, there were times when a burger or a slab of sirloin would have hit the spot.*

*"Madness. Total madness," came the not unexpected response from the small green goblin at his side. "If you think such a plan will work then you've got one less brain cell than I thought you had," he said, dramatically.*

*Roger paused for a moment. Sentences like that took a few moments to sink in properly. He looked hard at his companion then shrugged. "There's nothing wrong with this plan, or my brain cells. It should work... with a bit of luck," he said with a sniff.*

*"Nothing wrong? There's nothing right with it," said Tammy, slowly. "And it doesn't really qualify as a plan either. Just saying that the two of us should run as fast as we can towards the main entrance of*

*the Dragon King's lair shouting very loudly is not really a plan at all."*

*"Just because it lacks your sort of cunning doesn't mean it isn't a good plan," said Roger, feeling a little hurt. "It would have the element of surprise."*

*"That's certainly true," agreed Tammy. "For about five seconds. Then we'd be toast. It's just an insane way to commit suicide and certainly won't help rescue Bunty at all."*

*"Do you is better than that."*

*"I'm waiting."*

*"Well, first we have to assemble a carefully-chosen team to tackle the Dragon King's minions. Then we need to hold a meeting to discuss ways of getting inside the Dragon King's fortress as quietly as possible. Possible draw a SWOT diagram or too to see how things… balance out. Good points against bad ones, if you see what I mean."*

*"Where's the honour in that?"*

*"There'll be plenty of time for honour, shouting and killing later on, don't worry. I just think we should make a watertight plan and conserve our resources for as long as possible so we can get to the Dragon King without being detected. If we can get to Bunty without too much fuss, then all we will have to do is fight our way out after grabbing her. And that's where your singular talents will come in very handy. Remember that it's not just getting down ten levels or so, it's the getting back out again that sorts the men from the boys."*

*"I'm never wearing a jacket and a tie again, you know," said Roger.*

*"What?" asked Tammy.*

*"I wouldn't be able to do any of this dressed like a monkey in a suede suit. Just wouldn't work."*

*"Oh," said Tammy. "Well, if we get out of this one alive then I promise never to try to civilise you again. You can wander around the new shopping mall in a loincloth and toting a broadsword, for all I care."*

*"I'll hold you to that, my little friend."*

*Tammy the Goblin sighed deeply and stared at the map again. "The Troll's gate should be about a mile away. I just hope that that elfette has found it as well and hasn't got lost or distracted the way elves do. Hope she's managed to recruit a few more quest members too."*

Following what had become known in police circles as 'The Battle of Box Hill' there had been a lot of changes in the police force in south London. First, most of the officers who had been involved in that traumatic night had either taken early retirement or had had six months sick leave to get over the psychological effects of the battle. None were left unscarred.

In the higher echelons of the force it had been decided that a new broom should sweep the slate clean and that south London should have a new type of police force to protect it. Gone were the American-style squad cars which had decimated the area from Croydon to Reigate and had terrorised every man, woman, child and pet. Even the pigeons had fled the area and had not returned for weeks.

Pringle's chase to Box Hill had levelled three supermarkets, nine shops, twenty bus shelters and fourteen telephone boxes, as well as wrecking countless cars, vans, buses and anything else that had ventured near his route of destruction.

Ironically though, the public had seemed strangely subdued after the incident. The police had expected a violent outburst on the streets, riots, brick-throwing and car-overturning. What they got was nothing.

Nothing at all. A very British nothing. In fact, the really odd result of the mayhem had been a coming-together of the community and a steep downturn in crime across the area. It seemed that if you create a mini-holocaust, the man-in-the-street will quickly tow the line and become a model citizen.

And the police had not even been blamed either. That had been another strange thing. The sight of Inspector Pringle walking down what looked like a hillside in Hell itself on the front covers of all the daily newspapers, accompanied by a large and very friendly panda, had struck a chord with the British public.

Always willing to forgive anyone who was kind to animals, Pringle had been given a hero's billing in all the tabloids following the chaos.

The great British public went about clearing up their streets and rebuilding their lives with happy smiles, knowing that London Zoo's panda was fine and dandy.

But that was then.

In the months after 'The Battle' it was decided to build a spanking new police station in Bromley, very near to the train station - and to try to give the police a new image.

Bobbies were put back on the streets again and people began to feel relieved rather than worried when an officer in a dark blue suit and tall helmet walked past them with a cheery wave and loud 'Good morning!'.

Everything seemed to be going remarkably well until two years later when rather odd things began to happen all over central and south London. And not very nice things at all.

What made everything a lot worse was that this sudden outburst of criminal activity was aimed at just one section of the community. Police profilers and analysts were completely baffled. There did not seem to be any motive at all and yet crimes started to occur the length and breadth of London, from Acton Town in the west to Leytonstone in the east, in just one particular industry.

And the object of these strange crimes – the vast swathe of private language schools, which occupied all the nicest corners of each suburban area.

The crimes were odd too and police detectives called in to look at the crime scenes discovered computers had been tampered with and nasty viruses introduced, files removed or destroyed, accounts information left open on very selected pages, so that even the most unmathematical detective could smell the books cooking gently.

Detectives assigned to the cases were totally baffled. Why would these private enterprises be subjected to this type of crime?

The police were also not at all sure what to do. Certainly, it was a crime to destroy a few computers, but when subsequent investigations uncovered even worse offences being committed by the victims of the crimes, then it was difficult not to applaud whoever was undertaking these acts of vigilantedom.

And so, the police began to look forward to the next crime committed at a language school and arrived at the crime scene accompanied by a certified accountant, several computer experts and a few sniffer dogs. You never could be too careful where teachers were concerned. The fact that the staff and teachers were the victims gradually receded into the distance as all manner of misdemeanours were detected by the forces of law and order.

Language school owners started quaking in their collective moccasin sandals as well. Some sold up immediately to car park developers or people who wanted to put a Pizza Hut where the school was, while others carefully hid any embarrassing skeletons in far off cupboards, by employing a large and expensive team of their own accountants.

Still others employed squads of burly security guards or introduced draconian regulations on gaining access to their schools. Metal detectors were installed at main doorways, students were issued with identity cards with swipe chips and fire doors were locked and bolted on both sides except on the days when the Fire Department carried out its twice-yearly inspections.

An uneasy period followed as language schools adopted a fortress attitude and preferred to treat everyone, including their own staff and students, as potential criminals.

It was at the height of this paranoia that a certain young detective constable called Martin Ford came across a startlingly interesting fact. It was something that all the forensics teams which had processed each and every crime scene had missed. Something that was completely inexplicable and something that was totally impossible.

DC Ford had decided that he needed a little advice on his revelation and so it was, one bright Wednesday morning, that he paid a visit to New Scotland Yard to see a senior detective, who seemed to be an expert in crimes concerning language schools.

He made his way to a large fourth floor office just off a massive open-plan area, knocked on a polished wooden door and entered. He sat down at a large and conspicuously empty teak desk upon which there were just two phones and an ornamental nineteenth century police truncheon.

He waited for five minutes and was just beginning to get rather impatient when a side door opened and a tall and balding man with a moustache walked in. DC Ford got up and saluted.

"No need for that," began the senior inspector.

"DC Ford, sir," said Ford quickly.

"No saluting here, Ford. We're not in the public eye now. Just colleagues trying to do a difficult job as best we can," said the senior inspector confidently. "Please sit down and tell me what all this is about. Coffee?"

DC Ford sat down and relaxed. Stories of this man had become almost legendary. It was good to see that even a demigod liked instant coffee, had dandruff and a bad taste in ties.

"It's these cases involving language schools," said Ford, after supping at his coffee a few minutes later.

"Ah, language schools again," murmured the senior inspector distantly. "What of them?" he asked, putting his cup down and taking out a notepad and pen from a drawer in front of him.

"Something really strange about these cases, which I thought you might be able to help us with," said Ford, reaching for his briefcase. He then pulled a thick wad of files from the bag and placed them onto the desk.

"How many cases are we talking about?" asked the frowning senior detective.

"Thirty-three."

"Thirty-three," repeated the senior man.

"Yes, sir, thirty-three."

"And you think I can help you with this problem?"

"I think I have proof that they are all linked," said DC Ford flatly.

"Linked?"

"Yes sir. All linked. I think the same person is responsible for every single one of the crimes."

"You mean we have a serial vandaliser on our hands?" quipped the senior man.

"Indeed sir."

"Are you serious, Ford?"

"I'm afraid so, sir."

"And why do you think this?" asked the inspector, easing back in his chair.

"Well, the local detectives just catalogued all the data and filed their reports. Probably pleased just to get such petty stuff out the way so they could get back to the more serious and interesting crimes. Plus, I think that there was a certain reluctance to catch the perpetrators of these... misdemeanours."

"And why do you think that?" asked the senior man, his frown deepening.

"Well, sir, I believe that our detectives think that they would be providing a greater service to the community by not nabbing the blighter responsible for all these crimes."

"A greater service?"

"In all cases," continued the younger man, "Our men discovered evidence which was far worse than the initial crime - evidence which always incriminated the victims. Accounts fiddling, tax evasion, slave labour, prostitution rings and in some cases straightforward theft and deception. The vigilante who uncovered these crimes seemed to know what he was doing when he broke into the schools."

"Oh dear," said the senior detective. "We can't condone this sort of public vigilantedom, of course. A crime is a crime, you know."

"Yes sir," agreed the younger man slowly. "But you have to admit it's a dilemma, sir. Sort of acting outside the law to bring villains to justice. Like Spiderman, sir."

"Spiderman?"

"You know sir, a superhero who gets the job done by any means available and without all the red tape and reporting afterwards," said the young detective.

The senior detective leaned forward and put both hands onto his shiny table. "So, why are you here now, DC Ford? You're not going to tell me that Spiderman has moved to London, are you" he asked slowly. There was no reply. "Have you discovered anything else?"

"Yes sir. I ran a check last week and discovered something that is impossible."

"Impossible?" The older man picked up a thin ballpoint pen and began toying with it.

"Yes sir," said DC Ford enthusiastically. "The only fingerprints ever found at the scene of each crime were those of one person."

"So?"

"Well, sir, he would have to have been very fast to have committed some of these crimes, sir."

"Fast? And why is that?"

"Because three schools were vandalised on the same night last November. In totally different areas of London, miles apart at roughly the same time. Now unless our man has suddenly mastered how to fly or teleport, then we have a mystery on our hands," said DC Ford flatly.

"Do we have any idea who this person is?" mumbled the senior man slowly. He was beginning to get a nasty feeling about this whole thing for some reason.

"Well, this is the really strange bit and the reason why I came to see you," said Ford, leaning onto the table a little more confidently. "According to police records, it's someone you've run into before."

The senior detective frowned deeply and looked hard at the young man sitting in front of him. "A name please?" he asked, croakily.

"Percy Raymond Gabbitt," replied Ford.

It was the reply the senior man least wanted to hear, but somehow most expected. He snapped the pen he was holding. Chief Inspector Pringle's morning had taken a savage turn for the worse.

Not a million miles away and on the other side of the planet, the man with very active fingerprints was sitting on a bench looking at a gaudy tourist barge chugging past. He was feeling worried, if truth be told.

Percy Gabbitt watched a man on a bike pedal past his bench and spit voluminously over his shoulder and into the canal. This was clearly a prime spitting spot. He sighed deeply.

"So, have you decided yet?" asked a bright voice.

"Not sure... Bob," he replied truthfully. "Seems like a shedload of trouble, when all I want is a quiet life in a classroom during the day and watching bootleg DVDs in the evening."

"Sounds great," said Irwin. "Mornings trekking all over this city teaching classes stuffed with screaming kids, followed by afternoons with businessmen whose only reason to learn the language is to chat up American girls. Really does sound like the perfect life."

"It's better than being chased round London by madmen who want you dead," said Gabbitt, with feeling.

"What about a more meaningful life?"

"Not possible," murmured Gabbitt. "My life has lost all meaning."

"Suppose it were possible. Suppose we could give you... meaning," said Bob Irwin leaning closer and patted Gabbitt on the back. "Would you be interested?"

There was a very long pause as another group of spitters strolled past.

"What about visa things and sponsorship? Don't I need a Chinese boss who can sort all that out? My Chinese boss."

Irwin just chuckled and continued the patting. "You just leave all that to us," he said. "The big question is: would you leave all that behind and join the crusade?"

"I'll have to think about it. Sounds plain crazy."

"Don't forget about the other perks too," said Irwin.

"Other perks?" asked Gabbitt.

Yes, other perks. Like being able to move to a four or five-bedroom apartment on the top floor of the best place in town?"

"Really?" squawked a wide-eyed Gabbitt, as another man on a luminous green electric bike sailed past and spat expertly over his other shoulder.

"You can leave that little hell-hole you currently call home far behind and move in today, if you like. You only have to say the word," beamed Irwin. "We'll even get a few men round to pack your stuff up for you right now. We can go to the bar, have a few drinks and then go to your new place afterwards. What do you say?"

There was a pause as the two of them watched a man in an ill-fitting suit unzip his pants and begin urinating on a small grassy area beside the path just ten feet from where they were sitting. The man smiled and waved at them. Irwin returned the wave as did several mothers and babies who were walking past their bench.

"Well, I'm still not sure. Joining some outfit which seems to be a cross between a Bader Meinhof cell and a refuge for anyone called Bob seems dangerous on any scale, despite the offer of a penthouse suite," said Gabbitt, standing up. He looked at the urinating man and sighed. On the other hand.

"No hurry," said Irwin, standing up as well. "Take all the time you need. And you don't have to change your name to Bob either. Percy will do just fine," he chuckled, happily.

"But what would I do? I only know how to market things badly and teach even worse."

"Exactly, mate," said Irwin and patted him on the back again. "Just what we need at the moment."

"I can't agree to join any madcap group without knowing more." Gabbitt smiled thinly.

The two of them then walked slowly back towards Suzhou city centre.

<It's a large vegetable which grows in trees and has to be supported on a plank until it's ripe enough to be picked. In the same family as the cucumber. You see them all over the place in semi-tropical countries>

<Never knew that. Taste nice?>

<Like a used bath towel I'm told - hence the name>

<Who would eat a towel gourd?>

<The Chinese apparently. Tastes OK if you saturate it in soy sauce>

<Doesn't everything?>

<Even bath towels apparently>

<What now, boss?>

<Don't call me that. I still think we should wait for Percy to turn up. He's got lots of strength and shielding points. With him around we stand a pretty good chance of sending that troll packing>

<OK. Do you think he'll approve of the new team?>

<He doesn't really have much choice, does he? But an elfette, a magician and... what do you call yourself, Joe?"

<A dwarf shaman>

<What in god's name is that?>

<A dwarf that can do a bit of magic... on the side>

<But we've already got a magician. And isn't a dwarf meddling in the dark arts a bit dangerous?>

<I'll be very careful, but I have to admit that I'm not sure what will happen if I throw a six and go berserk>

<Lord help us!>

<Couldn't you just be a normal dwarf?>

<Not much fun in that. Being a dwarf shaman I

reckon I might just end up being the linchpin of the group, what with all my fireballs and double-bladed axes. I can sell stuff too>

<?????>

<His schematics say he's ace at bartering and getting knock-down prices at the weapons shoppe>

<God in heaven. I have to agree that not many people would argue with a freak like that. Shoppe?>

<It's what it's called in the game>

<Sigh>

<Not sure about the name either>

< Shortie? Yoda? Paddingon?>

<Li Bang Cho>

<?????>

<???????>

<Chinese I think>

<A Chinese dwarf magician salesman. You've excelled yourself this time, Joe>

<Thought Percy would appreciate the gesture>

<Not sure about that>

<Well, I like it. Sounds mysterious>

<Thought Chinese didn't have any body hair. Sort of an anathema having a Chinese hirsute dwarf>

<A what?>

<An anathema>

<He's got an inhaler>

<Will you two shut up?>

<But a Chinese dwarf? You really can't have a dwarf without a beard. Goes against the grain of dwarfdom. And slitty eyes too? He's not a pint-sized Bruce Lee dwarf, is he?>

<Now there's a thought. A dwarf that can kick-ass as well as fling fireballs around, while slicing up what's left with his axe and then selling the detritus to the local abattoir. Gets better and better>

<We could've done with a thief who can spot traps in dungeons, or a ranger with invisibility options>

<I've got enough strength points to wade through all that, take everything on the chin and still survive>

<Christ. Does he do feng-shui as well?>

<Every night. Gets his strength points back to maximum quicker>

<God above!>

<Will you stop being profane, Dave? Not allowed on the site. You could get us banned>

<Sorry Cas>

<And don't call me that either. It's Caroline and nothing else. And Joe, have you ever considered stealth as a better option? Wading through all the traps and alarms might just send every orc, zombie and pit snapper within a two-mile radius scurrying to where we are in a matter of seconds?>

<Isn't that the point?>

<What's the point?>

<To fight the sods in every corridor and massacre them mercilessly>

<Glory be>

<Have you had a bad day at school, Joe?>

<How did you guess?>

<Just a hunch>

<What I can't understand is why anyone would call the thing a towel gourd? Sort of a downer before it gets anywhere near your plate, isn't it? Like calling a carrot -'bog-brush root'>

<Thanks for that, Dave>

<Ah, look at the bottom of your screen everyone. Guess who's here?>

<At flippin' last>

*Roger the Norse Fighter marched up the forest path and towards the small group of adventurers who were sitting under a large yew tree in the shade. Tammy the Goblin trailed in his wake, looking apprehensive.*

*"Hail, friends and welcome! Good to see you once more, noble Snark Maiden," said Roger and waved at the group like a junior Conservative minister.*

*"You're late," said the elfette, standing up and brushing dust off her short green skirt. She did not appreciate being waved at like that either, being a staunch socialist.*

*"Bit of a problem with a sadly-inadequate map," said Roger frowning hard a Tammy, who was about to say something and then decided that silence was the more sensible option.*

*"Whatever," sighed the elfette. "I've managed to get a group together," she added, a little unenthusiastically.*

*"Well met, all of you," beamed Roger bowing at the odd-looking dwarf and the magician in the pointed hat.*

*"And, err, who might you two be?" asked Roger, slowly. He had not come across either of the odd-looking adventurers in the village before.*

*"Li Bang Cho," said the dwarf, springing to his feet and bowing deeply.*

*"A truly wondrous sight!" murmured Roger, as he surveyed the figure, critically. "Er, without causing offence, my friend, what race art thou?"*

*"I art a dwarf," smiled the dwarf.*

*"A dwarf without a beard?" queried Tammy.*

*"We've been there," said the Snark Maiden, tiredly. "His name's Li Bang Cho for some strange reason which I don't want to try to explain either. And this is Endymion," she said, gesturing to the tall figure in the pointed hat and dark purple robe.*

*"A worthy name," said Roger honestly, though he had no idea where such a name had come from, but it sort of sounded right for a wizard. "Well met, my friends. And now the quest begins. Let us proceed with haste to this troll's gate and make acquaintance with the troll there. Perhaps he is a sound and cheerful fellow who will let us pass with a cheery wave and a laugh or two."*

*"Doubtful," said Endymion through gritted teeth.*

Three hours later and the insanity had switched to a different location.

Gabbitt sat in a small room tucked away on the eighth floor of an impressive looking glass and metal structure quite near the lake in eastern Suzhou. He was perched on a red plastic chair and looking a Chinaman called Bruce in the eye.

"But teacher Gobfish," remonstrated Bruce, wearily. "I no have no hobbies. No time. Just work, sleep and eat."

Gabbitt sighed deeply. Teaching Chinese businessmen was turning out to be a rather harder task than he had anticipated. All they wanted to do was stumble through grammar books and repeat everything, chorus-fashion. Free conversation was a total anathema to them, with or without inhalers.

His class consisted of three employees from Suzhou-Solingen Tool Suppliers. It was a German concern staffed by about thirty locals and managed by two obese Rheinlanders called Kurt and Franz, who reckoned that their employees would benefit from two evenings a week learning survival English. German had only been briefly considered by the two managers, whose English was probably better than the average Englishman.

Apparently, Kurt and Franz had decided that their own language would be their own private domain for as long as possible and that English would be the Lingua Franca. Chinese, not surprisingly, had never been an option.

The other two employees down for three hours Business English that evening were Boot and Mouse.

Boot was a mid-level manager who listed his interests as western toolboxes, Chinese chess and westerns. He had very short-cropped hair, wore round glasses and always appeared for classes in a smart grey suit and orange company tie.

He had already had his turn and had just told the small group that John Wayne was the greatest man that had ever lived. Gabbitt had hastily moved on.

Mouse was a secretary. She had very long hair, a heart-shaped face, surgically-widened eyes and wore lacy-white blouses. To the man in the street she was quite a 'looker'. Mouse knew this and generally sneered at most males. Her interests were shopping, shopping and more shopping, preferably with her many girlfriends.

"What do you do in your spare time, when not shopping?" asked Gabbitt as he turned to face Mouse's massive eyes.

Mouse giggled and went red. "I like texting."

"Who do you text?" asked Gabbitt, trying to stave off terminal boredom.

"My friends."

"What do you text about?"

"Shopping and things."

"What things?"

"Every things."

"For example?"

"Nice things."

"What sort of nice things?" asked an increasingly mesmerized Gabbitt.

"Dresses," said Mouse, after a thoughtful pause.

"Ah," said Gabbitt, not at all sure where to lead the conversation next.

"Nice dresses," added Mouse seriously.

"Anything else?" said Gabbitt trying to stifle a yawn.

"Wedding dresses," said Mouse, suddenly becoming very animated.

"Are you getting married?" asked Gabbitt, waking up a little.

"No," squeaked Mouse, in embarrassment. "But I like wedding dresses. They very pretty."

"Oh," said Gabbitt, slowly.

"I like texting my friends about wedding dresses."

"Are they getting married?"

"No."

"So... why do you text about wedding dresses?"

"They pretty."

Percy Gabbitt cleared his throat and turned back to Boot. Perhaps an examination of his interest in western toolboxes would alleviate the chronic apathy slowly rigamortising everyone in the room.

"So, which tool do you like best, Boot?"

"The Colt-Root Model 1855 percussion repeating rifle."

# FIVE

*"My hobbies are tennis, golf and fast cats"*
**(A Chinese student trying to impress his teacher)**

Chief Inspector Pringle got out of his car and walked towards a set of imposing gates set in a high red-brick wall. The place looked like a fortress, the only difference being that this place prevented people getting out rather than in.

He flashed his ID and stepped through a small door to one side of the main entrance. He then signed the Visitors Book and then walked down a heavily-disinfected corridor accompanied by a man in a black peaked cap and clutching a fistful of jangling keys. Every twenty feet a door had to be unlocked, opened and then locked again behind them.

Pringle rather liked visiting prisons. It was like an artist looking at all his previous masterpieces or a novelist flicking through a pile of published novels. There was a sense of a job well done, a sense of completion.

Wormwood Scrubs was built in the late nineteenth century and looked like a prison ought to look. It was thoroughly Victorian and a place that you really did not want to spend too much time in, not like the modern ones, which tended to resemble a cross between Disneyland and the Marriott Hilton.

The current population of the Scrubs was one thousand, two hundred and thirty-nine. Strangely, this was a fact that Chief Inspector Pringle knew well and was intensely proud of.

He was ushered into the Visitors Centre and to a tiny room containing just two chairs divided by a simple vinyl-covered table. He stared at the walls while he waited for prisoner Number 34802 and was a little disconcerted to see a notice-board upon which were pinned small pieces of paper exhorting the prison population to enrol on a variety of month-long courses.

Pringle frowned. Even this place had been infiltrated by the do-gooders. He scanned the list of available courses and his frown deepened.

Some idiot was actually running relationship courses, for heaven's sake. He shook his held slowly. Why would a serial killer want to learn how to handle his relationships better? Maybe fraternising with his next victim would somehow help both parties understand the deep emotional problems percolating in the criminal's mind, as he began bludgeoning the poor sod to death, thought Pringle glumly. Total madness.

His gaze wandered from the notice-board to a magazine rack near the door and he frowned again. That was another thing. The prison even had their own monthly glossy magazine. What was the world coming to? Something called 'Life in Scrubs'. Life indeed, thought Pringle.

The door opened and a warder walked in.

"Sorry to keep you waiting, Chief Inspector, but the prisoner was attending an English 'A' Level class and we didn't like to interrupt."

Pringle did not reply. His sour face said it all though. A villain who had once run an English language school in central London now doing an English 'A' Level. Totally barking.

A moment later and a man in late middle-age with greying hair and a large paunch marched into the room. He sat down and stared at the Chief Inspector. There was a moment of silence as both men weighed up the unusual situation before them. The man then coughed bronchially and pulled a packet of cigarettes from a top pocket.

"Hello, Chief Inspector Pringle. What a pleasant surprise," he said, over-emphasising the 'Chief' bit and then lighting up and blowing the smoke into Pringle's face.

"Good morning Handsworth or Danvers or whatever you're calling yourself nowadays," said Pringle, grumpily.

"What do you mean, they're my fingerprints?" asked an indignant Percy Gabbitt in a place called the *'Moon Shining Brightly Through the Branches of a Flowering Cherry Tree.'*

It was a traditional Chinese tea house and Gabbitt was sitting in an enclosed booth opposite the beaming smiles of Bob Burley and Bob Irwin. Burley was in a jacket and tie, while Irwin sported a Hawaiian shirt which looked like a road accident involving a lot of pineapples.

"Don't you see, it's absolutely perfect," enthused Burley happily. "The police will be totally baffled and, more importantly, we'll have made an important point."

"That I'm a serial school destroyer who is hell-bent on single-handedly wrecking the entire industry in the UK, despite living in China. Is that what you mean?" fumed an increasingly upset Gabbitt.

"Absolutely," came the slightly odd response. "You see," continued Burley, leaning forward in his seat, "You have become an icon in the fight against corruption in the industry, as we've told you before. A legend in our time. Teachers and sales people everywhere mutter your name in hope. The police grudgingly admire you. The…"

"I've heard the sales talk," interrupted Gabbitt, tiredly. "I just like it. Are you trying to get me onto the UK's most wanted list in record time?"

"Don't you see, Percy? Even a particularly dozy detective will quickly realise that you can't be responsible for all of these crimes and that something is not quite right. Then they'll do a bit of research and will find that you're here in wonderful China. They'll take you off the list immediately. An obvious frame-up. Don't worry about it."

Burley then sat back and supped hard at his green tea.

"But why my fingerprints?" exploded Gabbitt.

"Because you're Percy Raymond Gabbitt!" replied Burley equally loudly. Burley was never a man to be easily cowed. He took a deep breath and continued: "You're the hero of the oppressed, the vanquisher of…"

"Stop. Please stop. I don't like it. You didn't ask me first. And how did you get my prints anyway?"

"Sorry about that, Percy. Thought you'd approve. Anyway, we produced these washing-up gloves."

Burley fiddled with an inside jacket pocket and pulled out a pair of Marigolds. Gabbitt frowned hard.

"Why am I staring at a pair of yellow washing up gloves?" asked Gabbitt, wearily.

"Incredible, isn't it?" marvelled Burley, as he snapped them on. "The wonders of science today. Each finger tip has your fingerprints embossed on it," he murmured, in admiration.

"How many?" demanded Gabbitt, feeling that he had to know the extent of the horror unfolding before him.

"How many what?"

"How many crimes have I committed?"

"Not that many," said Burley.

"How many?" insisted Gabbitt.

"Thirty-nine, if you add that job in Canada and the other one in South Africa," said Irwin bluntly. "Any more tea?" he sniffed. "My throat's drier than a wombat's todger."

Dave Springett was standing on a wooden crate by the statue of Eros in Piccadilly Circus. He was wearing a new outfit. Gone were the goggles and the silver suit. He had happily thrown them into the rubbish skip after Box Hill and had decided on a totally new incarnation - something that would somehow reflect his present mood, whilst at the same time intriguing the general public. And, most importantly, attracting a brand-new audience.

A group of about ten Americans had gathered around him and were taking turns to have their picture taken with him on their minute Japanese digital cameras. They were clearly intrigued and attracted.

Springett smiled – inwardly of course, and continued his silent vigil. The cardboard box at his feet also reflected the happy state of the public's mood that afternoon.

Several children ran up to him and squeezed his paw. Springett felt a glow of pride and delight as more coins clinked into the box. Life was really good at the moment, he thought, and tried to ignore an itch which was creeping along one furry ear to the other.

A man in a grey raincoat approached his plinth and stared hard at him. Springett stared back and suddenly began hearing alarm bells ringing in the far distance and getting closer with every second. He looked at the man tried to work out if he knew him.

"DC Ford," said the man flatly and flashed what looked like an ID of some sort. "We need to talk," he continued. "Man to panda."

*The troll had eventually seen it Roger's way though it had taken twenty minutes of persuasive arguing done mostly with the point of a spear and the blade of a sword.*

*Roger stood breathlessly by the bridge and wiped sweat from his brow. It had been one hell of a fight. Trolls were supposed to roll over after one or two pointless charges, but this one had been a little different.*

*The troll in question leaned against the bridge rubbing a bruised elbow.*

*"I like a good fight," he wheezed in Roger's direction. "Sort of adds meaning to life," he added and blew on a throbbing thumb.*

*"You certainly know how to wield that axe, my friend," said Roger, ever the one to congratulate a worthy adversary.*

*"You don't learn that sort of thing at troll's school, I can tell you that," murmured the troll. "Comes from countless encounters with the likes of your kind. A troll gets to learn the more complicated moves."*

*"Indeed," agreed Roger. "You certainly gave my friends something to think about," said Roger,*

*looking at his battered party as they recovered on the path some thirty yards away. "I particularly liked the way you took that wizard's hat off. No one was expecting that. Least of all him. "*

*"Should have been his head as well," chuckled the troll. "Must be getting sloppy in my old age. It's called the 'Bump-and-Grind' manoeuvre, just in case you ever come up against something likethatt in the future. I hear it's all the rage in troll circles down by the coast at the moment."*

*"I'll bear that in mind," said Roger and sheathed his sword.*

*"So, to business," said the troll, and spat copiously into the river by the bridge.*

*"Absolutely," agreed Roger.*

*"For form's sake, I have to ask you three questions. If you get them right I allow you and your mates across. If you don't, then we have to go through all this again…blah blah, blah. You know the rest. OK with you?"*

*"Yes, no problems. Let's have question number one, er…"*

*"Incidentally, the name's Toby Cudgel," grunted the troll. "Pleased to make your acquaintance, sir."*

*"Roger the Norse Fighter," said Roger and extended a hand.*

*"No, no, no," said the troll in a hoarse whisper. "Can't have the two of us hobnobbing like that. Best we keep our distance and preserve the… order of things. Trolls shaking hands with heroes? Whatever*

*next… a goblin companion?" he said and gave Roger a large knowing wink.*

*"Right," said Roger. "Understood."*

*The Snark Maiden, Tammy the Goblin and Endymion the wizard approached the two of them. The wizard was limping slightly and did not look very pleased with life.*

*"Did you see where the other half of my hat landed?" he asked indignantly.*

*Li Bang Co, the oriental dwarf, trotted up to the group and stared at the troll. "Two more minutes and I would have had you, you know," he said huffily. "'Dragon-over-Waterlilies' beats most moves hands down."*

*"That's old hat," snorted the troll, as he picked up the pointy bit of Endymion's hat and tossed it to him. "They teach you that in troll junior school.*

*"Tiger-jumping-through-bamboo-trees?" tried Li Bang, Cho a little less confidently.*

*"You'd be orc fodder if you tried that one on me, mate. 'Crunch-and-Smash' gets through all those fancy, namby-pamby moves any day. And if that they don't work then 'Twist-and-Squeeze' always carries the day."*

*Li Bang Cho sat down on the path feeling a mite taken aback. He had spent good money purchasing the best and most complicated killing moves possible from the Buddhist temple in the village just prior to leaving on this quest. Now it seemed that dragons and tigers leaping all over the place just were not good enough in the modern fantasy world. He would have a word with the head monk when he got back, though he doubted that a refund would be in the offing.*

*"Question number one," said the troll, clearing his throat.*

*"It's a multiple choice one by the way, so don't but in with an answer till I get to the end. I had a barbarian do that last week and had to fight him all over again, just because he was too impatient to let me finish. A lot of wasted energy on both sides over a simple question which he would have got right had he just waited a few seconds before answering.*

*"Understood," said Roger.*

*"And you have to answer it by yourself, mate," said the troll, staring threateningly at the Snark Maiden and Endymion, unless you wish to use up one of your three 'lifelines'."*

*"Lifelines?" queried Roger.*

*"You get three lifelines and then I have to have your answer. One lifeline is: 'Ask any friend you like'. You then get thirty seconds to confer with a mate of your choice. The second is for me to remove two of the wrong answers, leaving it a straight fifty-fifty choice. And the third is to ask all your mates which is the right answer. You have ten seconds to listen to their points of view and then you give me your best choice. Ready?"*

*"Er, yes," said Roger," who was a little confused by the breadth of choice. He far preferred the simple and more direct way.*

*"Right," said the troll. "Question number one: An angry dragon flies from its cave at a speed of thirty miles an hour towards the village, which it is terrorising. If the village is ten miles away and there's a head wind of five miles an hour against the dragon, what did the dragon have for breakfast?"*

*"What?" asked a totally baffled Roger.*

*"Wait for the answers, please," said the frowning troll. He cleared his throat again and looked at Roger. "(a) nothing; (b) corn flakes with chopped banana in high fat milk; (c) porridge and (d) muesli."*

*Roger mulled the question over for a few moments and was about to answer when the troll interrupted his thoughts.*

*"The clue's in the question, you see," he said with a smile and another wink. "You can have fifty-fifty if you want, you know."*

*"d," said Roger slightly worriedly. He fingered his sword hilt expecting the worst.*

*"Correct," beamed the troll. "Who wouldn't be angry if all you had for breakfast was something that looked like the bottom of a parrot's cage? Well done."*

*Roger relaxed. The Snark Maiden raised her eyebrows a little and was about to say something in defence of muesli, but then thought better of it.*

*"Question two," said the troll. "And remember that you still have all three lifelines left. Some adventurers forget that in all the excitement," he added with a chuckle. "And this is a straight question, by the way. No multiple choice thingie."*

*"Right," said Roger, feeling a little happier.*

*"Why does my dog smell so bad?"*

*"What?" grunted Roger, feeling for his sword again.*

*"You heard the question," said the troll with just a hint of menace in his voice. "I'll confer with one of my friends," said Roger quickly and looked at the sad group gathered behind him. "But which one," he murmured to himself.*

*After a long moment, he chose Endymion, feeling that his slightly odd way of looking at life might serve him best with a question like this one. The Snark Maiden would probably come up with a really plausible and logically perfect answer... that would be quite wrong, while Li Bang Cho would probably spend the entire thirty seconds trying to understand the question, let alone attempt an answer. Tammy the Goblin looked at him hopefully. Roger smiled at his friend chose the wizard.*

*Endymion grinned broadly and looked at the troll. "Because he has a cold," said the wizard smugly.*

*"Correct," said the troll and clapped his massive hands together in delight. "It's one of them trick questions, you see,' he said gleefully. "You're the first party to get that right in such a fast time. I am impressed," he said. "It won't help though because question three is a bit of a stinker, I'm afraid."*

*"Just a minute," interrupted the Snark Maiden. "You've got it wrong. It should be something like: How does my dog smell? That way you have the choice of answering both ways, the funny answer being: 'Badly', of course. Your way," said the Snark*

*Maiden moodily, "can only be answered in one way, unless you're being totally ungrammatical."*

*The troll narrowed his eyes. "There's always one," he murmured and began hefting his double-handed battle-axe menacingly.*

*"Quite," said Roger hastily. "Can we have question number three, please?"*

*"But..." began the Snark Maiden, determined to have her say.*

*"Quite," said Roger, slightly louder.*

*"Oh whatever," sighed the Snark Maiden. "But you all know I'm right."*

*"Question number three," said the piqued troll. "And I should say that nobody has ever got this one. It's one of those impossible ones which you either know or you don't, like: 'What's the capital of Surinam?' or 'What's my grandmother's name?"*

*"Oh great," mumbled Li Bang Cho, getting ready for another spat in the dust with the massive troll.*

*"Paramaribo," said the Snark Maiden primly.*

*"What?" said the troll dangerously. He had suddenly taken a strong dislike to the elfette.*

*"The capital of Surinam is Paramaribo," said the Snark Maiden, raising both eyebrows imperiously. "And I would think your grandmother's name is something like, er...Bijou," she said and readied herself for the inevitable attack.*

*The troll took a step back and his mouth fell open. "How on earth did you know that?" he spluttered in amazement.*

*"Obvious really," came the reply. "It had to be something so unlikely that it actually becomes very likely. A large trollesse, if you don't mind me saying, is everything that someone who is traditionally called Bijou, is not. On the other hand, trollesses are famous for liking jewellery and, as such, is a pretty logical name."*

*"Well, I'll be..." muttered the still shocked troll.*

*"Is it really Paramaribo?" asked Endymion, equally amazed, but for other reasons.*

*"Of course," came the Snark Maiden's reply.*

*"Please can we have question number three?" asked a weary Roger. "We haven't got all day, you know."*

*"Right," said the troll, returning to the business in hand. "Get this right and you not only get to pass over my bridge, but you also get twenty gold coins too, as a reward for your good fortune."*

*Good fortune has nothing to do with it," murmured the Snark Maiden.*

*"Quite," said an exasperated Roger.*

*"Number Three... and I can only accept your first answer," said the troll seriously. "What is a towel gourd?"*

"You know what they say about the enemy of my enemy," began Chief Inspector Pringle.

"Is still my bloody enemy," puffed Nero Handsworth stubbornly.

Pringle stared at the former gangland boss and decided that it was time to lay his cards on the table. He had had enough of being smoked on and then treated like an idiot. Who did this man think he was?

"Percy Raymond Gabbitt," he said and watched the reaction.

Nero's mouth opened and his cigarette fell out and into his lap where it smouldered dangerously. He appeared not to notice. It seemed that no physical pain, no matter how acute and no matter where applied, would have the same impact as the name just uttered in his presence.

"I have your attention then," said Pringle with a thin smile.

"What the f..." began Nero, his face turning a worrying shade of crimson.

"Careful, Handsworth," said Pringle. "Remember that your heart is not quite as it should be."

"What the f..." said Nero again, his eyes bulging out of their sockets.

"I think that for once we have a common interest," said Pringle airily. "I know of your ... dislike for the gentleman in question and as such, would like your views on a hypothetical situation concerning Mr Gabbitt."

"What the f..." spluttered Nero again.

"You see, Handsworth, we have a certain predicament on our hands which concerns our mutual friend. It seems that he has crossed the line once more."

Nero loosened his tie and sat back in his chair. All pretence at being in control of this meeting had evaporated upon hearing that hated name.

"Now I know that you have certain connections in the... outside world. Perhaps if we can come to some sort of loose agreement, then we may both be able to solve a little problem we are now faced with. How would you like that, Handsworth?"

"Certain connections? I don't know what you're talking about. I don't know anybody on the outside," growled Nero.

Pringle looked hard at the former gangland boss and noticed a curl of smoke rising from his trousers. He waited a few more seconds then leaned across the table so that his nose was almost touching Nero's. He then whispered very slowly: "Pants on fire."

"So, what's your dream?"

Percy Gabbitt stared at his class. It consisted of fifty-one sixteen year olds and they all spoke some English...more or less. This was Gabbitt's third week attempting to get them past the Present Perfect. It had proven to be one fence just that little bit too high and Gabbitt had decided on a bit of free conversation to get them all back into the mood again.

The boys at the back stopped throwing a tennis ball around, while the front row girls all beamed back at Gabbitt with eyes wide-open and hair immaculately pinched back in bright red scrunchies. They would not miss a single word from their new hero no matter what he said or did. It was a typical morning at Experimental School Number Nine in the eastern part of Suzhou's new district.

Gabbitt let the question hang in the air for a long moment. He watched as his flock of teenagers chewed over possible answers. He remembered quite clearly that when asked this question when he was sixteen he had instantly replied that he wanted to win Wimbledon, score the opening goal in a Cup Final, go out with Anne Percival and be the first Englishman to step on the Moon. All pretty modest ambitions for a teenager, but ambitions nevertheless. He readied himself for their dreams.

"Teacher Goblit," said a girl with large glasses at the front. She then stood up and addressed the class as a whole: "I will am be maybe good wife for rich husband maybe. Cute."

The class all clapped as one and the girl sat down.

"Thank you, Britney," said Gabbitt, uncertainly.

Another girl stood up.

"Yes, Lily?" tried Gabbitt encouragingly.

"I am same as Britney, but maybe need more rich husband," she said and waited for the applause. Then she sat down again.

"Anybody else with a slightly different dream?"

There was a long pause as if Gabbitt had asked them to explain Newton's law on gravity.

A boy at the back got to his feet. He had moderately short hair that looked as if it been subjected to an electric shock in the three-thousand volt range. It was gelled in lots of spiky directions.

"What's your dream, Sylvester?" shouted Gabbitt. He then added under his breath: "To buy a comb?"

"I want America go," bellowed the boy loudly.

The girls at the front all drummed their feet on the floor in excitement. This was clearly a popular dream.

"Why?" tried Gabbitt, feeling that at last he had something to latch onto which would waste the next ten minutes.

"I want gun," came the disconcerting reply.

"Yes, me too," said another boy, followed by two more. After a few seconds the whole back four rows were dreaming of guns.

"A gun? Why?" asked an incredulous Gabbitt.

"It cool and all Americans have," shouted the boy, knowledgeably. "I see on TV."

"But what do you want a gun for?" persisted Gabbitt, immediately regretting his question.

Sylvester did not mind. He raised his hand in the air and pretended to mow down the girls to his right.

"So, I shoot girls I no like," he cried, happily.

"Me too," agreed another boy also with a short-crop simian haircut, who looked as if he had had serious girl problems in the not too distant past.

"I want cat too," continued Sylvester.

"You mean car?" queried Gabbitt. Liking a gun and a cat did not seem to be a logical combination, whereas a gun and a car somehow did.

"No, I mean cat. I buy many and then I shoot them with my gun."

There were murmurs of approval from the back of the room. Shooting cats was definitely the way to go among the teenage fraternity in Suzhou

"OK, Sylvester, no problem," said Gabbitt.

"No problem?" repeated a baffled Sylvester.

"No problem at all. You can have a gun if you go to America."

"I can?" squawked Sylvester. His friends were all listening now. This was evidently a very important piece of information.

"Only..." started Gabbitt slowly. He then deliberately let out a long, vocal sigh and walked back to the blackboard.

"What, teacher Gabblock?" shouted Sylvester. He was almost on the point of running down the aisle between desks to get the low-down on gun purchasing in the States out of his teacher, no matter what the cost.

"Only," said Gabbitt tantalisingly slowly, before turning round. "You have to be able to speak English very, very well."

"Why teacher?" hurled Sylvester, impatiently.

"Well," said Gabbitt, spinning it out as long as possible. "At all airports in America you have to do a simple English test on arrival. Those Chinese students with high marks and no mistakes are given really big guns. The Chinese who make many mistakes get given a knife or something that you can put into your pocket."

There was pandemonium at the back of the class as the group of sixteen-year-old boys all suddenly realised that Lily and Britney on the front row of the class would be walking away with Kalashnikov assault rifles and Magnum pistols, while they would have to make do with a flick-knife each.

Clearly Sylvester did not really approve of such a thing and began voicing his disgust, while standing on his table and gesticulating wildly at the world rather like that monkey in '2001'.

The noise died down a little and the back row settled into a moody silence.

Sylvester crawled back into his chair and put his hand up slowly. Gabbitt nodded to the gun lover.

"It not fair," said the boy sulkily. "Now I learn Perfect Present, Present Continuous, Past Simple, Future Perfect and all the others so I get big gun and not small thing for back pocket. I lose much face if this happen."

Gabbitt sighed deeply. An optimist might say that such a tactic had worked brilliantly. He now had the undivided attention of the whole class for a topic which was unbelievably dull and difficult to understand at the best of times. He tried to imagine what a pessimist would think, but gave up very quickly.

He rubbed his board clean and was about to launch into the difference between 'I have eaten my tofu wrap' and 'I ate my tofu wrap,' when a little voice in the front row chirped:

"Can I have nice big handbag instead? I no want gun."

It was at this point that Percy Raymond Gabbitt realised that perhaps teaching English was not such a great career move and that Arapacana Associates, no matter how insane their motives and methods were, was probably a better and more worthwhile place to spend his immediate future. He turned round and looked at the big, beaming face of Britney Jordan Zhang.

"Yes, Britney,' he said slowly. "You can have the biggest handbag in the world all studded with diamonds and rubies and with not one, but three mobile phones with limitless credit."

Britney squeaked in ecstatic delight as she suddenly realised that America really was Paradise on Earth.

"I've got a licence, you know," mumbled Springett, as he picked up his money box and followed the man in the grey suit.

"I've no doubt that you have," said DC Ford. "Anyway, I'm hardly going to arrest you for impersonating a large black and white bear, now am I?"

"Stranger things have happened," said Springett, warily. He pulled his head off and ran a grubby paw through his sweaty hair. "Hot work in there, you know."

"Then let me buy you a drink," said DC Ford, amicably.

Several minutes later and the two of them marched into the Drum and Monkey in Curzon Street.

"Sorry, I don't serve bears in here," said the barman jovially.

"That's all right," said Springett. "I'll have a pint instead."

There was a cheer from a couple of drunks at the bar and someone gave Springett a round of applause.

"Always like a bear with a sense of humour," continued the barman, as he reached for a glass.

"What's life if you can't have a laugh?" said Springett as he installed himself at the bar.

"Can't see what you're laughing about, especially if you're an endangered species that only eats bamboo shoots and has sex once a year," said the chuckling barman as he pulled the pint.

"Well, tonight's the night," said Springett, now really entering into the spirit of things.

There was another cheer and some claps.

The barman placed two frothing pints of real ale onto the bar. DC Ford went for his wallet.

"Wouldn't dream of it," said the barman. "Those two are on the house," he said gesturing at the pints. "Never charge bears or coppers in this place," he said looking warily at Ford. He then walked slowly to the end of the bar whistling the theme tune from Laurel and Hardy.

"I do wish they wouldn't do that," said DC Ford staring at his pint. "Never really understood what it has to do with being a policeman."

"And therein lies the reason why the police will never understand Joe Public," said Springett, taking a large gulp. "So, Mr Policeman, what can a large Chinese bear do for you?"

"It's Detective Constable Ford," said Ford. "And I need you to tell me something."

"Last time I told a copper something I had just been locked in car boot, shot at and then rolled down a small mountain," said Springett reaching for his pint again.

"Box Hill is hardly a mountain," said Ford quietly. "And anyway, you have every reason to be grateful for the actions of the police force that day."

"Well, DC Ford," said Springett, as he downed the last two inches of his pint, "I'm not so sure about that."

"Anyway," said Ford, leaning forward. "I need a little help on a slightly touchy matter."

Springett indicated to the barman that he needed another pint and looked at the policeman.

"Now let me get this absolutely straight, Detective Constable Ford," he said slowly. "You want my help?"

"Indeed. Actually, it's nothing that important really. It just would assist us in a current investigation, that's all."

"What's he done this time?" asked Springett suddenly.

"What? Who?" asked Ford.

"Percy flippin' Gabbitt, that's who," replied Springett, as he supped deep into his second pint.

"Ah," said Ford also taking a swig at his.

"Ah indeed," said Springett. "What do you want with him this time? He hasn't blown up any more schools, has he?"

When DC Ford did not smile, Springett stared long and hard at the policeman. "He hasn't, has he?"

"I just need to have a word with him, that's all," said Ford quietly.

"Well, that might be a bit difficult," sniffed Springett. "He's in China."

"We know that," said Ford slowly. "It's just that he doesn't seem to answer his phone or respond to emails."

"Hates the phone, does our Percy," said Springett, starting on his third pint, "And never looks at his Hotmail account either. Doesn't like emails, does our Percy."

"So how do I have a word with him? It really is most important," said DC Ford. He cleared his throat and put his beer down on the bar. "Do you know any way I can talk to your friend?"

There was a short pause and then Springett put his pint down and turned to the detective constable.

"Have you ever heard of Dark Dawn Three?" he asked, seriously.

# SIX

*"The Chinese will never finalise any business deal until they've had a vast banquet and tried to get you completely plastered. A large brown envelope stuffed with cash helps grease the wheels of negotiation rather well too."*

**(Sales negotiations with the Chinese according to Bob Burley, Managing Director of Arapacana Associates)**

Percy Gabbitt needed a haircut.

In other cities around the world this would be a fairly innocuous and humdrum task. Not so in China and especially not so in Suzhou.

First of all, never search for anywhere that looks like it cuts hair. Second, make sure that you know exactly what you want doing to your hair. Third, expect the unexpected.

Gabbitt, of course, did not know any of these useful pieces of advice and had just walked into a rather cosy looking place just a stone's throw from the ferry terminal along the south side of the moat which encircled Suzhou. This was his first mistake of the day.

"You American?" enquired a particularly pretty-looking girl wearing little more than ten red silk handkerchiefs.

Gabbitt stared at the girl and wondered if she were going to be his barber. He rather thought not, but he had learned that in China you never take anything for granted.

"No," he replied a little curtly and sat down on a yellow velvet couch near the door.

"Nice day," said the girl, beaming a massive toothy grin at him.

"Looks like rain," responded Gabbitt, honestly.

"Why?" was the rather unusual question which this observation prompted.

"Dark clouds to the south," said Gabbitt, knowing full well that neither knew what the other was talking about.

"My name Madonna," said the girl and started giggling.

"Ah, another material girl," smiled Gabbitt.

The girl muttered something in Chinese and disappeared behind a long velvet curtain which led to the back of the hairdresser's. A few moments later and whispered voices could be heard behind the curtain. It sounded like two more girls had joined the pop star. The curtain fluttered slightly and half a face appeared for a short second and then bobbed back to safety. Gabbitt sat back and thought of England.

A slightly older woman in a lemon-coloured dress and wearing green Nike sneakers then pushed through the curtain and looked at Gabbitt. "You American?" she asked.

Gabbitt frowned and thought about this. Clearly, to have a haircut in Suzhou entailed being an American for some odd reason so, after a pause, he bit the bullet and said:

"Yes, I am an American and I want a haircut, please."

"How many?" was the response from the woman.

"Just the one," said Gabbitt, rapidly reconsidering the wisdom of getting his hair cut that evening. Clearly, this was a major task in downtown Suzhou.

"How long?" asked the woman.

"Just above the ears and collar and not much off the top," said Gabbitt wondering if this woman really understood the Queen's English.

"Five hundred. One hour," said the woman rather harshly.

"Ah," said Gabbitt, as the penny slowly dropped.

A moment later and two girls pushed through the curtain and stood in front of Gabbitt. One was Madonna, who was still wearing the red silk handkerchiefs, though she seemed to have lost three of them, the other was a slightly smaller girl with very long, electric blond hair and wearing what can only be described as a fabric glitterball.

"Ah," said Gabbitt again, realising that there was not going to be much action on the hair front in this establishment.

"Nothing fancy," said the older woman and wagged a finger at him.

"I think I'll be going now," said Gabbitt and stood up.

"You no like?" asked the woman, incredulously.

"No, they're very nice," said Gabbitt inching to the door and freedom.

"OK. Three hundred," said the woman, realising that this American might just be a harder bargainer than she had initially thought.

"Thank you," said Gabbitt and reached for the door handle.

"One hundred, OK?"

"Not really," said Gabbitt.

"Fifty?"

"Bye bye."

"Twenty?" squawked the woman, as Gabbitt stepped onto the street.

"Ten?"

Percy Gabbitt began striding away as fast as he could. He heard the door to the hairdresser's open and a voice rang out,

"Five and fancy OK too."

He rounded a corner and reached for his mobile phone.

*The village was relatively quiet. A rather thin fellow wearing a cotton jerkin and with a heavy sack slung over one shoulder walked purposefully from one small shop to the next. He opened the door to what looked like an armoury and… opened the door… opened the door… opened the door... opened the door… opened the door… opened the door… opened the door...door...door...door...door...doo...doo...do...do...d... d...d...d..................*

*FULL REBOOT REQUIRED........*

*SHUTTING DOWN.......>>*

The Screen went very black.

"Shit!" expleted DC Ford with feeling. He tapped at the buttons on his keyboard and started to lose his temper.

"Bloody viruses," he muttered to himself and banged the side of his VDU in an attempt to unfreeze his computer. The thumping of his computer in various novel ways lasted about ten seconds and then he angrily played his keyboard the way Beethoven probably did when composing the Ninth. He then got up and went to the pub for a double whisky and a fume.

As he left the police station, a small box beeped onto his screen telling him that he had contracted something called the 'Viper Trojan ESL 69' and that his Virus Doctor had kicked in to have a grapple with this particularly nasty serpent.

Chief Inspector Pringle looked up from a thick file on his table in the next office. He stared through a large window and wondered for a few minutes about the suitability of allowing DC Ford into his newly created task force. The man was certainly keen, but seemed to lack that certain doggedly patient attitude so important in today's policeman. Pringle also did not generally approve of emergency trips to the pub to solve emotional problems either. That smacked of what a seventies detective might have done.

Times had moved on and the Force nowadays looked down on the drinking, smoking, swearing and fast-car type of copper so popular in the past. Today, the modern policeman had to be a thoughtful, non-emotional, problem-solver... or a computer programmer that wrote copious reports. It was also far better for career prospects to be a good listener who related to criminals in a calm and soothing manner. Punching the shit out of them and then locking the bastards up was apparently not an answer. Talking to them and then releasing them after a damn good counselling was.

He made a note to have a word with Ford later that day. He then sighed from the bottom of his boots and stared at the buff file on the table. It had Percy Raymond Gabbitt written in felt pen on the front.

Pringle ran a finger over the name and caressed the file the same way that you would stroke a tiger. His fingers lightly brushed the file ready to leap away at the slightest hint of a snarl. Pringle frowned. Why did this man have such as effect on him? It was not that he was a particularly nasty villain. In fact, it had been proved that he had been the innocent dupe back in those heady Box Hill days and was not a villain at all.

But still... there was something about this man that made Pringle uncomfortable. Something that was not quite right. It was like an annoying itch in the middle of your back, which you can't get rid of no matter how often you give the thing a darn good scraping with the bathroom loofah.

He just had to be guilty of something, thought Pringle and frowned. To go through all that without a blemish to his character... well, it was just not possible. And now, his fingerprints were turning up in every crime scene the length and breadth of the country, not just in London. It was as if this Percy Gabbitt was giving the police two fingers all over again.

Pringle sat back in his chair and stared at the ceiling. And after all this time too. Two peaceful years during which he had policed London, perched at the top of the pyramid of law and order. Two lovely years during which no one had uttered the name of Percy Raymond Gabbitt.

But why now? What on earth could this miserable swine want? Hadn't he inflicted enough pain and suffering?

Pringle flicked the file open and looked long and hard at the photograph of his nemesis. The man seemed innocuous enough. 'Ah, but don't they all?' said a little voice inside him. Brown hair, a side parting, innocent blue eyes and a slightly daft expression.

The worst ones always looked as innocent and vulnerable as a kitten, thought Pringle. Forget the big, bald-headed and tattooed homicidal maniacs of the past. They were chicken feed compared with this new breed of criminal.

Chief Inspector Pringle sighed again and began looking through the file. Gabbitt had been a junior marketing executive at that dreadful school in Mayfair, the school run by Fingers Danvers and his cronies. He had not really made a success of even a job as basic as that. The man was mediocre through and through… and yet, there was something tucked away in his character which made him the most appalling villain Pringle had ever come across. Of that he was certain. It was just a matter of finding out what the crime was.

Pringle leafed through the thick file to the last page where some dedicated copper had actually stapled a copy of the airline ticket Gabbitt had used to fly off to China along with several pages of his passport.

China, thought Pringle. Another mystery. Why would he fly off to the other side of the planet and disappear?

Pringle's brow furrowed. He had just attended a seminar in Brighton on how various terrorist groups recruited weak characters from targeted countries like America and Britain and then whisked them off to somewhere in the desert and brainwashed them, before teaching them how to shoot a gun or make a bomb. They would then be released back into New York or London society a few months later, primed and ready for mayhem.

Surely Gabbitt was not being shown, at this very second, how to become a suicide bomber somewhere deep in the Gobi Desert? Pringle shuddered. The Chinese didn't do that sort of thing, did they?

The thought of Percy Gabbitt striding down Shaftesbury Avenue with a pipe bomb tucked under his arm sent Pringle into a cold seat. The Chinese might be a people capable of many things, but encouraging terrorism. No, not possible.

Even the recent visit to that appalling criminal, Fingers Danvers, in Wormwood Scrubs had not helped produced any answers. He shook his head slowly. Whatever had he been thinking? Letting Handsworth in on the game was like giving the keys to the banana plantation to the head monkey. If anyone knew of his little 'agreement' with the swine then it would be curtains for what was the rest of his career and retirement.

Another ridiculous problem caused by Percy Gabbitt. The man was a walking infection which messed with the mind and made you do things you would instantly regret. Madness. Whatever had he been thinking?

Pringle's eyes strayed to the framed commendation that he had been presented with after Box Hill. His bottom lip puckered.

He was still a policeman and a damn good one, he thought. There was still time to save the day… and his career. He closed the Gabbitt file and stood up.

It was time to get to the bottom of the whole current Gabbitt business which would lay all his ghosts to rest for good.

*<<FULL REBOOT…*
*WELCOME TO DAR………*

*…and opened the door. He walked into the shop and straight up to the counter.*

*"I want the biggest and most lethal weapon you've got," said the thin man, calmly.*

*A large fat man with a beard turned round and stared at his latest customer. He frowned.*

*"Oh yes? And what would you be using for cash then? I don't really think selling your jerkin would get you more than a fruit knife. It's not covering that much at the moment either," he said with a smirk, as he stared at the man's knobbly knees and bare feet. "I have a few small daggers over by the window," sniffed the shopkeeper, dismissively.*

*"A man has to start somewhere," said the thin man and heaved a heavy sack onto the counter, which clinked metallically.*

*The fat man's attitude changed, as he did a quick mental sum calculating the total possible amount of coinage in the sack. A normal person would have asked the obvious question, but the fat man had learned simply to accept everything at face value, ask no questions, never joke with the clientele and finally, always give the most vicious weapons available to those heroes with the biggest sacks of gold – especially the weedy-looking, thin ones. They were always the worst.*

*"I think this might be to your taste," he said, as he gingerly placed a long object nicely wrapped up in a crimson, velvet cloth on the counter.*

*"What does it do?" asked the thin man.*

*"Just about everything," murmured the fat armourer, rolling his eyes rather melodramatically. "And there's not a lot left behind afterwards that can't be scraped into one rather small bucket."*

*"That sounds like the sort of thing I'm looking for," said the thin man.*

*The fat man unwrapped the object and stared reverently at it.*

*"It looks like a sword with a blue tip," said the thin man in a not-very-impressed way.*

*"It does that, doesn't it?" said the armourer, who was still rolling his eyes and staring at the sack of coins.*

*"What does it do, apart from the obvious?" asked the thin man.*

*"This is the titanium-coated, chromo-sealed, obsidian-layered, vanadium-handled, gold-plated, platinum-forged, stainless-steeled, multi-rechargeable Level Fifteen Golden Dragon Slayer," said the fat man. "It also has a personalised hand grip which, when synchronised with its owner, will not allow anyone else to wield it without severe consequences. There's a homing beacon in the handle just in case you happen to mislay the thing and… and it all weighs as light as a feather. They say…" continued the armourer, leaning closer, "that it can cut the todgers off a mosquito at seven paces without it feeling a thing… for a few moments anyway. It can also fillet a heavily-armoured blood orc with just one flick of the wrist. This, my friend, is the future of adventuring. It's nickname is The Winged Avenger of the Nether Regions!"*

*"Can it fly?" asked the thin man, who was wondering about the winged bit in the sword's title.*

*"Only if you throw it," came the reply.*

*"And how much is this amazing weapon?"*

*"Twelve hundred gold coins... cash. It comes with a one week warranty and a guarantee of at least two hundred kills or you get fifty per cent cash back... well, fifty per cent to whoever brings the sword back here again," said the armourer, pointedly.*

*"Can I take it out on a test run?" asked the thin man.*

*The armourer sniffed. "OK. I'll give you an hour out back in the Haunted Forest. That should prove the value of the thing."*

*The thin man smiled and picked the sword up. He swished the air a few times and listened in awe as it thrummed past the armourer's left ear, neatly splitting a million molecules as it sliced through the air.*

*"Careful, sir," said the armourer ducking. "Best you do that sort of thing outdoors, I think."*

*"And the blue tip? What's that all about?" asked the thin man, examining the pointed end of the Winged Avenger.*

*"Maker's logo" replied the fat armourer. "Some put stripes down the length of the sword, others mess with the handle, but this one has the blue tip of Snuffhammer the Bastard."*

*"Is he any good at making swords?" asked the thin man innocently.*

*"Any good?" squeaked the armourer, in astonishment.*

*It was like asking a musician if he had ever heard of some bloke called Mozart. The armourer frowned deeply, tugged at his beard and leant over the counter. "With a name like Snuffhammer the Bastard," he said, rolling his eyes again, "Could you ever doubt that the maker of this sword is... any good?"*

"Jesus wept," muttered DC Ford sweatily. He pressed the Pause button and slid back in his chair. "The things I do for Queen and country," he said quietly.

"How's it going, Ford?" came the imperious voice of his boss, Chief Inspector Pringle.

"I think I'm in now, but this programme is a real swine. It's packed with viruses and all manner of stuff to screw up your computer. It also doesn't help when you get told that over thirty thousand sad weirdoes could be online at exactly the same moment as you all out for blood, mayhem and destroying your computer. There's a lot of cheating too sir, apparently."

"Which is exactly what we're going to do," said Pringle happily.

"It doesn't seem right, sir," said Ford, slowly. "I mean, to join a game wearing nothing more than a sack and to be toting half a million in gold around. And us being the police and all..."

"If you want any more, just get Andy from downstairs to tweak the system again. It's not real money so I don't care how much you have to spend in that ridiculous game. I don't care what you have to do to make contact with Percy bloody Gabbitt, just make sure you manage it in the next twenty-four hours. I want results, Ford, and I want them now," he shouted and slammed the door to his office.

A moment later and his door opened a fraction and Pringle's head poked back in.

"And buy yourself some top-notch armour or the mediaeval equivalent of Kevlar. Can't have you getting killed in the first fight. Remember that a twenty-first century police officer never enters a danger zone without full body armour and a loaded truncheon."

Pringle smirked for a long second. The door then shut again.

"Half a million gold coins," said DC Ford to himself. "Wish I had that in real life. I certainly wouldn't go round small villages trying to persuade fat cartoon bastards to sell me swords or armour," he said quietly to himself. "Wish I had a life," he whispered a little forlornly.

"Why Arapacana?" asked Bob Burley, rhetorically. There was a short dramatic pause as his listeners thought about that.

"I'll tell you why," continued Burley, happily. This was clearly a pet topic.

They were sitting on some rather scenic rocks in a rather secluded part of The Master of the Nets Garden in central Suzhou. They being the two Bobs and the one Percy.

The Master of the Nets Garden is one of the most popular gardens in Suzhou – well, popular among that group of slightly lazy and overweight foreigners out to enjoy a bit of ethnic Suzhou but not overdo it too much. The garden is the size of an average back garden in England, but is jam-packed with interesting stuff. There are many twisting narrow paths which double-back on one another all the time and give the illusion of the place being bigger than Hampton Court.

It is also just a stone's throw from all the major hotels and, as such, is an easy destination for the large parties of French and Germans who want to fit in a garden between visits to the silk shops and bootleg DVD stores in the nearby Shiquan Street.

Not much is known why the garden is called Master of the Nets. It implies a man who had a professional interest in fishing, but considering that the place is a considerable distance from the nearest possible patch of decent water, it is a bit of a mystery. However, since the garden first came into existence a good thousand years ago, or something like that, it is more than likely that there was a decent pond nearby then, long before the real estate people moved in with their shovels, hammers and bags of cement.

Nowadays, it is a rather pleasant retreat jammed in among a series of tight back alleys and very ethnic old Suzhou houses. In other words, it is the perfect place for Manfred and his camcorder. Not only can he capture the carp ponds, the weird Suzhou rock formations and strange circular doorways but, upon leaving the garden, he can also zoom in on Mrs Zhang doing her washing, while baby Zhang plays in the street with his plastic replica assault rifle. It is the ideal marriage between tourism and reality and a great way to introduce the folks back home to the wide and untamed diversity of modern China.

"I'll tell you why," said Bob Burley leaning into Gabbitt's personal space. Gabbitt moved back and frowned.

"Arapacana Manjushri was a Buddhist Bodhisattva who represented the wisdom of all the Buddhas of the Ten Directions," he said and nodded knowledgeably.

Gabbitt nodded back, as if he understood.

"He was the Bodhisattva who developed understanding through wisdom. Students of this brand of Buddhism devote themselves to all manner of literary studies, including logic and the improvement the memory," continued Burley happily.

"Really," chipped in Gabbitt, feeling that he ought to say something. He was not that sure what a Bodhisattva was and, to be perfectly honest, did not care that much either.

"At least, that's what it says if you look it up on the internet," said Burley leaning back on his rock. "I chose this as our name for several reasons, which you should understand. Percy. First, it is an important symbol of power and study. The Buddha in question is unique because he holds a book in one hand and a sword in the other. Education and strength rolled into one deity. Not bad, eh?" he said, beaming at Gabbitt. "It also," he said with a flourish, "begins with the letter 'A', which invariably means that we are seated at the front at language shows or exhibitions. I added 'Associates' to make this a little more potent. 'AA' will not be beaten, even in the alphabet."

"Aaardvark," contributed Bob Irwin.

"What?" queried Burley, a little taken aback.

"There's an agent up north in Beijing called Aaardvark. And they deliberately mis-spell it with three 'a's to make sure they get the top spot at shows."

There was a longish pause as the three thought about South American reptiles, language shows, interesting company names and Buddhas with swords and books.

It was a lot to take in at one time and Gabbitt reached for a plastic bottle of lychee juice (five per cent fruit) and took a swig. It tasted like liquid plastic laced with industrial amounts of sugar, but Gabbitt did not care. It was fluid - that was the important thing.

A group of French tourists ambled past, toting zoom lenses and wearing khaki shorts. One of them threw a used sweet wrapper into the ornamental pond. A carp the size of a small badger rose laconically to the surface to see what all the fuss was about and then slowly submerged, disappointed by the wrapper.

"Whatever," said Burley dismissively. "The important thing is that Percy understands that we are a force of… good."

"How did you end up here in Suzhou?" asked Gabbitt.

"Because of you, Percy," said Burley and patted him on the back. "Because of you."

"Because of me?"

"Indeed," said Burley, suddenly serious.

"I don't understand," said Gabbitt.

Bob Burley sighed and stared at the pond before him. There was a moment of silence and then he looked at Gabbitt. "You met my brother two years ago and that changed all our lives."

"Did I?" asked Gabbitt.

"Yes Percy, you did."

Burley then got up and strolled away from the bench looking sad and tired.

"He doesn't like talking about it," whispered Irwin.

"Talking about what?"

"The Big Switcheroo Caper."

"I have absolutely no idea what you are talking about," said Gabbitt. "And I can assure you that I would remember meeting his brother, if he were as crazy as he is."

"Martin Burley," said Irwin and raised his eyebrows.

"No," responded Gabbitt. "Still in the dark."

"Mayfair alleys? Any bells ringing now?"

"What?" queried Gabbitt, as bells really did start ringing. "His brother?"

"His brother."

"But how?"

"Martin got caught in that alley."

"His brother," mumbled Gabbitt.

"But you came along and saved the day, mate," said Irwin, patting Gabbitt on the back.

"But he died, didn't he?"

"Well, disappeared, mate. But... you tried to help him. Bob will always remember that. Still eats him up that he was never found. The police said that he was ninety-nine per cent dead, but… Bob is always niggled by that one per cent."

"I could have done more. I just ran," said Gabbitt.

"No, you couldn't. We realise that now. It was just lucky that you got away."

"I only took those damned newspapers from him. I did nothing else."

"Which probably saved western civilisation, as we know it," said Irwin brightly.

"I wouldn't say that."

"If those bastards had realised that Martin Burley had not swiped anything then history would have been very different," said Irwin.

"And my life would have been a lot simpler," added Gabbitt quickly.

"Indeed," chuckled Irwin. "But you took the papers... and ran. And saved the day!"

"I still don't see how."

"Well, for starters, Bob got clean away with the five million. He would have happily swapped it for his brother to be in the next seat on the plane, but… that's life. He wasn't."

"So Bob's here in China with the five million and..."

"A vision," said Irwin. "You see, he blames himself for losing Martin like that. So... he had a long think about everything and decided to get his revenge in a very different sort of way."

"It was hardly his fault that his brother got... killed," said Gabbitt thickly.

"You and I may think that," said Irwin, "But Bob hasn't managed... closure yet. And that's why he created AA with the intention of wreaking havoc in the industry which killed his brother."

"Shit," said Gabbitt. "You really are just a bunch of terrorists. Slightly strange ones, but terrorists all the same."

"Don't worry, Percy, mate. We're only interested in the bad guys. So, not really terrorists at all. More like an unofficial police force… of the grid. Just doing the right thing. Following in your footsteps."

"But I only decided to come here recently. How did you set up everything so quickly? It looks like you've been here for years."

Burley returned to their bench and sat down heavily. It was he that answered. "That was the easy part, Percy," he said, with a thin smile. "Five million pounds buys you a lot of things very quickly over here in the People's Republic. We actually had decided to set up in Shanghai, but then Bob the Third discovered that you had moved to Suzhou. Well, when we found this out, we just had to up sticks and come here. We couldn't believe our luck. The great Percy Gabbitt living in a neighbouring city."

"You came here because of me?"

"Yes."

"And you exist purely to destroy corrupt language schools?"

"Yes," replied Burley. "Only the really bad guys, I hasten to add. We don't wander the industry meting out carnage, willy-nilly."

Gabbitt frowned. "So...you're a force which weeds out all the corrupt and nasty people in English language marketing?"

"Well... it's not as simple as that, but..." said Burley.

"But very nearly," interrupted Irwin. "You have to remember that these bastards deserve what they get, as you should know, more than most. We only go for them. We don't mess with anyone who's not screwing with the teachers or students. We leave them well alone. It's the ones who drag the industry through the mud and make everybody's life a misery - we go for them."

"And who decides who's good or bad?" asked Gabbitt, surprisingly astutely.

"Exactly," replied Burley, missing the point.

"Someone has to," grumbled Irwin, who had not missed the point.

"So, who monitors what you are doing?" asked Gabbitt. "What happens if you make a mistake and bring down the wrong man?"

"Never has happened... and won't happen," said Burley. "We research each case rigorously and only act after at least three teachers or employees have complained about their treatment."

"And how do these disgruntled people know about you?"

"It's really very easy," said Irwin. "First, we attend workshops, fairs, exhibitions shows or infiltrate little sales gatherings like MAGPIE or LINNET... in fact, any sort of jamboree which gets a load of language school people together where tongues wag. And we simply keep our ears and eyes open. It's surprisingly easy to spot a total bastard. We also keep tabs on seven or eight chat sites which attract teachers anonymously. Places where they can vent their spleen about a particular school. You may have heard of 'www.stitchedup.com'," said Irwin innocently.

"I may have," said Gabbitt, honestly. Several teachers he had met at his second job at the Sino-Canadian Institute had been giggling over it in the staffroom a few days previously.

"That's one of ours. We put it up there," said Irwin airily. "Anyway, even then we don't just act. We first visit once or twice to get the lie of the land and see if the school really needs... special attention. Only then do we formulate a plan directly commensurate with the crimes being committed."

"Commensurate?" Gabbitt was frowning again.

"Well, we won't blow the place up if the owner has only stopped a tea-break or made teachers start paying for their photo-copying. That would be silly."

"So, what do you do?"

"Probably something rather small at first, like break a few windows or steal his personal computer. Something that will get him thinking about life. We're not vengeful vigilantes who close a school down at the drop of a hat - you have to understand that."

"But," interrupted Burley, "If we find a serious problem at the school, like deceiving agents, unfair dismissals, or a refusal to pay agreed bonuses, then we act a little more..."

"Vigorously," said Irwin.

"Exactly," said Burley. "Vigorously."

"And all the while the whole world simply views us as just another language travel agent with a rather silly name sending students to schools in the west and trying to make a fast buck," said Irwin. "Which incidentally we do as well. We have an office at the street level which helps comrade Zhang get his daughter a degree from Alabama University or student Zhao to et a visa to study in Hong Kong. But it's the offices on the upper floor which handle the real work of the day," he said almost proudly.

"And the local police are happy with this arrangement?" asked Gabbitt incredulously.

"Well, first, they don't know about our secret operation," said Burley, "And second, Bob here has regular meetings with Captain Wu down the road. They discuss the legality of our education licence every month."

"Legality?" queried Gabbitt.

"It usually involves a nice fat brown envelope and a jumbo pack of imported cigarettes," said Irwin, bluntly.

"Oh, I see," said Gabbitt quietly. "It seems you've covered all the angles then."

"Which brings us back to our question, Percy," said Burley.

"Yes, all right," said Gabbitt, with a shrug.

Being moral about the stuff of life was fine when you had a nice apartment to go back to and did not have to teach gun-toting ten-year-olds or office ladies whose only interests in life were texting and shopping. He looked at Burley and rubber-stamped his next life-altering decision. "It beats teaching and sounds like you're doing the right thing, I think. Plus, I need a hot bath and a decent internet connection."

"Perfect!" exclaimed Burley happily. "Welcome aboard," he said vigorously shaking Gabbitt's hand. "We'll get you moved tomorrow. Now, has Bob told you about your first assignment?"

"What?" asked Gabbitt. He had only just rather reluctantly decided to join this band of insane fools and a moment later he had an assignment.

"We need your skills as a teacher, Percy," continued Burley. "You're going to get a job teaching Beginners English up the road at the Shine School of English."

"But I've only just decided to quit my four teaching jobs and join your company," remonstrated Gabbitt, unhappily. "And now you want me back in a classroom? I thought that the idea now was to get me all dressed up as James Bond with dynamite strapped around my chest."

"Very good, Percy. I think I'm going to like your brand of humour," said Burley, unsurely. "But I should quickly add that this is a teaching job with a slight difference. Explain it to him, Bob," he said, staring at Irwin.

"No problems, Bob," replied Irwin. "But he'll need a haircut and a new suit," added Irwin breezily.

Gabbitt sighed. "That's another thing I could use a bit of advice on," he said quietly.

Behind them twenty Hong Kong Chinese shuffled down narrow paths looking bovinely at the carp pond and rock formations, while listening to a woman, who shouted pithy anecdotes about the peace and tranquillity of the Master of the Nets Garden into an electronic loud-hailer turned to maximum volume.

*A fireball exploded in the air just above Endymion and sent him effortlessly over the low stone balustrade and into the moat far below. Several crossbow bolts thrummed through the air and buried themselves into Roger's shield, while three cave trolls wielding cudgels the size of small hippos waded into and through the heroes' rather weak defences. It was beginning to look rather desperate.*

*"I say we retreat," shouted the Snark Maiden, above the deafening clamour.*

*"I say, if only," came the reply from a besieged Roger.*

*"It's the end," wailed Tammy the Goblin as he cowered in a dark corner beside a guard tower. "I knew straight-forward fighting would not pay off in the end."*

*"Oh shit!" exclaimed Li Bang Cho, the Chinese dwarf, with feeling, as he realised that two of the cave trolls were homing in on him.*

*The party had been ambushed as they had crept through the first gateway leading to the Dragon King's Lair. It had not been an auspicious start in the quest to save Bunty the Goblinesse.*

*It had all started quite well until someone had dropped a sword and then all hell had broken loose. True, the heroes had managed to overcome a platoon of ratmen, three Minotaurs and four beastmen without too much effort, but the noise of all this heroing had obviously attracted the bigger and meaner stuff.*

*The Snark Maiden fired her last arrow and started to look for a way out. Roger the Norse Fighter took a deep breath and had a last flurry of swipes at the nearest troll and then prepared to leap into the moat after Endymion. Li Bang Cho did not have that luxury though as he tried to weather the storm of blows from two of the largest cave trolls ever seen.*

*Then something quite extraordinary happened.*

*Suddenly, one of the cave trolls stopped mid-swipe and stared at his chest. A thin line of blood extended from his neck to his stomach. He seemed perplexed for a moment and then toppled forward.*

*Li Bang Cho stared in disbelief as the second troll suffered a similar fate, this time the line of blood stretching from armpit to armpit. "Wow," he cried, in astonishment.*

*"Two pit snappers then fell to the ground followed by an undead Minotaur and giant blood orc.*

*A small man appeared out of the carnage and approached the heroes.*

*"Obby the Gladiator, at your service," he said and bowed deeply.*

*"Who the fuck are you?" asked a panting Li Bang Cho.*

*"Someone who has decided to join your quest. Thought you could do with a bit more oomph up top," said Obby.*

*"A bit more what?" queried Roger, as he wiped blood and gore from his face.*

*"Oomph," said Obby flatly. "You clearly have the makings of quite a good team. A barbarian, an elf, a*

*dwarf, I think, and a magician.... but you lack adequate firepower when set upon by the really big stuff. I'm the answer to your dreams," he said quietly.*

*"I say we don't look a gift gladiator in the mouth," chirped a very relieved Tammy, as he dusted himself down and began scurrying among the dead, looting all the gold he could lay his little hands on.*

*"Well, whatever," said the Snark Maiden. "We can discuss this later. We need to get off this drawbridge as quickly as we can. There's no telling what will appear if we stay here any longer."*

*"True," said Roger and started for the dark entrance on the other side of the drawbridge.*

*"That's quite a chopper you have there," said Li Bang Cho, staring at Obby's sword admiringly.*

*"It does the job," Obby replied, simply.*

*"I'll say," said Li Bang Cho. "But why the blue tip?"*

*"Don't ask," said Obby, with a sigh.*

*The party jogged to the entrance of the lair and was about to enter into the gloom when a far-off voice wailed, "I could do with a hand getting out of this moat, you know."*

"Could I speak to a Mr Ronald Chipchase?"

"Who's asking?"

"A friend who wants to give him twenty grand."

There was a gasp at the end of the line. A moment later a voice said:

"I'm listening."

"I need a job done."

"Just a minute. We're a legitimate security firm only interested in doing an honest day's work protecting other people's money. We don't 'do jobs' unless it involves our armoured car, two blokes with truncheons and another inside with his finger on the nine button, so unless you just want to move large sums of money around London, then this call is at an end."

"One grand just to listen to what I have to say and a further thirty-nine if you agree to do the job."

There was another gasp and then a distant sigh as financial greed took precedence over morality.

"OK, I'm still listening."

"I'll set up a meeting. We can't speak on the phone."

"You're not the police, are you? We don't want no more trouble, do you understand?"

"Look, if I were the police I would hardly tell you now, would I?'

"Sounds a bit iffy."

"Fifty thousand pounds in cash and all you have to do is find someone. That doesn't sound very iffy to me."

"That sounds very iffy to me," came the suspicious reply.

"All right, obviously I have the wrong person. Sorry to have bother…"

"Wait!"

# SEVEN

*"I'm not certain if there's a God or a Heaven, but I'm sure there's a Hell and its other name is Box Hill."*
**(Nero Handsworth... on Box Hill)**

Alfred Fennell was doing a spot of gardening. To be precise, he was having a spot of trouble with the gardening, some ivy to be precise, which had decided to wrap itself around the Princess Diana in the front garden. He was also muttering to himself about his lot in life.

A window opened and a head poked out. "Tea-time," a voice proclaimed, loudly. Alfred sighed. Everything stopped for tea. He got up slowly, wiped his secateers carefully and placed them in a shiny-clean wheelbarrow next to a well-used hedge trimmer. As he made his way to the front door, the window opened again and a voice shouted: "I'll pour it down the sink, if you don't come immediately!"

Alfred chuckled to himself as he went inside.

"Did you know that there are over five hundred types of ivy," he said, as he pulled off an old pair of black leather shoes which were caked in soil and grass.

"Very nice," replied Hilda Fennell.

"Hedera," said Alfred and sat down on a chair in their small kitchen.

"Yes dear, that's right," said Hilda as she placed a large white mug of PG Tips on the table before him. "Would you like one or two custard creams?"

"It's the Latin name for ivy," persisted Alfred. "And the Algerian variety is one of the worst. A real brute, apparently. We've only got the English stuff, I'm pleased to say."

"I'll take that as a yes," said Hilda placing two custard creams onto a small saucer besides Alfred's mug. "And don't eat and talk at the same time. You know it gives you the wind," said Hilda seriously.

"Still grows like wildfire and chokes Princess Diana something rotten," mumbled Alfred, as he chomped his custard cream.

"I want some nice blooms from that bush this year," said Hilda in a way that implied Alfred would be to blame if the Princess only produced a few small and disappointing buds.

"Should be fine now. Lovely rose bush that," said Alfred and settled back in his chair.

"So," said Hilda. "Time to think about the summer."

"But it's August now."

"Then time to start thinking, sharpishly."

Alfred and Hilda Fennell were in their twilight years. Both had retired about a hundred years previously and were living a contented life in their terraced two-up and two-down in Bromley, south London. They were Percy Gabbitt's neighbours – on the left-hand side.

Alfred spent his days gardening and generally making sure that the local teddy-boys, did not throw footballs, crisp packets, chewing gum or cigarette ends into his front garden.

If someone, unwise enough to commit such a crime, did this in Alfred's line of fire then the miscreant would live to regret it. Alfred was rather good at swiping offenders on the backside with his shovel / rake / hedge-trimmer, or whatever was near to hand. The police had virtually given up on him and generally steered well clear of fifty-one, Greenway. The Fennells were well-known eccentrics, especially Alfred.

Hilda spent her days making apple pies and washing the bed sheets which she hung out to dry every other morning at about five o'clock. Like most geriatric survivors of many wars, they were criminally early risers and went to bed promptly after watching News at Ten every night.

"Holidays," said Hilda, sitting down and then smoothing her section of the wisteria-print tablecloth.

"Ah yes," said Alfred frowning. As a rule, he did not really like holidays much. It seemed to him like a lot of stress and bother – all that packing and unpacking and then spending far too much money. He far preferred to spend his days protecting Princess Diana in his garden and supping PG Tips in his kitchen.

"The Scillies again, dear?" he asked, resignedly.

"I rather think not," said Hilda, with a twinkle in her eye.

"Clacton-on-Sea?" asked Alfred, a slight tremble in his voice.

"No, not this time, dear," said Hilda, pulling some colourful brochures out of a large brown envelope. "I think something a little different this year. Young Percy has given me an idea."

Alfred surveyed the pictures on the front cover of the brochure. It certainly did not look like the Scillies or Clacton. There was a picture of what looked like a long garden wall stretching over some impossibly high mountains next to a photo of a lot of smiling Orientals under a huge painting of Chairman Mao in a massive town square. Alfred frowned and looked up at his wife.

"Bognor?"

<It's me>

<Hello you>
<You OK?>
<Not bad. Usual day at the office. Boss a sexist pig>
<One reason I'm happy to be over here>
<Just the one?>
<Errrrr. Yes>
<Bad day for you?>
<Quit all four jobs>
<Sounds like a really bad day>
<Got a new job>
<Yes?>
<Working for a professional hit-team>
<Perfect>
<Seriously>
<Percy, I can't take anything you say seriously. One minute you tell me you're on the run from the police again and the next, you say you've joined a team of hired assassins>
<Not really assassins. We're the good guys>
<Oh yes>
<Really. It's an outfit dedicated to restoring good in a bad world>
<Hello all>
<Hi Dave>
<Hi Dave>
<Are we going to get to Level Two tonight?>
<Percy's become a professional killer>
<Cool.>
<No joking, Dave. He's quit his teaching job>
<Mega-cool>
<Sigh>
<We just terminate bad schools and get the owners arrested. That's all. There's no killing>
<Really cool, but shame about the no killing>
<Terminate?>

<Well, closed down.>

<Percy, what's going on? You've joined a company dedicated to the destruction of language schools. How mad is that? Is this just a bad joke?>

<They approached me. Said they admired what I did on Box Hill.>

<?????>

<?????????>

<Gave them inspiration to sort out other bad bosses in the industry.>

<You really have been on the joy juice over there>

<Did you read about that raid on the school in Holborn? That was one of ours>

<One of yours?>

<God Percy. Be careful>

<Careful? When I try that, people come shooting at me. Better to have a team of madmen on my side this time round>

<Who are they? What do you know about them?>

<Nothing much. Just that they're keen to give me a new flat with a bath and great internet speed. That'll do me>

<And what do you have to do?>

<Lend a hand, now and then, I think. I may disappear from time to time>

<You think?>

<They call it 'going dark' nowadays, Caroline>

<What, Dave?>

<Percy's going dark>

<Whatever. Why can't you just have a normal life doing normal sane things, Percy?

<Things just seem to happen to me wherever I go>

<Even in the middle of China! Just go back to the teaching, Percy and give these losers a wide berth.

That's my advice. Not that you'll listen to me, of course>

<Anyway, I've got to start another teaching job on Monday …and learning Chinese as well>

<I thought you said you'd just quit all the teaching jobs>

<My first mission>

<Teaching?>

<it's a seriously bad school>

<OMG>

<Got to get it closed down in a week. That's the target>

<I don't believe this>

<And I've got to learn survival street Chinese too>

<I know I'm going to regret asking this question but… why?>

<The three Bobs think that I should be able to buy a bag of loquats or watermelons without resorting to sign language and looking stupid. Also should help with the job if I can say a few words>

<The three Bobs?>

<They're all called Bob here>

<Have you had a breakdown, Percy?>

<Did you know that the farmyard pig has orgasms which can last for over thirty minutes at a time?>

<Thank you, Dave>

<I want to come back as a pig next time round>

<Hi everyone>

<Hi Joe>

<Hi Joe>

<Hi Joe>

<Can't believe it. All of us here on time for a change. You ready for the next level?"

<Aren't you forgetting somebody?>

<?????>

<Obby, the new member of the Roger War Band>

<Not sure about him>

<Nice chopper though>

<Couldn't have done without him last time>

<Do you know anything about him? And do you think he'll turn up for round two?>

<Said he would. Says his name is Marvin in the unreal world>

<Marvin???>

<Never seen him around the village beforehand. Have any of you?>

<No. Seems OK though. And very… enthusiastic to get stuck in>

<Which is the important thing>

<Probably fancies our Snark Maiden here>

<Poor sod>

<Thank you>

<Hi everyone.>

<Hi Marvin>

<Hi Marvin>

<Hi Marvin>

<Hi Marvin>

<We ready to go get hunt some orc?>

<Orc? Not many orcs down here, I think>

<Then what are we up against?>

<It's a mass of undead weirdoes, I reckon. The game dynamics will have created a stock batch of your common-or-garden zombies, mummies and vampires, but it's the other gamers I always worry about. Generally, there's a corner in most of these dungeons teeming with sad geeks from Arkansas and Alaska, who've messed with the character-creation programmes to spawn vicious bastards with names

like Hades Wolfman or Satanic Sister. They're the ones we'll have to overcome... and it won't be easy. The game system has about forty thousand people online at any given moment with another fifty thousand logging on when America hits the weekend>

<And it's Saturday night here in China>

<OK. We ready then?>

<Oh and welcome to the team, Marvin>

<Call me Obby. Trying to get into character>

<Did you know that the male praying mantis can only achieve orgasm after the female has ripped its head off?>

<If only that were true of humans!>

<What!>

<Don't worry about them Obby. It's just their way of saying hello>

Nero Handsworth was busy getting through the day as well. He was feeling particularly pleased with himself for a change. His cell had just been cleaned by three new 'fish' who had had it explained to them that mucking out Mr 'Andsworth's cell would be in their best interests. Two had readily agreed, while the third had seen reason after two minutes of having his head thrust into a dirty toilet bowl.

Nero had then retired to the library to continue writing his memoirs and pondering about recent events, especially the visit by Chief Inspector Pringle and the phone call to his erstwhile 'colleagues', Chipchase and Bibby.

It was the two security guards who occupied Nero's mind as he sat scanning his personal copy of The Times which lay on a broad oak table in front of him. Two large men with bald heads and tattoos on their tattoos sat on either side of him. Both looked like the sort of characters who communicated with their fists rather than their mouths.

This suited Nero perfectly. There was nothing he hated more than a 'gabby' underling – someone who 'walked the walk' and kept telling everyone that there were no problems and that everything was 'sorted'. Nero had had enough henchmen like that. They invariably failed and always ended up on the ground with their faces in the dirt with a truncheon up one nostril and a pair of handcuffs being snapped on their wrists.

He shuddered as the memories came flooding back.

"Enough!" he exclaimed loudly.

The two bulldozers turned to look at their boss. Small, piggy eyes stared hard at Nero.

"Time to start planning the next chapter," said Nero quietly.

"Ah, your book," grunted Bulldozer One on his left.

"Something like that," replied Nero, absent-mindedly. "I need to make sure that tracks are covered and the trail leads well away from here," he muttered and began writing a few notes in a small notepad.

"Anything you say, boss," said Bulldozer Two on the right. He then resumed picking a nostril.

"I need to make a few calls now," said Nero quietly. "See to it that the phone is free in about five minutes' time, will you?" he said, without looking up from his notepad.

"Sure thing, boss," said Bulldozer Two and trundled out of the library.

"And you," said Nero, looking at Bulldozer One intently. "I need to arrange a meeting with Fred the Throttler."

"Sure thing, boss," said Bulldozer One, and lurched to his feet.

Chief Inspector Pringle was staring out of his office window at a windswept car park in central London. But he was not really looking at anything in particular. In fact, his mind was far, far away. He had come to an important decision and was about to tell his team about the next phase in their investigation. It would come as a surprise to them all, of that he was sure, but he felt that there really was no other way that the complexities of this case could be sorted out.

It was all very well to let DC Ford have a go at chumming up to Percy flippin' Gabbitt in their ridiculous fantasy world on the internet. Ford might get some information from the swine, but Pringle knew that Gabbitt would not roll over so easily. The man had single-handedly managed to avoid the clutches of about six different police forces across the planet as well as five crime syndicates. Percy Gabbitt was not the sort of a man to let his guard down, even when faced with a smiling glyph holding a big sword with a blue tip. No, this villain would only be defeated face-to-face, in the flesh, one-to-one, 'mano y mano'.... or something like that anyway, thought Pringle, his chin puckering slightly.

He would have to venture into the lion's den and drag the bastard out feet first if necessary. There could be no other way.

There was a knock at his door.

"Come," he said, quietly.

DC Ford walked in, looking pleased with himself.

"So, have you managed to make contact with him yet?" asked Pringle, sitting down at his desk.

"I can report that I have managed to infiltrate their cell without rousing their suspicions."

"Wonderful," growled Pringle.

"They communicate with each other via the game. Sort of like conference texting where they can all talk together for as long as they like. I told them my name was Marvin Law. They don't suspect, of course. No one would with a bland name like that. Nice touch though, the Law bit, don't you think?"

Pringle sighed. "Have you learned anything new?"

"Only that the male praying mantis reaches sexual climax after its had its head torn off by its mate," said Ford with a frown.

"So, you've met our Mr Springett then," murmured Pringle quietly.

"Seems a slightly dysfunctional sort of character," said Ford, slowly.

"Dysfunctional," repeated Pringle, shaking his head slowly. "The man's a deranged psychotic. Probably has an attic stuffed with assault rifles and pictures of small boys in swimming trunks."

"I wouldn't like to go that far, sir," squawked Ford. "He might be a little strange, but I haven't detected anything more than a slight… eccentricity."

"And therein lies our major problem," said Pringle getting up. "The whole crowd of them radiate eccentricity in all its more colourful forms. Dressing up as pandas in public, teaching at a Comprehensive School in south London, working in foreign companies and now, living in China. You might say that they all behave in outrageously eccentric ways, Ford, but you would be wrong. This is all a front. A cover. A game. Their whole lives are a game. But only on the surface."

Pringle paused and looked hard at the detective constable. "Don't get sucked in by them, Ford. It's always the danger when going under cover and trying to win their confidence. Remember that if you scratch the surface they are all villains. Scratch your surface and there's a copper waiting to jump out and biff them with his truncheon. Remember that at all times, Ford, and you'll emerge from this relatively unscathed."

"Oh absolutely, sir," came the instant response. "But I'm going to have to fight a few more battles with my virtual sword and become a trusted ally before I get to hear anything juicy, I think, sir. Got to live and breathe Dark Dawn Three now," he finished breathlessly.

"Fight away, Ford," said Pringle, airily. "But remember to watch your back at all times or, to coin a teenage phrase, you'll be toast. These people may seem as soft as teddy bears, but mark my words, Ford, they'll be scraping you off the walls in not just fantasy land, but out here too, if you don't watch your step."

"Indeed sir," said Ford, hotly.

"Well, I think you'd better get back in there then. And try not to crash Scotland Yard's computer system again, will you?"

"The game's riddled with Trojans sir," said Ford, enthusiastically.

"I don't care if the thing is stuffed with Greeks, Carthaginians and Spartans. I just don't want them rampaging across the Yard's databases and deleting all our files. Forensics is still not talking to us, you know."

"Sorry about that, sir. I've got two top-notch firewalls in place now. We should be protected."

"Well, I hope so," said Pringle, wondering what a firewall was and whether he should start reaching for the nearest extinguisher.

"Leave it to me, sir," said Ford, standing up. "It'll all work out without a problem. I'll have it sorted before you can say: 'Bob's your Uncle.' That's a promise, sir." He then walked out of the room and closed the door behind him.

Pringle steepled his fingers. Yes, he thought resignedly, he would have to step in and take a more active roll. He turned to a small side-table and pushed down the 'Play' button of an ancient tape recorder. Moments later and the room was filled with the deep bass chords of the late middle-aged, thinking man's modern music – namely Pink Floyd's Dark Side of the Moon.

Pringle settled back and let Roger Waters and his ex-mates sail him away to a far better world. He always thought much more clearly when some long-haired but well-intentioned (and totally un-drugged) progressive rock musician was synthesising in the background of his thoughts.

Yes, he ruminated, DC Ford was well-intentioned, but if he had learned just one thing in his twenty years as a copper, it was that when a junior constable started telling him not to worry and that someone called Robert was his uncle, it was most definitely time to worry.

*Roger the Norse Fighter was panting hard as he leant up against a damp and mossy cavern wall. It had been quite a busy day for the members of the quest to rescue Bunty the goblinette.*

*"You should have listened to me," said a small and slightly irritating voice a little below his eye-line.*

*Roger gasped in exasperation. "Well, yes, that's easy to say in hindsight."*

*"I have a nose for danger in dark caves, as you well know."*

*Tammy the Goblin adjusted a shoulder bag and sat down on the floor. "We should also find a safe place to stow all this stuff," he said and kicked a bulging sack of gold coins. "Hampers our movements and could get us all killed."*

*"Indeed," said Roger and took a deep breath.*

*"I'm nearly out of healing potions," squeaked a third voice from the shadows a little further down the corridor.*

*"Wizards are always complaining about something," muttered Tammy.*

*"And I need more arrows," said a fourth and very female voice."*

*"A beer for me," added a fifth voice.*

*Roger sighed. "There'll be time for quaffing when this little adventure is over, my friend," he said, as calmly as he could.*

*"I could do with a good quaff now," murmured the voice again.*

*"All clear!" exclaimed a sixth voice, slightly further down the corridor.*

*"All clear," repeated Tammy quietly. "Sounds like a law man on a raid," he muttered, wryly.*

*"You have to admit that we wouldn't have got very far down here without that sword of his," said Roger, with more than a hint of admiration in his voice.*

*"Should have taken the right fork when the tunnel divided, like I said," said Tammy. "Undead creatures tend to prefer things on the left-hand side. Thought everyone knew that. Most are left-handed. Bet you didn't know that."*

*"Did you know that left-handed people generally live up to nine years less than right-handed people?" said the wizard, perkily.*

*"No, I didn't," replied Roger, irritably.*

*"That's seven rooms explored, fourteen corridors explored and two underground rivers forded," said the Snark Maiden.*

*"And nothing we couldn't handle… as yet," said Tammy.*

*"Right," said Roger. "Check all your weapons and get the Snark Maiden here to heal any light wounds. Li Bang Cho, go back to that last room and search the bodies again. We may have missed something important. Endymion, I could do with a bit of light over here. Any chance of illuminating that staff of yours?"*

*"Certainly, my friend," said Endymion. There was the sound of a match being struck and suddenly the cavern corridor was filled with a peachy glow.*

*"I wish you wouldn't do that," said Tammy. "Wizards are supposed to mutter a silent incantation and gently pass a hand over their staff to make it*

*light up - not strike a match like a tobacco-addicted dwarf."*

*"Works just the same," sniffed the slightly upset Endymion.*

*"We need to stock up a bit," said Roger, as he surveyed his bedraggled party. "A few more healing potions and some food would also help," he added quietly.*

*"And some more arrows wouldn't go amiss," said the Snark Maiden, rattling a nearly empty quiver.*

*"Go and see if those dead beastmen in the room back there have any."*

*There was a noise of boots scraping on mossy flagstones and the thin figure of Obby emerged from the gloom.*

*"Big room with gold knockers on the door at the end of the corridor. All other rooms, clear."*

*"Well, this looks like it," said Roger. "We'll have a few minutes to get our breath back and then it's show time, I reckon."*

*"One thing," interrupted Endymion, looking hard at Obby. "Do you have to shout: 'Come out with your hands up!' and 'Clear' every time we enter an unexplored room?"*

*"Sorry," said Obby in embarrassment. "Just a habit I seem to have got into."*

*"Well, it's a bit silly, if you ask me," continued Endymion. "No sense in giving the blighters any warning, is there? And anyway, I hardly think that undead ratmen vermin will take your advice and meekly come out with their hands in the air, a task*

*made all the more difficult because most of them don't have their full compliment of arms… or hands."*

*"Thought it was a rule," sniffed Obby.*

*"Not down here," said Roger. "No rules."*

*"Right, Tammy," said Roger, feeling that it was time to get professional. "You find a place to put all our gold so we can collect it on the way out."*

*"Easier said than done," muttered the goblin, as he pulled a large sack off down the corridor to find a place where thieving eyes would miss.*

*"We'll all sit here and wait for Tammy to return. Then we'll have a look at those gold knockers."*

"They call him Doctor Death," said Bob Burley dramatically.

"Nice," said Gabbitt simply.

"The teachers hate his guts because he treats them like dirt, never pays them on time and sacks them if they ask him about money. He's also extremely sexist with his female office employees – less said about that the better. And he only uses teachers with no real training so he can pay them minimum wages and fire them without too much trouble. He's a truly nasty piece of work and…"

"Needs taking down," interrupted Bob Irwin.

They were sitting in Burley's heavily air-conditioned office on the first floor of Arapacana Associates. Beyond the plate-glass window separating them from the hustle and bustle of the main office, a mixture of Chinese and western employees scurried about on various doubtful errands.

"And you're the man to show us how it's done," beamed Burley, in Gabbitt's direction.

"Really?" said Gabbitt.

“My I suggest something?” chipped in Irwin, enthusiastically.

“Certainly,” said Burley. “Let’s have a few ideas.”

“We could try the straight-forward and well-tested ‘tantrum gambit’.

“Not subtle enough,” said Burley. “And probably not really Percy’s cup of tea. I think he prefers something with a bit of style and… panache.”

“The tantrum…” squeaked Gabbitt worriedly.

“Not this time, my friend, don’t worry,” said Burley, patting Percy on the shoulder.

“Well, considering that the school is due an inspection from their head office in the UK this week, we could try the ‘banana stratagem’.”

“Sounds good, Bob,” said Burley.

“Thought you’d like it, Bob,” said Irwin.

“Bob the Third tried it last month in London at that place where the boss refused to pay overtime bonuses. Brought the place to its knees within three days.”

“Bob’s the master of the ‘banana stratagem’, Bob,”

“I know, Bob.”

“The bana…” began Gabbitt.

“Definitely keep that one at the front of our minds, Bob,” said Burley talking over Gabbitt. “I rather like the ‘flu flimflam’ for this one.”

“Nice one, Bob,” agreed Irwin, nodding in agreement.

“Could go with a combination of the flu and banana, just to make sure,” he suggested.

“Don’t usually like gilding the lily,” frowned Burley. “When you over egg the pudding, there’s a strong likelihood it’ll backfire on you.”

“And no one likes backfiring egg on your lily, gilded or not, Bob,” said Irwin.

"Indeed, Bob," said Burley, not too sure if his namesake was attempting a little Australian sarcasm.

"Can I have a word?" tried Gabbitt, feeling like a drowning man in a sea of tortured metaphors.

"I think I know what you're about to say, Percy," said Burley jovially.

"You do?" asked Gabbitt, genuinely intrigued.

"You want to do the thing in you own inimitable way and not rely on poor imitations," he said and patted Gabbitt on the back. "We are so in awe of how you do it, Percy," he added with admiration in his voice.

"Now look, I..." began a worried Gabbitt.

"I still can't work out how you managed to get a van load of bad guys to blow up their own school, Percy. Pure

genius. They say you were even in the crowd of onlookers afterwards, standing right next to the police who were blaming the Welsh for some incredible reason. Utter genius."

"That's not quite how it happened," mumbled Gabbitt as he thought back to those heady days when he worked at RELI in Mayfair, central London."

"You're too modest, my friend. But I for one can't wait to hear all about what really did happen, from the horse's mouth," said Burley.

"And to get that bastard owner put away for three years for tax evasion – how did you manage that?" chipped in Irwin, shaking his head.

"But first, Percy," said Burley, happily, "We have to get you in there so you can start working your magic. I need to make a phone call now and, if all goes well, I think the Shine school will have a new part-time general English teacher turning up tomorrow morning. And don't forget that you're down to start a crash course in Chinese in the evening. Bob here will pick you up from your new apartment and take you to your class for your first wrestle with this appalling language."

Gabbitt sighed. He decided not to say any more. He would just have to go along with the whole daft venture and play it by ear. Something would turn up, he thought. It always did.

"Not you again," came the muffled voice of Dave Springett from deep within several matted folds of black and white fur.

"Care for a chat when you... come off duty," suggested DC Ford amicably.

"Only if you're buying the drinks," said the panda moodily.

"Mummy, the panda just asked that man for a drink," piped a little girl with lilac bunches and a purple dress.

"Nonsense, princess," came the slightly bored reply of a mother more interested in the innards of a deep handbag.

"It did. But I thought pandas couldn't speak or understand English because they're from China," said the little princess happily.

"You're quite right, Snowflake" said the proud mother.

"It says it wanted a drink... in English," persisted the girl, pulling at her mother's arm the way children do when they want to make point.

"Better give it one then," said another voice.

The girl, her mother and DC Ford all looked round at a rather fat teenager with a baseball cap on sideways. He was holding a massive KFC paper cup. However, it was what was in the cup that had captured the attention of the small crowd. Whatever it was radiated a sickly green colour with creamy blobs floating on the surface.

The fat boy then had a last long suck at a bendy straw and then hurled what was left at the panda. He shrieked with laughter as the panda turned a rather putrid peppermint colour and shuddered in shock.

"Daft bugger moved!" shouted the boy and then ran off, hooting with glee.

"Poor thing," said the little girl and attempted to stroke a sopping wet, fluffy green ear.

"Don't touch, Pudding, you don't know where it's been," said the mother, frowning critically at the panda's eye-slits.

Dave Springett was having a really bad afternoon. What had started swimmingly well had rapidly deteriorated as crowd upon crowd of slightly drunk and potentially very dangerous onlookers had passed his podium and decided to have a bit of fun with him.

The golden rule in any motionless artiste's handbook was always: never for any reason at all work on a Saturday or Sunday afternoon in central London no matter how financially tempting. Springett was beginning to understand why.

Piccadilly Circus thronged with weekend shoppers, day-trippers and football fans. It had all the makings of a disastrous afternoon for any endangered species brave enough to venture out with begging bowl in paw.

He had already been punched once, had a bag of chips placed on his head, had a cigarette pushed in his mouth and had even been urinated upon. The KFC drink episode was the final indignity and Springett had had enough for the day.

He decided to finish the day's performance with a dramatic flourish, so he shook himself vigorously and let out a low and extremely alarming growl.

The mother threw a protective arm round the girl and stared daggers at the panda. Even DC Ford took a pace back.

"It's all right," said the girl with the bunches. "They're vegetarian and they don't growl like that. Pandas only make noises like horses whinnying. And my teacher says they only do that when sexually-active."

"Sweetums!" exclaimed the mother, in alarm.

"What does sexually-active mean?" asked the little girl, loudly.

"Time for an ice-cream, Pumpkin Pie," said the confused mother, deciding on a quick diversion to defuse a potentially embarrassing situation.

"Anyway, they're not dangerous," said the little girl, studiously ignoring the bribe. "They only eat bamboo shoots and never attack human beings."

"This one does, Snowflake," said Springett and leapt from the podium.

The girl let out a rather predictable high-decibel scream. The mother approached the panda as it picked up its money box.

"You should be ashamed of yourself," she said, loudly, jabbing a finger at him. "Frightening little children."

"Shenme dong shi!" said the panda.

"What was that?" asked the mother, above the growing cacophony of child's wailings.

"It's a Chinese insult," said the panda. "I'm from China, you see. All pandas are," it added and started to walk away.

"Oh," said the mother and returned to Pudding, feeling a little baffled by events. Somehow a Chinese-speaking panda could be excused rudeness. It seemed more excusable than just a Londoner in a furry suit.

DC Ford caught up with Springett as he tore his soggy green and black head off.

"Bastard day!" exclaimed Springett and kicked a tramp, who was sleeping in a doorway.

"Bugger off!" shouted the tramp and hurled a half-eaten hamburger at him. It missed and hit DC Ford on his shoulder.

"It's looking up now though," said Springett as globs of ketchup and pickles started snaking down Ford's left sleeve.

"Drum and Monkey?" sighed Ford, as he picked the sodden detritus from his jacket.

"Why not?" said Springett. "Could do with something a bit stronger than bamboo shoots today. The suit needs a good dry clean, anyway."

Five short minutes later and Springett had sunk his second pint. DC Ford was still on his first pineapple juice. The barman approached them with a mischievous grin. He was pretending to wipe a beer mug with a grubby tea towel.

"You escaped again?"

"Yup," said Springett, supping hugely.

"Hope you're not going to cause any trouble in here like last time," said the barman, with a gleam in his eye.

"Just a bear and his pint quietly relaxing at the end of a rather long day," said Springett quietly, although he knew the barman was somehow leading to something he considered wildly amusing.

"Wouldn't want your sort of pandemonium in here, now would we?" said the barman, getting the tortured metaphor off his portly chest. "Might have to ring the police to take you away in their panda car. Can't bear your sort in here," he added and then laughed long and loud. "And I hope that's not blood on your jacket, Mr Plod. Wouldn't want you to mess up my upholstery with some villain's gore," he concluded, brightly.

"Are these drinks free?" asked DC Ford, bluntly.

"No," replied the barman, suddenly very serious. "Can't expect free drinks every time you turn up here, you know. We're not a charity despite your mate being an endangered species."

"Well, what about a search of your cellars then? Anything endangered down there?" asked Ford, warming to the task. "I hear there might just be a touch of French Legionnaire's Disease breaking out down there all of a sudden."

"Right," sniffed the barman. "I get the picture. No more bear jokes or allusions to police brutality, OK? And free booze anytime you want, as long as it's not shorts. I was just having a laugh, you know. No harm in that."

He then walked slowly back down the bar back to his other customers. He was not whistling any tunes this time though.

"So, what do you want?" asked Springett, clearly impressed by Ford's methods of procuring free alcohol, whenever he wished.

"Two things," said Ford, crisply, as he took a manly swig at his pineapple juice. "First, what did you say in Chinese to that woman with the little girl?"

"Does it matter?" asked Springett smirking.

"Not really. I just wondered if you made it up or whether you really did have another string to your bow."

"It actually is another string," said Springett. "But a pretty thin one. And I don't know any other Chinese expressions before you ask. Percy used it in fantasy land the other day and things like that tend to stick with me."

"So, it's an insult in Mandarin, is it?"

"Not bad, Mr Copper," said Springett, nodding. "It means something like: 'What a thing you are!'"

"Which is fairly strong stuff in downtown Beijing, I take it," murmured Ford into his pineapple juice.

"You better believe it. Causes no end of fisticuffs, if you use it at the wrong moment."

"Thanks for that," said Ford, thoughtfully. "Never like a mystery. It would have bothered me all night."

"And your second question?" asked Springett, feeling that this policeman was actually not such a bad sort after all.

"We want Percy Raymond Gabbitt back in England immediately," said Ford. "And you're going to help us, Mr Springett."

"Is that a question or a statement?" mumbled Springett, already knowing the answer.

# EIGHT

*"There are three things you must never talk about in an English classroom in China: Tibet, Taiwan and the events surrounding the Tiananmen Square 'incident' a few years ago. And saying nice things about Japan, fanatical religious organisations and cheese is not advisable too."*

**(Solid advice given to teachers arriving on Day One at the Shine School of English in Suzhou)**

Percy Gabbitt was feeling really nervous. D-Day had arrived and he was at the controls of a new electric bike and wobbling down the Renmin Road towards his first day at the Shine School of English in central Suzhou.

Things were moving a little too quickly for Gabbitt. Just a week ago he had been holding down four jobs and living in a grubby apartment in the smelly part of Suzhou. Now he had just one job, a new apartment on the fifth floor of a respectable block in the south and decidedly un-smelly part of the city. He also had this brand-new, racing-green, electric bike – top speed 25kph (with a snazzy twist-grip throttle to access the turbo accelerator which moved the machine up to the dizzying speed of 28kph).

Gabbitt might have felt quite the 'easy rider' as he hummed down the street of Suzhou, but all these recent improvements to his life in China were not at the front of his mind, as he trundled northwards.

He was feeling rather worried and a little guilty, since his new-found luxury depended on him destroying somewhere he had never visited and had absolutely no axe to grind with.

Gabbitt swerved to avoid a three-wheeler which shot out from a side-street without any warning. The owner shouted a musical 'hello' in Gabbitt's direction, as he sailed past, clearly pleased to be able to practice his one word of English.

Three cars then drove at high-speed through a red light, one of them grazing Gabbitt's back mudguard. The driver waved happily at Gabbitt and shouted another cheery 'hello' through an open window as he shot by. Happy maniacs, thought Gabbitt. He slowed to avoid a battered-looking bus which lurched towards him on the other side of the road. It was belching large clouds of black smoke as it accelerated past him. Three occupants of the rear seats were all leaning out of their windows and spitting in synchronised volley fire at the road.

He came to a sweaty halt a few minutes later, just in front of a two-foot deep hole next to a tall building. The inside lane appeared to end here. A confetti of cigarette ash and butts then rained down onto Gabbitt from an upstairs apartment followed by another copious blob of spit.

Gabbitt pulled his bike back a few feet and shook his jacket clean of the detritus. He then attempted to get back onto the road again.

A motorised three-wheel truck clanked past wreaking of something powerfully awful. As his stomach started to lurch northwards, Gabbitt noticed that there were two large oil drums perched on the back filled to the brim with a glutinous dark syrup which smelt of rotting elephants. It chugged past and disappeared down a side alley slopping its evil contents all over the road.

Gabbitt twisted the throttle and accelerated way. He was now determined to reach the Shine School as quickly as possible. The road cleared a little and Gabbitt relaxed. He seemed to have weathered the storm. According to Irwin's instructions, he only had one more street to go and then he would arrive at his new place of employment.

A man with a cigarette dangling from his mouth and wearing a dirty white vest suddenly appeared out of a fruit shop and hurled the contents of a red washing-up bowl into the street splashing Gabbitt's suede shoes expertly. He then looked at Gabbitt, smiled widely and shouted a gleeful 'hello'.

The Shine School loomed on the horizon. It was situated on a street-corner next to a building-site full of Japanese bulldozers all waiting for a day of noise, dust and hole-digging.

The school itself had quite a humble-looking entrance. In fact, it was really just a glorified shop-front with a grubby plate-glass window and a large faded Union Jack hanging in the middle. Gabbitt pulled his bike onto the pavement and tried to find a parking slot among the million other cycles already wedged into every spare spot.

He pushed his bike further up the road and eventually found a place next to a rather well-polished black Buick. Feeling rather pleased with himself, Gabbitt parked the bike and chained the front wheel to a red fire hydrant conveniently situated nearby. The bike then promptly fell over, the handlebars scraping noisily down the side of the Buick, leaving silver scratches.

A man in a suit and a peaked cap appeared from nowhere and started berating Gabbitt and pointing at the car door.

"Hello," said Gabbitt and pulled the bike upright, making one or two more dents in the car door.

The man continued to shout angry things.

The door to the school then flew open and a short, bald man in shirt-sleeves bundled onto the pavement and hurried up to the man in the peaked cap. There then followed a brief conversation which seemed to involve quite a bit of apologising by the bald man for some reason. Notes then exchanged hands and everything calmed down.

Gabbitt frowned at the two of them and set about balancing his bike by the hydrant again.

"Hello," said the bald man, turning in Gabbitt's direction.

"Hello," responded Gabbitt, smiling.

"No problem. Policeman happy now."

"Policeman?" sighed Gabbitt.

"You hurt police car," said the bald man. "I school owner - Zhang. You new teacher, yes?"

"Yes," said Gabbitt simply. He was beginning to sweat as he stood on the dusty pavement.

"I pay Chief of Police, so no problem."

"Chief of Police?" mouthed Gabbitt.

"He student here. My client. He big shot!" said the bald man. "I take money from your pay. So, no problem now."

Gabbitt shrugged and sighed inwardly. He had not even set foot in the place and had already had his pay docked, not to mention vandalising the Chief of Police's car.

Mr Zhang, the Chief of Police and Gabbitt then walked in silence to the school. A few minutes later, Gabbitt's bike toppled over again, leaving a fresh trail of scratches and grooves in the police car door.

The staff room was located at the back of the building next to a line of very public and extremely odoriferous toilets. It was rather narrow in shape – rather like a short corridor with a door at either end. Next to the door at the far end, was an old refrigerator, upon which perched a plastic tray covered in coffee jars, powdered milk and boxes of jasmine tea bags. There was also an electric kettle with a long flex plugged into an overloaded socket. Two chairs with torn plastic seats stood on guard on either side of the refrigerator.

A wooden table was wedged up against one of the walls upon which were several stacks of ancient-looking text books. And to complete the postmodernist image, an empty water cooler with the taps broken off, teetered on three legs by the table.

Two teachers were standing with their backs turned when Percy Gabbitt walked in. They were discussing food-poisoning quite animatedly.

"I was on the can for three days," said one, rather bitterly.

"Well, I did warn you about going there. They wash the plates in the canal, you know," said the other.

"Oh, gross!" exclaimed the one with the gastric problems. "I'm still feeling rather fragile."

They turned as one when Gabbitt cleared his throat.

"Hello," offered Gabbitt, with a thin smile.

"Oh god, Doctor Death's captured another one, Terence," said the one with food poisoning.

"Percy Gabbitt," said Gabbitt, extending a sweaty hand.

"Terence Thatcher. No relation I hasten to add, although I do have an aunt in Finchley. Welcome to the madhouse," said Terence, picking up a dirty white mug containing what looked like either coffee or mud.

"Ivor Frotmint," said the other teacher. "Leader of the escape committee."

"Pleased to meet you," said Gabbitt, with a frown.

"Looks like it'll just be the three of us this morning I'm afraid," said Terence with a sigh. "George, Barry and Arthur rang in earlier saying they'd gone down with malaria, SARS and Chicken Flu. So, it's backs to the wall today. And, I am told, there's a team from head office visiting later today too. That should give Zhang a heart attack by teatime."

"Hopefully," murmured Ivor, as he re-arranged a pile of textbooks on the table.

"Are you free on Wednesday afternoon?" asked Terence, looking at Gabbitt.

"Why?" responded Gabbitt.

"There's a day trip to some caves nearby and they need a foreign teacher to make the thing seem like a proper excursion. I would have gone, but I'm claustrophobic and Ivor has a fear of glass."

"A fear of glass?" asked Gabbitt, slowly.

"Can't stand being near glass, or it gives him the colly-wobbles," said Terence. "So, no bus trips for him, I'm afraid. And you wouldn't get me anywhere near a cave complex either. I get hot and sweaty in a lift."

"Oh," said Gabbitt.

"And I also need a day off to catch up on a bit of serious sleep," added Ivor, rubbing his face the way you do when you're trying to stave off imminent collapse due to sleep deprivation.

"Zhang said he'd find us an apartment by the end of the week. We just have to hold out till then," said Terence, quietly. He too looked exhausted.

"Where are you staying at the moment?" asked Gabbitt.

"Tell him, Terence," said Ivor, bottom lip quivering. "I can't seem to put into words without getting all emotional."

"We sleep here," said Terence, flatly. "Right here, in the school. Ivor has Room Two and I have Room

Four. We arrange the chairs in a row and try to get a few hours' sleep lying on them. It's very uncomfortable."

"Zhang told us that he was providing free accommodation. Only we both rather stupidly thought that meant an apartment," muttered Ivor.

"It's also no fun having stand-up baths using that broken water cooler," said Terence wearily.

"And don't start me off on the toilets," added Ivor.

"You stay here all the time?" asked an amazed Gabbitt.

"Yes, my friend. We're like modern-day galley slaves chained to our place of employ and only allowed out into the fresh air at weekends," said Ivor grumpily.

"Why don't you leave?" asked Gabbitt

"Why indeed?" came the sad response from Terence. "Because we need to keep renewing our visas, since Zhang has only given us temporary monthly ones. It's his way of trapping us here."

"But sleeping here? In the school? That's completely insane," said Gabbitt.

"You haven't heard the worst of it," said Ivor, now with the wind of revolution well and truly in his sails. "Poor old Terence had a nightmare trip over here on three different planes which took over thirty-six hours and then, when he arrived, Zhang collected him at Shanghai airport and drove him straight here."

"Well, wasn't that nice of him?" asked a perplexed Gabbitt.

"He dropped poor, dazed and jet-lagged Terence off so that he could immediately teach seven lessons of total beginners. He didn't even have time to have a wash and get a bite to eat."

"That's incredible," gasped Gabbitt, now beginning to understand what Arapacana Associates was all about.

"Right, we can chat later, but I've got Complete Beginners in Room Three," said Ivor, marching out of the room. "Pleased to meet you," he cried slightly maniacally as he walked out. "Hope you make it to Tuesday."

"And I've got False Beginners in Room Two and Elementary One in Room Four," said Terence and motored off after Ivor toting a huge pile of yellow text books with *'My Best English Book - One'* written rather immodestly in italics on the cover. "And don't ask how I manage to teach two classes at the same time either. We've become dab hands at that sort of thing here."

There was a pause as footsteps receded into the distance. A sigh followed and the steps retraced a few feet. "That leaves Forever Beginners in Room One," came Terence's tired voice. "Don't be late or they tend to wander off and wee in the corridor," he added resignedly.

Gabbitt looked all around him and wondered what to do next. All he knew about the school was what he had just been told by Terence. Mr Zhang had simply said he should go to the staffroom and 'settle in'. He sighed and looked at what was left on the table. There was a pile of texts all called 'Quality Immersion English' with a picture on the front of a smiling Chinese girl wearing large old-fashioned headphones. Gabbitt picked up the pile and headed for Room One.

Deep in the bowels of Wormwood Scrubs prison in central London, Nero Handsworth was putting the finishing touches to a plan which he liked to call: 'the Irish stand-off'.

He had just explained how this worked to Nearly-Mad-Mick from D Block, with limited success. Mick had a very short attention span at the best of times.

This is how it works. First. it is very similar to the Mexican stand-off in that it requires four or five trigger-happy villains, arranged in a rough circle, with each participant pointing his weapon at someone else's head. No-one pulls their trigger for the obvious reason.

The Irish stand-off is different in a small but crucial way, namely that they all pull their triggers.

Nearly-Mad-Mick in D Block had considered this as a racist remark and had kicked two of Nero's bodyguards where it had hurt them most. Considering that Nero had six other burly bodyguards present, such a violent reaction might be seen as slightly ill-advised and indeed, ten minutes later, Nearly-Mad-Mick had been stretchered off to the prison hospital with a badly broken leg, a torn ear and lacerations to the neck.

Nero had then decided to resort to Plan B, since using the unique talents of Nearly-Mad-Mick were now off the table. After a conversation on his illegal mobile phone with a gentleman called Slicing Sammy, he felt that he now had everything in place.

He smiled happily. It would take a pretty intelligent policeman to work out the circle he had just created – a circle which began with Percy Raymond Gabbitt and Fred the Throttler and ended with Three Knives Nigel and Slicing Sammy.

Nero felt particularly proud of his handiwork. What made the circle satisfying on almost all counts was that Nero did not like any of the participants either. It was the perfect way to clear the field of all the people he least liked in one masterstroke - a masterstroke which also had the tacit backing of the police force as well. Six deadly degrees of separation, chuckled Nero to himself.

That daft inspector did not realise he had released the beast of revenge onto Percy Gabbitt's world.

"Lunch-time, I think," Nero murmured and stood up. "I think the beef today and a Merlot," he announced to the world, airily.

Inspector Pringle was sitting at his desk with fingers steepled on the table before him. He had been in this position for the last ten minutes and was just reaching the conclusion that the world really was a totally insane place.

In the background, his trusty tape recorder was smoothing its way through Pink Floyd's 'Wish You Were Here'. DC Ford sat opposite him, explaining all about the quest to rescue a female goblin called Bunty in a world ruled by undead beasts and creatures from the black lagoon. It would have been too simple to dismiss all this as just plain idiocy and madness, except that it was in the line of duty.

"Now that I'm well and truly in, I'm going to have to upgrade," said Ford, with an avaricious twinkle in his eye.

"And what does that entail?" asked Pringle, in a slightly bored way.

"I need better armour and some ranged weaponry, sir," said Ford.

"Well, go to the armoury there and get yourself kitted out. You have the required clearances and enough fictitious gold,' added Pringle, with a sigh.

"No, you don't understand. I need mithril armour plating, invisible arrows and a bow made of dragon bone, sir," said Ford, enthusiastically. "So, I'll need an extra five hundred coins for the bow, sir."

"So..." began Pringle.

"And a further fifteen hundred for the other stuff, including a Healing Potion upgrade."

"Just get the tech boys to jiggle the system to give you..."

"No, I need real money," interrupted Ford.

"Real money?" queried an incredulous Pringle. "Not something from the Bank of Noddyland that our chaps can knock up for you?"

"Not this time," said Ford slowly. "This is big business, sir. People now live their whole lives in these fantasy worlds and actually buy upgraded weapons from other heroes using their Mastercards."

"And you want Her Majesty's police force to start spending tax payer's money on dragon bone bows and invisible arrows?"

"Not forgetting the mithril armour," added Ford.

"Oh no, we wouldn't want to forget that, now would we?" quipped Pringle, and sat back in his chair.

"It's all getting pretty intense in there," continued Ford.

"Indeed," said Pringle.

"The Snark Maiden also fancies me," said Ford, colouring slightly.

The Chief Inspector stood up. It was clearly time to call an end to the proceedings.

"And I think I can persuade Gabbitt to get on a plane back to Angleterre," said Ford suddenly, more as an afterthought.

"You can?" Pringle sat down again.

"Just a matter of pressing the right buttons," said Ford.

"And this button-pressing requires me to authorize the spending of two thousand pounds on make-belief weaponry, does it?"

"Absolutely, sir," said Ford.

"I'm also well in with this Springett fellow. We've had a few pints in Piccadilly and generally got to know each other. He doesn't know that I've infiltrated his little gaming circle as Obby the Gladiator. Just thinks I'm a tired old copper needing a drink and some company."

"What?" murmured Pringle. "Not only have you been spending all your work time chasing dragons, but you are also drinking, while on duty?"

"I had a pineapple juice last time, sir," came the rather injured reply.

"You've got a week," said Pringle and stood up again. "I'll authorise a budget not exceeding five thousand pounds, you understand, but I want results, Ford, or you'll be pounding the beat again."

"Five grand, sir!" exclaimed Ford breathlessly. "I can get an extra quiver of golden wyvern arrows for that," he marvelled happily. Ford almost floated to the door and exited Pringle's office, determined to get back into Dark Dawn Three as quickly as possible, and to upgrade.

Pringle's battered tape recorder started playing 'Shine on You Crazy Diamond'.

Mr Chipchase and Mr Bibby were at their best when given a difficult task which involved hefting heavy duty weaponry.

But their experiences on Box Hill had caused even them to step back and take stock of things. Having a bazooka on your shoulder usually simplified things rather well, but on that occasion, it had only confused everything. Chipchase and Bibby had departed that debacle thoughtful… and realising that it was time for a change.

The result had been the creation of a security company based in Leytonstone in east London – a company which made a very rapid impact on the business of protecting other people's money and valuables. Whereas most security firms relied on armour-plated vans and men in smart-blue uniforms toting lead-lined nightsticks, Chipchase and Bibby usually used a standard transit van with no added defensive features. Strangely enough, they never seemed to have any problems with the criminal fraternity or gangs in east London, mainly because it was well-known that the two of them were sadistic psychopaths who actually looked forward to the day someone tried to 'do them over'.

It only happened once and never again. A gang from one of those northern cities where people eat fish and chips all day and drink cheap beer all night, descended on London determined to make an impression. They soon found out about Chipchase and Bibby's operation and could not believe their luck when they discovered that large sums of money collected from market vendors and local betting shops were being ferried to banks across London in a knockabout transit van. They immediately set about planning a robbery – this was their first mistake.

The heist, when it came, seemed to go off without too many problems. The van was cornered in a backstreet near Aldgate, the drivers given a token thumping and sacks of loot were removed from the van.

It all had gone rather too well and the gang had settled back into their five star suites at the Savoy Hotel, where they had drunk their minibars dry, while agreeing wholeheartedly that southerners were soft and namby-pamby and certainly no match for the brutal and violent northerner. This was their second mistake.

However, their third and most important error was when they then decided to celebrate their good fortune at various clubs and pubs across London's West End the following weekend.

Mr Chipchase and Mr Bibby had moved quietly into action. They had not called the police after the robbery. Such a move would have been construed by all and sundry as a weak and dishonourable thing to do. No, this sort of thing had to be settled in the traditional way.

The northern gang had consisted of six members. Chipchase and Bibby's had consisted of two.

By the end of the weekend only two northerners remained alive, the other four meeting their ends in creative and highly-visible ways. One went off the Millennium Wheel as it reached its apex. A second was found naked and hanging upside down from the railings of Buckingham Palace with a chip butty in his mouth.

A third and fourth were found without heads rather appropriately in the Tower of London. The tabloids had loved that.

The final two members of the gang had scarpered back up north to Doncaster or Leeds, or wherever they had come from. They had left what remained of the stolen money in a pile in their Savoy Hotel room which Chipchase and Bibby had collected a few hours later.

The two had not bothered to pursue the fleeing gang members, having decided that a message had been clearly sent.

They had had no problems after that and business had thrived. They had even attained a certain respectability in east London circle and knew several of the cast of Eastenders, had a box at West Ham United's football ground and were said to be mates of both the Lampard and Redknapp families.

However, all was not peaches and cream in the Chipchase household that morning as Ronald Chipchase stood sweating slightly in his hallway and speaking into a mobile phone.

"You want to give us fifty large," he mumbled quietly. "We've had harder and more dangerous tasks than this for a lot less money. I don't see what your problem is."

"Look, if you don't want to do it, then fine. I'll find…" said the man at the other end of the line.

"I'll talk to my colleague and get back to you," said Chipchase and hung up.

Bob Burley was standing by a large computer screen and staring intently at the information it conveyed. Bob Irwin was at his elbow making the sort of noises people make when they are amazed by what they are reading. It was a normal sort of day at Arapacana Associates.

"We're going to have to keep them in England," said Burley slowly.

"But they're due on a plane back here today."

"Well, they'll have to 'undue' themselves," said Burley. "This is more important."

They were looking at an email sent by Bob Brand from London, which contained details of another language school which had 'gone bad'.

"Are they are absolutely sure that this marketing manager has had the balls to do... this? asked Burley quietly.

"Bob's checked everything twice over. It seems that our Mr Gabriel of the Happy Snappy School of English in London has excelled himself this time. And the owner of the school is completely in the dark, apparently."

"I always knew he trod the narrow line between the legal and the not so legal," murmured Burley, "But... this?"

"I reckon he's going for the big one this time, so that he can retire to that little cottage he's been dreaming about in Broadstairs."

"You have to admire him. It's certainly novel."

"But screwing with the Iranians is a tad dangerous for a simple marketing man, don't you think?"

"Well, we'll have to do something, of course," said Burley. "Get your team to return to their hotel and work something out. I want this given top priority. If the Iranians get wind of this, then there's no telling what sort of jihad they'll declare on language schools."

"Maybe some of their people are in on it?" offered Irwin.

"More than likely," agreed Burley. "The wobbly jelly of corruption stretches far and wide, especially when there's a shedload of cash to be made."

"Cunning sod," muttered Irwin.

"Cunning, but also rather stupid. To open a dummy company as a midway house to stash all Iranian money earmarked for educational purposes and then to cream off thirty per cent, before transferring the remainder to individual schools' coffers, is pretty audacious," said Burley.

"And going off-piste to set it all up. Got to love that. Not even his own employers know."

"The scam is worth something in the region of half a million a month," muttered Burley. "He's probably sharing some of the profits with a contact at the embassy."

"I want us to come up with a plan to scupper this scheme in the next three hours. Ring Bob now. And then find out how Percy is doing."

"I rang his school twice and he's still teaching."

"But it's gone nine, Bob," said Burley. "That means he's been in class for nearly twelve hours straight and has missed his first Chinese lesson. Find out what's happening, will you?"

"We need to have a quick talk about that Japanese agent, Bob?"

"It'll have to be quick, Bob. I need to talk to the team about the 'armadillo shuffle' in Madrid."

"That again?"

"I'm afraid so."

"Right," said Irwin. "I'll ring Percy's school and see if he's intending to teach there for the next month without stopping."

The man in question was well on the way to completing his first day at the Shine School and was dreaming of a large, cold beer. He had not realised that teaching at this questionable institution required all teachers to take extra lessons in their lunch breaks and teach two or three classes at the same time.

Percy Gabbitt was breathing hard as he looked at his watch for the millionth time. It said half past nine.

He should have been attending his first Chinese lesson hours ago, but Mr Zhang had saddled him with four extra classes as part payment for the Chief of Police's car vandalism.

"Excuse me, I'm down to see your next class," said a willowy voice from somewhere behind the refrigerator in the staff room.

"What!" squawked Gabbitt, turning to face the owner of the vaguely familiar voice.

"Inspection week," came the disconcerting reply. "I'm Jane Bobbin from the London office."

Eyes met and eyebrows were raised. Both Gabbitt and Jane Bobbin gasped audibly as unpleasant memories came flooding back.

"You?"

"You!"

"Oh no."

"Oh God!"

There was a slight pause as both of them stared in horror at each other.

"You can't be working as a teacher here. You're one of those sales people. You're not a teacher. You're not qualified for anything," said Jane Bobbin, as distastefully as she could.

"Ah," murmured Gabbitt. "How long have you been in China?"

"One day. One awful day," said Bobbin, with a tear in her eye. "And now this happens. I've been spat on, smoked on, given a plate of meat, even though they know I'm a vegan and now they're throwing you at me!" she squeaked a little pathetically. "It's just not fair."

"I'm a teacher now," offered Gabbitt, a little limply.

"At this school?" asked Bobbin, still in shock. "I only got this job so I could forget everything that happened two years ago. I've had four nervous breakdowns since then, you know."

"I'm sorry, but it wasn't my fault, entirely," began Gabbitt.

"Not your fault! You damn near got us all killed with your messing about, not to mention those offensive courses you insisted on selling without prior authorization."

"That's just normal selling. Everybody does it. Anyway, Nero didn't seem to mind," muttered Gabbitt.

"And look where he is now!" exclaimed Bobbin, hotly. "I was nearly trampled to death by a bull, you know," she finished.

"I'm really sorry," said Gabbitt again, feeling that this was becoming a day of permanently apologising for everything in his life.

"I still get nightmares," said Bobbin, a little wildly.

"So, are you working for Shine now?" asked Gabbitt, attempting non-confrontational, small-talk.

"I most certainly am not," replied Bobbin, angrily. "I inspect schools for the British Council. That's why I'm here at the Shine School. And I should say that up to about two minutes ago I always thought this was an excellent organisation with excellent teachers - a million light years away from that appalling place we both worked at in Piccadilly," she said, shuddering slightly.

"Oh dear," said Gabbitt quietly.

"Oh dear, indeed," said Bobbin smiling a little cruelly. "My turn now, I think," she added, slyly.

"This is my tenth class today," tried Gabbitt, as he picked up a pile of Beginners text books.

"Then you've certainly had enough practice," said Bobbin.

Gabbitt stared at the class record sheet. "According to this, the class has been having English lessons for a year now. It also says they are still total beginners with one girl hovering on the brink of breaking into the False Beginners category. But nobody seems sure when this will happen."

"I think I'm going to enjoy this," said Bobbin, eyes twinkling maniacally.

"Couldn't you watch Terence in Room Two? He's got a far more interesting group. Senior transport police wanting street English, so they can break up bar fights and sort out traffic accidents involving foreigners. Should be much morefun."

"No, I don't think so," snapped Bobbin, after a very short pause. "And anyway, I'm not here for fun, Mr Gabbitt, as you are about to find out."

Gabbitt sighed and headed for the corridor.

Room Five was inhabited by six students. All were sitting patiently at their desks as Gabbitt and Bobbin entered the room.

It was then that the fun really started.

Caroline Williams was attempting a bit of fun of her own. She had entered Dark Dawn Three and was busy scrutinizing the game options. She was getting a funny feeling about this particular game and had decided to make it less funny.

It was all very well to start marching around a strange landscape biffing anyone who came too close for comfort, but when odd characters suddenly appeared out of nowhere and started actually helping you, then it was time to do a spot of investigating. The fantasy world was a brutal, nasty place where nice things happened all too rarely and horrible things happened all the time. People were like that in this alternate existence. It tended to bring out the worst in mankind – not the best.

And yet, here was this Obby character striding up to them in the middle of a drawbridge and basically saving their bacon. He had not even demanded any sort of immediate recompense. It was all most unsettling.

Caroline stared at the game schematics and noted that over three hundred thousand addicts were currently online adventuring in their own grim little corner of Dark Dawn Three. What an odd world, thought Caroline and scrolled down the page looking at the list of dangerous locations, unsavoury characters and possible nasty events.

There were three locations to venture into in a virtual continent the size of America, plus over fifty computer-generated monsters, another thirty creatures added by various ingenious players and about one hundred game-generated beasts, equipped with two thousand possible weapon permutations. Very nice.

There was also a choice of over ten possible adventures including their own 'Rescue Quest' with Bunty's name written in the appropriate slot.

She scrolled on and came to the hero creation pages. It only took a few moments of tapping to get through to the page which held all the details concerning their new companion, Obby the Gladiator.

Ten minutes later and Caroline had signed off and closed her machine down. She then sat cross-legged on a deep velvet sofa in her apartment and held Barchester close. Something was not right – not right at all.

"It says here," said Alfred Fennell from the depths of his well-worn television armchair, "that Suzhou is paradise on earth. A place with lots of canals, gardens and nice weather. Sounds like Bedford."

It was late morning in Bromley and Alfred and Hilda Fennell were having their elevenses. They also had a selection of guidebooks and travel agency brochures spread out on the dining table among the custard creams and Rich Tea biscuits.

"Bedford doesn't have very nice weather," said Hilda, as she supped hard from a cup of iron-red tea. "It's a windy place with a crowded shopping centre and too many charity shops."

"It's near Shanghai," muttered Alfred, as he examined a map closely.

"Bedford's not near Shanghai," said Hilda, worriedly.

"No, this Suzhou place," muttered Alfred, irritably. "It's just a bit up the road from Shanghai. And on a large lake, too."

"Well, Percy wouldn't go to a nasty city," said Hilda, taking a small bite out of a bourbon.

"Says here that it was founded in 600BC by an emperor called He Lu. It's also on the Grand Canal, whatever that means. Probably a bit like the Manchester Ship Canal. Also, famous for silk factories. You can get yourself a new pair of shiny pyjamas."

"Drink your tea before it gets cold, you daft ha-peth," said Hilda. "Silk pyjamas indeed. At my age. Whatever are you thinking?"

"I like the idea of a place with gardens. Says here they combine balance, harmony and proportion. That sounds like ."

"Whatever, I'm sure it'll be a memorable holiday," said Hilda, nibbling the last crumbs of her bourbon.

It was also to be a memorable night at the Shine School of English in central Suzhou.

As Percy Gabbitt began a tired and ultimately unsuccessful attempt at breaching the walls of the Present Perfect tense with six wide-eyed students, the evening seemed to be winding down in a totally unspectacular and dull way.

Just down the corridor in Room Three, Terence Thatcher was introducing his policemen to the delights of shouting menaces at the general public in fluent Queen's English.

Meanwhile, Ivor Frotmint, in an adjacent room, was currently scribbling on his whiteboard a few communicative but semantically questionable sentences like: 'This is a violet watermelon', and 'Where is the beautiful toilet?'

Outside the school, the night shift had just arrived at the adjacent building site and were busy cranking up diggers and distributing spades and hammers for a night of noise, dust and industrial spitting.

Just another normal evening in downtown Suzhou.

However...

"You cute kid," said Pageboy slyly.

Percy Gabbitt's misery had been compounded by the fact that he knew his class already. Well, perhaps 'knew' is a little strong, unless you count meeting them in a bar a few days previously.

"I have eaten lunch today," said Gabbitt, reading slowly from a prepared sheet. "Have you had it yet?" he asked the class.

"I get it very often," chuckled Deranged Pony mischievously. Her English might not have been top-notch, but her knowledge of double-entendres was quite impressive.

Gabbitt blushed and turned to the board. Fate could be extremely cruel, he thought unhappily. To have most of the employees of Big Boy Bar sitting in front of him at any other time would have been traumatic enough, but on inspection night it was a little unfair to say the least. And why on earth did they all need to learn English anyway? American or Australian style bars only needed two or three stock phrases involving money, love, beer and sex and you were home and dry as a bar girl. Gabbitt was feeling angry, tired and considerably anti-China at that moment. He sighed and decided to give his class another chance. After all, it was not their fault.

"Have you ever been to Beijing?" he asked loudly and dabbed the question on the whiteboard with a bright blue marker pen.

"Yes, I been," came the happy reply. Afro-Cut had decided to enter the fray.

"Me too," agreed Pimply Moon, from her place by the window.

"And Tiananmen Square? Have you been there?"

Silence greeted his question. It was the sort of silence which implied that the class was totally unaware that he was attempting to speak a Chinese word. They all looked at one another and whispered: "Tian-an-em-an-suck-where" as if it were a complicated English idiom.

Gabbitt smiled and turned back to the board. Time for a bit of art, he thought and began drawing what he hoped looked like a massive town square with a picture of Chairman Mao on the wall in front of The Forbidden Palace in Beijing. After a few moments, he turned to face Deranged Pony.

"Tiananmen Square!" he exclaimed proudly and pointed at the board.

"Ah," said the class as one, wondering why the teacher had drawn a picture of a monkey on the board. Gabbitt was not very good at drawing.

"Have you ever…" he began slowly.

"Teacher… this boring," said Pimply Moon, suddenly. "You have Chinese girlfriend… yet?"

The class all seemed to perk up at this question. It was the kind of terrain that they were all fascinated with.

"Maybe we find one for you," said Afro-Cut, giggling wildly.

Gabbitt was about to reply when he heard Jane Bobbin clear her throat and turn to a fresh page on her clipboard.

"She your squeeze?" asked Pageboy, pointing a finger at Jane Bobbin. "She OK girl. Not pretty but…"

"Well lived in," interrupted Afro-Cut. "My New York boyfriend last month said all Chinese women looked well lived in."

"You have man?" asked Pimply Moon to Jane Bobbin.

Silence resumed except for increased scribbling of a biro on a clipboard.

"Maybe she deaf?" chipped in Deranged Pony. "You deaf?" she shouted, as loudly as she could.

"No," came the quiet and slightly irritated reply.

"That top not suit you," said Afro-Cut happily. "Make you look….. like frumpy girl."

"I beg your pardon," said Jane Bobbin, looking up from her pad and taking her glasses off.

"Look better in pink tank-top," said Pimply Moon, as she scrutinized the inspector closely. "Make you look more sexy. Anything better than that crap."

"Teacher, what tank-top?" asked Deranged Pony.

"What?" squeaked Gabbitt, as he realised the lesson was well and truly off-track again.

"What tank-top?" persisted the Pony, looking as though she damn well knew and was being mischievous.

Gabbitt sighed and began drawing a rather nice looking student in a tank-top waving from the middle of his picture of Tiananmen Square. He then drew an arrow pointing at the girl's top and wrote in block letters 'TANK-TOP'.

A moment passed and Gabbitt suddenly had an idea. He turned to the board again and began drawing once more. This was what teaching was all about he thought, as inspiration filled his every fibre.

A minute later and he had drawn a passable picture of a Chieftain tank with a particularly large gun barrel.

"This is another sort of tank," he said and drew another arrow on the board pointing at the tank.

"Ah." The class breathed as one.

"Have you ever seen a tank?" he said, feeling that he had somehow managed to fight his way back to the high ground again. The Present Perfect tense was nicely on the rails again.

"Teacher, that wrong pen," came the somewhat unexpected reply.

"What?"

"That not board pen," said Afro-Cut, knowledgeably.

"Does it matter?" asked Gabbitt, feeling a little irritated.

"It not wipe off," said Afro-Cut, pointing at the tank.

"Oh shit!" exclaimed Gabbitt, as he realised that he had mixed the board-markers with the very indelible markers.

The class all giggled at the expletive and Jane Bobbin began a new paragraph in her note pad.

"One moment," said Gabbitt and bolted from the class to get a towel, some hot water and a bottle of bleach he thought he had seen in the staffroom.

"We help," said Deranged Pony and slid off her chair. In a moment, the room was empty of students.

Further down the corridor, Percy Gabbitt had just reached the staff room and was beginning a frantic exhumation of any cupboards that might contain cleaning materials.

The door to Terence Thatcher's room opened and the senior police official with the scratched car door emerged looking rather unhappy. He was clearly having a torrid time with the Communicative Approach and needed a toilet break.

Jane Bobbin was looking at her clipboard. She smiled happily. A report on this lesson would probably not only get Percy Gabbitt a severe reprimand and pay deduction, but he might even get the sack. It could not be any better.

She thought of all those sleepless nights and sweaty nightmares involving exploding schools, psychotic bulls and brutal policemen with machine guns. Payback time, she thought and underlined the words: 'Totally Unprofessional' on her pad.

A few moments passed and Jane Bobbin looked at her watch. She wrote another sentence onto her observation sheet and looked at her watch again. Five minutes of the lesson frittered away looking for cleanser. She tutted in delight. She waited another minute and then stood up to stretch her legs.

It was at that moment that the door to her room opened and a man in a blue shirt with receding hair strode in.

"Hello," beamed Bobbin, in his direction.

"Sorry, wrong room," said the man in embarrassment.

"That's OK," said Jane Bobbin airily. "What room are you looking for?"

The man was about to respond when his eyes lighted on the whiteboard and Gabbitt's pictures there. It took a few moments as he took everything in. He then made a low gurgling sound followed by a loud gasp. He looked at Jane Bobbin and shouted something very aggressively in Chinese.

"I know. Silly man used the wrong markers," said Bobbin, with a sly smirk.

The man in blue then opened the door to the classroom and shouted something down the corridor. Jane Bobbin sat down and picked her clipboard up. Clearly, the man had a problem. Best to let the moment pass, she thought and smiled weakly at his back.

In the staffroom, Percy Gabbitt had managed to pull a likely-looking bottle from behind the refrigerator and was examining it closely. It was all in Chinese, but did have a promising picture of a cockroach lying on its back at the bottom of the label. Gabbitt wondered if it would be all right to swab his board with the stuff.

Outside the building, Deranged Pony, Afro-Cut, Pageboy and Pimply Moon were exchanging giggles and having a secret cigarette break. They were clearly very pleased to be getting a little fresh air in the middle of a lesson.

Someone shouted something in their direction and someone else laughed loudly. The four looked at the building site. The driver of the nearest bulldozer appeared transfixed by the sight of four young women in short yellow and pink skirts within ogling distance of his cabin. He shouted something at the four and put his tongue out.

Pimply Moon shouted something back and put her tongue out too. The man in the bulldozer seemed quite taken at all this attention and revved his engine accordingly. Maybe the girls would be impressed by his powerful machine, he thought, rather simply. The bulldozer revved again and lurched forward as the man's foot slipped off the brake.

Back in the Shine School, Jane Bobbin also felt like putting her tongue out. Something was clearly very wrong. Gabbitt's classroom was full of men in blue all shouting loudly at each other and gesticulating wildly. One was even taking photos of both her and the whiteboard on his mobile.

Mr Zhang then appeared. "Why you do this?" he murmured in horror at Jane Bobbin.

"Do what?" tried Bobbin, anxiously.

"You want me sent to prison?" he squawked at her.

"What?" asked Bobbin.

"I…" began Zhang.

He never finished his sentence. Two policemen suddenly grabbed him and started handcuffing his hands behind his back. A third policeman attempted the same treatment with Jane Bobbin. Predictably, she started screaming loudly and kicking out at the man with the handcuffs.

It was at that precise moment that a section of Gabbitt's classroom wall suddenly toppled inwards and onto the two policemen and Zhang. They all disappeared very quickly under a pile of brick ends, dust and plaster. A man with a cigarette dangling from his mouth appeared in the large gaping hole in the classroom wall. He was sitting at the controls of a massive yellow bulldozer, smiling congenially and mouthing "Hello" to the dusty occupants of the room.

The corridor filled with thick clouds of dust and Gabbitt started coughing. A moment later and two large shapes pushed past him followed by a smaller and whimpering shape in handcuffs, still clutching a clipboard.

Gabbitt made for the exit. He had been teaching for nearly twelve hours straight and now the place was collapsing around his ears. There was also that miserable woman. Gabbitt had had more than enough and decided that staying at this dreadful school was not an option any more no matter what the infernal Bobs wanted him to do. They would have to realise that he was not quite the person they imagined him to be.

He picked his way over a few bricks and part of another wall which had just collapsed into the main reception area.

As he stumbled onto the pavement, he noticed Terence and Ivor had escaped as well.

"Lord love a duck!" exclaimed Terence, with feeling.

"Shit on a stick!" was Ivor's succinct contribution as he brushed grey powdery dust from his tired, corduroy jacket.

"There goes the overtime bonus," said Terence, as another wall collapsed into a pile of rubble and a fire sprang up from a leaking gas pipe somewhere in the middle of all the devastation.

"There goes all our stuff," said Ivor.

Gabbitt got to his bike and wrenched it into an upright position, gouging another deep line into the police car door. He swore under his breath and pulled the bike away from the car and the fire hydrant it was chained to.

Unfortunately, the exertion of yanking a stout bike chain off a rusty fire hydrant had rather dramatic results. There was a sudden loud, watery explosion and the top of the hydrant tore loose.

# NINE

*"Business today is a war. We have to fight dirty to get to the end zone, while covering our asses if it all goes tits up by circling the wagons and waiting for the cavalry to arrive."*
**(Bob Burley talking idiomatically to his sales staff)**

Rain was steadily falling in London and a cold wind was blowing. It was one of those grey late summer days which had autumn written all over it.

Nero Handsworth was staring out of the prison library window and thinking deeply. He had a lot think about. Stuff like his sentence. He had already served two years and had a maximum of one year to go.

In fact, his meeting later that day with three stout members of the parole board might even shave a few more months of that year. He smiled weakly at the leaden skies and watched the rain bouncing off the tiles of 'D' Block, which faced the library.

Things were going pretty well, he thought warily. But he had learned to his cost that counting one's chickens before they were hatched could be a disastrous thing. He frowned and his thoughts turned to Percy Gabbitt.

He would have to be extremely careful. There would be no chance of the slightest error this time round. He could not even contemplate his final year at Her Majesty's pleasure being lengthened to a further five or ten years. Nero shuddered. No, that was not an option. His original sentence of just two years had already been increased to three following some meddling in high places. Nero had been extremely upset at that.

Perhaps it might have been better to call the whole thing off with this Inspector Pringle and just bide his time. Mr Gabbitt would still be there like a tethered lamb when he strode out of Wormwood Scrubs in twelve short months.

On the other hand, this police inspector had handed him a really juicy opportunity to get even with the swine with virtual total police immunity and while still behind bars. Virtual. Nero frowned. How virtual was this agreement? Did it extend to Messrs Chipchase, Bibby and Fred the Throttler? He rather thought not. It was a slippery dilemma facing Nero that morning.

"You got a visitor, boss," said a voice that could chop firewood without the aid of an axe.

A bulky man in a sleeveless t-shirt and with bovine muscles covered in dark tattoos, stared thickly at him.

Nero sighed and thought about the 'Irish stand-off' he had constructed over the last few days. It had been a pretty ambitious plan to get a whole crowd of vicious psychopaths in a line all waiting to drop one another at a given moment.

The worrying thing was that the plan seemed to be working. Working rather too easily. Nero existed in a world where nothing got solved without a lot of sweat, anxiety and pain. But he seemed to have covered all the angles this time and just had to wait for the first domino to fall. It all depended on just one thing – timing.

He strode to the door where the man with the muscles and a prison guard waited to escort him to the Visitor's Room.

Fred the Throttler was not a very savoury man. In fact, some might have said that he transcended the boundaries of savouridom and drifted into that rather murky area inhabited by things which defied categorisation. Being savoury invites comparison with being sweet. Fred the Throttler was very much neither. It might be better just to say that he was distinctly inedible and leave it at that.

Fred sat in a red plastic chair and stared at the world through narrow, furtive slits of eyes which were red and puffed like small, saggy balloons. He had a dull blue bruise on one cheek and a long cut on his forehead, which made him look as if he had just picked a fight with a very upset gorilla. He also smelt as though this gorilla had then dragged him back through a dung-heap filled with month-old rotting cabbages. He was truly a very unsavoury and unsweet person.

Nero entered the room with the guard and sat down.

"What the hell happened to you?" he squawked, as he surveyed the mess in a trenchcoat sitting before him.

"Bit of bovver in the car park," mumbled Fred, unhappily.

"I'll leave you to it, then," said the guard and beat a rapid retreat, trying not to breathe in too deeply.

Nero stared at Fred and wondered not for the first time if he had made a terrible mistake in getting involved with someone who was almost human, but not quite.

"The car park?"

"Best you don't know," came the reply. "You being in the nick and all. Don't want them to think you had anything to do with it."

"Right," said Nero quickly.

"And me allergic to cats an' all," continued Fred, sadly. "Just lucky I have long pockets."

"Quite," said Nero, wondering briefly what Fred's allergy to felines and the fact that he had long pockets had to do with things. "To get down to business," he continued. "You understand what you have to do?"

"No problem," sniffed Fred, professionally. "Collect the three packages from the airport, then throw away two of them and bring the third to that warehouse on the Isle of Dogs. Piece of piss."

"What!" exclaimed Nero, a little non-plussed.

"Three packages," repeated Fred in a furtive whisper, looking pointedly at the ceiling.

"The place is not bugged, Fred. You're the only thing in this room with a bug problem. Please speak plainly, I haven't got all day."

"Thought the one thing you did have was all day," murmured Fred, with a small smirk. He had not liked the bug quip.

"If you're trying to be funny, I would seriously suggest a sudden change of mood," said Nero, dangerously.

"Right," said Fred, sitting up in his chair and undoing his coat buttons. A new selection of odours drifted around the room before sinking below nostril line.

Nero narrowed his eyes and decided to make this meeting as brief as possible. "You will meet the three gentlemen at the airport and then accompany them to the aforesaid Isle of Dogs. I don't know how you intend to do it, but between the airport and the warehouse on the Isle of Dogs, you will manage to lose two of the gentlemen and only will bring the third to the destination. Is that clear?"

"Yes," said Fred, confidently. "Not a problem. Just tell me which is the lucky one and I'll be fine."

"Oh, you won't have any problems with that, I can assure you. The person I want looks like an idiot who couldn't punch his way out of a paper bag. The other two are built like brick shit-houses with the combined brain power of a small rodent."

"Oh, I see," said Fred making a mental note of this important piece of information.

"That's all you have to do," said Nero. "You will deliver the man who looks like an idiot to my people at the warehouse and then leave with your payment of five thousand pounds. That's four for dealing with the two men and one for delivering the third."

"What do you want him for?"

"Do you want to live beyond next week?" asked Nero.

"Ah, I understand," said Fred, tapping his nose and winking hard. "Need to know stuff, eh?"

"I'll get someone to phone you the arrival details at the appropriate time. Until then, keep you mobile on at all times and be prepared to go at a moment's notice."

Nero stood up and made for the door and fresh prison air once more.

"One problem," said Fred.

"What?" said Nero, impatiently, without bothering to turn round.

"Don't have a mobile phone. They always break after a few days in my possession."

"Why does that surprise me?" asked Nero. "I'll get my people to give you one." A thought suddenly occurred to him. "You do know that they need re-charging, don't you?"

"What do?"

"Mobile phones."

"Not very good with this new technical stuff," said Fred, feeling slightly confused. "Prefer to leave all that to the young 'uns. I'm a more hands-on, practical sort of bloke."

"Quite," said Nero, as he looked distastefully at Fred the Throttler's large, pudgy hands.

"OK," sighed Nero. "I'll get someone to phone you at that public phone box in The Bun and Trumpet near Orient's football ground every night at exactly eight. Is that clear?"

"Clear as custard," said Fred, smiling. He then tapped his nose again.

"Just don't make any mistakes and be at that pub every night, without fail," said Nero.

"Do I get a beer allowance, seeing as I have to be in the pub every night?" mumbled Fred, as the door closed.

There was no reply. Fred sighed, wiped his hands on his trousers and stood up. "Piece of piss," he muttered croakily and then spat onto the floor. He trundled out of the room just as three prison warders ran down the corridor.

"Do you know where the warden's cat is?" asked one of them.

"What? Me? Don't know nothing mate," said Fred and plunged his hands into his coat pockets.

"Because there's blood on the ground behind a clapped-out Vauxhall Viva in the car park which I believe belongs to you. And the warden's cat is missing."

"Got me there, mate," said Fred, trying not to sneeze. "Funny things happen in prisons."

"What's that smell?" asked another warder, as he inhaled some of Fred's air.

"Must be my aftershave," said Fred.

"If I find out you've got anything to do with that cat's disappearance, I'll be coming after you," said the first warder menacingly.

"Should keep wild animals safely locked up," said Fred, as he sneezed wetly, sending a huge glob of mucous onto the shoulder of the third warden. "Not right having them mucking around in car parks. Anything could happen," he said and shuffled his way to the exit door, still with his hands in his pockets.

The clapping and cheering took a full five minutes to subside. It was only then that two large magnums of Chinese champagne were popped followed by more cheering. The office had a jolly, festive air to it.

At the very centre of all this mirth and happiness sat a rather bemused Percy Gabbitt. He had only decided to return to the offices of Arapacana Associates at the very last minute after a lot of soul-searching. He rather thought that the mood there would be slightly different when he stepped through the door.

"I have to hand it to you, Percy," beamed Bob Irwin, swigging back his third glass. "I wouldn't have thought it possible. You were only there a day."

"You're an utter genius, my friend," chipped in Bob Burley, slapping Gabbitt on the back and refilling his flute. "I only said to discredit the bastard. But not only did you manage to get the swine arrested and his school levelled to the ground, but then you set fire to what remained and even managed to turn the water on yourself to put the goddamn fire out! Is there no end to your powers?"

"Don't forget that he pissed off the Chief of Police too," said Irwin, chuckling into his sixth refill.

"Vandalising his car right in front of him and then getting away with it. Priceless," he said, shaking his head in disbelief.

"Most of us manage to chuck just one or two spanners into an evil machine, but you manage to throw the whole toolbox in. It's just..." said Burley, his voice starting to crack.

"Awesome," said Irwin, completing his sentence.

"Exactly," said Burley, almost in a whisper.

"It wasn't quite what I planned..." began Gabbitt.

"You mean there was more!" exclaimed Burley.

"Surely that was enough?" tried Irwin, attacking another flute with gusto.

"No, that's not what I meant," said Gabbitt.

"Of course, it's not," said Burley, smiling widely. "And we're not forgetting that you got that British Council inspector from London expelled from China as well. How could you achieve so much in such a short time? It's just..." said Burley, for once lost for words.

"Awesome," repeated Irwin.

"Exactly," agreed a moist-eyed Burley.

"We are not worthy," said Irwin, reaching for the champagne magnum and taking a swig straight from the bottle. He had had enough of dinky flutes and had decided to drink the stuff the Aussie way.

"Old Zhang won't surface again for a few months, I reckon," chuckled Burley happily. "Probably on a fast train to a Mongolian Correction Farm, as we speak."

"One less nasty, corrupt piece of..."

"Quite," interrupted Burley quickly. "But there's lots more where he came from," he said and sighed deeply.

"You mean you want me to go to another school and do the same again?" squeaked Gabbitt, worriedly.

"There's no stopping him," said Irwin, patting Gabbitt on the back. "Easy there, fella.... take a breath and let the others do some of the work."

"That's not quite what I meant," began Gabbitt again.

"I'm sure it wasn't," said Burley. "Anyway, our task is never over."

There was a long pause.

"Can't you give me a few days off?" asked Gabbitt, "I would really like to just close my eyes and think of nothing for a few days. Is that too much to ask?"

"And you can," answered Burley. "After this one last mission."

Gabbitt sighed from the bottom of his soul.

"It's not a school this time, but an agency which is giving us a spot of trouble," said Burley.

"An agency?" mumbled Gabbitt.

"Yes, in a city in the far west of this odd country. A place called Chengdu. Bob will fill you in with the details."

"Chengdu?" squawked Gabbitt. He had never heard of the place and was not at all keen on trekking to the other side of China to wreak more unintended mayhem.

"Place where the pandas live," interjected Irwin. "Big panda research base there churning out the cute little critters like a sausage machine."

"You want me to go to a panda farm?" asked Gabbitt.

"Heavens above, no. Not the pandas. You can leave them well alone. I don't think they're quite ready for you yet," said Irwin, earnestly. "No, we're having problems with a local language travel agency that's suddenly... gone bad."

"Gone bad?" repeated Gabbitt. He did not like the sound of that.

"We're getting reports that they're enrolling students in large groups at a university in the UK, then sending the groups off for their courses, but neglecting to pay the fees. The students finish their courses and return home. The UK university is a bit stumped as to what to do next, because suing a Chinese agent from the UK is a bit… complicated."

"What do you want me to do?" asked Gabbitt, supping miserably at his champagne glass.

"Keen as mustard," said Irwin. "We need to put together a strategy which will basically get back all the owed money."

"Which university is it?" asked Gabbitt, feigning interest.

"Northampton," came the slightly surprising reply.

"I didn't know they had a university there," said Gabbitt, honestly. "Thought it was just one of those red-brick technical colleges."

"Not now, Percy. As we all know, anywhere can call itself a university nowadays. Not that Northampton is a two-bit place, I hasten to add. I can think of at least one worse place. However, the point is that it's been right royally ripped off by this agent in Chengdu - where the pandas come from," said Irwin.

"So, you want to steal the money back," said Gabbitt, flatly.

"Well, hardly steal," said Irwin. "The lolly is not really theirs. We're just making sure that it's given to the rightful owners, like Robin Hood."

"And, to do this, we have to rob a Chinese company miles from here."

"Where the pandas come from," added Irwin.

"Yes, where the pandas come from," repeated Gabbitt. He did not like the sound of this at all.

"You leave tomorrow on the early morning flight to Chengdu," said Burley, from his desk. "The tickets have just been bought and are being sent to us now. And I want this to be a two-man operation. Both of you are to go," he said, looking at Irwin and Gabbitt. "You have three days to get the money back here."

"Why the rush?" asked Irwin. He never liked to be hurried.

"Need you back here for a meeting on the latest developments in London. Bob's still after the Happy Snappy School of English. He'll need a bit of help, I think."

"Three days is cutting it a bit fine," said Irwin.

"Yes, it is," agreed a beaming Burley. "But you have the Gabbitt factor with you. Should be more than enough time. But please don't bulldoze the building this time."

"I keep trying to tell you, that was an..." tried Gabbitt, a little desperately.

"And you'll be going dark as well," interrupted Burley, in a whisper.

"Going what?" enquired Gabbitt.

"Not in touch with anyone at all from head office until the mission is completed," said Irwin. "We'll be on our own, just in case it goes pear-shaped."

Percy Gabbitt took a deep breath. Not only were these sad and dangerous people indulging in some extremely dubious activities, but they were now talking a completely different language to him.

"Going dark," he repeated. It sort of summed up his whole role in the cosmos. Gabbitt stared at Burley.

"Well, I hope nothing does go wrong," he said, a little lamely.

<Are you there?>
<Yep>
<Thought you were 'working' this afternoon>
<Panda's day off. What about you?>
<Got the week off. Owed holiday>
<Brill. So, are we having a go at this Level One boss then?>
<Just waiting for Percy to get online>
<But we're all here. Maybe we can get this done without Percy and his irritating goblin friend. He's probably laying waste to Shanghai as we speak. Far too busy for the likes of us>
<Not funny, Dave. Anyway, it didn't work out that well when we went it alone with the troll. Better wait, I say>
<But we've got that new guy with his big chopper>
<What? Obby?>
<Yep>
<Still say we wait. Don't know what will happen when we go through that door>
<Chicken>
<Just being careful>
<Hello>
<Percy!>
<Great! Can we go in now?>
<You OK, Percy?>
<Just about, Caroline>
<Any more fallout after the mess at that school>
<You don't want to know>
<Sounds like a madhouse over there>
<That's putting it mildly>

<And I'm off on another job tomorrow in the place where the pandas come from>

<How sweet>

<The pandas?>

<Yes, Dave. The pandas>

<Any chance of getting me another panda suit while you're there? Any old pelt that might be lying around would be OK. Mine's gone a bit green>

<Green?>

<KFC Slush Puppy problems>

<What do they want you to do this time?>

<Steal some money>

<You're mad, Percy. Stealing in most countries is bad enough… but in China???>

<Might also be coming home soon too>

<??????>

<??????>

<There's been some trouble at a few schools in London but we're sorting them out apparently. One of the Bobs is busy on a job in Oxford Street right now. We're international madmen, you see>

<Which school?>

<That you, Obby?>

<Yes>

<Something called the Happy Snappy something or other. Rubbish place that's screwing teachers, they tell me>

<So what's this Bob going to do?>

<Not sure Obby. Probably blow the dump up or set fire to the owner>

<So what do you have to do with that?>

<Nothing at the moment, Caroline. But they keep referring to me as the Gabbitt factor. It's all very disturbing. And they're still putting my fingerprints

all over the place too. Seems like I'm getting deeper and deeper into things I can't control>

<When have I heard that before?>

<I've also got to 'go dark' tomorrow>

<????????>

<Cool!>

<Go what?>

<Dark. It means undercover with no outside contact. No telephones or texting and stuff like that>

<Really cool>

<Dave, will you take this seriously? Percy's going to get himself killed… or worse>

<By the way… do any of you know what a flank two situation is?>

<?????>

<Flank two? Piece of cake. Don't any of you ever watch American cop programmes?>

<Oh god, Dave, you're beginning to frighten me>

<It means you're communicating over the phone while under duress>

<Under what?>

<Someone has a gun pressed to your ear and you're saying stuff you don't want to>

<Get out while you can, Percy. Come home. Nixon misses you, doesn't he, Joe?>

<That's a fact>

<I probably should walk away from all this, but can't see how. They've given me a new apartment, a big salary and a new visa>

<Madness, Percy!!!>

<Anyhow, no real damage done yet>

<Tell that to the owner of the school you just destroyed>

<I didn't destroy anything>

<Look, I hate to interrupt, but are we going to sort out the end of level boss or what. I have a lot to do tonight>

<Thought it was Panda's day off, Dave>

<It is, but I still have got to get the green stain out for tomorrow's performance>

<OK. Roger's never been readier for a bit of slicing and dicing!>

<Let's rock and roll. Lock and load! Time to go pitch black and take a sharp flank two turn, I think!>

<Be serious, Dave. Percy's getting into deep trouble over there and needs some serious advice>

<Sorry, Caroline. Just getting into the mood. Anyway, he can look after himself. Percy has the luck of the gods on his side>

*The door at the end of the corridor was wide open. It looked ominously easy just to saunter down the corridor, poke your head into the room and utter a few friendly greetings to the inhabitants inside.*

*Of course, it would not happen like that. It never did.*

*Roger the Norse Fighter adjusted his sword and tightened his thick leather belt. It promised to be a busy next few minutes. Behind him, Endymion the wizard was arranging his scrolls into a rapid-fire cardboard tube while the Snark Maiden and Li Bang Cho checked daggers, arrows and spare swords one last time. Obby the Gladiator stood motionless in the corridor with his monstrous sword already raised to shoulder height, cocked and ready. Nothing would catch him with his trousers down.*

*"We all ready then?" asked Endymion, wiping his nose on a sleeve. "I've got three fireballs and two acid rains primed and ready to go," he said and patted his scroll tube lovingly.*

*"I'll lead," said Roger, drawing Dune Blade and pushing past Obby. "You watch my flank, Obby. I don't want any nasty critter creeping up on me as I take on the big guy. Snarkie and whatever your name is…"*

*"Li Bang Cho," said the Oriental dwarf, sullenly.*

*"Yeh," said Roger, disinterestedly. "You follow close behind and use ranged weapons wherever possible. It would be nice to have a constant shower of arrows and darts keeping the irritating little sods busy while we tackle the big ones."*

*"Ready to go," said the Snark Maiden. "But please don't call me anything, except Snark Maiden. You know abbreviations irritate me."*

*"Right, let's do it then," said Roger and sighed.*

*He was about to march off to glory or destruction when a small voice next to him said: "What about me?"*

*"Err, you keep close to me," said Roger, with a frown. He did not like to be distracted by small goblins on the eve of a big fight. And Tammy was always a major distraction even when he did not speak a word. "Right then," said Roger. "Is there anyone else who would like to have his or her say before we get down to business?"*

*There was a moody silence and then Obby spoke. "I still think we should knock on the door, shout a warning and then enter. Seems fairer to me."*

*"Maybe we should offer whatever is in there a nice plate of jam scones and a pot of tea before we attack," said Roger, a little angrily. "The whole point of adventuring is to rush around and wipe out the bad guys. We don't have some strange code of honour which says that we start swiping the swines only after they've been nicely warned. What's the matter with you?"*

*"Just thought it was more... honourable," said Obby, footballing a small pebble down the corridor.*

*Whatever Roger was about to say was completely lost to posterity since at that exact moment, two massive blood orcs and three wiry ratmen suddenly tumbled out of the room in question and started charging down the corridor uttering low growls and high-pitched snarls. They did not look like the sort of creatures that would appreciate a plate of jam scones.*

*Wonderful," said Endymion. "So much for the element of surprise." He then hurled a full spread of fireballs over Roger's shoulder and into the faces of the rather surprised blood orcs.*

*"Fire in the hole!" he shouted and dived to the corridor floor with both hands over his ears.*

*A few moments later and a coughing and spluttering Roger staggered out of the thick cloying dust and smoke and back down what was left of the corridor.*

*The Snark Maiden was crouching on all fours and Li Bang Cho was sitting with his back to the corridor wall. There was no sign of Obby.*

*"What the hell are you playing at?" gasped Roger, at the wizard.*

*"I've been itching to see what a cluster of grade three fireballs would do in a confined space," said Endymion, enthusiastically.*

*"And now you know," said Roger, trying not to sound too angry.*

*"And now I know," agreed Endymion. "Not much left of the blood orcs," he added, happily.*

*"Except a lot of blood," said Roger with a frown, as he surveyed the corridor.*

*"Don't know what happened to the ratmen though," muttered the wizard.*

*"Not sure they do either," said Roger and turned to the rest of the group.*

*"After that little show I don't think there's much chance of surprising what's left in that room any more, so we might as well get stuck in," he said and marched down the corridor to the open door at the end.*

*"Here we go again," said the Snark Maiden, brushing herself down and knocking an arrow in her silver bow.*

*"Is it always like this?" asked Obby, as he emerged from a pile of rubble a few yards away.*

*"Oh yes," said the Snark Maiden resignedly. "Actually, it's usually a lot worse. Sadly, it's the nature of things that we end up with a schizophrenic,*

*impulsive and totally insane wizard. In the past, our wizards and magic users haven't lasted one level, so there's hope for us yet."*

*"Charming," said Endymion, as he started to unfurl an acid rain spell.*

Far, far away from the mayhem in Dark Dawn Three in a small terraced house in Bromley, south London sat Alfred and Hilda Fennell watching the evening news on the television.

Alfred was munching a bourbon, while Hilda pecked at a finger biscuit. Both were drinking tea from rose chintz cups placed on a tray on a footstool between them.

"Always wondered why they wear those white sheets on their heads," muttered Alfred as a newsreel film showed some sort of demonstration in a Middle Eastern city.

"It's to keep the sun off," said Hilda.

"Thought it was religious," said Alfred, after a pause.

"Religious sheets? Never heard anything like that before."

"We've got one as well," said Alfred.

"One what?"

"A religious sheet."

"Not in this house, we haven't," said Hilda emphatically.

"No, I mean us Christians. We've got that one in Italy with the face of god on it."

"What are you blathering on about, you daft ha'peth?" asked Hilda, having a small sip at her PG Tips.

"Never mind," sighed Alfred. "It's probably a fake anyway, knowing the Italians."

"Got to get the tickets tomorrow," said Hilda, suddenly.

"What tickets?"

"To China."

"China?"

"Alfred Fennell, do you ever listen to a word I say?"

"Oh China," said Alfred wracking his brains for anything recent on China.

"We have to get our aeroplane tickets to China from that nice travel agency in the shopping centre. We need to check the planes too. I'm not travelling on any funny ones."

"Funny ones?" asked Alfred, crunching deep into a bourbon.

"Only British Airways. They treat you decent. Not like those French or German ones with their funny food and rude waitresses."

"Of course, dear," agreed Alfred. There was a long pause and then Alfred spoke again: "What about those planes owned by that bloke with the beard who likes ballooning all over the place? He's English."

"I'm not going to China by balloon, you daft…"

"No, I know that, dear. They're called virgins or something."

"Sometimes I think your brain has turned completely to semolina, Alfred Fennell," said Hilda, finishing her cup of tea and turning the channel over to ITV so they could catch the beginning of the news there.

"British Airways it is then," said Alfred and reached for the newspaper.

"And don't forget to ask if there's anything off for pensioners?" said Hilda.

"Like bus tickets?" asked Alfred, with a frown.

"Well, I hope so," said Hilda. "We didn't go through a world war without picking up a few bonus points along the way."

"Perhaps you have to get tokens or something. Like those Green Shield stamps you used to collect," said Alfred.

"I don't think you can buy aeroplane tickets to China with Green Shield stamps, Alf," said Hilda, thoughtfully.

"I'll bring them along just in case," said Alfred, returning to his paper again and a column that had caught his eye on the history of the torpedo in modern warfare.

"Now we really are getting somewhere," said Chief Inspector Pringle, rubbing his hands and pouring himself a cup of instant coffee.

"Thought it would pay off," said DC Ford, a little smugly.

"So, you say that these terrorists are going to strike at a school just down the road from here in the next few days?"

"Exactly, sir. The Happy Snappy School of English on Oxford Street."

"The Happy Snappy..."

"Yes sir. Rather a catchy name, isn't it?"

Pringle stared into the eyes of the Detective Constable and realised after a short pause that he really did mean what he said. He sighed and supped at the coffee, burning his tongue in the process.

"Well, whatever it's called, we will be there and waiting for the bastards when they turn up with their box of vandalising tools," said Pringle, contentedly.

"Already onto it, sir," said Ford. "Got a team outside there now watching the doors and looking out for any funny business. Also, got a car guarding the back."

"Well done, Ford. But I rather think that these swines won't try anything till the dead of night. I think your team is in for a long wait."

"I've got a good feeling about this one, sir."

"Let's not count our chickens before they're hatched, Ford. I've been in win-win situations before that end up being lose-lose ones very quickly."

"I'll get an extra squad car out there immediately just to be on the safe side," said Ford, reaching for a phone.

"Right," said Pringle, sitting down at his desk. "That's the first leg of a three-point attack on the people behind all this."

"First leg?" queried Ford, as he put the phone down.

"We can't expect to catch then all with just one rather lucky raid, now can we?"

"It won't be luck, sir," said Ford, thickly.

"Whatever it will be, we can only hope to bag perhaps two or three of their foot soldiers in this little venture at the…"

"Happy Snappy School sir," interrupted Ford.

"We need legs Two and Three to make a serious statement, Ford."

"We do?"

"Indeed. And Legs Two and Three involve getting our friend Mr Gabbitt back here to face the full wrath of Her Majesty's legal system."

"How are we going to do that, sir?"

"Well, Leg Two is top secret. Need to now stuff and all that. I can't divulge the contents of that to anyone... except to say that it's already ticking away nicely."

"Ticking away, sir?" asked a slightly dispirited Ford. No one likes to be kept in the dark for the reason that they are not considered important enough.

"Yes, Ford. Ticking away. It's better that you don't know anything about it at this stage."

"I see, sir. Any chance of being told about Leg Three then?"

"Absolutely, Detective Constable," replied Pringle and opened a buff file on his desk. "I should emphasise that Leg Three does NOT in any way involve the Metropolitan Police Force in any highly secret and totally illegal kidnapping operation which is strictly off the record, of course."

Detective Constable Ford frowned and stared at his guv'nor. He had always been told to 'think out of the box' if he wanted promotion to the headier climes of the nation's police force. However, specifically being told about the police not getting involved in secret kidnapping operations totally off the record did not seem to be the best way of furthering his career prospects. In fact, he foresaw a slippery slope leading him back to pounding the beat once more… or even worse.

"NOT involve…" he began slowly.

"NOT even thinking about getting involved in something as illegal as this," said Pringle, with a smile. He then hit the Play button on his tape recorder and the strains of Pink Floyd's 'Us and Them' oozed mellowly around the office.

Ford winced slightly and sat down in the chair on the other side of Pringle's desk. He hated all kinds of old fashioned, overblown, over-rated and synthesised rock music. Anything which required twenty minutes of screaming guitars, tortured saxophones and whining keyboards grated on every fibre of Ford's being. You see, Ford was a traditionalist. He liked the Beatles, the Doors, the Stones and raw three-minute sound bites. Pink Floyd sat very uncomfortably in his world.

"So, what are we NOT going to do?" he asked, sighing.

"We are NOT going to do the one thing which will bring our friend Mr Gabbitt, running hotfoot back home on the next flight."

"So…we're NOT going to NOT arrest his friends?" asked Ford, trying to think out of his box. He was finding it increasingly hard to follow the logic of sentences which concentrated on what they were absolutely not going to do.

"Better than that," said Pringle, after a short pause. "We're most definitely NOT going to strike at the soft underbelly of Mr Percy Raymond Gabbitt's emotional stability," said Pringle, with an insane gleam in his eye. "And it won't even register as a serious crime either."

"NOT a serious crime NOT to have a go at his emotional stability, sir?" asked Ford slowly, also not liking the bit about soft underbellies. His own stomach gurgled in agreement.

"Yes…I mean no," said Pringle, himself becoming a little confused. "It will NOT NOT be a serious crime," he continued, getting more and more entangled in a downward spiral of negative double negatives.

Ford sighed deeply. The more he heard of this the less he liked. He had begun recently to think that his governor was one sandwich short of a picnic and now the man was trying to prove that he was two or even three hampers short. Ford thought quickly. He took a deep breath, stared at the ceiling for a few moments and then looked at Pringle. "Just do NOT NOT tell me what you do NOT NOT want me NOT to do, sir," he asked with a slight tremble in his voice.

Pringle took a few moments to work out roughly what the Detective Constable was trying to say. He then seemed to come to a decision and stood up, facing Ford.

"We are NOT going to kidnap Nixon, DC Ford!" he exclaimed and slapped the table.

"Why would we NOT do that, sir? Nabbing a dead ex-president is…

"His cat, Ford! His cat!"

"NOT kidnap his cat?" squawked Ford, in astonishment.

"Certainly NOT," said Pringle and gave the Detective Constable a broad wink. "It's genius," muttered Pringle. "He'll never NOT see this one coming."

"Won't he? I mean - will he, sir."

There was a long pause broken only by the dulcet tones of Roger Waters.

***<Up and down and in the end, it's only round and round and round…>***

# TEN

*"I try to divide my students into several parts in my lessons."*

**(Chinese teacher of English at a local primary School in Suzhou explaining his psychopathic teaching methodology)**

Percy Gabbitt's plane touched down in the city of Chengdu in western China late in the afternoon. As both he and Bob Irwin walked into the rather modern Arrivals lounge, Gabbitt was beginning to worry about something else. Something rather unusual and considerably un-nerving - he was suddenly beginning to enjoy himself. He was actually having a good time.

Gabbitt was not used to such a sensation especially when it applied to work. But here he was in a new city with an odd but not unlikeable person doing something which smacked vaguely of 'doing the right thing'.

Although he had not intended to destroy Mr Zhang's school back in Suzhou, it seemed in hindsight like justice had been served on a rather nasty person. Even Terence and Ivor had bought him a drink at Pulp Fiction. And then both had been found positions at a better school on the other side of the city, by Arapacana. They had even been given an apartment each. This had reduced Ivor to tears of gratitude. Gabbitt would never forget that. And all because of him too. He was a hero. The man of the moment. King of Box Hill.

So here they were, collecting their bags from a carousel in Chengdu airport and on the verge of nailing another unscrupulous bastard - a swine who was ripping people off and thinking he could get away with it with impunity. Gabbitt smiled. He rather liked being this avenger of good, this fighter for the little man - a real life Roger the Norse Fighter.

He sighed and took a deep breath. He had learned in the past that whenever he became happy about something, Fate had the nasty habit of puncturing that balloon very quickly.

And then there was Arapacana Associates and Bob Irwin. They were all clearly in awe of his 'methods', although he would be the first to admit that he had absolutely no idea what these were. They just happened and that was it. There was no grand plan or well thought out strategy. Things just occurred around him, things that generally involved walls collapsing, explosions and people getting wheeled off to hospital. Gabbitt shuddered.

He spotted his grey holdall emerging from beneath the plastic curtain and pulled it onto their luggage trolley.

"Should be a man meeting us, a local," sniffed Irwin, as he placed his own suitcase onto the trolley. "We're to check in at our hotel and then get to work immediately."

"Right," said Gabbitt, feeling like a cross between James Pond and Brute Willie. All he needed now was a large pistol tucked into his belt and Kate Beckinsale in black lycra waiting for him outside the airport.

They pushed through an exit door and immediately spotted a small Chinese man in a loud orange t-shirt holding up a piece of cardboard, upon which was written:

'Peewee Gobber, Bib Orweenie'

Gabbitt sighed again. Where was Ms Beckinsale when you most needed her?

The taxi ride into Chengdu was fairly uneventful for Chinese standards. Just one overturned bus, two head-on collisions and a van which attempted to climb a tree. Peopled milled around the accidents with a somewhat disinterested air about them. They had seen it all before and were expecting something a little more dramatic.

The Sichuan Hotel was situated in the middle of the city just a few hundred yards from the main square and a large smiling and incredibly white statue of Chairman Mao, which towered over the square and waved enthusiastically to new arrivals from the airport.

Gabbitt and Irwin checked in and then met twenty minutes later in the downstairs reception area.

The hotel lobby consisted of a large and very empty space in front of a long reception desk and a pot plant with bright red and yellow plastic leaves. Apart from a wooden brochure rack on a far wall – completely devoid of literature, and two wicker chairs by the door, there was nothing else.

Perhaps the proprietors of the hotel did not really want to encourage guests to hang about in the reception area. It was singularly lacking in any creature comforts.

"Don't like Chengdu," muttered Irwin, as he sat down on a creaky wicker chair by the main entrance. "Apart from the pandas, there's nothing much here," he continued, miserably. "The locals say that the place is situated in a mistily romantic valley, but they're pulling your leg. It's industrial pollution. You see, Percy, Chengdu is one of those Chinese cities surrounded by dozens of smoky chemical plants. That's where the romantic mists come from."

"Tell me more about the pandas," said Gabbitt, not really wanting to concentrate on the bad things. He was still in a reasonably good mood.

"Got the biggest research base in the world here. Panda cubs popped out of fertile females every other minute. A production line. Thirty-three born last year and more to come this year," said Irwin. "The Chinese realised a few years ago that it would have been an embarrassment on a massive scale if these cuddly bears died out, as they should have done in modern-day, industrial China. So, the government decided to approach the whole panda thing in the same way that it approached producing shoes, t-shirts or computers. Mass production. The panda research base is the nearest thing to a battery-farm as possible, where the result is lots of chubby, pink cubs. There's a large maternity hospital at the edge of the city here, while there's another one up in the mountains at a place called Wolong."

"Well I'm all in favour of not letting them die out," said Gabbitt. "I've always likes them."

"Everyone likes them," said Irwin. "That's the point. Pandas have nothing really going for them in the wild except that they look incredibly cute to us humans. And there's nothing that protects an endangered species more than being cuddly and cutiepie. I mean, look at them seriously for once. They have no camouflage in your average forest - they're large, clumsy and very black and white. As if that wasn't enough to wipe them out, they're the fussiest eaters ever known to man living on a diet of bamboo shoots, which contain hardly any vitamins at all. Finally, they turn their snouts up at sex, preferring to sleep all the time plus... they only live in China. It's a miracle they've survived this long."

"I never thought of it like that," said Gabbitt.

"If they were lizards, really rare ones, which spat poison darts at everyone who approached, the

Chinese would have wiped the blighters out years ago. They would not have cared about doing a dodo on them. But cute bears with big furry ears and large eyes are a different story. They're a marketing man's dream. So, what do you do? You churn the little critters out and open large zoos in China stuffed with them. Finally, when you have a good stock of the things, you hire out the nicest-looking ones to zoos in Chicago or London. This is when you really start coining it."

"But it is a good thing that they're protecting an endangered species so well, isn't it? It would be tragic to let them die out," said Gabbitt, speaking for the masses.

"Of course, it's a good thing in the short term," said Irwin. "But these pampered, furry bears have been bred for captivity and can never be released back into the wilds again. They tried it with one last year and it only survived six torrid months in the forests in Wolong, before being duffed up one too many times by wild pandas. It eventually crawled into a dark bamboo glade and died, miserable and traumatized.

"It got killed?" asked Gabbitt sadly.

"Yep. The funny thing is that the Chinese have now reacted in a totally Chinese way to the death, if you see what I mean."

"No, not really," said Gabbitt, clearly not seeing.

"They decided that the problem was a simple one. They thought that domesticated pandas were too pampered and ill-prepared for the real world out there, so they embarked on a programme of teaching their remaining semi-domesticated and home-grown pandas… self-defence."

"Are you serious?"

"Totally," said Irwin. "The western papers had a field day when they heard about it, one of them leading with 'Kung-Fu Lessons for Pandas'. Lots of chortling all round."

"Well, I like them and I think the Chinese are doing the right thing," said Gabbitt.

"Would you like to visit the research base here in Chengdu?" asked Irwin.

"I'd love to," replied Gabbitt, slightly surprised.

"No problem if we have the time," grunted Irwin. "No arguing that they're cute little fellows. Not their fault that humans dote on them. I myself would prefer the poison-spitting lizards though."

Gabbitt smiled. He was never really sure about Australians. One moment they sounded belligerent and callous about everything and the next they happily showed a softer and more vulnerable side. They kept you permanently off-balance.

"But first we have to sort out this agent," said Irwin. "Not going to be easy. The man's a suspicious bastard. Would spot anything out of the norm immediately."

"We could just walk into his office and see what happens," suggested Gabbitt, airily.

Irwin smiled thinly. After a few moments, he leaned over to where Gabbitt sat and patted him on the back. "I am in total awe of your methods, Percy. You really think that by just walking into his office and asking for our money back, everything will turn out peaches and cream?"

"Well, the direct approach has always worked for me," said Gabbitt.

Irwin lay back in his chair and laughed long and loud at the ceiling.

*Roger the Norse Fighter was running hard down a corridor. He was well and truly into level two of the Dragon King's Lair and had just filleted a particularly unpleasant undead pit snapper with extremely bad breath. Tammy the Goblin trailed in his wake, giggling wildly and clutching a bulging sack of heavy gold coins.*

*Just behind the two of them, ran the light-footed Snark Maiden and not so light-footed Obby the Gladiator. Endymion the wizard and the rather odd Chinese dwarf, Li Bang Cho, brought up the rear.*

*"Can we have a ciggy break?" gasped Endymion, as he came to a wheezing halt.*

*"Yeh, what about it, Rog?" shouted Li Bang Cho, also stopping. "I'm totally cream-crackered."*

*Roger skidded to a halt and turned round. "We need to get to the bridge at Shagrat's Doom before nightfall or…" he trailed off.*

*"Why is it always a mad dash for a bridge in these places?" asked Endymion, unhappily. "You'd think that the makers of these dungeons wouldn't construct just a few flimsy bridges from one area to another. Just asking for trouble, if you ask me."*

*"Makes for a more dramatic climax, doesn't it?" wheezed Li Bang Cho. "Couldn't have us strolling into a well-lit cavern and finding the treasure in a nice little pile. Has to be earned."*

*"Bollocks to that," muttered Endymion. "I'm not as young as I used to be, you know. Wizards don't generally have to run the hundred metres in ten*

*seconds in order to survive. Undignified is what it is."*

*"Well, can't you just turn yourself into an eagle and flap on ahead of us?" suggested the Chinese dwarf. "I know I would if I could. Maybe a cheetah or an antelope or something bloody quick."*

*"Never studied anthropomorphic translations at wizard school," said Endymion, with a frown. "I could probably manage a hamster or a small Guinea Pig if I put my mind to it, but I'm not so sure about the top speed of a worried hamster. Even in my present unfit form I could probably move quicker than an Olympic hamster breaking all hamster speed records if push came to shove," he concluded and looked up at the approaching Roger.*

*"What's the matter?" asked Roger, impatiently.*

*"We were wondering about how fast a terrified hamster could run if given the right motivation," said Li Bang Cho.*

*"What is it with you two?" asked Roger, beginning to lose his patience. "We have to get to this bridge before sunset or every goblin, ratman and undead zombie will be onto us in one massive attack. You both know that. It's the rules," he concluded, with a sniff.*

*"What I can't understand is how they know when it's sunset," said Endymion. "We're a couple of hundred metres straight down and it's pitch black in these caves. How on earth would they know when the sun is going down?"*

*"Must be in their genes," chipped in Obby, who had just joined the group.*

*"That's an interesting observation," said Endymion. Monsters with an intuitive 'feel' for the correct time. Wish I had that."*

*"You're a wizard," said Obby, flatly. "Can't you incant a spell or tear a scroll which will give the correct time?"*

*"They don't do spells linked to satellite chronometers," replied Endymion, ruefully.*

*"Have you all quite finished?" asked an exasperated Roger. "We have to get to Shagrat's Doom in the next few minutes or I'll be the one who you should fear. Forget the goblins and ratmen. Just concentrate on a very angry Norse Fighter with his sword drawn looking for an excuse to slice and dice any wizard or dwarf who happens to be passing. Do I make myself clear?"*

*"Crystal," said Li Bang Cho and stood up.*

*"There's no need to be unpleasant," mumbled Endymion.*

*"Look," said Roger, calming down a little. "This is not a picnic, you know. That last level nearly saw the end of us... again. If it hadn't been for a bit of inventive swordplay, most of us would have ended up as part of the next goblin banquet."*

*"There you go again," said a new voice.*

*"For pity's sake," said Roger. "Do we have to have this every time?"*

*"Yes," said Tammy the Goblin flatly. "Or until you understand that goblins are not ALL vicious, cannibalistic swines."*

*"Fine. Wonderful," said Roger and sheathed his sword. "I apologise for calling ALL goblins cannibals, although I can't remember actually accusing them of that kind of thing. Not even a goblin would eat another goblin, would it? All I thought was that it was in their nature to make a snack of any fallen hero, that all."*

*"Depends," murmured Tammy. "Most goblins have standards, unless exceptionally hungry. Then you have to watch your back. I'll agree with you there, but I myself wouldn't dream of snacking on another goblin. A bit too stringy for me, if I'm being totally honest. I should say, and I keep having to remind you of this, that the majority of goblins are kind, sensitive and peaceful creatures with normal gastronomic tastes… on the whole. And we're not vicious either… as a rule."*

*There was a long pause, broken by three metal arrows thrumming past Tammy's nose and burying themselves deep into Li Bang Cho's arm. The conversation on goblin cannibalism and viciousness suddenly became less important to the heroes.*

*The Chinese dwarf let out an enormous shriek and charged down the corridor waving his axe over his head.*

*"That's torn it," shouted Endymion. "The bastard's gone berserk now. It'll take him twenty*

*kills and several stiff black coffees to get him back down again. It never rains, only pours."*

*"Ah," said Roger, looking hard at Tammy. "If I'm not mistaken, those arrows seem rather goblinish to me, although what a race of kind, sensitive and peaceful creatures are doing with such things, I'll never know. It's a puzzle, isn't it?" he said, trying to ignore the growing mayhem further up the corridor.*

*"I told you, not all goblins are enlightened," said Tammy, sulkily. "We just always seem to happen across the unenlightened ones."*

*"And now it's our role to enlighten them, is it?" continued Roger breezily.*

*"Will you two stop bickering and get to work?" shouted the Snark Maiden, as she fired two arrows down the corridor and over the screaming dwarf's right shoulder.*

*"Perhaps a poetry reading might suffice?" suggested Roger.*

*Tammy kicked him hard on the shins and scuttled down to where Li Bang Cho was well into his seventh kill of the minute.*

*Things then happened rather quickly. It was one of those moments which are usually interpreted by film-makers as worthy of thirty seconds slow-motion.*

*It all started as Endymion the wizard tore three scrolls in half at the same time, while flinging two acid fireballs from his left fist. It was a combination that he had been itching to try out for a long time.*

*The idea had been to use the fireballs as ignition keys to the death spells contained in the scrolls.*

*Needless to say, the result was quite startling and rather unexpected. A dozen flaming skeletons sprinted down the corridor snapping fiery teeth at anything that moved. They then exploded spectacularly on several rather loose flagstones in front of two appalled goblins.*

*The cavern floor seemed to split and give way under them. There was then a sound of splintering stone and the whole corridor suddenly lurched downwards, taking all its occupants with it. It was like taking an elevator to the bowels of Hell itself. Level two rapidly became level three, four and finally, five. The descent ended there, probably because there were no more levels left.*

*Now normally to get to the final level in such a fast manner would be viewed by the gaming novice as a really good thing, but to weathered heroes it only signified trouble. Trouble on a far larger and more lethal scale. To get to the final level with weapons designed for level two monsters was not good news at all. Taking on creatures here with their current weaponry would be rather like having to face a pack of hungry tigers in an enclosed valley with just plastic picnic forks for company.*

*The dust began to clear and the heroes and remaining goblins all lay in panting heaps for a few moments. There was a pause as they all took stock of things. It suddenly seemed reassuringly quiet. And very dark.*

*However, you are bound to attract attention when steering a whole stone corridor straight down to the bedrock of the cavern complex.*

*Roger opened his eyes and rubbed a grubby hand through his hair. He moved his legs and arms. Good, he thought. No immediate problems. "Can you light your staff or something?" he grumbled loudly. "Can't see a flippin' thing."*

*There was scraping sound from a few feet away as Endymion did his wizard's thing. A dull glow lit up the corridor.*

*It was only then that Roger realised that his nose was about two centimetres from the largest dragon's snout he had ever seen.*

*"Oh crap!" he uttered, as the dragon started inhaling deeply.*

"We want two returns to China," said Alfred, slowly.

Alfred and Hilda Fennell were at a travel agency in Bromley in south London. It was five to nine, which made it late morning to the two geriatric survivors of countless wars and scrapes with various local authorities.

They were talking to a certain Gregory Bendall, their designated sales and travel co-ordinator, at Boomerang Travel. Five to nine to him was early. Very early in the morning. He was clutching a paper cup of hot coffee.

Alfred was beginning to lose patience with him, which was definitely not a good thing. Alfred never trusted men who wore green suits and had funny haircuts which involved never having to reach for a comb.

"You have to give me the name of your gateway city and the dates of your visit, sir... and madam," said Gregory Bendall patiently. He was feeling in control despite it being so criminally early in the morning. They were just a couple of harmless pensioners, after all. Gregory reached for his coffee. He had a little sip and stared at his computer.

"Sue-Joe," said Hilda. "That's the place where our young Percy said he's working. We want to have one of your gates to there."

"Where?" asked Gregory.

"It's a city near Shanghai," chipped in Alfred, looking at the young sales assistant, as if he had failed his geography 'O' Level miserably. "In China," he added with a perceptible tut.

"There's no airport called Sue or Joe," said a mystified Gregory.

"We'll take it to Shanghai then and catch a bus or something after," said Hilda and snapped her handbag open. "And I want a seat near the driver. I always sit behind the driver on buses. Can't see why planes should be any different. Stops me getting the janglies."

There was a short pause as Gregory considered telling his two customers about the recent terrorist actions which very much restricted passenger access to anywhere within twenty feet of the pilot. He also wondered briefly asking them what the janglies were. Again, he decided that discretion was the better part of valour and cleared his throat.

"And we want something off as well," said Alfred and gave Gregory a goosy wink.

"Something off?" queried Gregory.

"For being pensioners who made this country a safer place for the likes of you youngsters," said Alfred, loudly, and sat back in his metallic, plastic chair.

"Ah, a discount," said Gregory, relaxing again. He looked up from his computer and tried to assess the earning power of the two wrinkled and raincoated old-timers seated before his desk. "It's your lucky day," he said slowly. "We're offering a massive three per cent discount on Premium Economy and Upper Class seats bound for Shanghai on all weekdays this month. Would sir and madam be interested?"

"How much is this going to set us back?" asked Hilda, as she scrutinized the man and wondered why his mother had allowed him out with a striped shirt with a paisley tie.

Gregory tapped at this keyboard and then announced happily, "Three thousand pounds return to Shanghai, leaving on the twelfth at two in the morning and returning on the twenty-fourth at four-thirty in the morning… a real bargain."

"How much?" asked Alfred.

Gregory repeated the super-discounted price.

"In my day, you could buy a Rolls Royce for that," said

Alfred, through pursed lips. The last time he himself had spent that amount of money had been on their house fifty years previously. He was not about to blow their entire savings on a couple of tickets to Chinky land just because this ten year old with silly hair said it was a real bargain.

"I can look at other airlines and … cheaper seats," said Gregory, emphasising the word 'cheaper' in not a very nice way.

"I don't mind standing," said Alfred, honestly. "Just give one seat to Hilda here and I'll be happy prop myself up somewhere near the back out of harm's way - if it makes everything easier, that is."

Gregory Bendall stared at the two of them. He was not at all sure if this old man was joking or not. He had a horrible suspicion that he was not. He frowned and tapped away again feeling slightly worried for some unfathomable reason. "I can get you two tickets on an Aeroflot plane. Five hundred pounds each but there are two stopovers."

"Aeroflot?" queried Alfred.

"The Russian airline," said Gregory, airily.

"I'm not travelling on a Russian plane," said Hilda emphatically. "You don't know where we'll end up."

"In Islamabad, Beijing and then Shanghai," said a puzzled Gregory.

"Or in Siberia breaking stones in a labour camp and then getting shot at by the Red Guards," said Alfred, loudly.

"I rather think not..." began Gregory, feeling slightly sweaty.

"I'm not going on a cheap Russian aeroplane," repeated Hilda, clutching her handbag close to her chest. "It's British or nothing!" she exclaimed and stared at the ceiling.

"And that's final!" added Alfred and sat back in his chair.

Gregory Bendall had another long look at his customers. He could not quite work out how it had happened, but somehow, they seemed to have assumed the position of power. It was as if he would now have to find a suitable replacement to this perfectly adequate Aeroflot plane or...

"And we're going straight there and not making stops in Timbuktu or... Bombay."

"What?" squawked Gregory.

"We want British Airways and at a sensible price for pensioners."

"But BA will cost you over two thou..."

"Then we will take our custom elsewhere," said Alfred, as loudly as he could. Several sales assistants and one manager looked up from their consoles and gave Gregory disapproving stares.

"Boomerang Travel offers the best bargains in the High Street. We are never beaten on price," Gregory said equally loudly. The sales assistants and the manager relaxed and continued with their own work.

"I don't care how clever you are at getting lower prices here at Bodybag Travel," hissed Alfred. "We just want you to find us a way to get to Shanghai without us having to sell everything we own for just a pair of damn silly aeroplane tickets."

"I'm doing my best, sir," squeaked Gregory. "Those are the prices..."

"Do you sell boat tickets? Is that cheaper? But I want a seat this time. I'm not standing for six months."

"No sir, we don't sell boat tickets anywhere," said Gregory, rather too firmly. "This is the twenty-first century, you know."

There was a long pause as Alfred and Hilda took in that last comment. Neither liked being reminded that it was the far future and not a civilised period like the thirties or the forties.

"I don't think you understand," said Alfred, raising his walking stick and waving it menacingly in Gregory's face.

"I'll see what I can do," said the increasingly sweaty Gregory, after a large gulp of his cooling latte. He tapped away again and, after five minutes of tutting and whistling at his screen, he looked at Alfred and Hilda.

"I can get you two round-trip tickets on Virgin Atlantic for the cut-price fare of just nine hundred pounds," he said quietly, as he imagined all his commission disappearing on this ultra-low fare. Anything to get rid of them, he thought, a little unkindly.

"That's more like it, even if it isn't the proper British one," said Alfred, settling back in his seat again. "I don't mind one with virgins on board, as long as their British ones," he said and put his stick down on the floor.

"And I don't want a seat near the lavvies," added Hilda, firmly. "All that flushing every other minute will get me going… and them virgins certainly don't want that."

"I think I can arrange that," said Gregory, hastily opening up various boxes on his screen and punching in data. "All I need now are your names, your address and dates when you would like to travel."

Five minutes later and Gregory Bendall had entered all the relevant information and was looking at a screen entitled 'Method of Payment'. He turned to the old man in the cloth cap.

"And how would sir and madam like to pay for the tickets?" he asked, a little tiredly.

"Alfred, the bag!" exclaimed Hilda, imperiously.

Alfred reached for a large bag which rested safely between his legs. He pulled it up onto his lap and carefully unzipped it.

"You're paying cash?" asked an astonished Gregory. No one ever paid cash nowadays.

"Better," said Alfred with a gleam in his eye.

"Better," repeated Gregory, now totally confused.

"I'm not sure how many books there are in here," said Alfred, as he rummaged around in the innards of the bag, but there should be enough to cover the cost of both tickets with a bit left over for a cup of tea and some biscuits," he said, flatly.

He then emptied about fifty books of Green Shield stamps onto Gregory Bendall's keyboard.

At about the same time that Gregory Bendall was reaching for his telephone and asking for managerial assistance, Ronald Chipchase was entering the details of his credit card into a computer programme which would ensure two tickets to Shanghai for Mr Bibby and himself.

Had he known that two other survivors from the now infamous Battle of Box Hill had just bought tickets on the same plane, he would definitely have changed the airline and the date of travel. In fact, he might have also changed the whole plan entirely and not bothered getting on a plane there at all.

Memories of that day made the normally unflappable Mr Chipchase extremely flappable.

It had all seemed a pretty simple case to solve, thought Detective Constable Ford, as he sat in the driving seat of his Ford Orion and bit hard into a Triple Cheese Bulldozer Burger with extra relish. Simple and fairly routine. Just nab the buggers as they ransacked another school and that would be the end of it. Case solved and the lawyers could take over. Closure and they could all move onto pastures new.

But now it had all got a little more complicated. There was something he did not like. Something which his boss was keeping from him and something which was gnawing away at his insides.

He bit deep into onion, pickle and something yellow which tasted like a thin bar of soap. He swallowed the mouthful after a few cursory munches and reached for a can of luke-warm Sprite. Something was not right at all.

Three ridiculous tasks. Three mad undertakings. Three things which should have had him reaching for a resignation letter.

He looked in the rear-view mirror and stared with undisguised loathing at what was lying on the back seat. What lay there was the uniform of his third and most ludicrous task. The whole world had gone completely mad. Tasks one and two were daft enough – to capture a gang which was ransacking language schools and to steal a cat. A cat, for god's sake. He shook his head slowly. Madness.

But then there was this. Task three. The worst of the lot. Pringle must have taken a severe dislike of him. He looked at the back seat again. What was the Chief Inspector thinking? Madness!

He finished his burger and belched loudly at the world in general. He should have been sitting in a squad car outside a school in Oxford Street waiting for the school gang, not in south London about to undertake a spot of catnapping and do... this.

It was not just a ridiculous plan, but it was also plain insulting. It was the sort of job that a junior constable should have been doing, not a detective.

Still, he had to gain entry to the Slimm household somehow. Catnapping would be hard enough without a cunning plan. He realised that. And task two depended quite heavily on task three being carried our successfully. Why it had to be this though, he would never know. A simple boot through Slimm's door and a hit squad to grab the cat would surely have been simpler.

He sighed and reached for a rectangular piece of apple pie wrapped up in a cardboard envelope. He stared angrily at the school gates in front of him as he gulped down the pie. A battered metal placard proclaimed in faded grey letters on a yellow background: 'Turpington Comprehensive School'.

He just hoped that no one back at the station would ever find out about this. He frowned hard and finished his Sprite. He certainly would never write anything down about this little caper. A written report? Sod that.

DC Ford reached over to the back seat and pulled a dark purple jumpsuit towards him. After several minutes of heaving and pulling in all directions he sat sweatily in his new outfit.

"Well, here goes for nothing," he said to the cruel world out there and pulled on a large purple head piece with a wobbly triangular antenna attached to the crown. Ford then reached for a bright red handbag and opened the car door.

Inside the suit was a seething policeman about to enter the grounds of a London middle school, but to the outside world he was Tinky-Winky the Teletubby.

"Morning Mr Winky," said a muffled voice somewhere to Ford's left. "Or may I call you Tinky?"

A muffled stream of very un-Teletubby-like expletives mumbled from the purple head. There then followed a short pause during which the purple creature could be heard slowly counting to ten.

Tinky-Winky tried to turn in the direction of the voice, which was remarkably difficult given the position of the two small peep-holes in the suit's neck area. He was about to respond when the owner of the voice spoke again.

"Hel-lo," said the voice ludicrously slowly, rather like a Swede at the start of lesson one. He then waved at Ford in slow motion and said 'Hel-lo' again.

"Who the fuck are you?" asked the irate Teletubby, waving his handbag in the face of this irritating man in a tweed jacket and faded Marks and Spencer slacks.

"The name's Slimm. Joe Slimm. Are you the policeman giving the talk on drugs to the fifth year this afternoon?" he asked, trying to stifle a smirk.

"It's called Merlin the Magician and it's bloody brilliant!" shouted Chief Inspector Pringle into his telephone.

His tape recorder was playing what sounded like a twenty-fingered Scott Joplin plonking out a tune at light-speed.

Pringle listened in total amazement. Wave after wave of key-hitting produced a cacophony which approached music, but then somehow ricocheted away and became something else. Something which could be described as either utter genius or a throbbing wall of discordant noise. Pringle liked it though.

After years of mellow Pink Floyd buttering the walls of his office, he had suddenly discovered a new pretender to the crown of progressive rock music. The name of the man in question was a certain Mr Rick Wakeman, wizard of the ivories and keyboard player of the Neolithic rock group, YES.

The fact that it was the early years of the twenty-first century and that all members of this rock group were now grandfathers, did not matter to Pringle one little bit. All he wanted to do was to push the Play button and listen in awe at the total excess of sound being thrown at him like musical chocolate cake with over-fudged, cherried topping.

The particular piece booming away was called 'Merlin the Magician'. Pringle sat down at his desk and shook his head slowly. "Genius," he whispered into the receiver.

"What?"

"Merlin the Magician," he repeated, louder.

"Do you want him arrested?" asked the baffled voice from the other end of the line.

"Who?"

"This Merlin guy."

"Err, no, Ford. You can forget about him."

"Thought he was a drug runner too. They all have names like..."

"Yes, Ford, I get the picture."

"What's that horrible noise?" asked Ford, trying to hold his mobile away from his ear.

"That's Rick Wake..." began Pringle. He sighed and hit the pause button. "It doesn't matter."

"I'm in, by the way," said Ford.

"In?"

"In the school."

"Excellent, Detective Constable," said Pringle. "This first stage of the day's action already underway then. Excellent."

"Indeed, sir."

"We now can get down to the serious business."

"In a Tinky-Winky suit," came the flat reply.

"In a what?" asked the confused Chief Inspector.

"In a bloody Teletubby outfit... with matching handbag," muttered Ford.

"Oh that," said Pringle, who had completely forgotten that little idea. "Rather clever if you ask me. Less confrontational with the kiddies when talking about serious issues. More acceptable. Their kind of culture. Excellent, Ford."

"But they're all fifteen or sixteen," said Ford, unhappily.

"Ah," said Pringle, realising the flaw in their plan.

"Ah indeed," said Ford.

"Well, it can't do any harm," said Pringle, clearing his throat. "Just talk to them about drugs ruining their lives. That usually hits home, even if you're wearing one of those suits."

"A policeman wearing a bright purple Teletubby suit might encourage them to take up the hard stuff," said Ford, bitterly.

"Very funny, Detective Constable."

There was a short pause.

"I've met Slimm," said Ford, slowly.

"Excellent," said Pringle, sitting down and examining the cover of the CD entitled: 'YES Live'. "Phase two of the masterplan."

"Masterplan," repeated Ford, a mite sarcastically.

"Masterplan, Ford," snapped Pringle. "Just make sure you ingratiate yourself with the fellow. I want you to become best mates."

"When will all this end, sir?" asked Ford, with genuine sorrow in his voice."

"When we've solved the mystery and banged up as many people as possible," replied Pringle.

"And the cat, sir?"

"Phase three," replied Pringle. "As we discussed here, earlier.

"Do I really have to grab the cat?" asked Ford.

"Yes, Detective Constable, you do. What would be the point of phases one and two if we didn't pinch the cat?"

"What indeed, sir?"

"I think we'll both look back on this ingenious plan as one of our better days, Ford," said Pringle.

"Time to get on stage," sniffed Ford, who knew he wouldn't.

"Well done Ford and, when you've finished there, get to Oxford Street. I have a strong feeling that tonight's the night when the school gang turn up with their crow-bars and hammers, ready to hit another school," said Pringle and hit the Play button again. He did not hear DC Ford's reply, which was probably just as well.

# ELEVEN

*"If it looks like a duck and quacks like a duck, shoot it."*
**(Nero Handsworth, in belligerent mood, explaining to his thugs how they should treat anybody remotely resembling Percy Gabbitt)**

Bob Brand was as English as fish and chips. And he had a stomach to prove it. He had longish black hair and a badly-trimmed beard which attempted to circumnavigate his mouth in a rather wide circle, incorporating a scrawny little moustache above his top lip. He also loved wearing t-shirts and jeans most of the time, which made him look like a cross between a brickie and a software designer. He was about twenty-three years old, but looked late forties. All this aside, his heart was in the right place…

It was three in the afternoon and he was standing in front of a 'Prêt a Manger' on Oxford Street in central London and staring through dark sunglasses at the first and second floors of a building which had a bookshop and a sex shop on the ground floor. Beside him was a taller man in a grey suit and a cream, Panama hat.

"Today's the day, I think," said Bob and rubbed his hands together happily. "I'll case the place after a frapuccino at Costa."

"And it doesn't worry you that there are at least two cars parked opposite, containing four bulky-looking men with bad haircuts," said the man in the Panama hat.

"Adds to the thrill of the thing," said Bob, with a twinkle in his eye. "Do the deed in full view of the Old Bill. Now that's what I call style. Sort of thing that Percy Raymond Gabbitt would appreciate."

"He never gets caught," said the man in the hat as the two of them walked slowly towards the frapuccino.

"And neither shall we," said Bob.

"And how do we accomplish that?" asked the man in the hat.

Bob Brand opened the doors to Costa Coffee and stepped inside. He always loved that first moment when stepping into a coffee shop. That sudden assault on the nostrils as fresh coffee overwhelmed the senses. He turned contentedly to his nervous accomplice.

"What's it to be, Jack?"

"Just a muffin and an orange juice," mumbled Jack.

"Live a little, my friend," said Bob, rubbing his stomach. "Have a chocolate croissant or one of those cream slices stuffed with jam."

"No thanks," said Jack, quickly.

Jack Melligan was as different from Bob Brand as was humanly possible. If an alien had landed and then beamed both Bob and Jack back to the mothership in orbit, then the alien dissectors would probably have come to the conclusion that Bob and Jack were a totally different species of animal, like the warthog and the giraffe.

Jack was tall and thin. Painfully thin. It had been remarked before that it would have taken four or five Jacks to make one Bob. That was not the only difference. Whilst Bob favoured the standard teenage t-shirt and jeans look, Jack went for sports-casual. This usually took the form of uneasy suits from M&S, badly-patterned golf shirts from Matalan, beige Burton's trousers and brown shoes from The Officer's Club.

The addition of the Panama hat was supposed to add a certain salubrious decadence to the whole thing. What it did, in reality, was to make Jack Melligan look like a gay, middle-aged loser.

They sat down at a window table.

"You were saying," said Bob, as he supped at his ice cool drink.

"Just how do we do it?"

"Well," said Bob, thoughtfully. "What we need is something so absorbing that it'll keep our friends in the cars extremely busy, while we go to work," said Bob supping hard.

"A diversion?" asked Jack.

"Yep, but it'll have to be one of our better ones," said Bob. "A real corker."

"Do you have anything in mind?" asked Jack. Doing Russian accents and getting angry in Reception areas was one thing, but trying to divert the attentions of a complete police stake-out was quite another.

"Indeed, I do," replied Bob breezily.

"Care to elaborate?" sniffed Jack, nervously bending the rim of his Panama up and down.

"You do know that that is not a Panama hat, don't you?" asked Bob suddenly.

"Yes, it is," was the knee-jerk response.

"Panamas have a crease down the middle and can be folded up and put in a back pocket. Do that to yours and it would fall to bits."

"Really?" Jack stared at the hat, feeling slightly crest-fallen.

"It's an Ecuadorian hat," continued Bob. "They make copies over there. Not very good ones."

"Doesn't sound as good as a Panama."

"Nothing wrong with taking a stroll in an Ecuadorian or a Chinese," said Bob, breezily. "Anyway, that hat is going to help us."

"Both suspects are in Costa Coffee drinking what looks like cold coffee and a juice," said a flat voice into a mobile phone. "Suspect number one is wearing a white hat."

"That should make it easy to spot him in a crowd," said the voice at the other end.

"Sometimes I wonder. The criminal fraternity today – one brain between the lot of them."

"You sure it's them?"

"No, but they have an air of villainy about them. They also walk like ex-convicts," murmured the constable in the car.

"I'll pass that on to the Chief Inspector."

"Copy that."

"Copy what?"

"It's American cop-speak."

"Isn't it easier and quicker just to say yes?"

"Not as cool though."

"Oh."

Percy Gabbitt and Bob Irwin were strode across a narrow street towards a well-lit shop front, above which was written: 'Big Bung Travel'.

It was mid-evening in deepest Chengdu in western China and most people were finishing their dinner. Not so the intrepid westerners marching towards the shop with the lights.

"Just walk slowly past," said Bob Irwin. "I want to see how many staff are still on duty."

"Why don't we just walk in and ask for the money they owe Northampton?" asked Gabbitt, innocently.

"You really crack me up sometimes, mate," said Irwin, trying to stifle a chuckle.

"There's no harm in asking," continued Gabbitt. "And it would save a lot of time. We could go for a beer afterwards and get something to eat."

This time Irwin did let out a short laugh hastily-disguised as a cough. "Please, Percy," he said, quietly. "I don't think I can do this, if you keep making me laugh."

Gabbitt sighed and followed his accomplice. As they passed the shop-front and counted just one tired-looking female employee sitting behind a desk at the back, he could not help thinking that all this clandestine creeping about was simply not needed. Most people responded far better to the open approach.

He suddenly thought about George Melrose, trustee of his old school in Mayfair, London and his views on principled selling and telling the truth, whatever the consequences. People will not suspect you if you come clean from the start, Melrose had said. In fact, they might be so surprised that they will instantly roll over and give you what you want. Gabbitt frowned slightly. That was then. In London. Not now. In Chengdu. In China.

Big Bang Travel, or Big Bung Travel, as it was mis-spelt on the shop fascia, was a travel agency catering for the small number of people who had managed the impossible task of getting a study abroad visa for places like America, Australia and the UK. It probably sent about thirty students to western climes every year and was run by a Mr Cedric Zhang.

Cedric had been in the student game for about five years and only just managed to make ends meet every year. It had not proved the cash-cow that he had envisioned when he had opened the agency during the height of the study-abroad frenzy in the early years of the new millennium. It was now more a dying dog.

Business had steadily declined to the point when he had decided to concentrate his attentions more on the internal market and package tours for Chinese tourists wanting a weekend's shopping trip to Shanghai.

Then came along the Chengdu Teaching College and all that changed. It had been something of a surprise to Cedric, since he had not initiated this business opportunity himself, because he had more or less given up on schools and students wanting to study abroad.

More baffling still was that he had not had to slip the CTC manager a 'present' for the business offered – a present in a large brown envelope. It had all been extremely disturbing. Business never came your way in China without a lot of brown envelope action and yet here it was.

Cedric had then had many sleepless nights wondering how and why the contract had come about and feared that there may be a knock on his door in the middle of the night by shady people demanding their cut, which he had somehow overlooked.

However, the knock had not come and the contract had been signed and approved by the principal and director of CTC. Twenty Primary and Middle School teachers to study 'Modern Teaching Methodology' for six weeks at the University of Northampton in central England. And at twenty thousand RMB for each teacher, he stood to make a tidy profit from the commission.

But then greed had raised its ugly head. A type of greed which came about only because he had not to work for this contract. It had been too easy. And when things are too easy, people like Cedric wanted more.

The initial thought had come to him just after the college had presented him with a large holdall containing the entire amount for the group's courses in tight bundles of red one hundred RMB notes. Cedric Zhang had stared at the massive pile of cash and had suddenly had an idea. A rather naughty idea.

What if he did not send all this money to the English university for a few weeks? He could use the money to pay for a new car and a short holiday in Beijing with the missus.

This thought led onto another thought…

What if he never sent the money to the university?

It was rather a drastic thought. But…

Well, the university would hardly throw the teachers out of their classes. No, they would carry on teaching the course, patiently waiting for the money to arrive. English people were like that. Patient and polite.

Also, a university is a big place with many departments, thought Cedric. They probably would not know about the missing payment until it was too late and the teachers had all returned to the safety of China.

It all seemed so easy. Too easy. The Chinese teachers would have a great time and the teaching college would be delighted with the way he had organised the whole thing. As for Northampton University - he could claim he had already wired all the money to them and that there must be a problem at the UK end. More confusion would follow and gradually the thing would recede into a grey past, where no one really knew who had paid what. It seemed the perfect plan.

What Mr Zhang had not counted on was an unusually zealous sales assistant in Northampton called Emily Braithwaite and the involvement of Arapacana Associates. Had he known of these two factors, he would most certainly not have been out at an expensive fish restaurant in downtown Chengdu entertaining a possible client that evening, but would have been hastily packing his bags and boarding the first train to Inner Mongolia.

By mid-morning of the next day, he would be painfully aware of both of these factors.

"What's that place next door?" asked Gabbitt, as the two conspirators completed their pass of the shop front.

"I don't know. Does it matter?" asked Irwin.

"Just looks interesting," said Gabbitt, staring at an imposing building set back from the main road and with a row of small white vans parked outside the main entrance.

"A hospital of some sort," said Irwin, disinterestedly.

"You think?" asked Gabbitt.

"Right," said Irwin, tearing himself away from the distraction of what was next door. "We probably should wait till the woman in there has locked up and gone home. Then we go to work."

"But won't it be more difficult to get the money, if she's locked the place up and gone home? And won't the locals think it a bit suspicious when they see two foreigners jimmying the lock on a door in the street?" asked Gabbitt, innocently.

"You have a point. We could try the back," said Irwin, frowning.

"Let me go in and have a look," said Gabbitt. "It can't do any harm, can it?"

Bob Irwin stared at Gabbitt and thought very hard. When someone like Percy Raymond Gabbitt said things like: 'It can't do any harm', it was time to move very far from the possible blast zone and lie flat on the ground with your hands over your head. He sighed.

"If she meets you and then the next morning they discover that they're several thousand pounds light, it won't take a genius to put two and two together," said Irwin, nervously.

"And will that matter?" asked Gabbitt, airily. "It's ours anyway. We're just collecting. And you did say that companies like this rarely use banks for their ill-gotten gains. So, there could be a case in there with all our money in. Just lying there."

"True," said Irwin, a little perplexed at this rather cavalier attitude to stealing bags of cash.

"So, why don't I just walk in and ask for it?"

"Because she'll say no and then call her boss who will most definitely say no. He'll then come running hotfoot back here from wherever he is and all hell will break loose. It's not the best plan, mate. Believe me."

"She might say yes," persisted Gabbitt. He was a little tired of trying to act like a common criminal, especially when the people they were trying to 'rob' were the real criminals.

"All right," said Irwin, running a sweaty hand through his hair. "Go ahead and try, but it won't work this time, I can assure you. Not even for the great Percy Gabbitt. I bet you ten pints of beer that you don't walk out of there with the money. But have a go, by all means. I'll try to think of a quick back-up plan which will get us the money and out of here before the shit hits the fan."

"Whatever," said Gabbitt and walked towards the entrance of Big Bung Travel with his hands in his pockets and looking as cool as you like.

Bob Irwin looked on in disbelief as his accomplice walked into the agency. "You have to admire him," he whispered to himself under his breath and tried hard not to think of the really important issue of ten bottles of beer being on the line, if Gabbitt's mad plan actually came off.

"And that concludes my little talk about drugs inside and outside the school gates," said Detective Constable Ford. He tried to look serious from within the confines of his all-encompassing Teletubby suit.

Someone sniggered on the front row.

DC Ford cleared his throat and tried to summon up as much dignity as appearing in public as Tinky-Winky would allow.

"Any questions?" he asked, with some degree of trepidation. He was not at all sure how an audience of street-wise fifteen year olds would react to a pontificating Teletubby.

"You the gay one?" shouted someone from the back. There were a few isolated laughs.

DC Ford tried to think quickly. Of all the questions he had expected, he had not listed this in his top twenty. He felt a little flustered. Teletubbies were created for little children. Surely they were asexual and did not have partner preferences, even in this day and age?

"You're carrying an 'andbag?" added the questioner, as if to clarify his question.

"Oh that," said Ford, feeling a little relieved. "Just part of the costume," he said. "Next question?"

"Have you ever humped La-La?"

More laughter.

DC Ford again felt perplexed. What on earth was a La-La and why should this lot of delinquents worry about his humping activities?

"He looks more like Po's type," said someone else from the side of the hall. The whole audience were in fits of laughter now.

Ford swivelled his head piece from side to side. It was not that easy viewing the audience through the small eye-slits. "Are there any questions about drugs?" he asked valiantly.

"Yeh," shouted the owner of the first voice – the one at the back. "'Ave you got any free samples in yer 'andbag?"

"THERE WILL BE A TWO-HOUR DETENTION FOR THE NEXT PERSON WHO LAUGHS OR ASKS AN IMPERTINENT QUESTION," shouted someone extremely loudly and rather too close to Tinky-Winky's right ear.

DC Ford had not been prepared for this. He jumped forward and toppled off the stage and into the front row.

*... and then the dragon exhaled.*

*Roger closed his eyes and awaited incineration. At least it would be quick and relatively painless. He held his breath. At last, a glorious end to it all.*

*A few moments passed. He coughed and felt like retching, which was odd given that he should have been dead. However, instead of being engulfed in dragon-fire the temperature of a small sun, he found himself still very much alive and almost totally unharmed.*

*'Almost' being the slightly picky word to describe Roger's general condition here, since he was now engulfed in a cloud of rancid, sulphurous air with whiffs of year-old cabbages. He coughed again.*

*There was a loud wheeze from nearby and then another strong gust of rotting old vegetables.*

*"I was hoping that that would stop him lighting up," said a triumphant voice from further down the corridor. Endymion was holding a broken glass phial in one hand and a torn scroll in the other.*

*There was then what sounded like a large dragon squeaking in astonishment, followed by the scraping of huge claws on the cavern floor, as the creature attempted to scuttle away with its tale metaphorically between its legs.*

*"Don't tell me," muttered Roger, as he got to his feet. "Another unique and never-tried-before spell combination."*

*"Indeed," said the excited wizard. "Never thought it would extinguish a level five critter this big though. Quite a coup I think. You all owe me a beer when we get out."*

*"Right then," said Roger, dusting himself down. "Would someone please tell me what just happened?"*

*"That idiot blew a hole through the floor with another of his daft spell mixtures and we sort of*

*ended up at the bottom of the Dragon King's Lair," said Li Bang Cho.*

*"Is this good news I'm hearing?" asked Roger.*

*"Well, there's good news and there's bad news," said the Snark Maiden, who had just joined them.*

*"There always is," said Roger, sadly. "The bad first, please," he sighed.*

*"Level five is crammed with really nasty swines, who will take a lot of beating even with weapons that we don't possess, as yet," said the Snark Maiden, knowledgeably. "We should have picked up upgraded swords and stuff as we progressed through levels three and four."*

*"Oh crap," said Roger.*

*"There's more bad news," said the Snark Maiden.*

*"Really?" sighed Roger again.*

*"We've just made the sort of noise which will have been heard by virtually every monster from here to the end of the dungeon dimensions. I reckon that in about a minute we're going to have some pretty unwelcome company, not to mention a very irate Dragon King, who will have some serious questions as to why we blew a massive hole in his home."*

*"And the good news?" asked Roger.*

*"Well, we're still alive and can't be too far away from where Bunty is being held," said the Snark Maiden, happily.*

*"That's the good news," said Roger.*

*There was a low rumble from a distant corridor and then the sound of extremely heavy footsteps coming their way rather quickly.*

*"Maybe time to beat a quick retreat back up to level four?" suggested Endymion, trying to hide a slight tremble in his voice and pointing upwards through the hole in the ceiling. There was general agreement to this very sensible idea.*

*"Rope," said Tammy, from somewhere beneath the heroes' eye-line. They all looked down. "We have a coil of rope which may help."*

*"We?" asked the Snark Maiden, voicing the thoughts of the entire group.*

*"Tubby and me," replied Tammy, simply.*

*A small and rather dapper brownish goblin appeared at Tammy's side and smiled toothily up at Roger and the other heroes.*

*"And I take it that we are not about to kill this new goblin, despite the fact that he is standing about six inches from my left foot?" asked Roger, slowly.*

*"You don't want to kill me," said Tammy brightly. "So why should you want to kill an old friend of mine?"*

*"I give up," said Roger, staring at what was left of the cavern ceiling. "I really give up."*

*"He's very nice when you get to know him," said Tammy.*

*"I am, you know. Very, very, very, very nice," mumbled the newcomer.*

*"So, now we have two goblins in our party," said the Snark Maiden, shaking her head slowly. "Why don't we adopt a Minotaur or a beastman to complete the set?"*

*"Don't be nasty," said Tammy. "You'd like him if you gave him a chance. He likes music and outdoor games, you know."*

*"Do you have many other friends down here?" asked Li Bang Cho. "Might be an idea to get a bit of a goblin warband together, fighting on our side, for a change."*

*"A goblin warband fighting alongside human and dwarven heroes?" squawked Roger, incredulously. "The whole world has gone stark, staring mad."*

*"He has a map of levels four and five," said Tammy, quietly.*

*"Keep talking," said the Snark Maiden.*

*"A complete map of every corridor, room, trap and possible ambush spot," said Tammy, as airily as a small goblin could manage.*

*Someone coughed, while someone else began whistling a tune.*

*"Welcome to the group, Tubby," said Li Bang Cho, reaching down to shake Tubby's hand.*

*"Right," said Roger. "Time to get up there fast," he said, pointing up at the smoking hole above them. "Then, we can assess the situation properly and have a proper look at this new goblin."*

*A rope was thrown up into the gloom. It caught hold of something. Roger gave it a firm tug. It still held fast.*

*"Ladies first," he said gallantly and looked at the Snark Maiden.*

*"Very funny," said a voice to his left, as Li Bang Cho grabbed hold of the rope and began pulling himself up into the darkness.*

*"What price gallantry today?" asked Roger to the world in general.*

*"Just reverting to stereotype," said Li Bang Cho, going up the rope like a monkey after a bunch of bananas. "We Chinese don't hold the rope for anyone except ourselves. Law of the jungle in the People's Republic," came the muffled voice of the Chinese dwarf as he disappeared into the dusty gloom above.*

*"Right, I'll try to keep the swines at bay, while you all get up there and join our Chinese stereotype," said Roger and marched down the corridor towards the approaching heavy feet. Time to be a hero, he thought, grimly.*

*"I'll give you a hand," said the Snark Maiden. "You may need a few well-placed arrows."*

*Roger grunted approval and the two of them prepared themselves for yet another scrap in a confined space.*

*"I'm happy to help too," said another voice.*

*The two heroes looked round and frowned as one. There in the gloom stood a dusty and slightly dishevelled gladiator.*

*"Thanks Obby," said Roger. "But I rather think that we need some firepower up there in level four. Can't let a wizard and two goblins deal with the stuff crawling around up there, even if it is just for a few moments and even if they do have a map."*

*"Understood," said Obby. "Only... in all the confusion and everything, I found this," he said and brandished a short but lethal looking three-pointed dagger at the two heroes. Must have been on one of the goblins who fell through with us."*

*The Snark Maiden gasped audibly. "That's a trillium homing dagger," she said, in amazement. "You don't come across them every day. They're worth a pretty penny, I can tell you, and are very level five," she added, eyeing the triple blade enviously.*

*"It's yours if you want it," said Obby, generously. "You're better at ranged combat than me."*

*"Are you serious?"*

*"Go on, take it," said Obby and offered the weapon to the Snark Maiden.*

*A few seconds later and Obby had disappeared up the rope and into level four. It was then that the Snark Maiden turned to Roger.*

*"I have to say that I'm getting very conflicting feelings about our recent recruit," she said, quietly.*

*"He's a god-send, if you ask me. And a lucky bastard too, if he can pick up stuff like that after cave-ins."*

*"Too lucky," said the Snark Maiden, eyes narrowing. "Something's not quite right with our friend Obby."*

*"Women," said Roger, more to himself. "They get given the best present a hero could want and then become suspicious about the motives behind the giving."*

*"It's not just the dagger," said the Snark Maiden. "There's more…"*

*Whatever she was about to say was lost to posterity as an enormous figure suddenly appeared out of the gloom and ambled towards the two heroes. It had a massive head, a long duck-like beak and huge malignant eyes. What made it extra-special though were the four arms brandishing a different weapon in each.*

*"Prepare to die, little humans," quacked the duck man.*

*"It talks," said Roger, simply.*

*"Soon I shall be feasting upon your flesh," continued the duck man, closing quickly on the heroes.*

*"I hate monsters that trot out tired old platitudes," said the Snark Maiden, knocking an arrow and taking aim.*

*"A duck-billed platitude," said Roger, rather pleased with himself at having thought that one up without Tammy's help.*

*"I also hate tired old puns," murmured the Snark Maiden, letting loose her first arrow. She sighed. "And finally, I hate having to fight these things in the first place. They're simply not natural in these caves. They just don't belong here… rather like Obby."*

*"Well, let's send duck man somewhere else and worry about Obby later," said Roger, with a smile and leapt forward at the four whirling arms.*

It was late afternoon in central London and Dave Springett had had enough. Another day of pretending to be a motionless panda in Piccadilly Circus had ended with a box full of coins and the populace of the capital being kind and generous to men in fluffy and cute animal suits. But Springett had had enough. Six hours of crouching on a wet pavement holding a plastic bamboo shoot out in front of him might be financially rewarding, but there were limits as to how long he could maintain interest, no matter how much money was raining into his collecting box.

He stretched to full height, yawned expansively and pulled his head off, much to the delight of a group of passing teenagers on BMX bikes. One threw a can of Pepsi at him – and missed. Yes, it most certainly was time to call it a day, thought Springett.

He unzipped the panda suit and tucked it into a bulging holdall and pulled on a crumpled and baggy sweat-shirt. In just a few moments he was standing on the pavement in his stained cream chinos and scuffed brown leather shoes, looking like any other member of the human race. He then put on a tatty Ecuadorian hat, which he too called a Panama.

"Ni Hao," said Percy Gabbitt, uncertainly. He was never that confident dipping into another language, even when it was just to say hello.

"Hello," came the disconcerting response from the woman behind the low counter.

Gabbitt frowned and cleared his throat. Perhaps the straight-forward approach was not such a good idea after all. He foresaw a few problems with this woman.

"Can I help you?" asked the woman in flawless English. She was about twenty-five years old, wore a fashionable pale blue dress and had her hair tied back behind her head in that no-nonsense way that women sometimes adopt when doing serious work or trying to show that they are not just office flowers.

Gabbitt cleared his throat again.

"Would you like a glass of water or some tea?" asked the woman, pleasantly.

"Thank you," croaked Gabbitt, huskily. He sat down in a small wicker chair, while the woman busied herself with the tea at a table next to the Reception desk.

Gabbitt looked around the office and tried to spot anything that looked suspiciously heavy that might contain a shedload of money. Nothing came close though. The place was devoid of packages, bags or receptacles of any kind.

The office was rather narrow with a set of five shelves running the length of one wall and containing a large selection of holiday brochures. The other wall had a massive framed print of a panda in a tree looking rather tired but incredibly cute. Gabbitt stared at this for a few moments and wondered if Irwin had been serious about taking him to the panda research base in this city.

"You like 'tsiong-mao'?" asked the woman, as she returned to Gabbitt, replete tea for two.

"It looks very nice," said Gabbitt, staring at the deep green tea. "Is it jasmine?"

The woman burst out laughing. "No, I was asking about the panda," she said and nodded at the picture. "Tsiong-mao is Chinese for panda."

"Oh," said Gabbitt, slowly.

"It means bear-cat," continued the woman.

"Does it?" asked Gabbitt, genuinely interested.

"You see, when they were discovered, no one was really sure what they were. They couldn't decide if pandas were cats or bears so, being Chinese, we called them bear-cats, to be on the safe side."

She laughed again and poured Gabbitt some tea. "And no, this is not jasmine tea. This is local green tea. A little strong perhaps for foreigners."

"It looks very nice," said Gabbitt, adopting a very English attitude to someone offering him a cup of tea.

"So…" said the woman.

"Ah, yes," said Gabbitt, not at all sure what to say next.

"You've come to see Mr Zhang, haven't you?"

"Yes," said Gabbitt.

"He's not here, but I can call him, although his English is not very good. He usually gets me to talk to the foreigners."

"You don't have to call him," said Gabbitt hastily. "You'll do fine."

"Are you from a school or a university?" asked the woman, perceptively.

"Yes."

"Do you want to do a presentation of your college?"

"Well…"

"I can listen if you like, but I have to say that I've heard it all before."

"Well…"

"But you're not here to do that, are you?" The woman looked deep into Gabbitt's soul for a few moments and then supped her tea noisily. "You're here for something else."

Gabbitt started to feel anxious. He never liked being read like a book. Caroline always said he had a face which could fool no one.

"Have you come for the bag?" asked the woman.

"What!" squawked Gabbitt, nearly spilling his tea.

"You have, haven't you? This really is my lucky day," said the woman, clapping her hands in delight. "I've received many emails from Miss Emily about the feedback forms. I have them all ready to send by post to her, but if you're here in person, then maybe I can give them to you."

"Well…"

"They are rather heavy and sending by post from China could take over a month to arrive in England, so it's much better for you to collect them now."

"Err…"

"I'll go and get them," said the woman, brightly.

She left the room and disappeared through a door leading to the back of the shop. Gabbitt tried to work out what was going on. He certainly did not want to lug a ton of feedback forms around China.

The woman returned, struggling with a stout cardboard box. It said 'Northampton University' on the side. She placed it onto the counter and patted it like a friendly dog. "Teachers have a lot to say," she said and rolled her eyes.

"I see," said Gabbitt. "It looks heavy."

"It is… a bit," said the woman. "But much better to take them with you I think."

"Well…"

"Please…"

Gabbitt looked at the imploring eyes and gave in. He was always a sucker for women asking favours.

"Many thanks. Mr Zhang will be delighted. He likes Northampton University a lot."

"I bet he does," muttered Gabbitt, under his breath."

"Would you like more tea?" asked the woman.

"Thank you," said Gabbitt, who suddenly had an idea. "Can I use your…washroom?" he asked.

"Certainly. It's at the back."

Gabbitt got up and slid through the door into the gloom of the back of the travel agency.

What he had expected to find was a large stockroom full of cases and stacks of brochures, the stock fodder of a travel agency. What he found though was a tiny room with just one large case in the centre of the room and a door beyond, which had to lead to the washroom.

He crouched down and slid his hand along the lid of the box and peered inside the box. He had hoped to find a pile of red bank notes. No such luck though, as all that seemed to be there was a lot of office forms. Gabbitt felt slightly deflated.

So, Cedric Zhang did not keep his money in the office, after all. Well, he wouldn't, would he? Such a massive amount of money would be already in a safe somewhere or in a bank vault in downtown Chengdu, well and truly under lock and key and out of the reach of greedy hands. So much for that, thought Gabbitt, and pushed through the door and into the toilet cubicle.

He looked down at the toilet and sighed again. Things were not going that well. He stood for a few seconds deep in thought. Suddenly, the small window just above his eye-line scraped open. Gabbitt jumped in surprise. No one wants or expects this most secret of places to be invaded, whatever the reason.

A face bobbed into view. It was Bob Irwin.

"How's it going?" he said.

"What are you doing there?" asked Gabbitt, a little irritably.

"Thought you might need some help."

"In here? You could hold my trousers up, I suppose."

"No, out there."

"It's not here, Bob," whispered Gabbitt. "I've checked everywhere and there're no cases of money lying about. There's not even a safe in the office. He's probably taken the money home or put it in the bank."

"Crap!" exclaimed Irwin. "We'll have to find out where he lives and have a look there. This is getting a bit more difficult than I thought. We need a bit of Gabbitt luck at the moment," he said and winked.

"I'm doing my best."

"Bob, how did you get back there?" asked Gabbitt.

"Got in through the place next door. We were right. It is a hospital of some sort and the receptionist was only too happy to help a foreigner with pressing bladder problems. Great minds think alike, you see. Thought I would be able to get round the back of the travel agency by sneaking through the hospital. And it worked."

Suddenly all the lights went out and everything went pitch black.

A Chinese power cut.

Both cursed rather loudly. A moment later and the lights in the travel agency flickered on again.

"Still dark over here," muttered Irwin. "Just my luck."

There was then a loud scream and the sound of running feet.

"All hell breaking loose here in the hospital," said Irwin, looking over his shoulder at a long corridor now filled with shadows and the flash of small torches. "Can you wait there for a moment and I'll go and see what's going on?"

Gabbitt was about to say that there was very little he could do to help from the confines of a Chinese toilet in a travel agency, but Irwin had already disappeared from sight.

Not for the first time that evening, Gabbitt sighed long and deeply. A good five minutes passed and Gabbitt was beginning to feel worried. He was also wondering what the nice Chinese woman in the travel agency would be thinking he was up to in her toilet. A wave of panic swept over him as he zipped up his trousers.

"Are you still there?" hissed Bob Irwin.

Gabbitt jumped again, this time hitting his head against the toilet cistern. "Yes, I'm still here," he said, rubbing his head.

"Good. Bit of a crisis here," said Irwin. "We need a little help."

"Help? What?" spluttered Gabbitt, uncomprehendingly.

"Nurse Chen and Nurse Zhang," said Irwin. "They're both here. Say hello to Percy."

"Hello," chorused two distinctly female voices.

"What?"

"It's a hospital without any electricity. Must be a serious power-cut. They need a bit of juice immediately or it's curtains for some of the patients."

"Don't they have a back-up generator? Most hospitals do, you know," said Gabbitt.

"It's not a proper hospital."

"What?" asked Gabbitt, feeling increasingly confused.

"It's a place where they incubate babies that have just been born," said Irwin.

"A maternity hospital?" squawked Gabbitt. "Without electricity? You have got to be joking."

"Well, it's not quite a maternity hospital either," said Irwin.

"What are you talking about, Bob?"

"Baby pandas," whispered Irwin, urgently.

"Baby what?" was all that Gabbitt could muster.

"Pandas. And they need electricity to power the air conditioners in the incubation room, or it'll be curtains for the little things. They'll overheat."

"Oh."

"So, can you plug this in?" asked Irwin.

"What?"

"Just pull this cable through and plug it in."

A cable waved around the window like a dancing cobra.

"In here?"

"Yes, it appears you have electricity. Be a sport, will you?"

"You have got to be joking."

"Nurse Chen says you have a nice voice."

Gabbitt sighed and pulled a thick black cable through the open window. Sometimes, there was no point arguing.

"What will the agency think about this arrangement?" hissed Gabbitt, as he found a socket just outside the toilet cubicle.

"Do you really think I care? And anyway, the nurses will sort it all out in the morning. This needs to be done immediately, without a debate, which is what they will get if they come round and ask for permission."

"This is madness, you know."

"I'm just happy that the travel agency had the foresight to have a generator which kicks in at times like this," said Irwin brightly. "Probably bought with money stolen from schools in England. Nurse Chen and Nurse Zhang say a big thank you," whispered Irwin.

"Don't mention it," muttered Gabbitt and strode back through the door and into the front part of the agency.

"You OK?" asked the woman, in a concerned way.

"I think so," said Gabbitt, rubbing his stomach. "Some tofu which didn't agree with me I think."

"You must be careful when eating Chinese food," said the woman. She was about to impart a little more Oriental wisdom on sensible eating in China when the lights in the shop dimmed slightly and then flickered. There was also the noise of an engine somewhere nearby straining hard to keep up with the power it was suddenly expected to produce.

"That is very strange," said the woman, with a frown. "The reserve generator should handle just a few shop lights and my computer without any problems. Maybe it needs servicing," she said, as the generator appeared to wheeze and then cough twice.

"Time I was leaving," said Gabbitt quickly and picked up the heavy box of feedback questionnaires.

"Please come again," said the woman, chirpily. "I'm sure Mr Zhang will be delighted to hear that you've dropped by."

"I bet he'll be beside himself," said Gabbitt, honestly.

"We will try to send another group of teachers next year," said the woman. "Have a nice trip back to England."

Percy Gabbitt stumbled onto the street and marched quickly down the road. He then turned to look at the hospital and his mouth sagged open. There, in front of him were seven brightly-lit floors standing out like a beacon in the gloom all about.

"Just a few air conditioners for the incubation room," murmured Gabbitt to himself.

It was at that moment that lights flickered on everywhere as electricity in the area seemed to have been restored. Gabbitt relaxed slightly and was about to walk into the hospital to meet Irwin when there was a loud explosion behind him followed by the unmistakeable crackle of fire breaking out.

Bob Irwin burst through the hospital doors and ran towards Gabbitt, oblivious of what was happening in the travel agency. "This, you have got to see," he spluttered breathlessly, grabbing Gabbitt's arm and pulling him towards the hospital where a beaming Nurse Chen and Nurse Zhang awaited them.

A few moments later and Percy Gabbitt was staring through a Perspex window at a three-inch long, delicate, pink creature, which lay on a powder-blue, fluffy towel. It flexed its tiny paws while its little heart beat almost as fast as Gabbitt's.

There was a very long pause as the two foreigners and stared at the wonderful sight.

"Only two hours old," whispered Irwin. "You saved its bacon, mate."

"I thought you preferred poison-spitting lizards," said Gabbitt.

"Yes, well I know, but…" began Irwin.

It was then that Nurse Chen turned to the two of them and bowed deeply. "You truly are friends of China," she said with a large, ear-to-ear smile.

# TWELVE

*"Always laugh when you can. It is cheap medicine."*
**(Lord Byron, who would have loved Percy Gabbitt)**

It was early evening in downtown Bromley and Tinky-Winky had a headache. The handbag had somehow been lost and someone had pulled the triangular antenna off his head.

DC Ford stood in the front garden of Joe Slimm's rented house and wondered if things could get any worse. True, he had managed to inveigle his way into Slimm's life on the rather flimsy pretext that he needed somewhere to change back into his normal clothes. And true, he had just spotted the reason for this ridiculous charade lounging among the pansies by the front door.

"Why does it always lead to sex and drugs?" he asked, as he trundled to the front door just behind Slimm.

"That's youngsters today. Sex and drugs is like bread and butter to them," replied Slimm, as he fumbled with his keys. "They want instant gratification for the least possible effort."

"In my day, you never mentioned sex to anyone or you got a thick ear from your dad. And as regards drugs, we thought that was just the jar of aspirin in the cupboard."

"Times have changed," said Slimm, opening the door and walking inside. "The kids of the twenty-first century know more about what's kept on the back shelves of a pharmacy than most pharmacist's do and... they've had sex in some form by their thirteenth birthday. It's just the new world order.

"I don't know why we bother," said Ford, walking into the lounge and sitting down.

"I feel like that every working day of my life," said Slimm, sadly. "The burden of the modern-day teacher, I'm sorry to say."

He gestured at a crowded shelf behind the television.

"Whisky, vodka, gin, tequila, brandy, sundry reds and whites… or a beer? I've got the lot. Take your pick. You need a decent stock of alcohol if you're going to cope with teaching nowadays."

"Just a beer, thanks," said Ford. "On duty, later."

"Think you should take the rest of the day off after your experiences at the school. Most people would take a week, after what you've just been through," said Slimm. "Falling off the stage must have hurt."

"Oh, I don't know. It was a bit of a relief, really," replied a glum DC Ford. "The whole thing could not have gone much worse up that point. At least they all left the hall laughing. To be honest, I couldn't have cared less by then. Just wanted it over and done with. I still don't know where the handbag went. I suppose I'll have to reimburse the suit-hirers. God, I hate the Teletubbies," he finished with uncharacteristic venom.

"Forget the beer. Have a double," offered Slimm, waving a bottle of Glen Fiddich in Ford's face.

"I wish," said Ford, needing a friend to confide in. "But I've got a stake-out in central London."

"Sounds interesting," said Slimm, pouring a beer for himself. "A bank robbery?"

"Something like that," replied Ford.

There was a pause as a rather overweight black and white cat ambled into the room, mewed moodily and then retreated through the door to the kitchen.

"Nixon wants his dinner," said Slimm, getting up.

DC Ford sat in the lounge and waited for a few moments. He then took something small out of his pocket and dropped it into Slimm's beer.

"Drugs today," he whispered to himself. "Disgraceful habit."

A few minutes later and Slimm appeared again.

"He gets a bit antsy if he doesn't get his salmon nuggets about this time," he said and took a deep draft of his beer.

"I know how he feels," said Ford, relaxing into his armchair. "Is he a friendly cat?" he asked nonchalantly, hoping that the answer was in the positive.

"Well, he generally gets on with everybody," said Slimm, having another sip. "Never seen him scratch anyone."

"That's good," said Ford. The last thing he wanted was an angry mass of claws going for him when he made the snatch.

"Does this taste all right to you?" asked Slimm, frowning at his beer. "Tastes like it's gone off or something."

"Mine tastes lovely," said Ford, hastily.

"Well, I've had enough of this," said Slimm and went back into the kitchen.

Five minutes later and Slimm had still not returned to the lounge. Ford sighed and got up. He walked into the kitchen and looked with some degree of sadness at the peacefully sleeping figure of Joe Slimm, sprawled slightly oddly on a kitchen chair. It was as if someone had dropped him there from a great height.

"Here kitty-kitty," said Ford, beginning the search for his quarry.

Ten fruitless minutes later and DC Ford was getting angry and impatient.

"Where the fuck, are you?" he snarled, a little unkindly and walked into the back room. The cat was not there either, but just as Ford was about to begin another search of the upstairs bedrooms he spotted a feline shape sashaying slowly across the back garden, the way cats do.

"Bloody thing," said the exasperated Ford, and pulled the sliding patio doors open. "How'd he get outside?"

A moment later and he was stalking the cat through the overgrown shrubberies and bushes which divided the Slimm's place from the next-door neighbours.

"There you are," said Ford and stepped through a bed of red hot pokers, over a low fence and onto a well-mown stretch of lawn. Nixon looked up into Ford's eyes and blinked tiredly. He then mewed loudly and began to purr.

"There's a good kitty," said Ford and reached down to pick the cat up.

The next few moments went rather fast for Ford. Instead of 'Operation Catsnatch' being successfully completed with the cat being stuffed unceremoniously into a shopping bag, DC Ford found himself suddenly facing a short and wizened old man.

"Bloody Teletubby," growled the figure, belligerently. "And on my lawn too!"

"What? But I…" began Ford.

"Should be dog-whipped," muttered the old man and began pulling the leather belt from his trousers.

Chief Inspector Pringle was sitting in an unmarked Ford Escort in a small side-street off Soho Square in central London. PC Johnson sat beside him humming a little tune. Pringle was feeling apprehensive for some reason and had attempted to quieten the tuneful Johnson on two occasions already. Pringle was not a Robbie Williams fan at all, whereas Johnson most definitely was.

"What's the time, constable?" asked Pringle for the fourth time.

"Just coming up to seven, sir," replied the constable, wearily.

"Where's DC Ford?" asked Pringle.

"Still not answering his car radio, sir. Shall I get a squad car round there to see what's going on, sir?"

"No, not yet, constable. We don't want to spook him if he's still undercover."

"Very good, sir," said PC Johnson, breaking out into a tuneless whistling of another Robbie Williams' hit.

"Constable, please," said Pringle.

"Right you are, sir," said the constable, with a sigh. "Would you like any chewing gum, sir?"

Pringle sat back in his seat and did not reply. A Chief Inspector chewing gum, indeed. Where did the man think he was? America? Next time he would make sure he brought with him a little YES or Rick Wakeman. That would knock spots off Robbie flippin' Williams.

Just about thirty metres away in a small shop which sold party novelties and all kinds of jolly fun items designed for distinctly adult parties, stood a smiling Bob Brand and a very nervous looking Jack Melligan.

"That's anatomically impossible," muttered Melligan, under his breath, as he stared at something long and bulky hanging in a vinyl wrapper from a rack inches from his nose.

"Mind-boggling," said Brand, staring at the monster in the plastic bag.

"Not just the mind, I think," said Melligan, in awe.

"Can I help you two gentlemen?" asked a very camp voice from rather too close to Bob Brand's left ear.

"Ah yes," replied Brand, hurriedly. "Indeed, you can."

"It's the 'Monster Mule Three'," said the voice again, as his professional eye noticed where his two customers' stares were held, almost hypnotically.

"Is it?" croaked Jack Melligan.

"I'm not surprised," contributed Brand.

"Would sirs like to see other items in the Monster Mule series? Perhaps the Monster Mule Five… or Six? They're just in from Thailand. You're staring at the Monster Mule Two – a slightly basic product, with none of the enhancements of the Five or the Six."

Brand and Melligan stared at each other, in amazement. They then turned to face the owner of the jolly voice.

"No thanks," they said, in unison.

"Perhaps a movie? We have the latest in the Donkeyman series. Again, just arrived from Thailand."

"Donkeyman?" tried Jack, almost in a whisper.

"Donkeyman meets the Pussycat," explained the shop assistant and waved the DVD under his nose. "Quite a meeting too, I can tell you," he said, rolling his eyes.

"No thanks," said Bob Brand, quickly.

"Then how can I be of service, gentlemen?" asked the man. He was dressed in a salmon pink shirt and yellow shorts with a dark blue belt. On his feet were two fluffy crimson slippers.

"Do you sell Panama Hats, like the ones in the window?" asked Brand, gruffly.

"Ah, party attire," said the man, clapping his hands. "Yes sir, we do. And in three different sizes depending on the size of your head," he said and sparkled a mischievous grin at Jack."

"Wonderful," said Brand flatly. "Can we buy a few?"

"A few?" asked the man in the fluffy slippers, pulling an Ecuadorian from under the counter.

"Thirty should do it," said Brand and opened his wallet.

At exactly the same moment that Bob Brand was peeling out a sheath of notes for a bag of Ecuadorians, Percy Gabbitt and Bob Irwin were sitting in a small hotel room in Chengdu and trying to drink the mini-bar dry.

It was three in the morning and neither of them cared very much if tomorrow arrived or not.

"A total waste of time," murmured Irwin and threw back another whisky miniature.

"What will Bob say?"

"He'll just tell us to stay until we find the dosh," replied Irwin, irritably. "Arapacana never fails, he'll say."

"So, what do we do now?"

"Get sloshed and then, in two days time, think about raiding Zhang's house, I suppose, though god knows how."

"Still, we did save the pandas," said Gabbitt, as he gulped down a lukewarm vodka.

"Oh yes," we did manage that," agreed Irwin. "And then we burnt the agency down. What is it with you and fire?"

"It was an accident," replied Gabbitt. "You know that. The plug must have overheated, because of the extra power it was expected to handle from your hospital."

"Chinese electrics," tutted Irwin, undoing the top of a small brandy bottle.

"I think only the back room got properly burned," said Gabbitt.

"You really are a one-man Armageddon machine, Percy Gabbitt," chuckled Irwin, chundering the brandy and putting his feet up onto the heavy Northampton University questionnaire box. "And I don't know how we're going to get this sod onto a plane back to Shanghai," he said, kicking the box.

"Can't we send it straight to Northampton?" asked Gabbitt. "They must post offices here."

Bob Irwin sighed and reached for an unmarked bottle, which looked like it contained water. He frowned and undid the cap.

"Bastard day," he said and kicked the box, the side of which flopped open.

"Chinese cardboard," said Irwin and slugged back the unknown liquid.

A wad of red bank notes spilled onto the floor by Irwin's foot from the torn box. They both stared long and hard at the pile.

"Well I'll be a wombat's scrotum," murmured Irwin.

"Those are not questionnaires," said Gabbitt, thickly.

The two of them scrabbled at the top of the box. A moment later and the lid had been torn off and they were staring at a top layer of tightly packed one hundred RMB notes.

"Fuck my wallaby!" exclaimed Irwin and sat back on the bed. "Perfect! Bloody perfect!" he continued, starting to laugh. "He won't even know he's had the money swiped. Percy Raymond Gabbitt, how did you do it?"

"What do you mean?" asked Gabbitt, the alcohol confusing rational thought.

"Zhang will think that the money went up in smoke in the back room," he chuckled.

"So, he won't be after us," said Gabbitt.

"Bloody incredible! How do you do it, Percy? You save pandas, get the assistant to give you all the cash, burn the place down and waltz away into the sunset without anyone thinking it's you. Bloody incredible!"

"But I didn't mean it," mumbled Gabbitt.

Bob Irwin lay back on his bed and laughed long and loud. Meanwhile, a confused Percy Gabbitt wandered into the bathroom to stare at himself in the mirror and frown a lot.

Chief Inspector Pringle was also doing a lot of frowning some five thousand miles away. He was standing on Oxford Street in central London with hands on hips and staring up at the first floor windows of the Happy Snappy School of English.

"I'll get you, you vandalising bastards," he muttered, under his breath.

"Sir," said a voice near him.

"What?"

"Bit of a problem, I think," said PC Johnson, woodenly.

"What is it?" snapped Pringle.

"Well, you remember that we are looking for someone in a white hat?"

"Yes?" murmured Pringle, still with his eyes on the first floor.

"Well, there seem to be hundreds of the blighters," said Johnson.

Pringle stopped looking at the language school and stared up the road towards the junction with Tottenham Court Road. Sure enough, it appeared that a Panama hat convention had descended on Oxford Street as dozens of men poured into the street from all possible entry points.

"Look lively," said Pringle, running back to the police car to get to his radio. "I want the lot of them arrested," he shouted, loudly.

"On what charge, sir? They haven't done anything yet," said PC Johnson, rather lamely.

Think of something, constable. Be creative," he said, staring at the bovine constable. He sighed deeply. "What about drunk in charge of a hat?" he cried, as he threw the police car door open.

In his wake, a confused PC Johnson was left wondering how he cold manage to arrest what look like half of Oxford Street on such a charge. "We might need back-up, sir," he croaked. "And vans too. A lot of them."

Two figures, both hatless, climbed a fire-escape at the back of the building which housed the Happy Snappy English School. There was a slight pause as one of the figures glanced through a small window which led into the ground floor sex shop. Then the climb continued.

They reached the first floor and were faced with a closed door.

"What now?" asked Jack Melligan, worriedly.

"Easy," replied a smiling Bob Brand.

"But that kind of door only opens outwards. Can't open inwards. That's the beauty of the thing. Perfect security. You can't kick it down."

"In a perfect world where no one trusts anyone and you discount the human factor then I would agree with you, Jack."

"So... how are we going to get in?"

"Don't worry, Jack. I've got us this far, haven't I? You have to admit that the hat trick was pretty brilliant."

"Yes," very nice," said Melligan. "One of your better diversions. Clever and with a certain... style."

"I have to say that I'm quite proud of that one," said Brand. "We even made a small profit selling them all on that street corner. Brought back memories of the good old days when I was a barrow boy in Wandsworth. We stole and sold everything in those days. Even managed to off-load my old dad's socks on one famous occasion... while he was wearing them! Now you tell me if that's not pretty sharp salesmanship?"

"So..." said Jack Melligan and raised his eyebrows in a way which indicated polite impatience.

Bob Brand started barking.

It sounded like one of those large, friendly Labradors which loved being stroked hard.

Nothing happened, so Bob barked a little more.

Jack Melligan said nothing. He just stared at his co-vandal. Had the man suddenly gone completely insane? Was he not only determined to get the two of them arrested, but also committed as well?

The door opened a little and a muffled voice spoke. Melligan jumped back.

"Here boy! Here boy! What's the matter then? Are you stuck on this fire escape? How did you get there?"

Bob Brand pulled the door open and flashed his Tescos Club card from a dangling wallet.

"Health and Safety Inspectors," he said gruffly and pushed his way into the school, pocketing the wallet as fast as it had been pulled out. "We take a very poor view of keeping pets on fire escapes," he continued, officiously.

"But it's not our dog," squawked the opener of the door.

"Gangway," muttered Melligan, elbowing his way after Bob Brand. He was very keen not to be left alone outside.

"But," said the man again. He was a thin-looking character with a bald head, large spectacles and an unkempt beard. He leant out onto the fire escape. "So where are you then?" he asked the very empty patch of air there. "Must have trotted off," he said to himself and closed the door, slightly disappointedly. He then walked back to the small staff room and began eating a hummus and carrot sandwich.

Bob Brand and Jack Melligan walked down a series of narrow corridors and round sharp corners. It was like a rat's maze.

"Can I help you?" asked a young woman in a pair of baggy green combat trousers.

"Thank you, madam," said Brand. "We are looking for the Director of Studies' office."

"The shit's not there," said the woman, airily.

"Then where can we find the gentleman?" asked Brand, with a large smile.

"He's hiding in the toilet," came the unexpected reply.

"And where would that...?" asked Brand, leaving the end to his question hanging in the space between them.

"Just down the corridor opposite the photocopy room," said the woman, waving to a distant door.

"Probably flushing the evidence," she muttered and then disappeared into an extremely small room which seemed to contain an impossible number of young foreign people.

"Did you see that?" asked a breathless Melligan. "About twenty students in a classroom only fit for three."

"It makes you think, doesn't it?" said Bob Brand, as he strode to the end of the corridor and the toilets.

"How do they get away with it?" muttered Melligan.

There was mayhem in the street outside the Happy Snappy School.

About thirty uniformed and plain clothes police officers were having an extremely one-sided wrestling match with an army of rather respectable-looking gentlemen all wearing white Panama... Ecuadorian hats - many had already been spread-eagled on the pavement.

"I arrest you for wearing a hat," said PC Johnson and snapped the cuffs on one bemused old gentleman. He then turned to two of his colleagues, who were grabbing other behatted gentlemen. "Just load the swines up into our vans and we'll sort out who's who back at the nick."

"Carry on," said Chief Inspector Pringle, eyes narrowing. He looked up at the Happy Snappy School and frowned hard. "Not this time, you bastards," he murmured under his breath. "Not this time."

And with that, he waved urgently to a group of constables guarding a small alley leading to the back of the building.

"You lot!" he barked. "Follow me! We're going in!"

Back on the first floor, Bob Brand and Jack Melligan had closed in on their prey. To be exact, they were standing outside a toilet cubicle and putting on funny accents.

The effect of this on the occupant of the toilet cubicle was quite dramatic. It was probably a good thing that he was sitting on the toilet with his pants down.

"Meester Gabriel, we not happy," said Brand, spitting the words out like a veteran Al-Qaeda operative.

"You try rip us on," added Melligan sounding more like a Greek waiter.

"You what?" squawked Charles Gabriel, through the toilet door.

"You theenk you can take our dollars, Allah be praised, and getaway from the jihad," said Brand, really getting into character.

"You must have made a mistake," said a blubbering Gabriel.

"You theenk we stoopid, Unbeliever Gabriel. Wahad ithnan thalathat, my friend. We keel you a leetle," said Brand, sounding extremely menacing.

"Look, I'm sure we can come to some sort of mutual understanding," squawked the terrified voice of the school director.

"Allah be merciful," said Brand, loudly and kicked the locked cubicle door. "The infidel now tries to bribe servants of the one god."

"No, I'm not," cried Gabriel, desperately.

"You take our feloos, Meester Gabriel. And don't try to deny eet, or I'll keek thees door down and cut your bortakalaats off."

"Oh Christ!" exclaimed Gabriel. "Sorry, I mean..."

"Hee makes religious jokes, Meester Abdullah," said Brand happily. "Never try to reeep the Iranians off. We keel for fun."

"Oh shit," wailed Gabriel.

"And... remember the name of great leader, Percy Raymond Gabbitt."

"Who... what?" came the understandably confused response.

"Allah be praised. Feel fear in your unbelieving bones!"

"Oh god..." squeaked a bemused Gabriel. "OK, I'll sort it out immediately. No more special accounts. I'll see that everything is OK. Just please don't hurt me."

Gabriel paused for a few moments. He then heard the unmistakeable snap of someone putting on rubber washing-up gloves. "Oh shit! I never expected this. I never meant to..."

Bob Brand and Jack Melligan were already thirty yards away and walking down the fire-escape towards the back alley.

"Nicely done," said Bob Brand.

"I have to hand it to you, Bob," said an admiring Melligan. "Two small questions though."

"Shoot," said Brand, as the two of them reached the deserted alley at ground level and walked slowly back to Costa Coffee.

"What are bortokalaats and feloos?"

"A bortokalaat is Arabic for orange, I think," said Brand. "Always rather liked that word for some reason. You can really get your tongue round it and make it sound very Arabic, if you see what I mean. Has a menacing twang to it, too. And feloos means money."

"I didn't know you could speak Arabic," said an awed Melligan.

"Just a smattering I've picked up over the years."

"And what were those other words? Wahad, Ithn…?"

"Arabic numbers, I think," said Brand, breezily. "One, two, three."

"No shit!" exclaimed Melligan.

They got to the junction with Oxford Street and both said exactly the same word again, in unison this time, as they came across the aftermath of 'Operation Panama'.

A row of elderly gentlemen was 'assuming the position' against a brick wall, one of whom appeared to have a rather grubby panda suit draped over a shoulder.

"Busy evening for the boys in blue," muttered Bob Brand.

"Is that what I think it is?" asked Melligan, as he stared at the panda suit.

"Amazing what the general public carry around, isn't it?" said Brand, as they watched the police herd the Panama hat criminals into three unmarked white Ford Transits.

They stepped into the coffee shop.

"And all because of those Ecuadorian hats," said Melligan.

"Indeed," said Brand. "A double cappuccino and whipped cream chocco doughnut, I think," he said, licking his lips. "Celebration time again."

"Allah be praised," said Melligan.

Chief Inspector Pringle and his task force had managed to gain entry to the Happy Snappy English School and were busy flushing everyone out of the place by use of lots of truncheon work and loud swear words.

In about thirty seconds the occupants of twelve classrooms – some one hundred and eighty foreign adults had flooded onto the Oxford Street and into a wide police cordon where more white vans were parked and awaiting passengers.

The school was almost totally empty. Almost. Pringle and four members of his squad inched their way down one of the last corridors still not 'cleared' by his officers. They could hear voices, or rather one voice.

Pringle tiptoed towards the voice. It was clear that something was not quite right. Pringle smiled smugly. At last, I've got you, he thought. Diversions with Panama hats, indeed. Who the hell did they think they were dealing with?

He slowly opened the door which seemed to lead to the toilets and listened to the muffled voice.

"… and so, I thought that by opening that account I could earn a little money on the side, as it were. It really doesn't harm anyone. Money for all and no losers. Well I suppose the Iranian government are technically the losers, but they have buckets of spare cash which they regularly throw around. Look, I can cut you in for a slice of the action, if you like. I can hear that you are men of business, like me. Just say the word, my friends. I honestly meant no harm. The money is totally untraceable so the police won't even know it exists. We are in effect laundering non-existent money."

Chief Inspector Pringle frowned and cleared his throat. He was about to introduce himself to the occupant of cubicle number three when the voice said one last rather surprising sentence.

"And I promise not to tread on the toes of Percy Gabbitt any more, either. Perhaps he would like a slice of the pie as well."

Pringle started at the mention of his nemesis and dropped his truncheon noisily onto the tiled floor.

*"So, tell us your story, young goblin," said Li Bang Cho to Tubby, the new goblin in their party.*

*The heroes were back on level four and feeling rather vulnerable. The fight with the duckman had not gone particularly smoothly and it had taken quite a lot of nimble footwork to keep the two heroes in the game.*

*Roger had finally managed to drive the monster, quacking angrily about the loss of his expensive weaponry, back down the corridor. The Snark Maiden had had to use up all her precious arrows as well.*

*The two had then quickly pulled themselves up a level and retrieved the rope in the nick of time. They had then looked down into the gloom of level five and watched as dozens of nasty looking beasts with shiny teeth scuttled back and forth looking for likely quarry.*

*A few moments later and Roger and the Snark Maiden had joined the other heroes and begun to examine the weapons taken from the duckman. It had been quite a haul too.*

*"Would you look at that?" marvelled Roger, as he hefted a particularly glittery throwing axe with horse hair sights. He cared little for goblins reciting autobiographies and far preferred to talk about weaponry, especially the really fancy stuff. "The*

*handle's covered in diamonds. Must be worth a small fortune."*

*"Let me see," sniffed Tammy.*

*Roger handed the axe over to the small goblin.*

*"Thought so," murmured Tammy, after a short examination.*

*"Thought what?" queried Roger.*

*"Onyx," said Tammy, flatly. "Often mistaken for diamonds down here," he muttered and gave the axe back to Roger.*

*"Are you sure?" asked a sceptical Roger, looking at the shiny handle very closely. "I thought onyx was black. They look like diamonds to me."*

*"Well, I'm sure they do," said Tammy. "Unfortunately, you haven't had the benefit of a goblin education, where lesson one on cavern gems concentrated on fluorescence, phosphorescence, thermoluminescence and triboluminescence."*

*"You what?" grunted Roger, thickly.*

*"Calcites," replied Tammy, simply. "Caves are stuffed with the things. And they all glitter beautifully."*

*"Calcites?" muttered Roger and sat down heavily.*

*"Fluorite, quartz, barite, spalerite, galena, celestite, sulfur, apatite, biotite, zeo…"*

*"Enough!" exclaimed Roger loudly, angrily tossing the axe onto the cavern floor.*

*"Still worth something though," sniffed Tammy. "Not as much as real d…"*

*"I said enough," moaned Roger, unhappily. It was just about all he could bear to have a goblin in his*

*war party in the first place and now to have the little fellow proving he was far more intelligent. Well, it was beyond the limit.*

*The heroes looked at the rest of the weapons in silence. Somehow the euphoric mood of the moment had been tarnished by Tammy's calcites.*

*Li Bang Cho did not care though and picked up a stainless-steel halberd with a rubber joint for jabbing enemies round corners, while the Snark Maiden looked quietly impressed by a quiver of obsidian tipped arrows.*

*Roger picked up a light weight centaur's shield and sniffed it suspiciously.*

*"Not made of calcium?" he asked, gruffly.*

*"Calcite," sighed Tammy. And no."*

*Roger licked his lips as he hefted the shield. He would like to see the look on the faces of some of the ghouls and beasts on this level when they came face-to-face with level five weaponry in the hands of a weathered hero, calcite or not.*

*"So, tell us your story young goblin," repeated Li Bang Cho, as he experimented with the ninety-degree halberd.*

*"I'm into treacle," said the goblin, thickly.*

*"Treacle?" asked the Snark Maiden, happy to be talking about things other than fake diamonds.*

*"It's the future," said the new goblin, knowledgeably. "A real seller's market out there at the moment. Would you like to see my brochure? I've done the odd SWOT analysis on treacle commodities and drawn up a few pie charts as well,*

*you know. I've even got a couple of real pies in my bag as tasters, he finished and waited for the customary chuckle from his audience. It never came.*

*There was a very long pause as the group of heroes began to realise that their new companion was not just from the vilest race on the planet, but he also had an occupation which most sane people would consider pretty vile too.*

*"And what are you doing in the Dragon King's lair, skulking in dark corridors where most heroes fear to tread?" asked Roger, scrutinizing the goblin and trying to ignore Tubby's comments on market forces in dungeon complexes.*

*Tubby was a little larger than Tammy, though most of the largeness went horizontally, not vertically. You see, Tubby was a slightly overweight goblin. He wore a smart white shirt, a bright red bow tie and khaki corduroy trousers. On his feet was a pair of rather dapper, patent elven leather shoes. He carried a small black briefcase with snazzy metal clips and the letters TG written in gold leaf across the top of the case by the handle.*

*Tubby was a walking enigma. He was most definitely a goblin, but that was about it as far as being goblinoid was concerned. There was certainly nothing about his demeanour which implied a traditional set of goblin activities, like eating dead rats, sleeping rough in damp caves and not washing your hands after going to the toilet.*

*Basically, Tubby looked like a goblin only when viewed really close-up. At all other times, he looked like a rather small green business creature, which defied any racial category. He also knew his treacle.*

*"Tubby was not skulking," said Tammy. "He never skulks. He is just here on… business. He's very good at business, is our Tubby."*

*"A business goblin," said Roger and put his head into his hands.*

*"And a very good one too," continued Tammy.*

*"I learnt it at school," sniffed Tubby and opened his briefcase.*

*"He has a briefcase," said Roger, noticing the case for the first time. His voice began to tremble a little. "One goblin is able to give us the comprehensive history of gems and the other… has a briefcase."*

*"I keep my samples and sales orders in here," said Tubby.*

*"Are you here selling treacle to the Dragon King?" asked Endymion.*

*"And what's wrong with that?" asked Tammy. "As I keep telling you, times are changing and the goblin of today has evolved into an entirely different creature. We're an economic miracle!"*

*"But can we trust the bastard?" asked Roger.*

*"Well, you can you trust me," said Tammy, chancing his arm a little.*

*"Just make sure you keep an eye on him," said Roger. "He's your responsibility. I don't want a knife in my back when we reach the treasure room."*

*"He's not dangerous," said Tammy. "There's not a lot of damage he could do to you with a briefcase and a rusty dagger, now is there?"*

*"Just keep him out of my way," muttered Roger, sulkily. The whole adventure had taken yet another sad downturn. Roger preferred his dungeons to be filled with salivating cave trolls and vicious dragons, not ridiculous duckmen and business goblins. He sighed long and hard and stared at his boots.*

*"Where are these maps?" asked Li Bang Cho, anxious to get a look at what level four held for them. "They in that briefcase of yours?"*

*"No," replied Tubby, with a sly smile.*

*"Then where are they?" asked Endymion, frowning hard.*

*"In my head," replied Tubby, tapping his forehead. He then smiled at the unhappy-looking group.*

*"Oh crap," said Roger.*

*"So…" said Tammy, "where next, my friend?"*

*"We could go down there?" suggested Tubby, gesturing into the gloom of a corridor to their left.*

*"Right," said Roger, getting up.*

*"But I wouldn't, if I were you," said Tubby, as he watched the Norse Fighter marching off.*

*Roger stopped mid-stride and then returned to the group. He sat down again and began counting one to ten to himself.*

*"The other direction leads to a series of rock pools and three treasure chests," said Tubby, with a gleam in his eye.*

*"Now you're talking," enthused Obby. "Treasure chests. Brilliant!"*

*"But…" said Tubby, slowly.*

*"Don't tell me," murmured Roger, as he reached ten for the third time, "They're guarded?"*

*"Just a bit," replied Tubby and he began to pick his teeth with a small toothpick.*

*"A bit?" tried the Snark Maiden.*

*"I can get you into a corridor which leads… to their rear," said Tubby.*

*"Their rear?" Roger frowned at the goblin.*

*"Well, what are we waiting for?" asked Obby, hefting his large sword.*

*"Whose rear?" asked Roger, voicing the thoughts of the other members of the group.*

*"Nothing that you should worry about. Piece of cake, I should think," said Tubby, a huge grin breaking out across his face.*

*"Let's get going then," urged Obby, impatiently.*

*"One other thing," said Tubby.*

*The group looked at him again.*

*"It's just a thought," Tubby continued, "But are any of you interested in a barrel of treacle? I can give you an unbeatable price with a good discount, because you are friends of Tammy here. What do you say?"*

*"Unbelievable," muttered Roger.*

*"Right," said Obby, smacking his lips. "Time to get our hands on some serious plunder."*

*Roger sighed and started off into the gloom.*

*"Just a suggestion," continued Tubby, adjusting his bow tie. "You have a good think about it and let me know if you would like a barrel… or two. It's an offer that you'd be crazy to turn down."*

"I want some answers and I want them now!" shouted Chief Inspector Pringle.

"I don't know what you're talking about," replied the man in the chair in interrogation room two.

"So, you're denying that you are part of a gang which enters language schools, vandalises them and steals confidential information… and their money."

"Absolutely. Why would I do any of that? I'm a respectable citizen."

"And walking the streets of London in a grubby panda suit makes you respectable, does it?"

"It's better than what some people wear," responded Dave Springett, moodily.

"Mr Springett, you may recall that we've met before in other circumstances. I had your card marked then and I still have it marked now. You're a villain, Mr Springett. I know it and you know it."

"We've met before?" frowned Springett, wracking his brain.

"In a robot suit on Box Hill."

"My robot suit," murmured Springett. "Those were the days..."

"Quite," snapped Pringle. "And now you dress up as a panda and stand around the centre of London begging all day."

"Begging?" spluttered Springett. "Begging," he repeated. "I'll have you know that the profession of motionless artistes is well respected and admired the world over. We do not beg. We entertain!"

"You stand about doing nothing all day and... that's entertainment?" quipped Pringle.

"You try standing perfectly still for hours on end. It takes a lot of skill and breathing control," said Springett, hotly.

"But you still just do nothing and expect people to give you money. That sounds very much like the definition of begging to me," tried Pringle again.

"There speaks a typical philistine who doesn't have a shred of art in his whole establishment body!" exclaimed Springett, passionately.

"I like going to see plays now and then," uttered a hurt Pringle. There was then a short pause as the police inspector wondered why this crook had called him a Palestinian.

"So... why am I here then?" asked Springett, folding his arms.

"Right, Mr Springett. How long have you owned a Panama hat?"

"What?"

"The hat?" repeated Pringle.

"The hat? I bought it at Camden Market last January I think."

"Mr Springett. You are in a lot of trouble," muttered Pringle angrily. "And I want to know all about Percy Raymond Gabbitt as well."

"Percy? Does he have a hat?"

"Don't play games with me."

"What's he been up to now? Nicking Panama hats?"

"Why don't you tell me?"

"I've no idea..."

"'Denial' is always the first reaction when you've been nabbed red-handed by the police," said the Chief Inspector. "Let's move quickly on through all the other phases to 'acceptance', shall we? It would save a lot of time."

"But I don't..."

"I believe that Anger is next, Mr Springett. Then bargaining followed by grief and finally acceptance. We are experts at handling phases one and two; we don't really care about three and four. We just wish all villains would just move straight to phase five. It would save an enormous amount of police time, energy and manpower. I know you're an intelligent sort of man, despite your rather eccentric outward behaviour. So, Mr Springett, let me ask you once more: what is Percy Gabbitt up to and when did you last speak to him?"

"I told everything I know to detective Ford," mumbled Springett. "At the pub," he added, limply.

"And you told him all about this gang of terrorist vandals who are attacking schools the length and breadth of the country?"

"No," said Springett, after a long think.

"So, we're still in denial, are we? Fair enough, Mr Springett. Let's play it your way then. It's going to be a long night."

"I thought denial was in Egypt," said Springett.

# THIRTEEN

*"One crowded hour is worth an age without a name."*
**(Sir Walter Scott, who must have met Percy Gabbitt in an earlier life)**

The flight back to Shanghai and subsequent bus ride to Suzhou had been fairly uneventful, although getting a holdall onto their plane stuffed with enough money to buy a small Chinese city had been mildly problematical. Both Irwin and Gabbitt knew that it would be highly unlikely that a policeman would stop and search them, but there was always a chance. Nothing happened though and the two of them sped out of Shanghai in their taxi feeling tired, but elated.

Gabbitt had not managed to get to the panda sanctuary, but he felt that he had actually achieved something better in getting to see new born panda cubs in the hospital next to Big Bang Travel. That image would live with him forever.

They arrived in Suzhou in one piece and were soon ensconced in Bob Burley's office at the back of Arapacana Associates. Needless to say, the champagne was flowing and people were clapping and cheering as well.

"Another bottle, I think," shouted Burley and reached into his own private refrigerator. There was a louder cheer from a group of employees gathered in the doorway to his office.

"Incredible!" exclaimed Burley as he popped the bottle and started refilling flutes. "Totally amazing," he added, as he reached for Gabbitt's outstretched glass. "You've only been with us for a few days and you've already levelled one school, burnt down an agency and retrieved a pile of stolen money. Unbelievable! The Gabbitt factor."

"It was poetry in motion," muttered Bob Irwin, seated to Gabbitt's left. "Just being with the master on a mission is enough. The man's a walking miracle," he said, downing his glass in one and reaching for Burley's bottle.

There was more cheering and then someone started singing: 'For he's a jolly good fellow…'

As the song finished and everyone started cheering and laughing again, Bob Burley sat down in his chair and stared at both Irwin and Gabbitt. "I've just emailed our good friend Emily at Northampton University to say that the money is being transferred today that all is well in the world. She will be one happy little bunny when she reads that, I can tell you."

"That's good," responded Gabbitt, quietly.

"Good!" exploded Burley. "It's bloody fantastic! We now have excellent relations with another university and have expunged the world of another dodgy agent. Arapacana strikes again!" he exclaimed loudly and held up his flute. "To Arapacana, Percy and Bob here."

There was another loud cheer and everyone guzzled their drinks.

"Bloody amazing," said Burley again, as he reached inside the refrigerator for another bottle.

"Pleased I could help," said Gabbitt, a little limply.

"And they called you a friend of China too?" queried Burley, still in a state of shock. "Even after all that?"

"Well, we did sort of save their baby pandas," murmured Gabbitt, feeling a little embarrassed for some reason.

There were a few 'Ahs' and the odd 'Bless' from the predominantly female presence in the room. Gabbitt had clearly struck a chord there too.

"Percy Gabbitt," cried Burley suddenly. "There are two types of people in this country. Friends of China and Foreign Big Noses. Not many of us move from the latter to the former without a lot of luck."

"Foreign Big Noses?" queried Gabbitt.

"That's what they call us when we arrive. You have to spend a lifetime trying to understand the Chinese way before one day a kind Chinese man or woman will decide that your long nose does not matter any more and will then welcome you to the Friend of China Club. Yet again you've amazed me, Percy."

"Oh, thank you."

"Oh, don't thank me, Percy," continued Burley, clearly onto a pet subject. "To the Chinese we are all lumped together into one group called 'Laowai'. No matter what we do or where we are from, we are all Laowai, which incidentally can be translated as Old Foreigner and is neither meant to be either complimentary or insulting. Within this category there are many subsections, two of which are, as I said earlier, the Big Noses and the Friends. Most of us, who have been here years, are still very much still in the Big Nose section or... I should add," Burley said, looking critically at Irwin, "in another section entitled Foreign Devil."

"And Friend of China is the best category?" asked Gabbitt blithely.

"You can't get much higher," beamed Burley. "You'll be telling us next that you've been invited to join the local Communist Party."

There was a rustle of nervous laughter in the room.

"You see, Percy," said Burley leaning back in his chair, "Most foreigners never really fit in here for a shedload of reasons. Never mind the spitting and the bad driving. It's other things too which you'll soon come across. Then there are others who take to it all like a duck to water and end up loving it. They come to realise that the Chinese are not so bad really and actually quite like it here."

There was a long pause while Burley and his audience took all this in. "Have a look at my wall," said Burley suddenly.

"Your wall?" queried Gabbitt in surprise.

"Just read this," said Burley, standing up and carefully unhooking a small picture frame from behind his desk. He handed it to Gabbitt, who stared at it uncomprehendingly. There were two poems written in bold ink behind the glass. Gabbitt started reading.

**Ode to the Laowai**

**I don't spit and I don't smoke**
**And don't understand when you make a joke.**
**In public parks I don't urinate**
**Or go to Pizza Hut on a first date.**
**I don't drive through red lights**
**Or get into silly pushing fights.**
**I don't shout into my mobile phone**
**Which has a very loud ringing tone.**
**I don't stare into other people's trolleys**
**At supermarkets when buying Hello Kitty brollies.**
**On buses and trains I don't push and shove**
**As if I have god given rights from up above.**
**I don't wear an English fox-hunting hat**
**On my electric bike, looking like a right prat.**
**I don't think foreigners are all American**
**Or call myself Gun, Carrot or X-Man.**
**I don't still think that London is foggy**
**Or throw stones at the neighbour's moggy.**
**In the streets I don't wear my jim-jams**
**Or buy from mucky barrows my hot yams.**
**I don't chuck my waste into the river**

**Or drink Great Wall wine to ruin my liver.**
**But I DO say thank you,**
**If kind things are what you do,**
**For I am Laowai.**

Gabbitt paused for a moment and considered criticising the way it scanned. To be honest, the poem was a structural nightmare. However, he decided that silence was probably the best reaction. After all, he did not know who had written the thing. It could even have been Burley himself, though some of the lines smacked of an Australian influence. He frowned and started the second poem.

**Ode to the Chinese**

**We walk the streets feeling safe and sound**
**No one thinks of mugging us from behind.**
**Everyone is part of our family**
**And chatting with strangers is not thought silly.**
**We like to be part of every conversation**
**And we really love our massive nation.**
**Everything in China is totally possible**
**And nothing is seen as instantly disposable.**
**We find a use for every little thing**
**Be it a duck's foot, beak or scrawny wing.**
**Of our history we are so very proud**
**And 'we are Chinese' we want to shout very loud.**
**We work very hard for our nation**
**Top country in the world is our destination.**
**And you may think it rather funny**
**But we simply love making lots of money.**
**Into the streets we like to go**
**Happily shouting at foreigners: "Hello".**
**We go about our work at a fast pace**
**Trying above all to save face.**
**For everything we charge an elastic fee**
**And wine and dine our bosses for added 'guanxi'.**

**Yes, China is certainly the place to be**
**If you love good food and RMB!**

"Very nice," mumbled Gabbitt, not at all sure what to say next, though he was sorely tempted to have a go at the author over the rhyming of 'possible' with 'disposable'. Nasty that. Very nasty, thought Gabbitt, gritting his literary teeth.

"The first was written by an ex-colleague here who hated every second and couldn't wait for his contract to end," explained Burley. "He was then back to Pittsburgh before you could say 'Welcome to Steeler Country'. The second was written by Pamela here."

"That's me," said a voice at the door. "It's not very good but sort of gets the message across," she said in breathless embarrassment.

"I see what you mean," said Gabbitt, honestly.

"Not very good at poems... and stuff," added Pamela, quietly.

Gabbitt turned to have a good look at the budding Arapacana poet laureate, but she bobbed back into the office where she busied herself with a hole-puncher.

"Very modest," whispered Burley and smiled broadly.

There were then a few quiet minutes as everyone seemed to drift off into their own worlds and thought about luck, modesty, Percy, Northampton, piles of money, burning schools, Big Noses, Friends of China, poems and, in Irwin's case, getting another refill. It was then that Bob Burley took a deep breath and leaned forward onto his desk.

"And now… to our biggest task!" he boomed, loudly.

Instantly, the noise died down and tipsy employees attempted to grapple with a situation which required serious thought and not cheering and clapping at the end of every sentence.

"I'm pleased you're all here," began Burley, putting his glass down and adopting a tone of gravity. "We have to start thinking hard about the ICAS exhibition in Shanghai next month."

"The what?" queried Gabbitt, thickly. The champagne was starting to take a firm hold of his senses.

"The International Conference for Agents and Schools," said Burley. "It takes place once a year and attracts about eight hundred delegates from all over the world, including, of course, a fair number of the ones we are trying to..."

"Whack," interrupted Irwin, aggressively.

"Well, not quite that," said Burley with a frown. "But probably whacking is not such a bad word, given our exploits this week," he said and grinned widely at Gabbitt.

"We need to draw up a battle plan," he said, suddenly seriously again. "I want to take down about fifty of the most corrupt swines in one go," he concluded and sat back in his chair as a dozen drunken gasps echoed around his small office.

"Yeh...whack the lot of them," gurgled Irwin, dreamily and took another slug at his champagne flute.

"OK. Clear your mind of everything. Have you done that?"

"I think so."

"Well you have or you haven't."

"OK. Done now."

"Sure?"

"Wait a second… yes, all clear now."

"Right. Without thinking about it, say the first three animals that come into your mind. Quickly! Now!"

"Err. Sloth, squirrel and fruit bat."

"And those really were the first animals that came into your mind?"

"Yes."

"Are you sure?"

"Absolutely. So, what does it mean?"

"Oh dear, Dave."

"Come on Cas. Does it mean I have unsolvable psychological problems?"

"And you need me to tell you that?"

"So, spill the beans, Cas."

"The first animal you say is how you see yourself, the second how others see you and the third, is your true self. And don't call me Cas. You know how much I hate that."

"So, you see me as a squirrel, do you?"

"Well…"

"And a sloth! Brilliant!" exclaimed Springett, happily, "They are probably the animal kingdom's answer to the motionless artiste!"

"I see what you mean," said Caroline, keen to move on.

"Did you know that the fastest that a sloth can move is five metres an hour? Isn't that cool? Five metres an hour. So, if it spots a tasty bit of food like a banana in a tree thirty metres away, it would take… err.. a pretty long time to get it."

"Six hours," murmured Caroline.

"Six hours to get a banana that close. The same amount of time it takes to fly from London to Chicago. Isn't that amazing?"

"Absolutely," commented the totally unamazed Caroline.

"A sloth's fine by me," said Springett.

There was a deceptively long pause.

"Also, if you shoot one while it's hanging upside down in a tree, it remains there, until it rots away. Its claws lock onto the branch, apparently." Springett chortled happily.

"Really," responded a bored Caroline, now wishing she had not mentioned the animal thing in the first place, although she did wonder somewhat fleetingly if shooting Springett would have the same results.

"They don't have any natural predators either," said Springett, wistfully. He was clearly beginning to see slothdom as a definite step-up from being human in central London. "I wish I were a sloth," he concluded and stuffed another shovel-load of chips into his mouth.

"Whatever..." began Caroline, taking another sup at her Earl Grey and looking longingly out of the window.

"Not sure where the fruit bat fits in though. I wouldn't fancy flying around totally blind all night and then hanging upside down in a dank cave all day. Sounds like a very unpleasant way to live out your life. No, that's not really me."

"You're not supposed to take it literally. The idea is to make you think about yourself a little. Think about your personality and how people might view you," said Caroline, with a small sigh.

"What were your three?"

Caroline frowned and continued supping.

"I told you mine, so it's only fair that..." started Springett.

"Rabbit, cow and gorilla," muttered Caroline, resignedly.

"Ah."

Caroline Williams and Dave Springett were sitting at a table in The Screaming Egg near Piccadilly Circus. Caroline was eating a blueberry muffin and drinking an Earl Grey tea while Springett was busy consuming a large pile of chips liberally laced with tomato ketchup and brown sauce. They were waiting.

"Where did you read that? Bella or Cosmo?"

"I don't read magazines."

"What? Never?"

"All right, I don't buy magazines. If they're in front of me in the Dentist's or the Doctor's waiting room, then I may just flick through them, as I'm sure you do."

"Never read rubbish like that. I prefer more intellectual stuff like History Today and The Economist," sniffed Springett and loaded another pile of chips onto his fork.

"Nuts, Tits, Chicks and Air-Head. You have a pile of them on a chair by the toilet in your flat. Are they intellectual as well?"

"I didn't know gorillas had such good memories."

"Indeed."

Springett burst out laughing and sat back in his chair.

"So, do you want to hear my story then?" he asked suddenly.

"What story?" responded Caroline, moodily.

"This sloth was arrested again yesterday," said Springett, happily.

"You're joking of course," said a rather weary Caroline.

"Nope. Grabbed by about twenty constables as I walked to the pub near Oxford Street. There was a raid going on and I was collateral damage."

"Collateral…" began Caroline.

"Caught up in friendly fire," said Springett, jabbing at a particularly large chip and dipping into the small lake of brown sauce at the side of his plate. "There was a raid going on at that school we were talking about while online the other day – the one with the daft name."

"The Happy Snappy School of English," interrupted Caroline, utilising her gorilla-like, photographic memory to the full.

"That's the one," agreed Springett, as he popped the chip into his mouth.

"The police were raiding the school as you walked by?"

"And arresting anyone in a Panama hat."

"You've lost me there, Dave," said Caroline, slowly putting her tea mug down onto the table.

"Me too," said Springett. "Anyway, I was thrown into a van and then carted off to Marylebone nick with about thirty other blokes in hats. Nice bunch too. One of them was a poet, another an actor at the National and…"

"I get the picture, Dave," said Caroline.

"So… we get to the police station and then I'm put into a room and asked lots of questions about vandalising property, breaking and entering and generally getting on the police's nerves. They even wanted to know where I got the panda suit from."

"What?"

"I know. I had absolutely no idea what they were talking about. Then, guess what?"

"I have no idea, Dave."

"That stupid inspector we all know only too well walked in and asked me straight out if I knew where Percy was and if I'd been in recent contact with him."

"No."

"Yes."

"Kept telling me that I was in denial."

"I thought that was in Eg…"

"Yes, I said that too. He didn't laugh."

"It's not that funny," sighed Caroline.

"I was then given a two-hour going over, which mostly revolved around our friend in China. They seemed very interested in him again."

"Whatever for?" asked Caroline, worriedly.

"Beats me. The inspector just wanted to know where he was, when I last spoke to him and if I knew if he had anything to do with vandalising properties in London lately."

"No, is the short answer," said Caroline. "He's in China, for god's sake. How could he wreck anything in the UK?"

They both looked at each other for a few moments.

"No, not even Percy could manage that," muttered Caroline, unsurely.

"Anyway, this idiot of an inspector then warned me that he's got his eye on me. I was then let go. Daft or what?"

"And you never found out what all the hat business was about?"

"No. Probably a case of mistaken identity. A sloth in a Panama hat. Now there's a picture. Anyway, I've decided to wear that hat at all times from now on," said Springett, loudly.

"Why? It might get you arrested again."

"Exactly," responded Springett. "A panda in a Panama hat. Really cool."

The door opened to the café and Joe Slimm walked in. He had a harried and bedraggled look about him. Even his trademark grey Macintosh seemed unusually creased.

"Sod it!" he exclaimed and sat down.

"Tea?" queried Caroline, as if a cup of Twinings would solve most problems which began with that exclamation. She then looked severely at Springett.

"Right, I'll get the teas in," he said, "although at five metres an hour, it may take a bit of time getting to the counter, ordering the teas and…"

"Then you'd better get going now," said Caroline with eye-brows high in the air.

Springett sighed and jabbed his fork into the middle of what was left of the chips. The fork stood up in the air like a thrown javelin. He then slowly stood up and pretended to walk to the counter in exaggerated slow motion.

"So, what's happening in your life, Joe?" asked Caroline, nibbling at her muffin.

"You wouldn't believe it. It's mind-boggling."

"More surprises. This is becoming quite a memorable lunchtime," said Caroline. "The kids at Turpington up to their tricks again?"

"No, not this time," shuddered Slimm.

"You haven't had another joy ride, have you?"

"If only."

"Not kidnapped by penguins?"

"No," shuddered Slimm again, as memories of that little incident flooded back.

"So?"

"Teletubbies. I really hate them, especially the purple one."

"The Teletubbies," repeated Caroline slowly. This was clearly going to be a long lunch hour.

"Ground-breaking kids programme," said Springett, as he sat down holding three steaming mugs of tea. "Actually, the purple one is the only soundly politically-correct one, being so outwardly gay. La La, the yellow one is just a stupid, vapid bimbo, while the red one, Po, is brain dead. I forget what the green one's name is or what he's like, except that he's supposed to be multi-racial and have had sex with La La when the cameras were off, while still on set. At least, that's what The Sun said."

There was a long pause as Caroline and Slimm stared at Springett.

"Tinky-Winky," said Slimm slowly.

"Yes, that's the fellow's name," responded Springett.

"What?"

"The purple one with the Afro-Caribbean face."

"Have you quite finished?"

"That's probably what La La…"

"Enough Dave! Enough!" exclaimed Caroline, putting her mug down loudly.

"Cow! Sorry, make that gorilla," muttered Springett.

Caroline frowned hard.

"I thought they were just blokes dressed up in daft costumes saying unconnected sentences and running around a hillside terrorising the indigenous rabbit population," said Slimm, happy to step into Springett's world for a few insane moments.

"Will you two please stop talking about the Teletubbies?" sighed Caroline, in exasperation.

"Very clever programme," continued Springett, after a long and noisy sup of his tea. "Tellies in their tummies, a thinking vacuum cleaner and a machine that makes toasted pancakes. Far ahead of its time, if you ask me."

Right," said Caroline. "Any more mention of the Teletubbies and I'm off."

"Not as good as The Clangers but…"

"The purple gay one was in my house," interrupted Slimm, quietly. "It then drugged me and tried to catnap Nixon."

"Right," said Caroline, taking a very long sup of Earl Grey. "I'm off."

"It's true. I'm not joking, Caroline. I couldn't make stuff up like this. I'm not Dave."

"That's true," said Caroline reaching for her mug of tea again.

"You haven't been smoking the happy stuff, have you?" asked Springett, as he finished his chips and began mopping up the grease and ketchup with a large slice of white bread.

"I wish I had," murmured Slimm. "It's too horribly true."

"What happened?" asked Caroline, feeling for once lost for words.

The next few minutes saw Slimm telling the whole sorry tale of DC Ford's visit to Turpington Comprehensive, the drugs talk and then the events in Gabbitt's house afterwards.

"I woke up on the kitchen floor with those two pensioners from next door standing over me. That gave me quite a turn, I can tell you. I don't usually sleep in the kitchen, you see."

There was a respectful few moments of silence as the three of them mulled over the obvious drawbacks of having a doze in a kitchen.

"They said that that bastard Teletubby had tried to grab Nixon for some mad reason. Steal the cat, for god's sake. What's the police force coming to? It's not even a stray."

"Did it get the cat?" asked Caroline, deciding to play along for a few more moments.

"Never mind the damn cat! What about me!" exclaimed Slimm.

"Well, you've clearly come through your ordeal in more or less one piece," said Caroline, sweetly. "But we don't know about Percy's cat, do we?"

"He's fine," said Slimm, after a short supping pause. "That mad old bloke next door beat the copper up with a garden rake and then sent him on his way. Apparently, he hates Teletubbies more than I do."

"He assaulted a policeman?" queried Caroline, worriedly.

"A detective too," muttered Slimm.

"Glory be!" exclaimed Springett.

"So more small cells and interrogations in the offing for Mr Joseph Bruce Slimm then?"

"Shit, I hope not," replied Slimm, unhappily.

"Did he say why he wanted to steal Nixon?"

"DC Ford, that's the detective's name, never got that far. We were just talking the usual rubbish about the school, the Teletubbies and life and then suddenly he spikes my drink and I'm out cold in the kitchen for the next two hours. Bastard! If you can't trust coppers nowadays, then who can you trust?"

There was a long pause and then a thoughtful Dave Springett spoke. "What did you say this copper's name was?"

"Detective Constable Ford," replied Slimm.

"Ah," said Springett, slowly putting down his knife and fork. "Then I think we all need to have a little talk."

"I think we need to have a little talk," croaked Detective Constable Ford and limped into Chief Inspector Pringle's office.

"What in god's name happened to you?" asked Pringle, as he surveyed the broken man before him.

"Don't ask," replied Ford, wheezily.

"You look terrible," added Pringle.

"Three broken ribs, heavy bruising on both legs and a sprained wrist," murmured Ford and sat down heavily.

"What the hell happened?"

"I'd prefer not to talk about it," winced Ford, as a shot of pain electrified his calf muscles.

"I thought you said you wanted to have a little talk. Did you get the cat?" asked Pringle, slowly.

"No sir, I didn't!" was the heated reply. "I was unable to apprehend the aforesaid feline, mainly because I was assaulted by a rather vicious member of the general public."

Not a slightly elderly member…" began Pringle, his voice trailing off.

"Yes sir," whispered DC Ford between painful gasps. "A positively ancient member of the general public. But a member who knows how to inflict pain in the maximum sort of way with a variety of garden implements."

It was Chief Inspector Pringle's turn for a wince as he imagined the one-sided confrontation between Alfred Fennell, weathered veteran of several wars and major participant in the Battle of Box Hill… and his rather 'green' and untried detective constable.

"Not that easy protecting yourself when you're still all dressed up in that ridiculous suit either," muttered Ford angrily.

"You were wearing the Teletubby suit in his garden?" uttered an appalled Pringle. It was a well-known fact that the homicidal pensioner had particularly strong feelings when it came to Teletubbies. It was in his file, underlined heavily.

"I only just got away from the bastard," squeaked Ford, trying to shift into a less painful position. "He chased me down the road all the way into Bromley Common. Only gave up when I lost him by dodging into The Crown and Cushion. And that wasn't very nice either. A man in a Tinky-Winky outfit should approach running into gay pubs with a great deal of caution, sir."

The Chief Inspector shuddered once more. He stared at the detective constable and could not help feeling slightly sorry for the man. He had obviously had a swine of a day.

"Go home Ford," he said quietly. "Take the rest of the week off."

"With respect, no, sir," said Ford. "I'm due into Dark Dawn Three in about an hour and feel that my new compadres will need the aid of Obby the Gladiator in level four. I can't just let the game 'dynamic' do everything for me. It would lack that personal touch and besides, I might learn something new about this Gabbitt fellow and his homicidal mates. We got that good lead with that language school through this, didn't we?" puffed Ford.

"Indeed, we did, Detective Constable," replied Pringle, uncomfortably. "Although that didn't quite pan out the way we had planned either."

"Shit, sir," said Ford with feeling.

"They're very well organised, Ford. Even used a rather inventive diversion to get us running in the wrong direction at the start."

"A diversion, sir?"

"It doesn't matter, Ford. We just have to be better prepared next time round."

"Bloody swines!" exclaimed Ford, through the pain.

"Hmmm," murmured Pringle. "We did however manage to arrest a particularly nasty fellow who seemed to have been running quite a high-level scam involving lots of Iranian money."

"But no sign of the gang we're after?"

"No, Ford. The swines just disappeared into thin air, despite a trawl of the area after the raid."

"Shit!"

"And there were Gabbitt fingerprints everywhere again."

"Christ, sir! How does he do it?"

"I just wish I knew," muttered Pringle, unhappily. "We fell nicely into their trap and did exactly what we were expected to - namely to arrest and charge the bloody manager of the school. Another success chalked up for the Language School Gang and another school cleaned of all corruption. Makes you sick," muttered Pringle.

"What next, sir?"

"Forget about the cat, detective Constable. I think we will have to shelve that idea for the time being. You get back into that dungeon, while I have a long think about how to get Percy Raymond Gabbitt back to the UK to answer a few of our questions. Phases one and three may have been slight setbacks but we still have phase two."

"Ah yes, the secret phase which only you know about," said Ford, acidly.

"Indeed," said Pringle through pursed lips, as he thought about Nero Handsworth and the possible violent contribution that he might lend to the proceedings.

The man himself was having high tea in his cell in Wormwood Scrubs. He was sitting by himself and feeling rather contemplative.

Thoughts of actually getting his hands around Percy Gabbitt's scrawny neck then invaded his mind for the millionth time. That bastard would pay dearly. His hand trembled slightly as he picked up a cucumber sandwich.

It had been a long day for Nero, but ultimately a satisfying one, all in all. Chipchase and Bibby were nicely booked onto a plane to the Orient while the other participants in his ingenious Irish Stand-Off had been informed of the likely time-line of events. It would be an interesting twenty-four hours when Percy flippin' Gabbitt eventually did set foot back in this country. Only Slicing Sammy was proving to be a problem – the maniac wanted to add a few unnecessary creative touches.

And now this. Nero picked up a rather nastily-designed magazine and flicked through the pages. What an incredibly dull piece of work? Who would spend even a minute of their lives dwelling on the articles in this piece of rubbish? He looked at the cover page again.

*'The Language Teacher'*

God, they were making magazines about this sort of thing now. What a sad and tired world it was, thought Nero.

The door to his cell opened and a large man with muscles bulging on his muscles, walked in.

"Finished your tea yet, boss?" he grunted deeply.

"Does it look like I've finished?" replied Nero, throwing the magazine onto his bed. It flopped open onto a centre page spread.

"Thought you wouldn't have much use for that fairy cake, boss," said the massive mountain of sinew, as he eyed the small sponge cake with bright red cherry perched on the top.

"What?"

"Never mind, boss," said the man and retreated out of the cell in a hang-dog and defeated sort of way.

Nero sighed. Prisons did odd things to people. He was about to put in an order for an extra pot of Darjeeling when his eyes strayed over the hated magazine again. He frowned and picked it up.

The centre page article which covered the two pages suddenly had his full attention. Nero read quickly and took it all in. He then sat down on his bed and smiled. Another nice little thread to add to his cobweb, he thought maliciously.

A conference.

And in Shanghai too.

What a nice coincidence.

Nero thought at a million miles an hour and then came to a decision. He would finish his tea first and then telephone those two idiots to tell them that they were about to be recruited as school representatives attending this damn silly conference.

Perfect, thought Nero. Perfect. An international conference in Shanghai for everyone in this hated trade. And all in one place. What an absolutely dreadful thought!

Percy bloody Gabbitt would not be able to resist such a ridiculous event. After all, he lived in China and it was a conference for teachers from all over China. It could not have been better.

It was just a shame that he could not arrange nuking the venue. On the other hand…

*"Well, for once, things are going quite well," said Roger the Norse Fighter. He looked at Tammy the Goblin and smiled in that way which implied a job done well.*

*"Thirty-five ratmen butchered and not so much as a scratch on any of us," sniffed Tammy, thoughtfully.*

*"As I said, the perfect bloody day," commented Roger deliberately belligerently and wiped his sword across the back of a dead ratman the way all heroes did after a bloody encounter.*

*"Told you they would be surprised," chirped a small figure in a red bow tie and clutching a briefcase to his chest."*

*"They were absolutely astonished," chuckled Li Bang Cho, as he looted the bodies of precious jewels, money and the odd food pouch.*

*"And I didn't have to use any of my arrows either," added the Snark Maiden, rattling a full quiver, contentedly.*

*"Not quite the heroically memorable encounter though, was it?" sighed Tammy. "More like a bit of ratmen extermination."*

*"Now look," said Roger, angrily. "I'm not getting into an argument about what's fair and what's not. We won a battle, all right. It was only a small one, but we managed to get our hands on three treasure chests and countless arrows for Miss Snark Maiden*

*here. And none of us got hurt. I call that a good day's work," he finished in a way that implied that he did not really believe what he was saying.*

*"Is he always like this?" whispered Tubby into Tammy's ear.*

*"He used to be worse," replied Tammy. "But I've only had a short time to educate him. He's a bit confused now, not knowing whether to be heroic or just be successful."*

*"What was that?" asked Roger, dangerously.*

*"Oh nothing," replied Tammy. "You get back to counting up all your well-earned plunder."*

*"So, what now?" asked a figure lounging by the entrance to the cavern.*

*"Ah yes, Obby," intoned Endymion, slowly. "What next indeed? What shall we all do now? What do you think?"*

*"Well, I'm not sure," replied Obby, uncomfortably. "Probably have a few more level four fights and then get back to level five and rescue that goblinesse."*

*"Sounds good to me," said Li Bang Cho. "We'll be able to raid the villains' safe house and then apprehend the swines."*

*"Well, not sure about that," said Obby, feeling acutely uncomfortable at the sudden police-speak.*

*"Enough of that," snapped the Snark Maiden. "I think we should immediately scout out those caves down there," she said, pointing at a very unwelcome and distinctly dark corridor leading savagely downwards. "And I think our best warrior should*

*blaze the trail. The hero with the biggest weapon. What do you think, Obby?"*

*"Well, I don't mind," he murmured. "As long as I have you lot right behind me."*

*"Don't worry," said Li Bang Cho. "You'll have all the back-up you need."*

*"That's all right then," grunted Obby and started towards the corridor.*

*"But that's..." began Tubby, the goblin map reader.*

*He stopped when he felt the tip of Roger's sword making its presence felt on the nape of his neck.*

*"But that's... a wonderful route to take," he said quickly.*

*The sword point disappeared as quickly as it had appeared.*

The police had just left.

Alfred Fennell sat down heavily into his favourite armchair and turned the television on. He was in a sour mood.

"I told you about getting violent," muttered Hilda, as she entered the living room.

"Bastard Teletubby. And in my garden too. The bastard," he repeated venomously.

"Yes dear, tried Hilda, using her best placatory voice. "Now you have a nice cup of tea and don't worry about silly men in purple suits."

"A Teletubby in my garden, if you please," repeated the appalled Alfred again. "I've never seen the like of it before."

"Well, he wasn't that happy either, dear," said Hilda, as she sat down and reached for a finger biscuit.

"What do you mean?" asked Alfred, belligerently.

"No one likes to be hit on the head with a rake, dear, not even a Teletubby," said Hilda, as she supped her PG Tips.

"I'd do it again, no matter what that young constable said," barked Alfred loudly, as if the said constable was still lurking at his front door, taking notes.

"You can't keep taking the law into your own hands. The policemen don't like it and it's bad for your shingles. You know that, dear."

Alfred shifted uncomfortably in his seat. "I'll fetch him a nice one with my shovel next time. I don't care if he's Sherlock Holmes or the king of England. He had no right to be on my lawn - and in a Teletubby suit too. The bastard! And then I'll get my belt to him, if he dares..."

"No, you won't dear," interrupted the voice of reason.

"In my garden," said Alfred again. "My garden."

"At least he didn't get his nasty Teletubby paws on Nixon," creaked Hilda as she tousled the chin of a deeply purring black and white cat which lay at her feet. "Don't you worry, my little friend," she continued. "We'll look after you, from now one. No one's going to take you away. And we'll get someone nice to look after you while we're away in China, don't you worry."

The purring seemed to grow louder to Hilda's ears and she settled back into her chair nibbling at the finger biscuit, thoughtfully.

"In my garden too, the little beggar," whispered Alfred to the world.

"And don't forget to remind me about stopping the milk and the papers while we're away, Alf," said Hilda.

"In my garden. My garden," whispered her traumatised husband.

"Yes, I know, dear."

"Would you credit it?"

"Yes, dear. Can you turn the volume up? Eastenders is about to start. I want to find out if that Darren really is the father of little Tracey."

"The bastard," muttered the voice from the other armchair, probably echoing the views of three-quarters of the nation, but for entirely different reasons.

# FOURTEEN

*"She'll never be popular because of her face. She must increase her personality to succeed."*
(Suzhou University student's view on her friend's 'plainness')

"But I don't know nothing about schools," said Ronald Chipchase thickly. "I always hated them as a boy and was pleased to be shot of them when I was sixteen."

"No one is asking you to go back to school," said Nero Handsworth, with consummate patience. "It's a ruse."

"A what?"

"Just a way of getting you into the damn place."

"We could just break a few locks off and get in that way."

Nero Handsworth sighed and then used the receiver as a makeshift hammer to kill a housefly which had perched on the window-sill near the pay phone he was using.

"Ouch," came a voice from the other end.

"Just listen to me," tried Nero again. "This stupid conference takes place in two short weeks and I want you two to enrol as representatives of a language school in London."

"But we don't work for a schoo..." began Chipchase again. There was another loud clang at the other end of the line.

"I don't care," said Nero, slightly louder. "I have just been online and you are now the official representatives of The Scrubs School of English attending an educational conference in Shanghai. Next week. And that's final. Do you understand?"

"The what?"

"The Scrubs... oh never mind. The important thing is that you have been registered and we have paid the necessary fees and stuff like that. All you have to do is turn up."

"But we don't..."

"Which is why I want both of you here today for a little... briefing. You seem to forget that I ran one of those god-awful places not so long ago."

"But..."

"Please don't say anything, Mr Chipchase... except yes."

There was a short pause and a long sigh from the other end. "We still haven't forgotten the... van incident, Mr 'andsworth," came the serious response.

"Ah... that," said Nero and slumped against a grubby wall. "The elephant in the room."

"The eleph..."

"It doesn't matter. I can only say that I am sorry. Very sorry. I really am," he said, a mite insincerely. "Luckily, you have both recovered. Maybe it's time to put all that behind us. See all this as the beginning of a new relationship together. A new page. Let bygones be bygones, Mr Chipchase. Forgive and forget. Time to move on. That was just a business decision then. It's ancient history now. And let's not forget that I'm also paying you quite handsomely for my misdemeanours of the past."

"When do you want us to come to your nick?" asked Chipchase, who had clearly not forgiven or forgotten.

"Be here about four,' replied Nero. "I have my sauna at three you see. "

"Right."

"And I've already got a couple of the lads in here getting a glossy brochure sorted out for you. Luckily, the prison newspaper has a pretty good graphics package. Am I making any sense to you, Chipchase?"

"No," came the reply.

"Well, in a nut shell, it's no use turning up at a place like that with nothing to put on your table."

"Brochures?" came the delayed retort.

"Yes, the sort of thing that people read when they want to get to know all about your company."

"We've never needed things like that for our security firm," said Chipchase, honestly.

"Just be here with Mr Bibby at four and try not to be late. I have a meeting at five."

"I thought you were in the choky. People don't have meetings in prison, do they?"

"Got to see the governor about my cable television link. It's still rather grainy and..." Nero stopped and sighed deeply. "Just be here at four, will you?"

"One last question," asked Chipchase, chancing his arm a little.

"What?"

"What's a ruse?"

Nero closed his eyes, slowly put the phone down, said a mildly bad word and walked back to his cell wondering whether it would be stewed lamb or Entrecote Bourguignon for lunch.

<So, what do we do now?>

<Well he has to go, of course>

<Why? He's saved our bacon more than once already.

<He's a copper for heavens sake. I've a million questions I'd like to ask him as to why he's infiltrated our little game>

<Just a minute... how did you tumble him, Caroline?>

<Not that difficult really. I'm angry that I didn't spot it earlier>

<Spot what?>

<His name>

<His name?>

<How did you work out that this sod was a policeman just by the name Obby? Tell me that, Caroline>

<Simple. Reverse the letters and you have Ybbo>

<?????????>

<Surely I don't have to explain the obvious?>

<Think you do, Caroline. Remember that you're dealing with a quite a low branch of the vertebrate family here>

<OK. Just look at the last two letters>

<BO>

<And now think like a policeman with a rather limited imagination>

<Well?>

<I'm still thinking>

<BO. What detective on the telly has these letters at the end of his name? Penny dropped yet?>

<Jesus, Caroline. What sort of mind have you got?>

<The sort that can spot a simple word game like that a mile off and can solve an 'Araucaria' crossword in The Guardian in about twenty minutes given no interruptions and a nice hot pot of Earl Grey and a Bourbon>

<You're not an alien, are you?>

<Do aliens like Bourbons? I never knew that, Dave>

<So… what are we going to do with Peter Falk then?>

<You got it then. Columbo>

<Yes. I'm not as daft as you think Cas. But to be serious>

<You Dave? Serious? This I have to hear>

<Right. OK. I just want to say quickly that I'm sorry about not telling you about him earlier>

<Yes, Dave. That wasn't very friendly>

<He had me by the short and curlies and I thought it wouldn't do much harm. After all, it's only a game. Thought it might be interesting watching how he managed to get Percy to come back to the UK using some sort of cunning, legal trickery. I would have told you all if it looked like he was getting us into any trouble with the police. The fact was that he's got that big sword and well, we needed his firepower>

<Still playing mind games are we, Dave?>

<Trying to>

<So when did you decide to draw the line and let us in on the secret?>

<Nixon>

<Ah>

<No one messes with your mate's cat>

<Indeed>

<And now?>

<We get him killed off I suppose>

<Not that easy with that enormous chopper of his and… I hate to say this, but he seems quite a nice fellow>

<He's a policeman who used intel gathered in one of our conversations to raid a school in London which nearly got some of Percy's colleagues arrested… and he planned a catnap!>

<There is that I suppose>

<There is another question>

<????????>

<Why does he want Percy to come back to England so much? I mean, the man has tried to get Dave drunk, then he's got all dressed up as a Teletubby at

Joe's school and he's been beaten up by your insane neighbour. It must be something really important to put himself through all that pain and suffering>

<Any ideas would be very welcome, Brain of Britain>

<Well, maybe they've got something on Percy now. They made no secret that they would be permanently after him after Box Hill. People like that Inspector have long memories and never give up. They're go at it like a dog at a bone especially with someone who so publicly rubbed their noses in it>

<And Columbo here is doing his level best to get Percy back using our little game?>

< The swine>

<So, how do we do him in then?>

<Just a minute everyone… I've had an idea>

<What a surprise! Caroline has an idea. That's certainly a novelty>

<Thanks Dave. What if… and this is only a suggestion. What if we don't try and get him killed off? We've already found out that the monsters in level four are simply not a match for that massive sword of his. It'll just be more carnage everywhere>

<So, we don't kill him off?>

<Well, he's a pretty useful member of the group and we might be able to … use him>

<Use him?>

<Yes Joe. We know that he's a copper, but he doesn't know that we know that>

<Ahh...>

<Pennies dropping>

<Not quite>

<We could actually use him by… feeding him only the stuff we want him to know>

<Dangerous, Caroline>

<Not really, Joe>
<But exciting>
<I thought you'd say something like that, Dave>
<Hello everyone. What's new?>
<Hi Percy>
<Hi Perce>
<Hello Percy>
<Have I missed anything important, or do we just strap on our weapons and get slicing? I could do with a bit of mindless chopping this evening>
<Well…> began Caroline.

Chief Inspector Pringle was in his office and feeling a little out of sorts. He stood by his window and stared out at the large car park filled with spanking white police cars. He tried counting them. Twenty-eight, if you added in the vans and tow-trucks. He sighed and turned round. Things were not going as well as they should.

He pushed the Play button of his small tape recorder and let Jon Anderson and Rick Wakeman waft him away to some environmentally-friendly planet a long way from New Scotland Yard. This one was all about something deep and serious happening in topographic oceans. It was like listening to something that Beethoven had trotted out, but with guitars and keyboards. Pringle rather liked the whole effect. Overblown, over-enthusiastic and over-indulgent, but somehow… good.

Pringle thought about the cases before him as Jon Anderson sang about everyone being a part of the sun in French. Pringle frowned. He was not so sure about that. It would get rather hot being part of the sun no matter how metaphysically you viewed the experience. And as regards singing about the whole experience in French…

He hit the Pause button and frowned. His mind turned to other things – slightly more unpleasant than standing on a star and speaking about the experience in French.

He would have to ring up that infernal blighter, Handsworth, and see how things were proceeding with phase two. In hindsight, it had been a rather desperate aberration getting that gangster involved as an active player in his team. Pringle shuddered.

Then there was Detective Constable Ford. The man was clearly enthusiastic about the whole detecting thing, but could he be trusted?

Pringle sighed again. Computer games indeed. What had gone wrong with the world? In his junior detective days, you disappeared to the local pub with notebook and pencil in hand and heard all about the 'word' on the street from Davey the Dip.

Nowadays, you logged on, created a daft persona with a massive sword and then went about chopping up make-belief creatures in nasty-looking locations. And somehow this constituted police work.

Pringle hit the Play button again and resumed listening to people living on the sun. He sighed deeply. Perhaps the good people of the YES had got it right after all. We really were all living on the surface of the sun, permanently in danger of being frazzled to a cinder if we put a step wrong. He was still not that sure about being French though.

There was a knock at the door and a sheepish DC Ford pushed his way into the room. He was still limping and had a very sad look about him. "Not sure how it happened, but I think I might have been rumbled," he murmured under his breath, as he sat down.

"Rumbled?"

"I think they know I'm a copper."

"Wonderful," responded Pringle.

"That Springett fellow may have grassed on me, but they could have worked it out for themselves. The Snark Maiden is a pretty sharp cookie when she's not firing arrows. And the cat incident could have really swung things against me too. They've also started using police jargon, like it's some big joke that I'm not in on. The whole thing is a bit dispiriting."

"Right," said Pringle. "And what does all this mean to the price of cheese, Detective Constable?"

"Well, I think I'll have to work pretty quickly, if I'm going to get Roger, I mean Gabbitt, on a plane back here. I might have to resort some plain, old-fashioned threats or blackmail, or something."

"But if we've just lost the cat factor, Detective Constable, I think we've lost the blackmail angle, I think. What am I talking about?' Pringle shook his head sadly. "And me, a police inspector, too. Resorting to catnapping to get people to talk." He stared out of the window, glumly.

"We're just thinking laterally, sir," said Ford, trying to justify the unjustifiable.

"Maybe you could jab him with that horrifically-expensive sword of yours," muttered Pringle, thinking laterally.

"It doesn't work like that, sir," said Ford.

"What about telling the truth. Maybe that would get them thinking."

"It would get me thinking too, sir. Tell the truth? That's not a serious option, is it, sir? Certainly, not standard police procedure. Could jeopardise the whole operation."

"What operation, Ford? I fail to see any coherent strategy at all at the moment. Telling the truth now might be our last halfway decent card in a very badly-dealt hand."

"It's not that bad sir. At least we have instant access to the prime suspect. It's not every day that that happens in an investigation. That's a pretty good card, sir. Like having the queen in your last three cards."

There was a thoughtful pause as both of them considered that one.

"But they appear to have two Aces and a King, Ford," said Pringle acerbically.

"Ah yes, but we have a few nice trumps, sir."

Pringle sighed and looked at his desk. He was not too sure how to continue this conversation without suddenly producing a real deck of cards and announcing that Diamonds were trumps and that the Jokers should be immediately removed from the pack.

"And it's our turn to play..." said Ford brightly, getting deeper and deeper into the undergrowth of the current metaphor.

"Enough, Ford," interrupted Pringle, tiredly. "Cards aside, it's not every day that the lead detective has to carry a sword and wander around a cave complex wearing nothing but his underpants over a leather jerkin."

"I've upgraded to a mithril vest and breeches sir," said Ford, proudly.

"Oh, I'm sorry, Detective Constable. Please make sure that you remember that vital piece of information when you write your report on the current situation of the case at the end of the day."

"Sorry, sir."

"I'm just saying that perhaps telling Gabbitt that a policeman is actually standing right next to him in a claustrophobic cave in Cloud-Cuckoo Land might make the swine realise that he's up against a more serious adversary than a computer-animated dragon."

"It's an idea, sir. At least then they wouldn't keep pushing me into pitch-black rooms filled with horrors intent on rending flesh from bone the first chance they get."

"Sounds like the police canteen, Ford," said Pringle, raising his eyebrows a little. "You should be right at home."

"It's not funny, sir."

"No, it's not, Detective Constable."

"But how would I tell them the truth?" asked Ford, thoughtfully. "I could say that we're just trying to eliminate Gabbitt from our enquiries. And I could also mention his fingerprints all over every crime scene in London."

"You could try that, I suppose," sighed Pringle.

"Time to play our queen," said Ford, with a satisfied smirk and limped from the room.

There was a moment of quiet reflection as Pringle considered everything from playing aces and queens to goblins and beastmen. The moment passed only after he had hit the Play button once again and listened to the first minute of something called 'Long Distance Runaround'. It seemed worryingly appropriate.

Pringle stood up and sighed deeply. It was time to bite the bullet. He punched in a number on his mobile and took a deep breath. Consorting with a high-profile convict, he thought hopelessly. Ridiculous and dangerous.

Ten minutes later and Chief Inspector Pringle's mood had lightened considerably. He pressed the buzzer which linked him to Ford's desk and ordered the Detective Constable back to his office.

Ford shuffled in and sat down.

"Detective Constable, I think we now have an alternative plan to the truth," said Pringle, with a worrying gleam in his eye.

"Yes sir?"

"Ii will require me taking a couple of weeks off to go undercover."

"You, sir?"

"Yes Ford. I think I've had the call of the Orient."

"The what, sir?"

"I'm going to China to attend a conference."

"Really, sir?"

"As official representative of the... Yard School of English."

"Ah," said a confused Ford.

"The ace at the back of the pack," murmured Pringle.

<We all ready then?>

<Yep>

<Let's get started. I haven't got all evening, you know>

<So, we're going to have a bash at level five, are we?>

<Never been a better time and we haven't lost anyone yet>

<Pleased if we can get this finished soon>

<Why Percy? Are you destroying Mongolia or attacking Taiwan single-handedly?>

<Not yet, Dave>

<So, what's keeping you away from the real world of Dark Dawn Three?>

<Got to attend a conference next week in Shanghai>

<A conference. My, we are moving up the food chain, aren't we? What's it for? Spies? Vandals? Terrorists?>

<For language schools and agencies. Seems we have to take out about a hundred of them at one stroke>

<Gasp>

<Awesome>

<Cool>

<You have got to be joking, Percy. This will end up with you in a Chinese prison cell>

<And I'm not paying for the bullet either>

<What?>

<Chinese executions are usually by firing squad with the closest relatives or friends having to pay for the bullet>

<Thanks for that, Dave>

<Bullets are expensive, even in China>

<How on earth do you know that?>

<Read it on the internet>

<When are you going?>

<Don't know yet, Obby. But probably in the middle of next week, so we can all settle into our luxury five-star hotel by the river>

<Cool>

<What's the hotel called?>

<The Shangri-La I think. It's the official venue for this event>

<Right>

<Why the interest, Obby?>

<Just jealous, that's all>

<Copy that>

<Pardon>

<Nothing>

<We're hitting a London school as well>

<What?>

<Well, not me personally. The team in London>

<Which school?>

<Why the interest, Obby?>

<Just making conversation?

<Hampstead>

<What's its name?>

<Not sure Obby. Does it matter?>

<Just inter…>

<I know. The People's Language Centre I think. It's somewhere on Haverstock Hill>

<That good enough for you Obby>

<Fine>

<Some of the lads are going to hit the place in the next three days. Apparently, there's an illicit drugs factory in the basement>

<A what???>

<You wouldn't believe the half of what I've been hearing goes on in language schools>

<They're making drugs? What kind?>

<The works>

<The works?>

<Yes Obby. Loads of 'E', weed, shit, smack, angel dust, grass, coke, pepsi, crack, spot, plank, banger, bleach, liquorish, Mr Whippy, dodo, spode and sponge>

<?????????>

<Wow! Can I get there before you blow the place up? Sounds like Heaven on Earth>

<No, Dave. Can't arrange that. Sorry>

<Jesus>
<What was that Obby?>
<>
<What's sponge?>
<Don't ask, Dave. You just need to know that taking too much of it will make you think that your eyeballs are sticking out on stalks ten feet above your head>
<Really cool. And Mr Whippy?>
<Makes you think your head has been stretched out and then squeezed onto the top of an ice-cream cornet. Not that pleasant at all>
<And then people lick you?>
<Sigh>
<And all this is in their basement?>
<Yes Obby. Why the interest?>
<Nothing really>
<Then there's the raid on the British Council offices in Spring Gardens?>
<What????>
<You have got to be joking>
<And when's this happening?
<Why? Are you taking notes, Obby?
<No, of course not. It's just that I'm int…>
<Interested. Yes, we know>
<OK Obby. The raid takes place tomorrow afternoon after our brave lads have finished the morning task of dropping smoke bombs into the air conditioning units of The Universal Academy of English in Acton Town>
<Acton Town?>
<Going to be a busy week>
<Lots of corrupt bastards in this business>
<Can I interrupt please? Can we get into level five?>
<Just a thought, but…>

<Oh God. Joe's had a thought. Stand by for something mind-blowing>

<It's just an observation. Why are there so few females in computer games?>

<Why are there so few females in our lives? Any ideas, Caroline?>

<And you really want me to answer those questions?>

<No, not really>

<And what about all these weird monsters? A duckman?>

<That's because this game has a 'dynamic' storyline. It allows players to create their own characters, whether it be hero or villain. The duckman was probably created by some friendless geek in Wisconsin>

<How sad>

<And distinctly worrying>

<I know. There's no telling what will walk or crawl around the next corner. The Dragon King is probably the least of our worries. Sad geeks tend to veer towards creating unstoppable, vindictive, ridiculous and very violent monsters. It's in their nature>

<Right, let's go and kick some perverted geek's ass>

*Li Bang Cho dropped down the hole caused by Endymion's nuclear blast a few hours previously. The others went down the rope after him, with Roger bringing up the rear.*

*Level five was slightly different from the other levels. The Dragon King had placed flaming torches every ten or so feet. The effect was quite appealing. Everyone prefers peachy fireside glows in their dripping dungeons to pitch black menace.*

*"So, where's the duckman's mates?" asked Endymion, jovially.*

*"A duckman," sighed the Snark Maiden, sadly. "Monsters aren't what they used to be."*

*"Don't think about it, love," said Obby, quietly. "Just get on with the job and stay breathing, that's what I say."*

*"Don't call me 'love', "said the Snark Maiden, knocking an arrow into her bow and pointing it menacingly at Obby's chest.*

*"Quiet," hissed Roger. "I thought I heard something."*

*"Should be nothing here," whispered Tubby the Goblin. "This part of the corridor is supposed to lead the heroes down to the main killing fields on a lower sub-layer."*

*"How comforting," muttered Endymion, nervously.*

*There was a faintest of noises from a distant and very dark corner followed by a lot of very silent and worrying nothing. The torches flickered, slightly.*

*"WHO'S FUCKING THERE?" shouted a squeaky voice.*

*"Show yourself," barked Roger. He didn't like being shouted at in caves, especially when bad language was used.*

*"Yeh, right. And then you blow my fucking head off," said the voice, who obviously knew her dungeons pretty well.*

*"Last chance," said Roger and drew his sword.*

*"OK. You fucking win. I'm coming out." said the voice.*

*A moment later and a creature of moderate human height dressed in a black, shiny and very close-fitting leather one-piece, slunk into view. The heroes all gasped as one. This was the very last thing that any of them had expected five levels down in the meanest dungeon ever created.*

*It was carrying a long, coiled whip and had a dark purple cloak draped over its shoulders. On its feet were crimson,n very high-heeled stiletto boots.*

*As the creature came closer still, they could see that it was most definitely a she - with all the trimmings, including rings, bangles and chains hanging from virtually every loose bit of skin and orifice. There was also a bulky necklace around her neck, which nestled heavily in the foothills of her breasts. She was a walking bondage accessory shop.*

*"Holey moley" uttered Endymion, dropping his scrolls.*

*"Gordon Bennett!" squawked Li Bang Cho, in a most un-Chinese way.*

*"Treacle tarts!" cried Tubby, rather observantly.*

*"Ay Caramba!" exclaimed Tammy.*

*"Smurfing Henry," blurted Obby.*

*"And who might you be?" croaked Roger, after the initial shock had worn off and he had pulled his sagging jaw shut.*

*"What the fuck are you lot staring at?" snarled the angel in black.*

*"Ah… well… not sure… hmmm…" tried Roger, a little limply.*

*"Is it a monster or a hero?" whispered a baffled Tubby.*

*"What race art thou?" asked Roger, clearing his throat and trying to sound as professional as the situation would allow.*

*"I'm a friggin' neo cyber-Goth, aren't I?" replied the creature, brushing back impossibly long, jet black hair from her face. "And what's all this 'art' stuff? You're not some sort of Monty Python knight, are you?"*

*The heroes gasped once again. A paper-white face looked at them. It had violet lips and coal-black mascara around her eyes, which looked as if a drunken blind man with an old toothbrush had applied it.*

*"Shall we just kill it?" queried a genuinely mystified Endymion, stroking his beard thoughtfully. Such creatures did not readily inhabit his world and get away with it.*

*"Maybe that would be cool," said the creature, disinterestedly. "At least it would be bit more exciting than living down here."*

*"What? Being dead?" spluttered Li Bang Cho.*

*"Yeh, why not? Try strangling me. They say that's a sexy way to go," said the creature, exposing her neck to the party.*

*There was a very long silence as the heroes wondered what to do next.*

*"Would you like a sandwich?" asked Tammy, deciding that offering strawberry jam on rye would somehow defuse a complicated situation.*

*"OK, why the fuck not?" was the reply and the creature sat down.*

*Tammy handed over the sandwich. Everyone then sat down.*

*"Where's the rest of your party?" asked Roger thickly, trying desperately to make conversation.*

*"All got cremated by a fucking dragon back there," was the jammy reply.*

*"Oh dear," said Roger, sheathing his sword. "So, you're all alone?"*

*"Fuck that!" exclaimed the creature. "Hated all of them, anyway. Bunch of weirdoes."*

*The heroes went silent again.*

*"And only one sodding arrow left too."*

*"Oh dear," repeated Roger. His brain had quickly turned to mush and he was rapidly losing all power of coherent thought. "The name's Roger," he said and extended a hand. "I'm a Norse Fighter. And this is my band," he said, gruffly.*

*"Fucking daft name for a Norse hero. Shouldn't you be called Thor or Olaf, or something like that?" asked the dark angel and then spat hugely into a dark corner of the corridor.*

*"Well, I…" began Roger, defensively.*

*"Are you here for the treasure or is it a rescue quest?" she grunted through the remainder of a crust.*

*"Rescue quest," said the Snark Maiden, who had been silent to this point.*

*"So, the chick's got a voice," said the dark creature.*

*"The what?" uttered the Snark Maiden, dangerously.*

*"You look hot, though."*

*"Do I?" squeaked the Snark Maiden, suddenly feeling a little disarmed.*

*"If you're into the elfish look... which I am, incidentally."*

*"Oh," managed the Snark Maiden.*

*"So, do you know your way around here?" asked Tammy, who was rapidly getting bored with all the human getting-to-know-each-other stuff.*

*"You've teamed up with fucking goblins! How cool is that? I am impressed," said the creature, clearly surprised.*

*"We're a different type of goblin," said Tammy, a little huffily.*

*"I can see that," agreed the woman, frowning hard at Tubby in his red bow tie."*

*"What's with the retro look, short stuff?" she asked him.*

*"The what?" grunted Tubby.*

*"The colonial, paedo look."*

*"I beg your pardon," interrupted Roger, hotly.*

*There was a short pause and then the woman in black burst out laughing. After a few seconds, she looked at Roger. "You know, of all the things I would have expected in this dungeon, it would not be you lot. Things are looking up."*

*"We like to keep an open mind on beasts and heroes when we come across them," said Roger, guardedly. "Not really my idea," he added, quickly.*

*"Great. So, where's the pet Minotaur?"*

*"Playing fetch back there," said Tammy, sarcastically.*

*The black angel again burst into peels of laughter. "And a goblin with a sense of humour too. Fucking A."*

*"You haven't told us who you are," enquired a curious Snark Maiden.*

*"Me? The name's Crystal. Crystal Meth."*

# FIFTEEN

"Stand and fight we do consider, reminded of an inner pact between us that's seen as we go. And ride there in motion to fields in debts of honour defending… "

**(The first lines of the song: 'The Gates of Delirium' by YES - a new favourite of Inspector Pringle's, loosely based on Tolstoy's War and Peace. The lyrics are best read very quickly and not dwelt on too deeply…. otherwise it doesn't really make that much sense, unless you're an unwashed teenager who can spot inner meanings, far more easily than cynical adults.)**

'*Citizen Kate*' starring Awesome Hells.

Percy Gabbitt was back in 'ock Stat on' and pawing through the bootleg DVDs.

He needed a break from madness, abnormality and the general wholesale destruction of things, so what better than to amble down the Shiquan Street and then have a flick through a few of the latest DVDs on offer. He was looking for escape.

Perhaps Awesome Hells could provide it. He looked at the DVD cover. It was of a rather fat man with an outrageous beard and wearing a silly-looking hat and dark cape. Gabbitt put the DVD back. He rather thought that Mr. Hells would not hit the mark this time round.

What about the large boxes on the top shelf? They looked interesting. Reefer Southernband in '34'. That looked interesting. The whole first six series packed onto four CDs, promising over six solid days of action with the Los Angeles Counter-Terrorist Unit and how they dealt with hourly Armageddon. Perhaps not. He had enough of that sort of thing in China on a daily basis.

After a long ten minutes, Gabbitt decided on 'The Sump-Sins' compendium. Every episode ever on two CDs. An ideal choice. He could do with a bit of top quality satire at the expense of virtually everyone who took themselves far too seriously. Roll on hours of cartooned mirth with Homo and Fart Sump-Sin.

"Train goes at twelve and we're supposed to be meeting Bob and Pamela at the station in forty minutes, mate," said a familiar antipodean voice next to him.

"I know," murmured Gabbitt.

Pamela. He briefly thought of the new addition to the Arapacana strike team – this Pamela person, the author of that dubious poem on Burley's office wall. He had never met her properly, but knew that she had worked in Hastings at a language school at about the same time that he was fighting the world in London.

"Disparate Mousewives!" exclaimed Irwin. "What's all that about, you think?"

"Worth a look," replied Gabbitt. "And it's dirt cheap too. Could be another of those politically-sound Disney things."

"Nah. I'll stick with this," said Irwin, waving the Director's Cut of 'The Donkeyman meets the Pussycat' under Gabbitt's nose.

"Not that again, said Gabbitt tiredly.

"Ten extra juicy minutes have been added, which were cut from the original," commented Irwin as he read the back cover. Director Randy Savage says, and I quote: 'This is how wanted it. Full on everything!' Definitely worth a dollar of anyone's money."

"Great. Hope you enjoy it," said Gabbitt wearily. "I think I need some fresh air," he added and walked out of the small shop and across a narrow street to where one of Suzhou's many canals wound its gluey way.

He stared at the dark and forbidding surface as it moved slowly passed him. Something hit the surface and bounced. One or two tired ripples attempted to do their concentric thing, without much success though – the stuff in this canal having the consistency of grey emulsion paint.

Gabbitt looked at the water and wondered if it would be possible to walk across the surface if you were quick enough.

Something else hit the surface and he turned round. An old man was standing at his left shoulder and obviously practising for a place in the Chinese spitting team at the next Olympics. He attempted, for the third time, a spitting feat akin to a pole vault of over thirty feet in the air. Yet again, Gabbitt was amazed by how noisily a normal man standing in a public place could empty the contents of his lungs. The wind-up to the event took about five long seconds of guttural and deep-throated gurgling, before something large and glutinous was expelled at the speed of sound.

An expert like this geriatric could judge the trajectory much like an archer at Agincourt could aim his arrow. This old man seemed to be a weathered expert after many years of practice probably at this very spot.

Gabbitt stared at the surface of the canal and wondered in horror if the contents of this part of the canal were just the expectorations of this one man over an eighty year period.

He started doing one of those wonderfully bizarre mathematical calculations, which people do when tired or bored. In this case the calculation revolved around the amount in millilitres of the average spit, at a rate of say twenty a day, over the said period of eighty years.

Gabbitt shuddered as he imagined the glutinous mountain as it built up over the years.

On the plus side though, it was probably very good for his lungs and might have counteracted some of the harmful effects of smoking sixty a day for possibly the same length of time.

Gabbitt shook his head and walked back to the DVD shop as a fourth spit plopped into the canal behind him.

"Right, let's get a cab to the station," said Irwin as he stepped from the shop toting a small red plastic bag bulging with hours of mindless watching.

He then started semaphoring at a string of parked taxi cabs nearby.

"Ladies and gentleman, this is the captain speaking. Would you make sure that your safety belts are secured, your seats are in an upright position and your tables folded away. We shall be landing in about fifteen minutes at Shanghai Pudong International Airport. The ground temperature is twenty degrees and it's raining. We hope that you've enjoyed your time with us and that Cathy and her team have made your flight a memorable one. Have a nice time in Shanghai and hope to see you on a Virgin flight soon."

Virgin Flight Number 250 touched down at Pudong airport and the massive airbus trundled heavily towards its parking gantry. It had not been an easy journey for most of the crew. Having about three hundred grouchy and squashed passengers on board for twelve long hours had pushed the flight crew to the limit, especially when the on-board entertainment system had crashed and they had run out of reconstituted beef for dinner.

Row 38 and 39 in Economy had been the epicentre of all the worst feeling though and the unfortunate flight attendant called Sharon, who was responsible for this area, was close to a nervous breakdown as the doors opened and passengers were disgorged. There had already been tears and a threat of resignation during the last two appalling hours of the flight.

Sharon was not the only dissatisfied person.

"I'm going to write a letter to that Mr. Branston," said Alfred Fennell truculently.

"It's Branson, dear," corrected Hilda wearily.

"That's what I said. He should stick to making pickles."

Hilda Fennell sighed. It would be no use correcting her husband again, especially when he was in such a foul and sleep-deprived mood.

"All I wanted was a decent slice of bread," grumbled Alfred to the world in general. "Not some silly soft roll that you wouldn't even give to the dog."

"I don't think dogs eat bread rolls, dear," said Hilda thoughtfully.

"Well, mine wouldn't eat these!" exclaimed Alfred hotly. "That's all I wanted. Decent bread. I didn't want any trouble. It's a man's right to have decent bread."

"The air marshal might disagree."

"That's his own fault," mumbled Alfred. "I didn't know the man was some sort of private detective. I just saw a suspicious fellow coming down the aisle with what looked like a funny bulge in his trouser pocket. You can't be too careful nowadays, what with all them teddy boys and Ali Baba terrorists going around blowing themselves up in shopping centres and all over the Lebanon."

"You didn't need to attack him though, dear."

"Someone had to do something and quickly."

"And it had to be you," murmured Hilda in a mildly reproachful way.

"He'll be all right," said Alfred airily. "Them trolley dollies have just managed to staunch the bleeding."

They both looked across the aisle to where a prone man was being tended by two highly-stressed stewardesses clutching a pile of bloody paper towels. Hilda sighed again and started to collect her things together.

"We'd better get off this plane, Alf. China's waiting for us, god help it."

Alfred Fennell shifted in his seat. For all he cared, China could wait. He wanted to have a decent wash and what he called a stand-up bath in the toilet before he left the plane. He had never in his life ventured into the outside world without having washed, shaved and brushed his teeth, discounting the war years of course. And he was not going to start now.

He got up and pushed his way up the aisle to the toilets in the middle of the plane, a task made all the more difficult because of the hordes of impatient passengers wanting to push down past Row 38 and off the plane. Alfred's attempts to get to the toilet were rather like the vain thrashings of a determined salmon trying to get upstream and home. He made it though after elbowing his way through a Chinese family and treading hard on a businessman's foot.

The occupants of Row 39, right behind the Fennells, were in similar disarray. To be quite honest, they appeared to be in some kind of mild shock.

"Are you absolutely sure it's the same bastard, Mr Chipchase?"

"There are some people you never forget, Mr. Bibby."

"He really was on the... you know what?"

"Yes, Mr. Bibby. He was there."

The two of them sat solidly in their seats as memories of those painful days surrounding the Box Hill Battle came swirling back. Although the incident got mentioned on occasions, the two of them never actually spoke the name of the place. It was too difficult, even for psychopaths like them.

"Are you certain?"

"I'll remember the faces of all of the people on that hill till my dying day, Mr. Bibby," added Chipchase quietly.

"Just saying that the chances of sitting behind one of them on a plane to China is a pretty remote coincidence, Mr. Chipchase. The memory can play funny tricks on people."

"Engraved on my subconscious, Mr. Bibby. Every last one of them."

"What are we going to do?"

"Nothing, Mr. Bibby. Nothing. We have no axe to grind with him. Anyway, if I remember correctly, he was actually on our side during that... event two years ago. Wanted the bastard dead almost as much as we did."

"Respect then, Mr. Chipchase."

"Indeed. Time to get our bags I think, Mr. Bibby."

The two bulky security guards then stood up, adjusted their ties and put their suit jackets on. Both stared with a certain degree of suspicion, anxiety and... respect at the empty seat in Row 38.

"Shit!" exclaimed Chipchase suddenly and dropped the bag which he was attempting to pull from an overhead locker.

"What?" squawked Bibby, quickly looking in all directions and bracing himself for a fight.

"I don't friggin' believe it!" exclaimed Chipchase in astonishment. "There's another of the bastards," he croaked and pointed a shaky finger at a thin man in a beige raincoat who was walking down the aisle on the far side of the plane.

At exactly the same moment that amazed, sulky, angry, bloodied and desperately tired occupants of Flight 250 dragged themselves into Pudong Airport and towards the baggage collection hall, four foreigners were boarding a super express train from Suzhou to Shanghai and having the traditional contretemps with a Chinese family who had appropriated their reserved seats at a previous station.

The family were eventually evicted after a lot of face-losing apologies. They then all smiled weakly and wandered up the aisle of the crowded train looking for a square foot or two that they could huddle together in for the remainder of the journey.

It took the Arapacana team a further five minutes to clean up the mountain of detritus left behind. Orange peels, sun flower seeds and biscuit wrappers were strewn all over and under the seats - there was also a suspicious pool of something unpleasant rippling threateningly in front of Gabbitt's seat. They all eventually sat down and settled in for the quick forty minute journey to Shanghai main railway station.

Bob Burley was holding court and trying to be social as the train slipped out of Suzhou station.

"So, Percy, if your fairy godmother suddenly appeared in a blinding flash of lightning before you now and offered you three wishes which were guaranteed to come true, what would they be? And you can't choose anything too politically-correct or involved with health issues. Just three totally selfish things."

"I'd want a million dollars, to marry Miss World, a bright red Ferrari and my own island in the Caribbean," interrupted Irwin after about two seconds serious thought.

"That's four wishes," said Burley flatly.

"Oh right," frowned Irwin. "Then forget the Ferrari. You couldn't get up to very high speeds on your own small island anyway."

"And you, Percy?" tried Burley again.

Gabbitt sat back in his seat and thought long and hard. He had never really given his dreams much thought and was surprised that nothing huge and wonderful came to the fore.

Burley decided to do the interrupting this time. He looked up at the carriage ceiling and said: "To own my own pub in old England, somewhere near a river, possibly outside Cambridge. That would be one of mine. A yacht would be another and maybe my own private jet."

"I suppose," started Gabbitt. "I would like to be a director of Northampton Town football club with my own seat in the West Lower Stand. Probably Row D," he said slowly and very thoughtfully. "That would be one wish, but I would need Bob's million to donate to them, before I was granted that I think."

"Not football, please," moaned Pamela, rolling her eyes the way women do when faced with a possible conversation involving the 'f' word.

"Number two," continued Gabbitt, ignoring the interruption, "would be to see my father's paintings hung in the Royal Academy, the Louvre and the Guggenheim in New York."

"Now that is interesting," said Pamela, warming slightly to the man she had heard so much about but had never met. "What's he paint? Animals, country scenes, nudes or lots of coloured squares and abstracts?"

"He's very good at oranges and apples in bowls," said Gabbitt slowly.

"Still life," said Pamela who appeared to know a little about art, as well as poetry.

"And trees too," added Gabbitt. "He's good at doing them."

"So," said Burley seriously, "you would use one of your wishes to get your father's paintings hung in the biggest art galleries in the world?"

"I think so," replied Gabbitt quietly. "He deserves some recognition for the pile of canvases in his attic."

"Probably not really the age for oranges and apples in bowls any more," said Irwin.

"Well, they're much better than most of the paintings hung in those galleries now. At least you can see he knows what he's doing. Successful artists nowadays only have to nail a pair of their dirty underpants to the inside of a cow's carcase and then exhibit the whole messy result in a glass case. That's not my idea of art."

"But it does shock," said Pamela.

"So would a kick between the legs, but that's not art," said Irwin ruefully. "Or is it?"

"Maybe," said Pamela, clearly getting into the subject at hand and giving serious thought to Irwin's suggestion.

Gabbitt stared at Pamela Henderson, the Arapacana official poet, for a few seconds. It was the first time he had properly met the ex-teacher from Hastings, who had joined Arapacana a few months previously after a disastrous year being exploited at an English school in the Philippines.

She had blonde shoulder-length hair and an expression which always seemed to teeter on the edge of rebelliousness. Gabbitt wondered briefly what Caroline would have thought of her. Probably would have got on together like a house on fire, apart from the poetry that is. Caroline would have definitely not resisted the temptation to put her right there. And now she was a member of this mad band of vandalising lunatics. Life could be very strange.

"And number three?" asked Burley breezily.

"Well, that would have to be winning Wimbledon," said Gabbitt finally. "After a five set classic in the final against someone like that Swiss bloke who's brilliant at the moment."

"Easy things then," commented Irwin. "All I wanted was an island, Miss World, some money and a fast car."

"And you Pamela?" asked Gabbitt.

"To nail every bastard who's ever exploited me, would be number one. Numbers two and three would probably be disqualified by Bob here, since they would involve politically-correct issues like building more refuges for battered women and making everyone turn vegetarian."

There was an extremely long pause as the three men stared at their shoes. Irwin then broke the silence.

"I see that England lost yesterday."

"Right," said Burley, firmly putting a full stop to the end of that conversation. "To business," he continued, as he extracted a weighty-looking file from his briefcase, "I have here our battle plan."

The three employees stared a little apprehensively at the bulky file before them. Even several bored Chinese passengers stopped talking about the price of onions and started watching the Foreigner Show instead. One spat copiously onto the floor and rubbed the mess with his foot to stop any other passengers slipping on it. He was then all ears for what Burley had to say next.

"Four hundred and fifty-three schools and institutions attending the ICAS show. Four hundred and five are well-run and a credit to the business."

"Which leaves… quite a few dodgy ones," said Irwin, licking his lips and trying hard to do the complicated calculation.

"Indeed," agreed Burley, flicking to the page one of the file. "Forty-eight schools which fall below the accepted norm, I'm sorry to say. And of those forty-eight, seven are truly dreadful."

"So many," murmured Gabbitt. "Just how did you evaluate them?"

"Good question. Percy," replied Burley, warming to the task. "We have a ten point criteria which we measure all institutions against. Page three will explain everything, I think. We have been extremely thorough, Percy."

"Ten points?"

"Yes, just ten, Percy," sighed Burley. "Spell them out for him, Bob," he said, looking at Irwin.

"Right Bob," said Irwin, clearly delighted to have been given the task. "We drew them up from your template after the Box Hill battle," he said with a gleam in his eye.

"But I..." began Gabbitt defensively.

"The Ten Rules of Gabbitdom," he said rather loudly.

"The ten what?" queried a weary Gabbitt.

"In reverse order, of course," said Irwin. "We'll have a countdown leaving the juiciest till last, like they do on the telly."

"A countdown..." repeated Gabbitt.

He looked at Burley and Pamela for support, but both just smiled weakly and then stared back at Irwin.

Rule Ten," said Irwin and looked at the carriage ceiling. "Are all teachers and employees happy? This may seem a silly one, but a happy school forgives minor discrepancies."

"Happy?" said Gabbitt. "Is anyone really happy at a language school?"

"There are some who take to the whole sorry business of listing important banking English words like a duck to water," said Irwin, shaking his head sadly.

"Too true," agreed Burley quietly. Pamela just tutted and shook her head too.

"I should add that this rule includes all the usual sort of mundane stuff like schools having pleasant social areas for students and staff alike, well-equipped classrooms and a decent library. The stuff that teachers reckon are important," said Irwin as if he didn't really believe in that sort of thing.

"Also includes a few subsections on schools having the correct number of fire exits, a decent and well-policed maximum class size, and a structured teaching method. Things like that," added Burley seriously.

"Rule Nine," said Irwin. "Is the quality of the canteen or restaurant food good enough for your grandmother to eat at?" Irwin smacked his lips as he finished Point Nine. This was clearly far more important than if a school had enough books.

Gabbitt shuddered as he thought back to the chicken in a basket offered by RELI most weekday afternoons.

"Rule Eight: Are the staff and teachers happy with the quality of the toilets? What we mean here is cleanliness and paper quality of course?"

Gabbitt again thought back to some of the more rowdy staff meetings at RELI and the ever-raging toilet paper debate. Clearly this was also quite an important thing for language school teachers the world over.

"Rule Seven: Coffee and tea making facilities," said Irwin. "What does management deem appropriate for its staff? Just a twenty year old kettle which scalds your hand when you touch the handle or an up-to-date cappuccino and latte machine in its own small room? You be the judge, Percy."

"Solid points," murmured Burley seriously.

"Rule Six. Nearly half way there, Percy. No mistakes on the monthly salary cheque. This is a common thing in a bad language school. Teachers and staff should not have to take a deep breath when opening their brown envelope. It should all be nice, tidy and correct."

"Indeed," said Burley, nodding slowly.

"Rule Five: Schools must have a sensible timetable. It's no use hammering a teacher to death with nine lessons a day to total beginners. Brains quickly turn to mush when teaching the Present Continuous hour in, hour out. Also, no more than five lessons a day and with a nice healthy lunch hour in the middle. And all classrooms have to be proper rooms, not converted church halls, cloak rooms, toilets or mop cupboards for one-to-one lessons."

"Tell that to my last school," chipped in Pamela, a mite bitterly.

"Rule Four: No delay in paying teachers. If it's agreed that's they get their wages every Friday, then that's the way it is. No prevarication or delaying till next Monday because a manager couldn't get to the bank in time."

"Big problem is Rule Four, especially in the summer," said Burley sadly.

"Rule Three," said Irwin. "A biggie. No surreptitious changing of contracts once you've joined a school. If you're down for a maximum of twenty contact hours a week, then so be it. Any more and you automatically get a nice fat bonus without having to beg for it on bended knee."

Gabbitt thought of Nero Handsworth and wondered how he would react to Rule Three. He frowned and looked back at Irwin.

"Rule Number Two: The student is always right. Again a pretty contentious one, but students are our bread and butter and, as such, should be treated like gold dust. If they are unhappy about anything then it is our job to put a smile back on their little faces!" exclaimed Irwin.

"Too right," agreed Pamela enthusiastically. She clearly liked Rule Number Two a lot.

"Again, this rule includes everything that concerns the student like sexual harassment or if a teacher has started sleeping with an under-age student," said Burley happily.

"And the Number One Rule," said Irwin with a flourish. "The most important of the lot: A simple one really and very easy to understand - No lying.

This may seem a bit of a bland one, but it covers everything from what the brochures and literature say all the way to what school directors tell their teachers and staff. Again, a big one and pretty difficult to monitor, but we do our best," said Irwin smiling broadly.

"We have quite a few sub-sections to this one as well," said Burley leaning forward seriously. "Stuff like watching if a school has become a visa factory for Chinese and Russian students or if it is using non-qualified and cheap slave labour teachers. And if a school says to agents and students on the verge of enrolling that it limits the size of each nationality percentage; then, when the bookings start flowing in, it gets greedy and accepts everyone, so that classes are eighty per cent Korean or Italian. In other words, all shades and colours of lying."

Again Gabbitt's mind wandered to his ex-boss, Nero Handsworth. It would have been a difficult thing to pin him down on anything that did not constitute a lie of some sort.

"And if a school breaks any of these, Arapacana swoop in and lay waste to the place?" asked Gabbitt worriedly.

"No, Percy, of course not," chuckled Burley. "They have to contravene at least five of these points including two of the top three. And most importantly, we keep every institution under the microscope for six months so that they can clean up their act up before..."

"We act," interrupted Irwin.

"Exactly," agreed Burley and sat back in his seat.

There was a short silence and Gabbitt stared out at the flat countryside sliding by the carriage window. Whereas in England there would be green fields and rolling hills, here in China it was one industrial wasteland followed by another - all under a rather dusty yellow haze. He watched in silence as a forest of chimney stacks marched past, all belching grey smoke out into an already grainy sky.

He sighed and mulled over the ten points that Irwin had so colourfully outlined. It all seemed very simple indeed, but he did wonder if there were any schools out there which did not contravene at least three of the rules. It was a sad industry. A very sad one.

"These seven schools?" asked Irwin suddenly.

"Our most important priority, of course. All our efforts during the two day workshop will be geared to bringing these institutions down, or embarrassing the buggers to high hell, at the very least."

"It seems a pretty tall order," said Pamela sceptically.

"Ah, Pamela," said Irwin, smiling benignly. "You clearly have not met Percy."

"But seven?" persisted the doubter.

"It'll certainly be a challenge," agreed Burley. "Pages six to thirty-three should help allay your fears, Pamela. I have outlined a thirty point attack list."

"Thirty points?" squawked Irwin, in a way which implied that he had never read so much in his life and was not about to start now.

"Thirty ways to bring a school to its knees."

"Wow," said Gabbitt in true admiration. "I wish I had had this two years ago."

"But you did, Percy, my friend. You did," said Burley with a twinkle in his eye.

"Did I?" queried a lost Gabbitt.

"All of our strategy comes from the Percy Raymond Gabbitt template. The Bible of the school avenger."

"But I didn't..."

"There you go again, Percy. Modest to the point of absurdity. You may sit there and claim innocence, but the hard facts are difficult to disregard. You single-handedly destroyed not only the worst school on the planet, but also had the owner incarcerated and his school blown up in the process. Not to mention about a million other minor and just as extraordinary successes. You can't do better than that, Percy."

"I wish everyone would forget about those times," sighed Gabbitt honestly.

"That's like saying we should forget Waterloo, Trafalgar, the Crimea and 1966."

"1966? Surely you mean 1066?" queried Pamela.

"England four, West Germany two," said Burley slowly.

"Oh no," mumbled Pamela hopelessly.

"A watershed moment, Pamela," intoned Burley seriously. "Something happened that day that changed the course of things in Europe. It wasn't just a football match. It was the turning of the tide. Someone had to put a stop to the resurgent German machine. And it was down to us again, of course."

"Excuse me for saying so, but it was only football," tried Pamela in vain.

"The third goal didn't go over the line," chipped in Gabbitt rather scurrilously. "It's been proved by computer graphics."

"Details, details," said Burley dismissively. "Shows that the gods were on our side that day, as they should have been."

"But we won by... cheating," persisted Gabbitt. "Like Maradona's hand of god and the Koreans in virtually every game of their World Cup in..."

"Can we please not talk about football?" interrupted an exasperated Pamela.

There was a silence as the four of them thought about cheating Koreans and hands of god.

"Did I say that England lost last night?" muttered Irwin.

It was late evening in Wormwood Scrubs prison in London and the inmates had just been subjected to the English equivalent of the American lock-down scenario so popular in prison dramas on the television. Basically, it simply meant that all prisoners had to return to their cells immediately and be locked in, usually because someone had done something violent to someone else... or escaped.

In Wormwood Scrubs though it was a little more benign. A toothbrush had been reported missing and one of the guards had suspected a bit of pilfering. And so, lock-down UK style.

Nero Handsworth sat on his bunk and scribbled in a large note pad. He was feeling increasingly contented with his latest machinations, especially with the addition of Barry the Bagman, a huge Nigerian called The Bear and the Shotgun Sisters to his ever-widening Irish Stand-off circle.

If all went well, then they would be dropping like flies from the moment that Percy flaming Gabbitt once again set foot on British soil. He rubbed his hands happily. It had been fortuitous indeed to discover that Sophie and Sal Squire had been free and very employable at the moment. Adding the Shotgun Sisters to any mix more or less guaranteed a fiery outcome. Nero smiled. That made it nine psychopaths in an increasing circle of violence, which began with those bovine security guards. All they needed to do was get Percy Gabbitt onto a plane back to London and then nothing could possibly go wrong.

He already had Fred the Throttler in place with Slicing Sammy looking over his shoulder – well, actually at a spot between his shoulder blades.

With the addition of Sophie, Sal and The Bear, he had managed to spice things up quite nicely. He placed an arrow on his pad between Three Knives Nigel and The Bear. He then put a similar arrow between the Shotgun Sisters and Stabbing Sid.

Very nice, thought Nero and put the pad down. Some might say that he was gilding the lily a little, but he had never liked lilies that much and rather thought they could do with a bit of outrageous touching up to give them a bit more colour. He chuckled to himself. It was time something went right in his life.

The small mobile phone in his trouser pocket buzzed like an angry bee caught in a jam jar.

"What?" barked Nero after pulling the phone out.

"There's been developments," said a tinny voice from what sounded like the planet Uranus.

"Where are you?" asked Nero, frowning.

"Baggage hall in China," came the slightly worrying reply.

"And is that the new development?" asked Nero innocently.

"No," came the curt response.

"Then what is it?"

"It's some sort of convention," muttered Chipchase.

"I know," replied Nero. "That's why you're there. You have to attend a teachers' fucking convention. You haven't forgotten that already, have you? Stone the crows! I really pick them."

"No, not that," came the whispered reply. "Another sort of convention."

"What the hell are you talking about?" grunted Nero unhappily. He never liked this sort of circuitous conversation, especially when half the prison populace had their ears to their walls trying to listen in.

"That police chief and the old geezer… they're both on this plane as well. It's really creepy."

Nero suddenly felt a wave a nausea shoot through him. He had managed to go from total serenity to dithering wreck in about one second. "What?" he squawked thickly.

"The policeman on that hill two years back is on this plane. And that old nutter who nearly killed us all. He's in the seat in front."

Nero's mind went into rapid rewind and he was soon conjuring up extremely unwelcome images of that appalling night when he had come face-to-face with that mad police chief and the psychopathic pensioner from Hell.

"What? On your plane?" he repeated incomprehensibly.

"Yeh. Well, not now. They're in this baggage hall waiting for their… bags," said Chipchase slowly. "What do you want us to do?"

Nero thought hard and fast. This certainly changed a few things. What the devil was that old man doing there and, more to the point, what was Chief Inspector Pringle up to? Perhaps he was not the only one attempting a little lily gilding. He frowned deeply and whispered: "Nothing. I repeat, do nothing. Stick to the original plan, but keep an eye on what they're all up to. I want to know everything that happens in the next three days. Do you understand?"

He then snapped the phone shut and lay back on his bed. So much to think about suddenly. What on earth was going on?

It was total chaos and mayhem at New Scotland Yard. Phones were ringing, detectives were pinning photos onto massive blackboards, coffee was being drunk by the gallon, computers were going into meltdown, the Yard's satellites were spinning from one location to another and groups of mean-looking policemen in black helmets and bulky bullet-proof vests were marching around car parks awaiting orders to kick a few front doors in.

Detective Constable Ford was at the centre of the hurricane. He stood in a first floor corridor holding a sheath of papers and two mobile phones. Grouped in a rough circle around him were about five senior policemen and a man in plain clothes carrying an enormous pistol.

"Six locations simultaneously?" queried one police chief in an impressive-looking hat.

"It's the only way," said Ford breathlessly. "The bastards must have a huge cell and are hitting all these places in one go. We have to be there to nab them all."

"And you're quite sure about all this, Ford?" asked another policeman sceptically.

"Yes Chief Inspector Grimmond. The bastards are having a full scale assault on all these schools over the next twenty-four hours. It's going to be Stalingrad in the language school industry today I think."

"Stalingrad?" repeated a baffled Grimmond.

"Well, Beirut or Kabul at the very least," said Ford, toning down the scale of expected destruction a little.

"Are you quite sure?" asked the man in plain clothes. MI5 haven't picked up anything like this on their radar."

"They're making Mr. Whippy on Haverstock Hill!" exclaimed Ford in exasperation.

"Are they?" asked a bewildered Grimmond, taking his hat off and running a hand through his thinning hair. "And why would they be doing that?"

"Because it's a drug factory and we all know what Mr. Whippy is," said Ford, as if he was speaking to a two year old. "Sponge, Dodo, bleach, Spode and liquorish? Ring any bells, Chief Inspector?"

There was a long silence as the team of senior policemen thought several things. First, this junior detective was clearly overstepping the line. Talking like that to police chiefs not just a few rungs up the ladder, but several ladders further up into the ether, was simply not on.

Second, this whippersnapper of a junior detective clearly knew something was up and was getting rather agitated by it, which was also a distinct no-no when addressing a superior.

Third, they were beginning to realise that they all were clearly out of touch with the contemporary drug culture, since none of them had any idea what dodo, bleach or sponge did to the system, though they could guess.

"Right, Ford. Better get to it then," muttered Grimmond seriously.

"Liquorish eh?" whistled one of the chiefs and stared at the ceiling as Ford walked off into the distance, once again barking into a mobile phone. "When will it all end?"

"Dodo's worse," added another chief, not to be seen to be outdone.

"At least it's not Crack Dodo," said the man in plain clothes.

There was a longer pause punctuated by a little tutting.

"And I always thought Spode was fine eighteenth century pottery," muttered an elderly member of the group.

They all laughed as one at the naivety of age. Grimmond then slapped the senior inspector on the back and said: "More pot than pottery nowadays, John, I'm sorry to say. Myself, I just think it's a crying shame that these swines take perfectly respectable and nice-sounding names and label their perverted addiction with them, Spode being a case in point."

More silence ensued. It was John, the elderly chief who broke it: "Like gay I suppose. Perfectly nice word and now look at it. Appalling."

They all nodded in agreement. The world could be an unforgivable place at times.

"Right, time to do the devil's work, gentlemen," said Grimmond and marched back to his office where a small éclair and a cup of Darjeeling awaited his inspection.

*"This is all getting totally ridiculous," said Roger the Norse Fighter as he trudged down a damp corridor towards yet another skirmish. He was about twenty yards up the corridor from all the other members of his party, except for the Snark Maiden, that is. She walked by his side nodding gravely. "The whole point of a quest like this is to have the main hero - no offence intended," he murmured,*

*looking briefly at his companion, "...pushed to the very edge of his endurance and then to emerge victorious. Possibly all by himself or, if he's lucky, with one other comrade in arms, "he said, winking in her direction.*

*"It does seem an odd sort of quest," said the Snark Maiden in agreement. "We seem to be collecting heroes by the hatful and not losing any of them!"*

*"Exactly my point," said Roger, slapping a thigh. "It's time to draw a line in the sand and say 'No more!'"*

*"But you can't turn people in distress away, can you? Goes against the hero code."*

*"Well, you'll have to explain that very quickly to me if we meet any more heroes down on their luck. I'm in the mood to skewer anything that comes in my way from now on. It all seems so different suddenly. I reckon the rot set in when I came across that first goblin."*

*"I told you about that," muttered the Snark Maiden. "There's a lot more to him than meets the eye. I wouldn't trust him at my back, I can tell you. And as far as his friend is concerned, well, goblins that believe in trade, commerce and poetry are a world that I for one don't want to venture into."*

*"I couldn't agree more," enthused Roger. "This other goblin, who wears a bow tie and carries a briefcase - if that's not natural, I'd like to see what is."*

*"A duckman?" queried the Snark Maiden.*

*"Ah yes," sniffed Roger. "Point taken. There's a lot happening in here that I don't really understand.*

*"And now the cherry on the cake is this foul-mouthed creature all dressed up in black with a ton of tasteless make-up on," sighed the Snark Maiden.*

*"Crystal Meth," murmured Roger and shook his head again. "She says she's good with healing potions."*

*"If I had a gold coin every time I heard that, I'd be…" began the Snark Maiden dismissively.*

*"We can only wait and hope," interrupted Roger. "Still, on the plus side, any monster daft enough to tackle us will have his work cut out. We must look a pretty strange group of heroes," he chuckled.*

*"And the quest must be nearly finished by now," said the Snark Maiden. "I reckon that once we start a few firefights in the area near where this sales goblin says the Dragon King is holding Bunty, then the whole thing will reach some sort of massive climax."*

*"Hope so," said Roger, drawing his blade quietly. "Could do with grabbing the goblinesse, as much booty as I can carry and getting out of here. Can't wait to be rid of this band of heroes. Bunch of jokers I call them."*

*"Well, I think you'll get your wish soon enough," said the Snark Maiden, knocking an arrow and dropping to one knee.*

*"Not sure what to do about my goblin though. He seems to think he's here at my side for good," mumbled Roger as he raised his sword.*

*"You have to tell him that enough's enough and that it's time to move on and for nature to revert to stereotype," said the Snark Maiden, letting loose an arrow, knocking and then loosing another. Two orcs with feathers behind their ears fell silently from ambush perches above them. A third groaned slightly as Roger's blade found its mark.*

*"I just look forward to the day when I can wander around a cavern killing as much as I can and not worrying about what Tammy calls the ethical dilemma of skewering a ratman or an ogre without a weapon," said Roger, hacking out at a beastman which suddenly lurched into sight.*

*"Ah, the good old days," chuckled the Snark Maiden, as she fired three more arrows into extra gloomy patches of darkness above and before them. A moment passed and then what sounded like three large sacks of potatoes falling from a great height echoed throughout the corridor.*

*Roger sheathed his sword and sat down. "Fancy a cheese and pickle roll?" he asked, offering a large bread bun to his companion.*

*"Don't mind if I do," replied the Snark Maiden, as she plopped the lid onto her quiver and hitched her bow onto her back once again.*

The baggage hall in Shanghai's Pudong International Airport is enormous. It's probably about four football pitches long and has carousels as far as the eye can see. There's also a rather spectacular roof as well, which looks like a swirling tent canvas in a gale, which is held to the ground by a series of enormous metal pontoon pegs, but only just.

"Reminds me of 'The Glades' shopping centre in Bromley. Grand piece of engineering. I wonder if the yellow devils did it themselves or if they got the Germans in. They're very good at big structures like this. Not like the French who are hopeless," remarked Alfred Fennell, as he stared up at the space-age roof, with hands clasped behind his back, the way old people do when admiring something.

"Yes dear. It's very big," said Hilda flatly. "Perhaps we should keep an eye out for our bags though, rather than admiring the architecture. I put a broad red band round our cases so we recognise them immediately."

Alfred was about to reply when a small and very friendly King Charles spaniel started nuzzling his leg.

"Well, where did you come from?" he said and bent down to tousle the friendly little fellow's head. The dog stared up at Alfred and wagged its tail hard.

"Strange," said Alfred to Hilda. "Thought they didn't allow dogs into airports."

"Maybe it's different in China, dear," said Hilda without removing her eyes from the small hole in the wall where the bags would shortly emerge.

"Thought the only dogs they allowed inside were served up on a plate," said Alfred a little too loudly.

"You!" barked a distinctly unfriendly voice suddenly. "You!" it repeated, only louder this time.

Alfred and Hilda swung round and were surprised to see not one but to official men in uniforms, toting impressive firearms.

"It's not ours," tried Alfred and patted the dog again. "Honestly, guv. It just came up to us and I was being friendly the way the British are with dogs. We're a doggie nation, you see."

"You! Come with us!"

"Steady on," said Alfred dangerously. "He never liked being addressed abruptly, especially by Johnny Foreigner.

"Bag!" said one of the guards, looking at Hilda.

The next few moments could have been totally disastrous for the Fennells had a tall and thin man in a rather official-looking raincoat not stepped in front of a belligerent Alfred, who was just getting ready for a 'dust-up' with a Chinaman who he thought had just called his wife a 'bag'.

"Mr. Fennell. Mr. Alfred Plantagenet Fennell of Greenway, Bromley Common, Kent," said the man in a booming voice.

Alfred took a pace back and gave the man the once-over. "Hilda! It's that daft copper from the hill," he said after a moment of brain-racking. "The one that brought down one of his own whirlybirds with that truncheon of his."

"Quite," said Chief Inspector Pringle in a clipped and annoyed tone. "But I think that you had better concentrate on the problem at hand rather than delve too deeply into... unpleasanteries in the distant past."

"Unpleasanteries? Is that a proper word?" asked a bewildered Alfred. "Anyway, I ain't got any unpleasanteries that I can't sort out myself. And you haven't got jurisprudence here, so I don't have to listen to you."

"Then you do know that this is a sniffer dog and that these are two Chinese Customs officials who want to inspect your hand luggage, don't you?"

Alfred stepped back and frowned at the dog which was still wagging its tail and demanding more strokes and pats. He looked hard at the dog and whispered in a voice only meant for canine ears: "Judas."

"Of course we knew that, Constable," said Hilda quickly, while Alfred was talking to the dog. "But perhaps these Chinese bag inspectors have made a small mistake. We aren't carrying any guns or drugs. Honestly. There were many more suspicious fellows on our plane who they should be inspecting. Take that man over there for example," said Hilda, pointing at Mr. Bibby. "If ever there was a suspicious fellow, he would get my vote."

The two customs officials, whose English was not that good, seemed to ignore most of what Hilda was saying, but suddenly went stiff at the mention of guns and drugs.

"Come now! Room!" barked the more erudite one and gesticulated towards a door about a mile away across the cavernous baggage hall.

Fifteen confusing minutes later and Alfred and Hilda were standing in a small room with Chief Inspector Pringle and the two Customs officials. In front of them was a large table covered with the contents of their hand luggage.

The officials were having a hard time discovering what had interested the sniffer dog so much. There seemed to be so much in front of them which they did not understand. It was like a caveman trying to understand the contents of an alien spaceship.

"What that?" grunted one of the men and poked a jar of marmite suspiciously.

"My mate, Marmite," said Alfred proudly. "Spreads very nicely on a piece of Wonderloaf, "he beamed happily. "Wouldn't go anywhere without a jar."

The jar was passed in front of the dog, which just stared disdainfully at the floor. Clearly it had taken grave offence at being called a Judas in public.

A packet of Weetabix was similarly examined as were Hilda's lumbago pills and Alfred's angina tablets. All seemed perfectly well with the world with these items. It was then that one of the inspectors unearthed a brick of Sainsbury's best Red Leicester cheese.

It was at this moment that the dog suddenly perked up and started barking, while attempting to climb the walls of the little room.

"Likes a spot of cheese, does he?" remarked Alfred generously. "Not surprising, it is top quality stuff."

"Not good!" exclaimed one of the officials, rolling his eyes in a very menacing way and desperately trying to restrain the dog.

"I take issue with that, young man," said Alfred. "It is very good, not like the stuff you get at Tescos or Safeway's, though you probably wouldn't know that, being Chinese and all," finished Alfred, frowning hard.

"Cheese not good in China. Very bad," said the man loudly and pushed the offending article to one side with the business end of his gun.

"It's good anywhere," continued Alfred, getting increasingly angry.

"Not allowed! Forbidden!"

"What!" blurted Alfred. He could not imagine any country in the world banning Red Leicester.

"Dairy food regulations," interrupted Pringle. "Can't bring anything like that into the People's Republic, I'm afraid."

"God's trousers!" exclaimed Alfred with feeling. "What sort of country is this?"

# SIXTEEN

*"I like Chinese.*
*They only come up to your knees.*
*They're cute and cuddly and easy to please..."*
**(The opening lines to the song about the Chinese by Monty Python man, Eric Idle)**

The Pudong Shangri-La Hotel is a massive five-star sprawling monstrosity sitting right on the banks of the Huangpu River, which bisects the city. The place is a typical luxury hotel, the likes of which can be found almost anywhere in the civilised world. Nine hundred and eighty-one award winning rooms with, as the brochure remarks: 'panoramic, floor-to-ceiling views of the historic Bund'.

The Bund is the area of Shanghai which nestles next the river on the opposite bank to the Shangri-La Hotel and attracts that sort of Sunday stroller who is deeply into marvelling at massive skyscrapers from afar.

The hotel itself has no real unique Chinese-ness about it, just a rather uneasy feeling that tourists with bulging sacks of money are checking in every minute of the day and night.

It has far too many restaurants with names like Fook-Lam-Moon, Ling-Bah-Fook and Gui-Hua-Lou, just so that the western tourist realises that he or she really is in China. There is also the inspirationally-named bar on the first floor called: 'The Bar', where smart casual dress is obligatory.

There are also spas, swimming pools and all sorts of coffee lounges located in various scenic nooks throughout the public expanses of the Mezzanine and first floor.

Finally, there is a pastry shop called 'The Gourmet' which offers takeaway ice-cream, cakes, cookies and pastries …that are certain to put a smile on your face', or so the hotel brochure proudly proclaims.

Delegates attending the many conventions held in the hotel's gigantic halls throng the place every week of the year. Needless to say, the only talk that graces the coffee shops, restaurants, halls, corridors and spas is of just one thing – money.

And it was here that the first International Conference for Agents and Schools – ICAS – was to be held. The organisers of the event, a company based in Denmark and run by a man called Teddy Jensen, wanted the whole thing to be a grand and unforgettable affair which would make its mark in the field of education not just in China, but globally.

Jensen was a rather tall man with a bald head and a look of cool but distant authority about him. He had built up his company from a back room in the small Danish town of Brondby to an empire covering all continents of the world and employing a workforce of over a hundred willing and thoroughly multilingual, mostly female staff.

The idea of an agents' workshop had come to him one afternoon when entertaining a delegation of Vietnamese tour operators in Copenhagen. He had suddenly had the brainwave that if he could get all the best agents in the world together under one roof with the biggest language schools and universities, then everyone would be insanely happy - and he would become insanely rich.

The Vietnamese visitors had quickly agreed with the idea, since having to trek around Europe for two hectic and expensive weeks, visiting obscure schools up back streets in Stuttgart and Newcastle was not really their idea of a good time.

Far better to fly all the managers and marketing people to a luxury hotel somewhere exotic and sit them all down in serried ranks in one large ballroom. Two days of lightning, speed-date appointments with the Vietnamese and their like, who could then spend the rest of the week shopping, eating, drinking and then doing a little more shopping. Everyone a winner.

Of course, there were drawbacks. First, it was extremely expensive. Two thousand pounds paid for one small table for the duration of the event. Teddy Jensen's brainwave did not come cheaply.

Second, the place was a goldfish bowl where there were no secrets. Everyone knew who was doing business with who.

Third, such a jamboree would naturally attract the big man or president of most of the companies attending. A luxury hotel was not to be wasted on a marketing or sales manager. This was unfortunate for two reasons. First, the big man had as much idea about business as the average Londoner has about the Nanjing ping-pong team. Second, presidents of companies generally have short memories and tend to lose business cards extremely easily.

There were other more practical problems with the event. For example, meetings were scheduled to last for only twenty minutes during the two working days, a bell being rung when a meeting was to end and another start.

This was all fine and dandy when you were doing business with a Danish or an Italian businessman, but to the Chinese businessman, who was more used to three hours chatting followed by a hearty dinner to seal the deal, these twenty minute sessions were both bewildering and somewhat meaningless.

And finally, there was always a rather aggressive feeling in the air from the ringing of the first bell rang on day one of the event, as squeaky-clean and immaculately-dressed marketing people from the west tried to bag the best agents from under the noses of their competitors.

It resembled the first hour of a Harrods January sale as sales executives jockeyed for prominence with the largest Chinese student providers, using any and all means at their disposal to get business cards exchanged and a meeting arranged.

It all made for a thoroughly sumptuous, luxurious, magnificent and totally confusing occasion - tinged with backstabbing and skulduggery in all its most fundamental marketing forms.

Detective Constable Ford was sitting with his back against a rather greasy wall in The Screaming Egg just off Piccadilly Circus in central London. Opposite him and scrutinising his every action and word were both Caroline Williams and Dave Springett, who was still wearing the bottom half of his recently-washed and very fluffy panda suit. The head-piece sat on the table beside him and was frowning at Ford.

Springett was eating his trademark plate of chips and tomato ketchup, while Caroline was nibbling at a plain scone. Ford had a heavily-stewed cup of tea for company.

"That was not a very nice trick," muttered Ford sulkily and had a deep draught of tea. "Probably cost the Met something like ten thousand quid in manpower and resources if you add up everything at the end of the day."

Springett could not help a small chortle.

"It's all very well for you jokers to have a good laugh, but this is serious police business, you know."

"It's your own fault," said Caroline, acerbically. "You should have checked all your leads much more carefully and not just raided every place we happened to mention during a casual conversation."

"Drug factory in the basement," sniffed Ford, unhappily. "You should have seen the look on the face of the director of that school when our SWAT squad confronted him with that piece of news. Damn near fainted!"

"I can't believe you just went ahead and took the place apart merely on a side remark from one of us," said Caroline. Springett stuffed a forkful of chips into his mouth.

"And I don't want to get into what happened during our visit to the British Council," grumbled Ford. "To raid the place is one thing, but to accuse the Director-General of having ladies of the night in the reception area of the building... well, let's just say that I think I'll be receiving a call from high up pretty soon I think."

"Sorry," squeaked Springett, unconvincingly.

"Anyway," continued Ford. "Your friend is up to his neck in trouble. I could probably already get him ten years just on what he's done up to now."

"Which is precisely nothing," said Caroline.

DC Ford sighed. It was not easy explaining policing matters to the general public, especially to pranksters like these two. He decided to have a another go. "For starters, we both know he's a member of an underground terrorist cell. That's ten years without even thinking about a court appearance. The government threw away the rule book when it comes to anything smacking of terrorism. We could lock him up forever if we wanted to."

"But he's is China," said Springett, through a greasy shovelful of chips.

"And that's our current problem," said Ford, truthfully. "We want to get him back immediately, so we can ask him what the devil he's playing at. The man's dabs are all over every crime scene from here to John o' Groats. There are people high up at the Yard asking very searching questions about Mr Percy Raymond Gabbitt, I can tell you. He's only just behind IS in the league table of most wanted terrorists, you know."

"But he could not possibly have done anything," said Caroline.

"Then are why his fingerprints everywhere."

"And infiltrating our little game is all part of finding out, is it?" asked Caroline, with both eyebrows on the ceiling.

"Well, yes," responded Ford, putting his mug down. "I have to admit that was a little… left-field. We had to think of a way of getting to him. We also wanted to know how you managed to collapse virtually every computer system at the Yard with this damn game. Piqued our interest."

"Really?" spluttered Springett.

"Viruses and Trojans ran amok in forensics. They had multiple contamination of whole real crime scenes with orc and beastmen statistics. Could have been very serious. Several very nasty villains nearly walked on technicalities."

"So," said Caroline, slowly. "What now?"

"Well, I have a meeting tomorrow morning to see if I still have a job after all those futile raids and, well, I need to apologise to you two, I suppose."

"Really?" sniffed Caroline, as she popped the last piece of scone into her mouth.

"And," continued Ford hesitantly. "You have to help me persuade Percy to come home."

Nero Handsworth was having a minor crisis as he sat in the library at Wormwood Scrubs and pretended to read 'Hard Times' by Charles Dickens.

He had just received a confusing phone call from Chipchase saying that the two of them had safely arrived at the hotel in Shanghai - the only fly in the ointment being the rather strange remark that some pensioners from the plane had tried to put the finger on Mr Bibby in the baggage hall. That was certainly rather odd.

Nero scratched his head and read a few more lines from his book. Someone had just spontaneously combusted. He knew how the poor victim must have felt.

He thought a little more about the phone call. Apparently, the world and his dog were now all holed up in the same hotel in downtown Shanghai. Every man jack of them.

Nero thought long and hard for a few moments. He had to keep a clear mind at times like this. Focus on the goal, he thought, and do not get sidetracked by irritating, but essentially unimportant, minor facts which would only muddy the waters. Chipchase's call might have muddied the waters, but he had to ignore these peripheral distractions.

But... what in god's name was Chief Inspector Pringle and those two old people from the battle of Box Hill doing there in China at the same hotel at exactly the same moment as his team? Nero shuddered. If only he could be there to have a good look around himself.

He put Dickens down. Given the constantly-changing circumstances over there, could Mr Chipchase and Mr Bibby be trusted? He bit his lower lip and came to the uncomfortable conclusion that the answer had to be a disturbing no.

He looked around the library and then, seeing that there were no warders present, he pulled his illegal mobile phone out and tapped in a number.

After a few worrying moments of idle ringing, someone was grunting a nervous 'What?' at him.

"It's me," said Nero, quietly.

"What?"

"I need you to get on a plane immediately."

"What?"

"I'll buy the ticket. But you have to be on the first flight out tomorrow morning."

"What?"

"Pack your bags, Fred. You're going to China."

"What!"

*They were getting very close indeed. Roger the Norse Fighter could feel it in his bones. And his bones rarely let him down.*

*They had been in level five for the last three hours and had cleared out two large rooms and several corridor sections of critters with sharp teeth and a nasty attitude. They now stood at the top of a flight of stairs which led to a gloomy area some thirty feet below.*

*"Looks like the big one, boys," said Endymion, breathlessly. "And not a minute too soon, either. I'm down to my last six scrolls and two acid rain*

*potions. I'll need a refill pretty soon or you'll just be relying on my expertise with a small dagger, which is not that proficient."*

*"Better have a few moments rest," said Roger, crouching down, wearily.*

*"That was a close one," said the Snark Maiden, as she joined him. "Thought at least one of us was a gonner that time."*

*"Hmmm," murmured Roger, in a way which signified that this would not have been such a bad thing.*

*"Fuck this for a game of soldiers!" exclaimed a voice from further back.*

*Roger frowned and tried to ignore the interruption. "I reckon we must be pretty close to the throne room of the Dragon King by now and hopefully near to where Bunty is being held."*

*"Just hope there's not a lot more between us and her," said the Snark Maiden quietly. "I've only got five platinum arrows left. Then it's back to the normal kind, which don't really cut the mustard in level five."*

*"Anyone got a ciggie?" shouted a voice from back in the gloom. "I'm fair gasping."*

*Crystal Meth staggered into view and sat down in a crumpled heap next to Roger. "I'm totally fucked!" she added a little obviously. "Never thought we'd get past Cedric back there. Fucking nearly roasted us. Don't know how we avoided the fucking flamethrower."*

*"Cedric?" queried Roger, as he took his sword out and began cleaning the weapon.*

*"Cedric – the pit dragon."*

*"Ah," said Roger.*

*"What I can't fucking understand," continued Crystal, "is why you keep asking me to enter dangerous rooms first. Surely it would make more sense for you or Obby to go in first."*

*"It's done on a strict rota basis," sniffed Roger, a little guiltily.*

*"A rota basis whereby I'm always fucking first?" asked Crystal, patting out a small fire which had been smouldering away in the copious dark layers of her dress.*

*Whatever Roger was about to say slipped away into insignificance as the Snark Maiden suddenly leapt to her feet and went into arrow-knocking mode. Roger was up and ready a moment later. Crystal Meth stayed on the floor though, looking moody and upset.*

*"Secret door," hissed the Snark Maiden, indicating a slight indent in the cavern wall.*

*"Trapped?" asked Roger, professionally.*

*"No," said Endymion, who had quickly joined the three of them and was waving a blue candle beside the indent.*

*"Lock and load," said Li Bang Cho, pushing his way the front.*

*"Not your turn," whispered Roger.*

*"You have got to be fucking joking," uttered a voice from the floor.*

*"I'll have a peep first," said another voice.*

*They looked down at the small figure of Tubby the Goblin, staring smilingly up at them.*

*Roger frowned yet again. "A pit dragon wouldn't even waste its breath on you," said Roger.*

*"Exactly," said Tubby, with a gleam in his eye. "A small goblin could slip in there without anyone or anything taking any serious notice at all. I could then have a quick root around and return here to report what's in there. Sensible or what?"*

*Roger frowned. Although the tactics were definitely very sound, it smacked slightly of being a little underhand. Heroes generally had no time for subterfuge like that. And anyway, they had been rather mean in getting Crystal to do the suicidal stuff on the last four occasions. "OK," he said, slowly. "Five minutes and then we're coming in though – firing in all directions."*

*"I'd best be going then," said Tubby, adjusting his bow-tie, as if he were about to step into a sales meeting. He pushed the door a little and was gone.*

*"He's like that all the time," said Tammy.*

*"Like what?" asked Roger.*

*"Impulsive," replied Tammy. "Suddenly he's up and doing things nobody would expect… or appreciate," he added.*

*"Well," mumbled Roger. "I have to admit it was a brave thing to do, although he probably isn't really in any danger, being a goblin and all."*

*"So says you," said Tammy.*

*"Well, all right. I'll say thanks when he comes out," muttered Roger, moodily.*

*"No one ever says fucking thank you to me," muttered a voice from the floor.*

*Five short minutes passed and the party arranged itself into its usual strike formation. Roger then signalled that he would go first, much to Crystal's relief, and began a silent three-two-one countdown sequence.*

*The door clicked open on two.*

*"Hold on there, fellas," said the now familiar voice of the sales goblin. "Just little me and... a few potential customers, I'm delighted to say."*

*The heroes relaxed slightly and retreated down the corridor as three rather bedraggled but grateful-looking black orcs wandered into the corridor behind Tubby. The heroes went into high alert pose again.*

*"Easy there," said Tubby. "Stand down, boys. I said they were customers."*

*"But they're black orcs," said Roger, thickly. "Renowned throughout the known world for sadistic cruelty and cannibalism, when vaguely peckish."*

*"Meet Arthur, Manfred and Julius. Customers. And they're artists, as well," said Tubby, as if that excused pretty much everything. The black orcs bowed, a little warily.*

*"They're what?" growled Roger, looking at the jet-black creatures, worriedly.*

*"They specialise in portraits. Often to be found at the entrance of new levels offering to paint the portraits of heroes for a groat or two. And they're..." began Tubby.*

*"And they're not joining us," interrupted Roger, firmly.*

*Tubby cleared his throat and continued as if he had not heard Roger. "They've been imprisoned by the Dragon King for sundry reasons of no particular importance for the last six months and are dead keen to get their own back, as soon as possible. They're not just good with a paint-brush. More importantly, they also each want to buy a tub of treacle from yours truly at an amazing three per cent discount. So, put your weapons down and give my new customers a little elbow room."*

*"Jesus fucking Christ," said Crystal Meth, with feeling. "Black orcs? How fucking cool is that?"*

Bob Irwin and Percy Gabbitt were busy settling in. They were sharing a room on the third floor of the Shangri-La and Irwin had just switched the television to the porn channel.

"Don't you think you should unpack your stuff first?" asked Gabbitt.

"Later," replied Irwin, as the opening credits flashed onto the screen.

"You'll never guess what's being shown today," said Irwin, lounging back on his deep, soft bed and jabbing away at the remote.

"I wouldn't even try to guess," said Gabbitt, as he hung two neatly-folded shirts onto coat hangers."

"Donkeyman meets the Pussycat," announced Irwin, dramatically. We can watch it again and again and again all day for just seven hundred RMB."

"And it won't show up on our bill?" asked Gabbitt.

"Ah, good point," muttered Irwin, his finger hovering over the Pay button.

"We could just watch the free one minute and see the rest back at my place on DVD next week. Sort of whet our appetites," he said and threw the remote onto an armchair by his bed.

"Or we could just not watch it at all and get ready for the official reception in exactly two hours time," came the voice of reason from the bathroom.

A minute passed and Irwin's head appeared round the bathroom door. "You missed a good minute," he said, slyly.

"What a pity," said Gabbitt, as he arranged his toothbrush and deodorant on the pink and grey marble sink unit.

"A classic preview minute which would rank up there with the best preview minutes of all time," continued Irwin.

"Better than the Star Wars preview?" asked Gabbitt.

"What?" That was a load of old tat," responded Irwin quickly. "Great film but the preview minute was dreadful.

"So, what's the best preview minute of all time, then?" asked Gabbitt from the bathroom.

"The Lord of War, starring Nicholas Cage."

"Never heard of it," said Gabbitt and walked back into their room.

"Brilliant film with a stunning preview minute. It starts in an armaments factory somewhere in the west. The camera focuses in on just one bullet. After lots of jiggery-pokery involving being melted, remelted, dropped onto a succession of conveyor belts, it's then packed in an ammunition box and shipped off to some African republic somewhere. Then, as the preview ends, it's fired into some poor bastard's head. Bang! What a preview! From factory to death in one minute. Genius."

"And that was all in the preview?"

"Well, maybe not, but that was the first minute of the film. Brilliant. Kill to see it. Percy."

Just two rooms down the corridor and a similar discussion on the nature of violence was taking place.

"It should only take a minute if we plan it carefully. Then it's grab, biff hard and run," said Mr Chipchase.

"We have to be careful, Mr Bibby. This is one slippery mother-f..."

"You don't have to tell me that, Mr Bibby," interrupted Chipchase, as he arranged his toothbrush and deodorant in their bathroom. "But if we do this by the numbers, we'll have the bastard and fifty gees will come sailing our way."

"I hope it'll be that easy and we can get out of here fast," said Bibby. "I don't bloody fancy having to sit in a hall downstairs for two sodding days talking to the Chinks about learning fuckin' English at... what was the name of our flippin' school again?"

"The Scrubs International Company... or SIC for short."

"You got that right," muttered Bibby, unhappily.

"Just have a look at our brochure. It'll tell you everything you need to know," said Chipchase, tossing five copies of a multi-coloured leaflet onto the bed beside the prone form of the gloomy and heavily-jetlagged Bibby.

"I could do with a fuckin' drink," said Bibby.

"The reception starts in two hours," said Chipchase, as he unzipped his suitcase and started stacking a pile of their brochures on the floor. "You can drink your fill there... and it's free too."

"Shame we don't have the bazooka," murmured Bibby.

"Indeed," agreed Chipchase. "That would certainly help."

In the next room, Bob Burley was having a nap and dreaming of sailing a yacht single-handedly around the world and trying to avoid the island inhabited by Bob Irwin and Miss World.

Strangely enough, in exactly the same room but on one floor above, Chief Inspector Pringle was standing by the window and staring out at the busy Huangpu River.

Boats of all sizes were chugging up and down the river laden with chunky dull-coloured containers, all intent on making the People's Republic that little bit richer. Pringle sighed. He had never seen anything like it. The place just thrummed naked and enthusiastic commercial energy.

He flicked open his cell phone and hit numbers. A long ten seconds later and there was the distant but distinctive English ringing tone.

Someone answered.

"How's it going?" asked Pringle, flatly.

"Fucking A," came the surprising reply.

"I do wish you would not use that sort of language," snapped Pringle.

"I know you do, dad."

"So, nothing to report?"

"Don't talk to me like that, dad. I'm not one of your fu... underling stooges."

"Sorry," sighed Pringle. "Everything going OK, then?"

"It's actually more fun than I thought, dad. They're weirder than I am."
"Don't tell me about it," muttered Pringle.
"Not sure if I'm one of the gang yet though. I think they're trying to get me killed off."
"Just do your best, Priscilla. That's all we can expect."
"And you still want this Roger dude to get his ass back to London, do you?"
"Err, yes, that's right."
"Just leave it to Crystal. She'll sort the fucker out."
"Pris."
"Sorry. Just getting into character."
"Don't. I've had enough of that from my detective constable. What race are you?"
"I'm a neo cyber-Goth."
"A what? Never mind. I don't want to know."
"Copy that, dad. Leave it to Crystal Meth. If she can't deliver, then no one can."
"Jesus Christ," muttered the Chief Inspector. "Is that your name?"
"Good, isn't it? Better than that creep, Obby. Is he your man?"
"That easy to spot, is it?"
"All he needs are shiny black boots and a truncheon, dad."
"God."

By a remarkable coincidence in the very next room to Chief Inspector Pringle, one of the two occupants was imploring the Almighty at exactly the same moment.
"God!" exclaimed Alfred Fennell.
"What now, dear?" asked a weary Hilda, from deep under a soft duvet.

"The only tea they have here is some green stuff that looks like washing up liquid," muttered Alfred, as he poured boiling water onto a green tea bag.

"It is China dear," came the sleepy reply.

"Don't I know it?" grumbled Alfred into the steaming cup. "And taking my Red Leicester too - the liberty," he continued, unhappily.

"Come to bed, dear, you're jetlagged," murmured Hilda, as she began to drop off.

"But it's only seven in the evening. If I sleep now, I'll be all over the place come two in the morning," replied a truculent Alfred. "I think I may go for a stroll," he said and reached for his coat.

"Yes dear," murmured Hilda, already three-quarters asleep.

Down on the second floor, Teddy Jensen was busying himself with a rapidly diminishing tower of red plastic folders. He was in a rather good mood and was enjoying a bit of harmless banter with a few of the delegates who were at the three long desks. They were registering for the ICAS event and collecting their folders and name badges.

"So, have you bought a Rolex watch yet?" he asked, with a twinkle in his eye.

"On my salary, I couldn't afford the case it's put in," muttered a thin man with receding brown hair and a goaty beard.

"You can buy one on the road outside the hotel," continued Teddy, happily. He liked to sound knowledgeable of local colour.

"Really?" asked the delegate, as he pinned his name badge to a tired corduroy suit lapel.

"All genuine fakes," laughed Teddy. "You wouldn't know the difference."

"Do you think they have a Bvlgari?" asked a woman who was leaning in on the conversation from a neighbouring registration station.

"Not sure what a Bvlgari is, Jane dear," sniffed the goaty beard man, in a very politically-correct way. No one was going to get him to start pandering to such designer nonsense.

"Oh, come on, Gil," said the woman called Jane. "Buy one for your boyfriend."

"He most certainly would not approve," replied Gil the goaty man. "He has an old-fashioned digital Casio which has never let him down and he's happy with that. If I were to buy him something made by a Bulgarian he would be appalled at the extravagance. It is merely a timepiece after all.

"The real ones can sell for about fifty thousand dollars. They're lifestyle statements," said Teddy, as he slit open another box of vinyl registration folders.

"That's more than my flat costs," muttered Gil. "What does that say about my lifestyle?"

"Well, I think it's disgraceful," said the Jane woman. "People that buy that sort of thing should have their money taken away from them."

"Which is why they sell perfect fakes here," said a smiling Teddy. "So that everyone can get a slice of luxury.:

"I wonder, purely as a point of interest and I totally disapprove, of course, but do they have any Gucci watches? My niece is going through a diamonique phase and well, you have to... well, you know..." she trailed off, unconvincingly.

"Of course," responded Teddy Jensen. "You can get anything in Shanghai, they say," he chuckled. "Have a walk along the path by the river and the purveyors of these watches will come to you with suitcases full of everything you can think of, don't worry."

"What about it, Gil?" asked Jane. "It'll be a bit of an adventure."

"As long as they don't nab you for soliciting, dear," said Gil and barked loudly at his own joke.

"Very funny."

"I wonder if they would take Switch. I'm a bit low on the local stuff," murmured Gil.

Teddy Jensen sighed and made a mental note of Mr Gilbert Grimm of the London Institute of Proper Spoken English or LIPSE and Jane Bobbin, the designated British Council representative attending.

He was about to move on to another small group of bewildered and jetlagged delegates when he suddenly became aware of a smallish figure standing rather too close to him and staring up quizzically.

"May I help you?" asked Teddy, with a disapproving frown.

"Any idea where the lavvies are? Got to get my bearings," said the man, loudly.

"The what?" squawked Teddy, in surprise.

"The lavatories," said the voice, flatly.

"Have you registered yet?" he asked, hoping that this creature was not a delegate.

"What? Register to go to the lavvy?" was the unhappy reply. "Do you have to register to have a wee? This country gets stranger by the minute. They take my cheese and now I have to fill a form in to have a pee. All right, it's your country, mate. Hand me a form. I only want a number one, this time round. But can you give me a couple of number two forms, as well? I think I'll need a few of them in reserve - foreign food and all that."

"Are you attending the workshop? Are you a delegate?" asked Teddy, desperately.

"You're having a workshop on weeing?"

"No!" exclaimed Teddy. It was time to put a stop to such idiocy. Several delegates within hearing range were already giggling at his expense.

"This is a language workshop, sir. But I believe that the nearest toilets are down the corridor, on the right. And now I have to attend to this gentleman here," he said and turned to a tall man in a dark suit who was scrutinizing him the way a scientist would regard a small but not that interesting creature.

"Thank you, kindly," said the old man to Teddy's back and then wandered off down the corridor, whistling a jaunty tune.

"Now sir, may I have your name and institution?" asked Teddy Jensen, recomposing himself after the toilet interruption.

"Pringle of the Yard," said the man, ominously.

"Pardon sir?" squeaked Teddy, worriedly.

"The Yard School of English. We're new to this sort of thing."

"Ah," sighed Teddy, in relief. "Then I bid you a warm welcome to ICAS and hope you have a successful and very profitable time over the next two days."

"Hmmm," was the noncommittal reply.

"Here is your folder containing all appointment slots and a list of the delegates attending. I believe you already have a full meeting schedule. It would seem that the Chinese are very interested in the Yard School, Mr Pringle," said Teddy, his smile returning. "You're already very popular."

"Mr Percy Gabbitt," said Pringle, slowly. He felt it was important to remain focussed and not get side-tracked by tall, sycophantic Danes.

"Who sir?" queried Teddy.

"Is Mr Percy Gabbitt attending?" asked Pringle.

"Ah," said Teddy and reached for a clipboard. After a moment of finger tracing up and down a long list, he tapped on the clipboard and looked up at Chief Inspector Pringle. "He's part of the Arapacana delegation, sir. They're down to meet you tomorrow afternoon at three, I believe."

"Right," said Pringle, wondering what the hell an Arapacana was. "Thanks," he said and began to move off.

"Don't forget the reception tonight, sir," said Teddy, as Pringle left the registration tables.

Pringle walked down the corridor deep in thought. At last he was just a few hours from meeting his nemesis again. It seemed slightly strange to be thinking about facing Gabbitt again. It had been a long time. But not long enough.

Something lurched into him and Pringle dropped his ICAS folder. It hit the floor and spewed its contents all over the floor.

"Nice lavvies," said a voice, as he bent down.

"What?" he grunted and looked into the eyes of the man with the bladder problems. "Oh, it's you again."

"You could eat your dinner off the floor in there," proclaimed Alfred Fennell to anyone within earshot.

"Indeed," murmured Pringle.

"The yellow devils know how to do a nice toilet. I could spend the afternoon in there."

"I'm pleased you like them," said Pringle.

"Got to get back to see how Hilda's doing now, then get ready for dinner."

"Very nice," said Pringle. "I hope you haven't had any more cheese problems."

"Don't get me started," mumbled Alfred and trundled off in search of an elevator.

"Very nice," said Hilda Fennell, and supped at a cup of green tea. "Has a rather earthy flavour to it. I rather like it."

She was sitting in her hotel bed with the duvet pulled up to her waist. Percy Gabbitt was sitting at the end of the bed, smiling benignly.

"I never thought you and Alfred would come."

"Neither did Alf," said Hilda and raised an eyebrow. "But I told him that we're not dead yet and still had a bit of kick left in us. He wanted to go to Bognor again, but I said no and that was that. So here we are in China."

"Are you staying long?" asked Gabbitt.

"Two weeks to see it all," replied Hilda and had another sip at her tea. "And you don't have to look after us either. We survived a world war and decimalisation, so I think we can survive a few days with these foreigners."

"I'll help as much as I can," said Gabbitt, warmly. "And it all begins tonight too."

"Tonight?"

"I'd like you to attend the reception as my official guests," he said. "It would be nice to have you there and the food's free. And there's dancing afterwards."

"Oh, I don't know about that," said Hilda, with a gleam in her eye.

"I would like the honour of the first dance," said Percy.

Hilda giggled like a schoolgirl.

The door to the room opened and Alfred walked in.

"We've got a visitor," shouted Hilda.

"Oh, aye," came the answer.

"Young Percy's here and we're going dancing tonight. What do you say to that?"

"You what?' was Alfred's response, as he came into the room and plumped himself down into one of the armchairs by the window. "You have got to see the toilets in this hotel. They're the Taj Mahal of loos."

Bob Burley was sitting in the bar with Bob Irwin.

"So, are we ready?"

"Never been better prepared."

"Arapacana's biggest two days ever."

"Should be fun."

"But I think we'll be the only ones laughing."

## SEVENTEEN

*"Marketing and Life are very similar. Sometimes, when all seems lost, you have to do something totally extraordinary. Rabbit out of the hat extraordinary."*
**(Professor Max Snaffle – Peckham School of Marketing)**

Teddy Jensen picked up a small bronze bell and shook it vigorously. A bright tinkling sound echoed around the cavernous hall and everyone started talking at a million miles an hour.

The first ICAS Shanghai Workshop had begun...

... which was something of a miracle, given the problems the previous night.

Teddy Jensen sat down heavily and poured himself a large mineral water. He gave all the delegates' tables a quick three-sixty from his position on the raised ICAS podium in the middle of the hall.

He took a tentative sip from a trembling hand and thought back several hours. Less than two hours sleep after an appalling official dinner which had ended with multiple complaints from vomiting and dizzy delegates. It had all been most disturbing and certainly not the way he had intended his showpiece to start. They were still investigating what it could have been. Teddy's money was on the fish. It had looked worryingly green.

That was not the only problem– he would never allow delegates to invite their own guests to official functions at future workshops – certainly not guests who were over a hundred years old, or thereabouts.

It had also been a minor miracle that the hotel had not cancelled the whole event following the old man's antics with the swan centrepiece on the buffet table.

The thing had only been meant as a table decoration, thought Teddy bitterly.

It had been the unofficial mascot of the hotel and had attended over a hundred similar functions up to that night. Then it had met Alfred Fennell. He shuddered involuntarily as he vividly remembered the old man attacking the swan with a steak knife.

The thing had been down to attend a presidential reception the following week in downtown Shanghai and then to be wheeled out for an official banquet to honour the Pakistani ambassador the following weekend.

Teddy wondered if some creative Chinaman could repair the damage. He rather thought not. The swan had had its day.

Then there had been the problem with the wine. Teddy Jensen made a mental note never to dip into the Shangri-La's wine vault again, unless he found something from a French or German vineyard. He would certainly never again break open six crates of Great Wall Bordeaux.

News from the front-line had been pretty grim that morning too as three schools' representatives had reported sick. Still, it might have been worse. He could have had a major food-poisoning outbreak on his hands. Fortunately, most delegates had avoided the fish and had given up on the wine after one tentative sip. But there were always a few brain-dead delegates, who would doggedly stuff themselves with anything set before them.

"Excuse me, Mr Jensen," said a pinched and nasal voice from a little below the podium's eye-line.

"Yes," said Teddy, on automatic, looking at one of his female student helpers.

"Bit of a problem on Table J8," she said.

Teddy Jensen sighed. You would think that delegates attending an event like this would act like adults and not ten-year-olds. He had already had to field one complaint about the bell he was using to end meetings.

Apparently, it had disturbed a woman delegate rather too near to his podium. Disturbed, for god's sake! That was the whole point of the thing! The old bat looked like she needed a bit of serious disturbing, Teddy had thought, as he had attempted a bit of smoothing, which involved promising to ring the bell a little softer in future.

Then there had been the problem of the Global English Enterprise Company and their position near to the stairwell and women's toilets. Teddy had had to mollify their grumpiness, by explaining that they were actually in the best position in the hall, since all agents would have to visit the small room at some time during the workshop and could be pounced upon by their delegates. Only then did they agree to stay in the same spot. Ten-year-olds, the lot of them, thought Teddy, unhappily.

And now a new problem on... Table J8. He scanned a large piece of A3 paper upon which was a grid showing where all the schools were located in the hall. He traced his finger down the J column and came to number 8... 'The Scrubs School of English.'

*Endymion tore three scrolls in half and threw the scraps of paper into the air. He had absolutely no idea what would happen next and dived into a dark corner. There was a loud explosion and four bull elephants with a line of extra tusks along their backbone plopped into existence. Needless to say, the room in which they suddenly appeared was not really geared to housing three large and thoroughly confused pachyderms.*

*A group of appalled zombies were instantly squashed against an unforgiving stone wall, while a pit snapper quickly realised that the advantages of slithering everywhere on its stomach did not really hold water when there are three huge elephants charging around in the dark.*

*The heroes did not fare so well either. The Snark Maiden had to use all her dexterity to avoid a heavy trunk swish, while Li Bang Cho achieved some sort of a first by leaping onto one of the beasts and attempting to ride it, rodeo-style.*

*Roger crouched in a corner and said a few unkind words about wizards. And then, just as suddenly as they had appeared, the elephants all popped out of existence leaving just a rather earthy aroma behind.*

*"And another winner, courtesy of Endymion the Flippin' Magnificent!" exclaimed the wizard, happily, as he dusted himself down and marched to the centre of the room, where Li Bang Cho lay sprawling in a heap, having hit the cavern floor quite hard after his mount had vaporised.*

*"You stupid..." began Obby the Gladiator, as he tried to knock a kink out of his once-mighty sword. Magic weapons might be pretty incredible in fights with cave trolls and blood dragons but they did not fare that well when trodden on by heavy elephants.*

*"Did you have to make them so big?" asked a grumbling Tammy. He had never liked the wizard*

*and this was approaching the last straw. He was sitting with his back to a wall next to his friend Tubby, who appeared to have lost his sample briefcase. The three artist orcs sat on Tammy's other side looking thoroughly traumatized, which is saying something for an orc.*

*"You nearly brought the roof down on us again," said Roger, angrily.*

*"It was the floor last time," responded Endymio,n with a wounded sniff. "All ceilings have been left in tact the whole time."*

*"No more spell combinations, all right!" said Roger dangerously. "I've had enough of your kind of experimentation down here. From now on, just stick to a standard repertoire of fireballs, acid rain and the odd healing spell. That's final. "*

*Endymion was about to remonstrate when a blood curdling scream echoed through the cavernous vault followed by what sounded like someone dropping one-ton sacks of cement onto the cavern floor. The place shook as though a top-notch earthquake had suddenly hit the place.*

*"Oh fantastic," murmured Roger, unenthusiastically. "Not even enough time to tend our wounds. That's what needless arguing does, you know," he said to no one in particular. "It wastes time."*

*More heavy footfalls echoed throughout the cave. Whatever was coming towards them seemed on the large side of massive and might have given*

*Endymion's elephants pause for thought had they been around.*

*"Mud dragon basilisk!" shouted the Snark Maiden authoritatively.*

*"Holy shit!" exclaimed Li Bang Cho.*

*"We'll just wait just here," squeaked Tammy. He then scampered off back to the entrance of the cavern, followed closely by Julius and his two artist friends, one of whom had a small notepad out and was getting ready for an action sketch of the basilisk.*

*"Not wise to look at the thing in the eye," shouted the Snark Maiden, as loudly as she could to everyone. "They turn you to stone, if they get a firm fix on you."*

*"A what?" squawked Obby, worriedly.*

*"A firm fix," repeated Roger. "And don't ask me what that is. Just don't look at the bugger! Isn't that clear enough?"*

*"Shit on a stick!' exclaimed the neo-cyber Goth of the party. "We have to fucking fight a fucking beast like that without being able to look at the fucker! What sort of fucking game is this?"*

*"One that we lose," said Endymion, quickly packing up his scrolls and retreating to the place where Tammy and Tubby now cowered expertly.*

*"You tie its legs up and I'll have a jab at it," said Roger to the Snark Maiden. "If I can take out its eyes then perhaps we have a chance."*

*"Good thinking," agreed the Snark Maiden. "Just one minor thing though."*

*"What?" asked Roger thickly.*

*"How do you reckon a small elfette with no magic arrows left is going to tie up a monster like that?"*

*"You'll think of something," replied Roger tersely. "You always do."*

DC Ford had had a tip off and was feeling cautiously pleased with himself as he sat at Chief Inspector Pringle's desk at the heart of New Scotland Yard in London.

The tip off had come from an unlikely source and Ford felt in his bones that this one was the real thing, not like the stuff fed to him by his 'friends' in Dark Dawn Three.

Percy Gabbitt had let the little nugget in question slip out just as they were about to call it a night following the mud dragon basilisk fiasco. It had been a chance remark which most people, not trained in the ways of policing and detection, would have missed.

Gabbitt had mentioned the names Brand and Melligan to Caroline after she had asked him about developments on her side of the planet.

He even knew that these two villains would be on a Virgin Atlantic plane back from Shanghai to London the following day. It had been almost too good for words. Ford would have a team of expert trackers shadowing both of them everywhere they went while in the UK and... then they would pounce.

Bob Brand and Jack Melligan would have been mildly disconcerted had they known of DC Ford's plans as they trundled through the mid-morning traffic towards Shanghai's Pudong International Airport. Neither spoke very much as their taxi moved from lane to lane sounding its horn vigorously and at every possible opportunity.

Their mission had been explained to them by Bob Burley on the phone a few hours previously and both Brand and Melligan were feeling a mite apprehensive about it all. It was to be a slightly different mission this time round.

"Not sure about this one," muttered Melligan.

"It's certainly a break from the norm," agreed Brand, as their taxi shot between two juggernauts and hit the breaks so that it could swerve within two inches of the back of a truck carrying about twenty massive tree trunks all stacked in an unsteady pyramid and sticking out the back of the wheezing vehicle by about thirty feet.

"Shit!" squawked Melligan and white-knuckled his door handle.

"Relax," said Brand and eased back in his seat. "These chaps know what they're doing. Insane maniacs, the lot of them, but with bloody quick reactions. Best to shut your eyes and think of England."

"Shit," hissed Melligan again, as the taxi shifted into fifth and nosed its way passed the tree trunks and into empty road again. "We've only just got back to this flippin' country and now we're off on another mad trip. Could have done with a few more days with my feet up in a bar downtown."

"Bob's a bit short-staffed what with this workshop thing. Just us again, I'm afraid."

"It's always us though," mumbled Melligan, as the taxi accelerated to overtake a lorry carrying two hundred cardboard boxes all tied together with one piece of string.

"Let's concentrate on the mission, shall we? Look at me Jack and try not to look at the madness all around us."

"Right," said Melligan, through pursed lips.

"So, it's a mission with a difference this time," said Brand slowly, trying to get Melligan thinking about things other than Chinese driving. "Should be interesting, whatever happens."

"Not sure I really understand the point," said Melligan, sullenly.

"Apparently, it's a personal favour for our friend, Mr Percy Gabbitt. A sort of present from Arapacana for all he's done."

"Why can't he just request a drink and a pay-rise like the rest of us?"

"Because he's Percy Gabbitt," said Brand, with a smile. "You have to expect something a little unique from someone like him."

"It'll certainly be a challenge."

"But..." began Brand, with a smirk. "If we pull it off, then I think our Percy will be mightily impressed."

"I'll be mightily impressed," said Melligan.

"First things first," continued Brand. "We have to hire a car on arrival and then get down to Cornwall, so that we can catch a helicopter out there as soon as possible."

"A helicopter?" squawked Melligan, unhappily.

"A chopper," said Brand.

"Can't we take a boat?"

"Too slow. We need to be out there as fast as possible to initiate part one of the mission. Time is of the essence, apparently."

"Time is always of the essence," muttered Melligan.

A couple of hours away as the Chinese taxi driver drives and on a large concrete patio veranda which looked out onto the main Huangpu River, those exact same words were being spoken by Bob Burley.

"Time is of the essence, everyone. I hope you all realise that. We have to hit all ten tables simultaneously to make the right... statement. Synchronise watches please. Ten o'clock. On my mark: three, two, one."

"Don't have to synchronise," sniffed Irwin. "Got a Samsung Galaxy. Does all that sort of thing for you."

"Aren't they the ones that explode in your pocket?" asked Pamela, frowning.

"Naa, not anymore," replied Irwin. "Anyway, wouldn't that be cool?"

They all stared at Irwin, but said nothing. Australians could be very odd.

"And this stuff really will work?" asked Pamela, raising a bottle of innocent-looking mineral water, after correcting her wristwatch.

"Should do. The chemist chappie back in Suzhou said it could clear blockages in drains within seconds, as well as being a grade A laxative. Sort of has a dual function, like most things in China."

"Jesus," uttered Pamela and hastily put the bottle down. "I thought everyone here already had dodgy tummies after last night's dinner."

"They do. This is to push them over the edge," said Burley, grinning insanely. "All thirty tables to get a couple of these bottles each at exactly the same moment. That's phase one."

"Sorry Bob, but how many phases are there again?" asked Irwin quizzically.

"I do wish you would listen, Bob," said Burley.

"Humour me, Bob," responded Irwin, with a smile.

"Thirty all told."

"Jesus," said Pamela again. "I thought we were just concentrating on the worst seven schools," she added, worriedly.

"We are," said Burley. "They will get the full treatment in due course, don't worry. But the other twenty-three need to have their wrists slapped a little too."

"Wrists slapped?" queried Pamela.

"Indeed," said Burley. This seems just too good an opportunity to miss. Right, positions please, lady and gentlemen. And... good luck."

It would be true to say that the following five hours would be indelibly imprinted on Teddy Jensen's mind for the rest of his life. Actually, there were about thirty other people, who would join him in the indelibly imprinted category.

Not three hundred yards away, but completely oblivious of what was about to happen inside the conference hall, two geriatric Londoners were taking a stroll along the Huangpu River near the hotel.

"Should be a cafe somewhere round here," said the woman.

"I could murder a cup of proper tea," growled the man.

"Well, I'm sure we'll find somewhere soon. It's not such an uncivilised a place."

There was another growl from the man.

"Nice to see young Percy again," said Hilda Fennell, changing the subject.

"He's doing very well for himself," answered Alfred Fennell. "And a very nice young gentleman, as well."

"He can take us round Shanghai, after this conference thing."

"What? The toilet conference," said Alfred.

"That's not really funny, anymore," reprimanded Hilda, primly. "It wasn't really funny in the first place."

"The bloke who's running it is a complete idiot. Couldn't answer a straight question. Forms indeed. All I wanted to do, was have a wee in the nearest lavvy," murmured Alfred, as he stared out at an overladen barge, chugging down the river towards somewhere else with an unpronounceable name.

"I do wish you wouldn't use that word, Alfred Fennell."

"I've always called it a lavvy and I'm not changing now," grumbled Alfred, quietly. "It's like napkins and serviettes," he suddenly continued.

"What's like napkins and serviettes?" asked a puzzled Hilda.

"Stuck up people always say napkins when serviettes is better. Less snobby," said Alfred, with a knowing sniff.

"You are silly, Alfred Fennell," chided Hilda. She then slid her arm through his. He might be a daft old man but he was her daft old man.

"Rolex? You want Rolex?" said a voice from nowhere.

"You what?" grunted Alfred Fennell, as he turned to meet the owner of the intrusive voice.

"Cartier, Omega, Bulgari, Gucci?"

"Me no speakie Chinkie," said Alfred, as slowly as he could.

"Watches - very cheap,' said the man with the watches, clearly not that deterred by Alfred's retort. "Cheap, cheap, cheap. Just looking, mister and lady?"

"What are you blathering on about?" muttered Alfred, dangerously.

"Ooo look, Alfred," said Hilda, clutching his arm. "He's selling those watches you hear about on Crimewatch."

"You what?" queried Alfred.

"Fake watches," explained Hilda, trying to get a good look at the man's collection, which ran up both of his arms.

"Why would I want a fake watch?" asked Alfred, bluntly.

"Never mind," sighed Hilda. "Can I see?" she asked. The man seemed suddenly very happy and produced two smart brown briefcases out of nowhere, which he snapped open and placed on a nearby low concrete wall.

"Gucci for madam?" he asked, happily.

"Don't they look lovely?" marvelled Hilda.

"They look expensive," murmured Alfred for her ears only.

"Very cheap," interrupted the man, who had not got where he was today without having ears like an elephant. "I give you best price in Shanghai. I like German old people very much."

It was actually reasonably calm at the table occupied by the Scrubs School of English. It was located in the centre of the hall quite near to Teddy Jensen's podium. Mr Chipchase and Mr Bibby sat squashed into their small chairs in front of a table dominated by a stack of about one hundred multi-coloured brochures.

They both looked supremely ill at ease in their dark grey suits and identical bright red ties and stared at the somewhat tacky luxuriousness around them with an element of suspicious mistrust. Above them a massive fake crystal chandelier glittered rather too brightly, while the crimson carpet beneath their feet glowed like the entrance to Hell itself.

"Do you know what we're doing here?" mumbled Bibby anxiously.

"Waiting for the moment..." came the reply from Chipchase.

"And then?"

"We strike."

Mr Chipchase was about to elaborate further on his plan to strike, when a tall, willowy man with a bald head and pained expression approached their table.

"Scrubs School of English?" he queried in a slightly disapproving voice. When there was no immediate reply, he moved closer and sat down in one of the two seats on the other side of the table from where Chipchase and Bibby sat.

"What you want?" asked Bibby, belligerently.

"There's been a small complaint," said Teddy Jensen with a warm smile.

"What the f..." began Bibby.

"What seems to be the problem?" interrupted Chipchase, quickly. He gave Bibby a deep frown.

"A Mr Chen from Happy Panda Tours in Chengdu has just issued a formal complaint to my desk saying that you told him to, and I quote, 'shove off, you yellow shit,' at the breakfast buffet. Is this true?"

"Yes," came the surprisingly honest reply. "He tried to push in front of us in the queue."

"Ahh," said Teddy, after a pause. "Are you new to these workshops?"

"Yes," said the two security guards, thickly.

"Well then. May I suggest a little more... tact, in future? We are guests in their wonderful country and it is possibly not that diplomatic to tell them to shove off, especially when they are here to do business with the likes of... you," finished Teddy, a little uncertainly.

As he spoke to the two representatives of this slightly odd school, he began to get a very uncomfortable feeling. Normally, marketing people smiled a lot and tried to speak all the time. These two just sat frowning hard and saying nothing at all, unless you counted the odd grunt now and then.

"So," continued Teddy, "Can I ask you to be a little more... tolerant in future?"

"No problem mate," said Bibby and blew his nose hard into a handkerchief which he had pulled from his jacket pocket.

Teddy was about to hammer home the point a little harder when something caught his attention on a table three rows away. One of the delegates had suddenly risen to his feet and was waving his arms at a small group of Chinese agents. Voices were being raised as well.

"So, I'm pleased that's sorted out," said Teddy and stood up. "If you'll excuse me," he said and smiled broadly again. "I have other...issues to deal with." He then walked off to see what this next problem was all about.

A moment later and a Chinese man with a wild haircut and in a grey, ill-fitting coat and Burberry scarf sat down at the Scrubs table.

"You tell me good points of school?" he asked and jabbed a finger at the pile of brochures.

"Push off, you yellow shit," said Bibby morosely and blew his nose loudly.

Teddy Jensen reached Table G9 just in time to hear another rather odd way of addressing a Chinese agent. Teddy suddenly felt very anxious. The workshop had started badly the previous night and appeared to be on a downhill slope that morning too.

"We don't have Green Monkey Disease at our school!" exclaimed a corpulent delegate.

"But we get email," remonstrated a small Chinese woman. "It say you close down because Korean students give it to you."

"Well, I can assure you..." began the delegate, trying to remain calm.

"We cannot send students to sick school," chipped in another woman. "This very bad for us and students."

"No, I understand that but we..." tried the delegate again.

"What is Green Monkey Disease?" shouted a man at the back of the group. "Like AIDS?"

There was a communal gasp from the group.

"We don't have AIDS or Green Monkey Disease at our school!" shouted the man a little too loudly.

Heads turned from tables a little further away from the immediate orbit of the man's table.

Someone in the C row was heard to mutter something about AIDS being discovered at a school in London, while another whisper, from a quick-thinking marketing shark, was along the lines that London schools were rife with exotic illnesses and that Bournemouth was the place to send students.

"Can I be of any help, Mr Er...?" beamed Teddy Jensen, affably.

"Allebone. Martin Allebone," said the large man with Green Monkey problems, morosely.

"What appears to be the problem here?" asked Teddy.

"Would you tell these people that our school is not infected with fucking Green Monkey Disease," whispered Allebone, trying to keep his voice down. "It was a malicious hoax a few weeks ago and has no substance at all," he spluttered, angrily.

"Green Monkey Disease?" repeated Teddy.

More heads turned towards the table with the exotic problem.

"We don't have it!" exclaimed the man, his face now turning a nasty shade of crimson. "And don't keep saying it so loud! It'll spook the punters!"

"Perhaps you would like to sit down and we can discuss this quietly... like gentlemen," suggested Teddy, meekly. He frowned, as he surveyed the man's desk and saw the name of the school – LICE.

"I don't want to fucking sit down!" said the man. "I want these Chinese people to understand that our school is not infected with some daft disease."

"Quite," responded Teddy, not at all sure who was the crazier – the group of open-mouthed Chinese agents all speaking in hushed tones about AIDS in the decadent west or this fat Englishman who would not sit down and be reasonable.

It was then that someone threw up in Row S and someone else fainted in Row B.

The police arrived about thirty minutes after the initial incident.

The promenade which wound its way along the length of the river and past the Shangri-La Hotel was not normally very busy at that time of the morning, but on this occasion there was quite a crowd gathered near the epicentre of the... incident.

Hilda Fennell was sitting on a low stone wall and shaking her head, resignedly. She was being questioned by a waiter from a nearby Starbucks whose only official standing in the ongoing argument was that he spoke elementary English, which was a hundred times better than most of the other participants in the debate on the path.

"What problem?" tried the waiter, with a smile.

"He shouldn't have said we were German," moaned Hilda, shaking her head, slowly.

"Welcome to our country," said the waiter, happily.

"No one tells Alfred he's German, unless they have a death wish," muttered Hilda.

"I like David Beckham," said the waiter, toothily.

"He gets so angry about things like that. Had the man said American, Australian or Canadian, then he wouldn't have minded, but not German!"

"William Shakespeare and Bilbo Baggins," said the man, after a lot of thought.

It was then that a squattish man in a dark blue uniform and a white milkman's cap strolled up to the crowd and barked something very loud. The police had arrived.

The crowd parted to let this official through. Alfred Fennell stood, jacket off and with sleeves rolled up.

"What problem?" barked the policeman, authoritatively.

"He called me a German," growled Alfred and stared loathingly at the watch salesman.

"Passport," snapped the official.

"No, German," responded Alfred.

Hilda appeared at her husband's side and opened a large cream-coloured handbag which contained all the couple's treasured possessions. Passports were flashed.

There then followed a heated exchange with the seller of the watches. The crowd got larger and, as in all Chinese confrontations, began to take an active role in the proceedings. Someone at the back started shouting at the policeman, while someone else began making aggressive gesticulations towards the English pensioners.

The policeman suddenly shouted something very loudly and there was silence. He turned to Alfred. "Why you throw his case in river?"

"Because he insulted me. He insulted all British people," said Alfred.

"Welcome to our country," said the policeman, after a lot of thought.

Alfred frowned and shook the policeman's hand slowly.

"He must not sell illegal things here," explained the policeman. "We try close these people down, but they always here selling to foreign tourists. Not good. He... hooligan," he said and shook Alfred's hand again.

He then turned round, picked up the watch salesman's other case and in one easy movement hurled it over the concrete wall which Hilda was sitting on and into the fast-flowing river. The crowd all clapped solemnly, while the watch salesman stared in disbelief at what had just occurred.

Then, out of nowhere a man with a camera appeared and insisted on taking a photo of Alfred and Hilda with the policeman and the watch seller. The photographer quickly arranged the group so that Alfred's left hand and the policeman's right hand were gripping the man's collar. The man was then ordered to bow his head in shame.

There was another round of clapping from the crowd and a few moments later three more policemen appeared in a white police car with flashing red and blue lights.

The cameraman then had a good look at the foreigners' passports, made a few notes in a notepad and disappeared as quickly as he had appeared.

Someone then handed Alfred his jacket and a woman offered Hilda a small bread bun and a paper cup containing green tea.

"How kind," said Hilda. "What nice people."

"You American?" asked the policeman, suddenly.

"What?" growled Alfred.

"American?"

"No. English and proud of it."

"Ah, Eng-er-land," said the policeman, after another thoughtful pause.

"That's right," said Alfred.

"David Beckham," said the policeman, with a huge smile and offered Alfred a cigarette.

Bob Burley was smiling contentedly to himself by the coffee table in the small corridor area which led to the main exhibition workshop hall. He had imagined that this would be a major operation for his team with the distinct possibility that rather a lot of things could do awry, but everything seemed to be going remarkably well that morning.

The event had only been three hours old and already four schools had succumbed to various forms of illness, not to mention the man from LICE who had just hit a Chinese agent for mentioning West Nile Virus at his table.

He sipped his coffee and watched as another delegate, groaning weakly, was led out of the hall by two of Teddy Jensen's helpers. The poor man appeared to have stomach cramps. Burley smirked and picked up a small finger biscuit from a shallow dish on the table.

Percy Gabbitt and Bob Irwin appeared at Burley's side with cups of tea in hand.

"Magic," murmured Irwin, as he took a sip.

"How many down, so far?" asked Gabbitt, in a state of awe.

"On my count, three schools are already out of action with another two… pending," said Irwin and pushed a whole gingernut into his mouth. "We got the delegates from The Jane Austen College early. Their table is devoid of life at the moment. They must have missed their first four meetings. Probably in their rooms throwing up, wondering if Mr d'Arcy will notice their disarray at the vicarage garden party."

"Any more?" asked Burley.

"The woman from Wombat University in Queensland has been in the toilets for the past hour. And the Hemel Hempstead University man has just vomited on his own brochures. Nice one that."

"Did you manage to get all those water bottles distributed?" asked Burley.

"Every single one," replied Irwin, with a smirk. "Even put two on the central podium. Never did like that Dane much. Too cocky by half."

"I got some suspicious stares from that American school when I tried to put bottles on their table," added Gabbitt, with a frown.

"What? The Elvis School of English?" asked Burley.

"Yes, that's the one," replied Gabbitt.

"The one that gives students discounts at Burger King?" sniggered Irwin.

A moment later and a man in sunglasses in a white suit and with one hand over his mouth, rushed past them to the balcony.

"Elvis has left the building," murmured Burley into his coffee.

"Also nailed the Bowler Hat School of English and Sheila's English from Adelaide," added Irwin, airily."

"Right," said Burley. "Time Pamela and yourself started getting those posters up on the walls. Percy and I will do a leaflet drop in about ten minutes and then we'll get that flag up at the back of the hall when no one's watching. That should get things nicely stirred up before lunch."

"The posters," repeated Irwin happily. "I like this phase."

"Thought you would," said Burley and handed him a large roll of A4 posters held together by a stout elastic band. "I suggest two on the wall by the main entrance and then five or six in the hall itself. I don't expect them to last very long given Teddy's security people, but they should be there long enough to get some sort of attention from the right people."

"A flag?" asked a bewildered Gabbitt.

"Page eleven of the strike list," muttered Pamela, after a tut. "Here it is," she said and handed Gabbitt what looked like a well-folded and brightly-coloured table cloth in a sealed plastic bag.

They were all about to move off in various directions when a loud voice from somewhere in the workshop hall boomed out: "We don't fucking have Weils Disease! And we don't have fucking rats either, you bastards!"

It was not quite chaos in the hall, but an impartial observer might say that it was approaching it. More than seven tables were now deserted and there were three teams of Chinese cleaners with mops and disinfectant sweeping up the grisly detritus of a marketing peoples' stomachs near the coffee urn at the back of the hall.

Several agents were also having tantrums for reasons which Teddy Jensen had absolutely no idea, not being able to speak guttural Mongolian. Five of them hovered annoyingly by the main doors and were gesticulating wildly at all and sundry who passed by.

Teddy decided to move in and try a bit of smoothing. This is what he was famous for and he was damn sure that a fat Mongolian woman and her colleague, a man who looked as though he had not had a bath for ten years, would not pose too many problems.

"What appears to be..." began Teddy, with his trademark beaming smile.

He stopped mid-sentence when he saw what the problem was. The fat Mongolian woman was holding a piece of white paper in her hand.

Teddy frowned. Posters were banned in the hall. Delegates knew this and would be severely reprimanded if caught. He stared at the paper and tried to see what it said.

The Mongolian threw her hands in the air and said something that sounded like: 'Cream crackers stuffed in my dachshund' and promptly threw the paper on the floor angrily. The group then left the hall as loudly as they could and headed for the bar in high dudgeon. None of the Mongolians had taken the slightest notice of Teddy Jensen throughout the little piece of drama.

Teddy bent down and gingerly picked the paper up. He stared at it for a few moments and suddenly felt rather perplexed. On it was a photo of a Chinese-looking woman with a sour expression under the simple one word caption: 'Missing'.

The rest was in Chinese and completely unintelligible to Teddy. He did get a sinking feeling though when he spotted the name of the largest and wealthiest school in the workshop at the bottom of the poster. Any problems involving them would be long, drawn out and messy. Their marketing team was famous for that. Teddy folded up the poster and decided to investigate it at another time. It was then that he spotted an identical poster on the entrance pillar. Then he saw another… and another.

Teddy Jensen said something rather uncomplimentary about God in Danish and set about hurrying around the room and tearing down the posters. It was clear that something was happening in his workshop. Something not very nice and something potentially very damaging. Teddy was suddenly a rather worried Dane.

# EIGHTEEN

*"The main difference between a developed country and a developing one is the number of times you have to resort to sounding your horn when driving your car around town."*

**(Bob Irwin in reflective mood after observing an incident involving an electric bike and a bicycle taxi in central Shanghai)**

Percy Gabbitt and Bob Burley were standing in front of a large wooden rack which resembled the pigeon holes you might find in an English post-office of old. It was quite an impressive rack too, housing about three hundred individual slots, meticulously labelled with all the names of the agencies attending the workshop.

The idea here was that schools could mass-mail every agent at the workshop with their literature, without ever having to meet them. It was a wonderful system for the lazy businessman.

Already, there were quite a few brochures with free pens taped to them, flattened stress balls, small teddy bears of sundry sizes, rammed into each hole by quick-thinking marketing people.

Gabbitt and Burley had a quick look around and then began the distribution of their own leaflets. Fortunately for them, not many agents or schools were that interested in two rather bland businessmen going about the dull tools of their trade at a time when there were far more interesting things happening in the hall.

The two of them moved about their task as fast they could, since technically agents were not allowed to use this service – it being the designated stamping ground of school marketing people wanting to deluge agencies with their material. And so, phase four kicked into action.

A short five minutes later and every slot had received the Arapacana leaflet and Burley and Gabbitt retired to the large balcony beside the main workshop hall.

No one likes to be thrown up on, especially when you are wearing your best dress uniform and have been drafted in for the day from a small town in the sticks.

Inspector Zhang had been expecting an exciting time mingling with foreigners and looking rather dapper in his dark suit and white cap - a day away from the mundane small town matters of Suzhou, a day when he could make an impression with his lower intermediate English skills and a day when perhaps he could gain the ear of someone high up in the prestigious Shanghai constabulary.

What he did not expect, as he stepped from his police patrol car and stood beneath the impressive facade of the Shangri-La hotel, was to be showered with what smelt like noodles, diced carrots and mushroom soup.

He looked up in amazement at a balcony just two floors above him and into the open mouth of Elvis Presley.

Back in the workshop hall, four more schools had closed down for the morning and agents with missed appointments mingled in bewildered groups around the entrance to the hall. No-one was sure what was happening, but whatever it was, it seemed to be striking down the delegates at dramatically regular intervals.

"They're going down like nine-pins," muttered Teddy Jensen, running a clammy hand over his bald patch.

"We think it's the water," said one of his bright and bubbly aides. "The outbreak should be containable now. We've told everyone not to drink it."

"But… can we be sued?" asked Teddy rhetorically and slumped down into his chair on the podium at the centre of the storm.

"What meaning this?" barked a crackly voice, rather too close for comfort.

Teddy jumped to his feet. "What appears..." he started, weakly.

"That school give this. Cambridge school. Not good. We angry. Maybe police see," continued the owner of the croaky voice.

"What..." tried Teddy again, not really believing that anything else could go wrong.

A CD case was handed to Teddy. He stared at the object and then back at the agent. On her name badge it read: *Sweetie Chao, Come Quickly Travel, Taipei.*

"Well... err, Sweetie," said Teddy, uncertainly. "It appears to be a CD or a DVD, probably containing material of the school and such-like..." he trailed off.

"I look on my laptop and… it not school. You look," crackled Sweetie and snapped open her laptop. She placed it on the table in front of Teddy and slipped the DVD into the appropriate slot.

A moment later and after the briefest of credits, a picture of a young woman with red lipstick and toting a long leather whip flashed onto the screen. Teddy frowned deeply. This clearly had nothing to do with the city of Cambridge, unless you counted a few back streets near the football ground.

He stared at the screen not knowing that he was just one tap away from the beginning of 'Donkeyman meets the Pussycat (Director's Cut).

Another agent approached, waving one of the posters which he thought he had expunged from the workshop.

"What this?" shouted Ribena Ping of 'Lollypop Kids' of Nanjing.

"I honestly don't know, Miss Ribena," replied Teddy, standing up.

"It say Mongolian student kidnapped in London and that agents should give money to this school to pay ransom or she become sex slave to German tourists. This not good. We not pay kidnapping fee for Mongolian bar girl. We only get ten per cent commission on courses from there. Cannot pay ransom fee. This not good business. I not send my kids there. Not in million month of Mondays!" she said emphatically.

Teddy made a small noise which sounded very much like a male bullfrog deprived of its pond for rather too long. He then started making short gurgling grunts. What was happening to his workshop? Had the world gone completely mad? First, a crazed geriatric ruins the opening dinner, then a food poisoning epidemic rampages across the place, followed by libellous posters pornographic CDs.

"I need speak now, Mr Jensen," said a new voice of complaint. Teddy sighed and turned to see what the problem was this time.

"This... big problem," said a large woman, with a bubble-perm.

Teddy hazarded a glance at her name badge - Britney Kim from 'Yoohak Uhak' in Korea. He sighed again.

"What appears..." he began, worriedly.

"This put in my hole!" exclaimed Britney angrily and waved a piece of paper under Teddy's nose.

"In your hole?"

"My hole," emphasised Britney, waving at the post-box, pigeon-hole rack.

"Ah," said Teddy. "What does it say?"

"All Koreans gangsters."

"What?" croaked Teddy.

"And it say Japanese are nicest people in all Asia. They bastards," shouted Britney, with passion.

"Yes, they very bad," agreed a Miss Zhang from Wuxi Student Tours in China, who just happened to be passing and wanted to have her say. "They did very naughty things in Nanjing."

"And in Korea," boomed Britney loudly. "We not gangsters!"

"Well, I'm very sorry for that," appeased Teddy.

"We not forget," said Britney waving a fat finger in Teddy's face.

"We never forget too," agreed Miss Zhang from Wuxi.

"We not bad now. We nice," said a new voice.

The name badge announced Tomoko Nakajima from Nagoya Bright Horizon Travel to the brewing argument. "All in past now. Everyone forget... so OK," she said with a broad smile and offered Britney and Miss Zhang a small pink candy each from a bowl she was holding.

There was a pause as Miss Zhang took two sweets from the dish. "I still hate Japanese, but candy very nice. And my little girl like Hello Kitty."

"Korean candy better," muttered Britney Kim, taking a handful of the brightly-coloured sweets.

Teddy Jensen rose to his feet and decided that enough was enough. First things first, he thought. He stepped down from the podium and began to make his way to the Cambridge Universally table to sort out the DVD problem. He would then instruct his team of helpers to scour all the agent pigeon holes for any more scurrilous leaflets.

It was as he trudged unhappily to the CU table that he happened to glance at the entrance to the workshop hall. There, surrounded by a group of large and heavily-armed Chinese policeman stood a man who looked like he had had an argument with a tureen of eggnog. In shock, Teddy staggered sideways, upsetting a large jug of orange juice and an impressively-high pyramid of Toblerone chocolate bars. A man whose name badge identified him as Brandon McTavish from Toby's English Club in Vancouver, leapt to his feet and said a few choice words about Danish people in general and Teddy in particular.

"He very rude man," said Ribena Ping, who had accompanied Teddy from the podium. "I not send my students there too."

There was a short pause and then an outraged voice from behind Teddy barked quite loudly: "And not Chicken Flu either, you stupid, mad, idiot bastards!"

"Not there either," muttered Ribena, who was beginning to feel she was rapidly running out of options for her groups.

Elvis Presley had for some reason been handcuffed and was being led away by two serious policemen. A woman with a green face sat in a slumped heap on a chair on the balcony with another delegate fanning her face with a Pudsey University brochure. Two other school delegates were nervously smoking in a far corner and rubbing their stomachs from time to time, while four Chinese clean-up crews, clad in powder-blue boiler suits, were busy mopping the floors and pouring disinfectant into waste paper bins which had recently been rushed into service for reasons which did not involve too much waste paper.

It was a sight of desolation as Burley and Gabbitt poured themselves a cup of coffee and helped themselves to an untouched pile of ginger biscuits on a silver platter.

"Best not touch any of the food, sir," advised one of Teddy Jenson's aides, as she passed by holding a large damp cloth.

"Oh, I think I'll take the risk," murmured Burley. "They do look rather tasty."

"Please yourself," said the aide. "But we're telling everybody not to eat or drink anything currently in the hall."

"How considerate," said Burley and reached for another biscuit. "More for us then."

Irwin and Pamela then appeared.

"On my count," said Pamela breathlessly. "That's eleven schools down, including all seven of our top targets. And a further three looking like they're on the way."

"A good morning's work," said Burley, brushing a few crumbs from his lapel.

"Do you think this was totally necessary?" asked Gabbitt, anxiously. "People are in a lot of pain, you know."

"Pain?" queried Burley, through his third gingernut. "Pain? These schools have inflicted more pain than you can imagine. And I can assure you, Percy, that we have only taken these most extreme measures against the worst offenders of our trade. They have all had warnings in the past and have simply turned their backs on them. So, don't worry about them. They thoroughly deserve a little ...shaking up."

"Just seems a bit over the top," mumbled Gabbitt, as a man limped past on his way to the lift.

"All right," said Burley, putting fifth biscuit down. "Let's take a few examples to put your mind at rest. Take the occupant of table A5 – Tom Griddle of the Bowler Hat School of English."

"Last seen calling god on the great white telephone," chipped in Irwin.

"Indeed," said Burley, with a frown. "Mr Griddle has a school in Tottenham Court Road in Central London and uses his school as a front to get visas for Russians, Arabs and the Chinese. Basically, he sells the visas via bogus acceptance letters to agencies in these countries at exorbitant prices. Students arrive in London and then simply disappear. They then turn up as waiters in Burger King and McDonalds are can begin a sad life in the west, working eighteen-hour days for an absolute pittance. If they get upset about this or become sick, they are then fired and fresh replacements are found. Many end up on the streets, or worse.

"Mr Griddle made about a million pounds last year from doing this and came to Shanghai to make a few more contacts at this workshop so that he could increase his nasty little global network. He will now be thinking of entirely different things in the privacy of his hotel room, I think.

"Then there's Table B6 and Table B9. The Cowboy School of English hailing from Dallas, Texas and Red Sox College of Art and Design from Boston. Both are private colleges with a short and colourful history.

Technically, they take large groups of teenagers from China or Russia and give them a wonderful summer of sports, social activities and fun in rolling American hills and magnificent purpose-built schools. At least, that's what their glossy brochures say.

"In reality, both institutions are situated in grimy backstreets with just one large classroom, no toilet facilities and no qualified teachers. The Cowboy School is actually in a church basement and only comes into existence for just three months a year. The rest of the time it's a storage place for Bibles and old wooden pews.

"And the college in Boston really is an old foot hospital which is due for demolition next January, because it's in danger of actually falling down.

"Both these places feel that it is perfectly all right to pocket a huge amount of money from Chinese and Russian parents, who genuinely think that little Zhang or Boris Junior will be experiencing the American dream for three weeks of the summer. I think that Ms Jodie Quick from Dallas and Mr Buck Hudson from Boston will be rethinking their Far Eastern strategy, as they nurse their stomachs after this morning's little demonstration. Need I continue, Percy?"

"But will they realise they're being... punished?" asked Percy.

"Good question," replied Burley. "All targeted school and institutions will receive a warning on the last day of the workshop that they should desist from future dubious activities or face further... actions."

"And you think that will work?" persisted Gabbitt.

"Probably not," nodded Burley, sadly. "But it will get them thinking about what they do. A first shot across their bows."

"But won't they just call the police?"

"What... and tell them that someone wants them to stop ripping off Chinese agents and parents and putting their children into mortal danger? I think not, Percy. It will, as I say, get them ... thinking."

"So... what's next?" asked Irwin, still hungry for action.

"Lunch, I think," said Burley and rubbed his hands clean of biscuit crumbs. "Lunch and then we can prepare for phases five and six this afternoon."

"Wow!" exclaimed Pamela, with stars in her eyes. "Isn't it exciting? Actually to be able to do something good in the world and not just talk about it."

"The Arapacana way," said Burley, as a woman in a pea-green jacket lurched over to a potted palm tree on the balcony and emptied her breakfast into the dusty foliage.

"Jo Tansy of the Neighbours School of English in Melbourne," murmured Burley, as he watched the woman in a rather distant way. "Didn't settle any commission to her South American agents for over a year, just because she could get away with it. Three agents went bankrupt as a result and one even committed suicide."

"She'll be settling early this year," remarked Irwin, as the Arapacana group strolled for the staircase and the restaurant area on the floor below.

*They had expected a large and very imposing cavern with a jewelled door lit by a hundred flaming torches... or something like that anyway. What they had not expected was a rather battered old wooden door riddled with terminal woodworm.*

*"I don't like it," said Endymio,n for the tenth time. "It doesn't feel right. End of level bosses are always surrounded by large treasure chests, even larger bodyguards and positively enormous spells of warding."*

*"Hmm," nodded Roger, thoughtfully.*

*"So, do we rush in and put everyone to the sword?" asked Obby.*

*"You really are getting to like this sort of thing, aren't you?" murmured the Snark Maiden, with a frown.*

*"Just can't wait to get to the end, so we can count up the winnings. Then we can all go home."*

*"And where would that be, Obby?" asked Li Bang Cho.*

*"Err, well... the village back there, I suppose," said Obby, uncertainly.*

*"Not sure I want to go back there," said Roger, as he oiled his sword.*

*"There's no place like home," said Obby, chancing his arm a little. "No matter where you end up in this crazy world, it's always good to get back home afterwards."*

*"Is that right, Obby?" asked Endymion, slowly.*

*"Well, I think so. Don't you Roger?"*

*"I reckon I might stay in the caverns with my goblin friends after this is all over," said Roger, airily.*

*"Good decision," mumbled Tammy.*

*"But won't you miss the people back..."*

*"Not at all, Obby," said Roger. "Most of my acquaintances back there would rob you blind as soon as look at you. Here in the caverns there's a certain degree of... honour."*

*"Goblins don't have honour," sniffed Obby.*

*"Says who?" interrupted Tubby, hotly. "At least we don't pick your pockets the moment you enter our warrens. There's always a fair fight."*

*"Well, I think you can't beat being... with your own kind," said Obby.*

*There was a nervous silence as the heroes took that last sentence in. Roger then spoke in a firm voice. "Obby, you clearly don't understand. I consider my good companions here as my friends more than some scruffy back-alley thief from Waendelsburgh, who, by quirk of fate, happens to be human. Such vermin have as much in common with me as that pit snapper back in level three. And I warn you to be a little more careful in future when selecting your choice of words regarding my friends."*

*There was another much longer silence.*

*"But you should go home at some time in the future,' said Obby pointedly. "Can't stay down here forever."*

*"Is that so?" responded Roger.*

*"You can't stay away forever," finished Obby.*

*"Maybe everyone will forget me, if I stay away for a long time," suggested Roger.*

*"No, Roger," said Obby, flatly. "We... I mean, people will not forget you."*

*"Indeed."*

*I bet they'll be a welcoming committee waiting for you when you decide to wander back into town. They will never forget someone like you."*

*There was one further silence and then one of the black orcs approached the party of heroes.*

*"Scuse me," it wheezed. "But can I draw your piccie?" it asked, almost politely. It was carrying a thin stick of charcoal and a grubby notepad.*

*"See, even orcs want a souvenir. You're a hero, who will never be forgotten," said Endymion, taking his hat off and blowing the dust off the rim.*

*Roger looked up at the black orc. "Of course, you can," he said. "How would you like me? Heroic or...normal?"*

*Oh, definitely heroic," said the black orc quickly, and started putting an easel up in front of Roger.*

*Five minutes later and it was just the Snark Maiden and Roger who were sitting quietly in front of the orc, who was scribbling away seriously. The others had drifted off for a rest before the big encounter at the end of the level.*

*"Was I convincing?" hissed Roger.*

*"A bit over-the-top," whispered the Snark Maiden. "All that stuff about living happily with your goblin friends forever. It was a totaly out-of-charucler."*

*"I wanted to get the message through to him. I'm not going back."*

*"Oh. I think he understood that at the end. He…"*

*Whatever the Snark Maiden was about to say was lost to posterity as a heavy, echoey voice resounded in the cave corridor.*

*"I am so pleased you are having such a good time here in my home."*

*The party dived in all directions, grabbing weapons and readying themselves for the inevitable onslaught.*

*"Why don't you come in? You're just in time for tea."*

*A moment later, two snarling hellhounds with their beastmasters appeared at the end of the corridor.*

*"Hello folks," tried Roger. "Who's a nice doggie, then?" The hell-hounds growled as one and strained at their leashes, salivating over sharp teeth.*

*"Here, go fetch!" shouted Roger and threw a stone at the lead beastmaster. The hounds seemed momentarily confused. One even wagged its tail a little uncertainly.*

*"Aaaaaaaaaaaaaagh!" screamed the beastmaster, mostly for effect and also because no one likes to be hit square on the head with a small rock.*

*The dogs all barked loudly. The beastmasters then let go of their tethers and the dogs hurled themselves onto the heroes.*

"So, what's going on?" whispered Nero into his cellphone.

"It's rather hard to say," came the reply.

"What do you mean? Have you spotted our man yet?"

"Not really," replied Chipchase.

"Would you like to be more specific?" asked Nero, with unusual patience.

"It's hard to explain in one sentence," replied Chipchase honestly, as two men ran past his table trailing vomit in their wake.

"Well try," said Nero, in as steely a whisper as he could muster.

It was about two in the morning in Wormwood Scrubs and the place was as silent as the grave. Silent everywhere except a certain cell. Nero Handsworth was lying on his bunk with the sheet over his head and whispering into his illegal cellphone.

"It's like a mad house here," said Chipchase, slightly worriedly. "I thought teachers' conventions would be boring, but not a bit of it. It's flippin' incredible here."

"But have you met Percy bloody Gabbitt yet?"

"Not yet," said Chipchase slowly, as a woman fainted across their table and rolled gently onto the floor. "He's down to see us this afternoon," said Chipchase. "Not sure that will happen though. People are dropping like flies here."

Nero Handsworth frowned into his cellphone. This was not the sort of call he had either envisaged or wanted. All he really needed to be told was that everything was in hand and that Percy Gabbitt was moments away from being biffed hard on the head, loaded into a car boot and driven as fast as possible to the nearest international airport. He did not want to be told that people were dropping like flies. It smacked of uncomfortable deja-vue.

"Get the job done, Mr Chipchase," said Nero, trying to control his temper. "Or I will make sure that you both drop like flies, as well." He then snapped the phone shut and sat on his bunk. A few moments quiet reflection passed, after which he was tapping away at the phone again. It rang distantly.

"What?" came the short response after being picked up.

"What's happening?" hissed Nero.

"All hell's breaking loose here."

"I don't care if the place is being attacked by platoons of Red Guards armed with rocket launchers," spat Nero in fury. "Just tell me what's going on!"

"There's some sort of madness breaking out in the hall. Everyone's either dying or throwing up."

"What?" squawked Nero.

"I can't explain it. It's like they've all gone down with a communal form of Mad Marketers Disease."

"Mad what?"

"Sort of like Mad Cow's Disease but affecting only salesmen."

"Are you trying to be funny?" asked Nero, thickly. He was not in the mood for this.

"I'm just telling you how it is," muttered Fred the Throttler, as another delegate ran past with a hand over his mouth.

"Anything else important to tell me?" asked Nero.

"I've just spotted your two at their table. And I've seen your Mr G as well."

"Well, that's something," breathed Nero, in relief. "Just make sure that those two idiots get the job done and... well, you know what to do."

"I've only just arrived and have jetlag," mumbled Fred the Throttler, through pursed lips as he reached for his water bottle.

"What was that?"

"Nothing."

It was mid-afternoon at the Shangri-La Hotel and what was left of the delegates were taking a short coffee and bikkie break in the area just outside the main arena and near to the expansive balcony overlooking the Huangpu River.

The representative of the Yard School of English was not concentrating on his custard cream though. He was deeply ensconced in a phone call back to the UK.

"Alert the rhino squads, Ford," he whispered conspiratorially into his small mobile handset.

"Yes sir," came the tired response.

"Are you all right, Ford?"

"It's seven in the morning, sir, and I did not get much sleep last night," mumbled Ford, miserably.

"Nice and bright here," said Pringle. "Just having a coffee and a biscuit."

"That's good," mumbled Ford. "Is there anything else, sir?"

"Of course there is, Detective Constable. I've just spotted two of the worst villains in south London. They're here on another table."

"What?" squawked Ford, suddenly wide awake.

"Unbelievable, isn't it? The last time I crossed swords with these two blighters they couldn't put together a single sentence without attaching the 'f' word to every noun."

"And now they're selling English courses?" queried Ford.

"Well, it does prove one thing," said Pringle.

"What, sir?" asked Ford, thickly.

"Solid proof that English schools and serious crime do go hand in hand."

"So, what now, sir?"

"Just get the boys ready for when this lot returns to Heathrow. I want every man jack of them tailed to wherever they're heading. We don't know what's happening yet, but if these two desperadoes are here along with Percy Raymond Gabbitt and his cronies, you can expect fireworks somewhere along the line."

"Will do, sir," said Ford and made a note to contact

the captains of the Black and White Rhino Squads. He thought he would also ring the newly formed Wild Elephant Squad and the reformed Grey Hippo team as well. That group of manic psychos would love a car chase from Heathrow and a firefight at the other end. DC Ford smiled to himself and sat back in his chair. For once, the forces of good were ahead of the game.

Back in Shanghai, Pringle was having a first sup at a tepid cup of Lipton's Yellow Label. Things were developing nicely, he thought, although he was a little concerned that three Chinese agents who had visited his table earlier that morning had seemed rather too keen on sending several students to the Yard School for executive English classes. He sighed. That was a problem for another day, he thought and idly stared at a group of delegates gathered in the balcony area beside the conference room.

He was about to put his tea cup down and get back to his table in preparation for his meeting with Percy Gabbitt when an appallingly familiar figure drifted across his field of vision.

"Jesus, it's Fred the Throttler," he said, under his breath.

In a small room next to the main hall, Teddy Jensen had also just implored the Almighty's son, although somewhat weakly. He was sitting at a table opposite the Chinese policeman who seemed to have had a fight with a tureen of eggnog. In the confined space of the room, it was beginning to smell rather strongly - and not of eggnog either. Teddy was turning a shade of green and staring at the wooden table surface and trying to persuade himself not to throw up.

"So, Mr Jensen, you know nothing of this poster or this flag?" The egg policeman waved a multi-coloured piece of cloth under Jensen's nose.

"Never seen either," replied Teddy, as honestly as he could, inwardly swearing as he recognised it as the free Tibet flag. "Don't know who would do such a thing."

"This flag... is a very sensitive issue at the moment. I could have this entire event closed down and everyone arrested," said Chief Inspector Zhang, threateningly.

"Oh, don't do that," responded Teddy, quickly. "Please don't do that."

"And this too," said Zhang, tossing a DVD onto the table.

"Ah that," muttered Teddy, as memories of 'The Donkeyman meets the Pussycat' swam back to the front of his tired mind.

"This not good, Mr Jensen," said Zhang and placed both hands on eggy hips.

"Maybe we can come to some sort of... understanding," said Teddy, thinking at a million miles an hour.

"What?" asked Zhang, with eyebrows raised.

"Perhaps an official invitation to tonight's dinner along with all your dry-cleaning needs taken care of? Plus... a small... present to show our appreciation..." he tailed off feeling that he was somehow walking a tightrope where falling to the left would bring a stiff prison sentence, while it would be peaches and cream to the right.

Chief Inspector Zhang grunted and flicked a nasty piece of yellow off a cuff. It landed glutinously onto the table near Teddy. Teddy ignored it and smiled hopefully. "And," he continued, "maybe a VIP room at the hotel at the expense of ICAS for the next two days, so you can monitor events at the workshop?"

"Perhaps... that would be acceptable," said Zhang, after a very long pause. He picked the DVD up and trousered it.

"I'll see to it at once," said Teddy quickly. "If you'd like to wait here, I'll have a room key in your hand within five minutes."

"And the posters and the flag?"

"You will never see them again," said Teddy, staring at the sad-looking photo of the missing student and the Tibet flag, lying accusingly on the table.

"Well... maybe OK then," said Zhang, slowly. Teddy was out of the room in a moment and mustering his forces.

In the workshop hall, everyone was settling down for the afternoon session. Delegates were starting to emerge from toilets, bathrooms and the fresh air of the balcony to get down to the serious business of making money again. Sad little groups moved gingerly about, arranging brochures and giveaway furry bears, ballpoint pens and next year's calendars.

Agents were getting read, as well. They circled the tables like hyenas out for an easy kill. Things appeared to be returning to a semblance of normality...

...and then the Arapacana team arrived back in the workshop hall. They were looking well-fed and ready for another few hours mayhem.

"Appointments time, lady and gentlemen," said Bob Burley, brightly.

"Right," said Gabbitt, nervously. "I've got Shakespeare's College from Walsall now and then this strange meeting with the Yard School of English."

"That should be fun," chipped in Bob Irwin. "Fancy calling a school that.

"I've then got a place called the Scrubs School," said Gabbitt, very dubiously.

"Don't forget," interrupted Burley. "These appointments have been carefully selected. All of them are guilty of something nasty, or potentially nasty, so give them the full treatment."

"Even this Yard place and this Scrubs outfit?" asked Gabbitt, slowly. "It says here that they've only been in business for a couple of months. Seems too short a time to get a bad reputation."

"That's true," frowned Burley, checking his notes. After a few moments, he whistled through his teeth and looked at his small entourage. "Well spotted, Percy. There seem to be about six schools on our appointments lists who have actually requested meetings with us, not the other way round, as is normal at these affairs. The Yard School and the Scrubs place are two of these institutions. Just go easy on them, Percy," said Burley. He then looked at all of his comrades in arms. "And make sure all of you check your notes to make sure you're not condemning the wrong outfits. That would never do," he concluded, with a twinkle in his eye. "Where's your official workshop badge, Percy?" asked Burley suddenly. "Have to wear them at all times or you run the risk of being thrown out you know."

"What?' replied Gabbitt, fingering his chest for something that clearly was not hanging there.

"Well, never mind," said Burley. "You're in the hall now, so probably don't need it. Just make sure you find it before stumps this evening."

"Must have left it in the toilets," mumbled Gabbitt.

"Right... to action everyone," said Burley, clapping his hands enthusiastically. "I do believe the bell for our two-thirty meetings has just sounded."

As the delegates and agents all began sitting down and starting the rather odd verbal mating dances which constitute business meetings at the workshop, a pair of cunning eyes were staring at an agent's badge by the sinks in the men's toilets on the third floor of the hotel.

After a moment of hesitation a sweaty hand reached out and trousered the badge. The figure then beat a hasty retreat to a cubicle and locked the door.

Jane Bobbin narrowed her eyes and folded her arms. She had seen some pretty strange things whilst in China and was now in an almost permanent state of wariness. Her recent experiences at that dreadful school in Suzhou and the meeting with that appalling man from her past – Percy Gabbitt, had made her extremely suspicious of everything.

She had decided long ago that she would be on maximum alert while attending this conference and would try to avoid all contact with the aforesaid Gabbitt, or anyone who looked vaguely shady.

Needless to say, Bobbin had not been one of the poor unfortunates who had supped at the drugged water earlier in the day. She only drank from bottles she had bought herself and were preferably of an un-Chinese origin.

She stood eying the workshop hall critically and thinking of the moment when she could fold up her British Council stand and march to her room, well away from this ghastly conference.

Why she had been asked to attend was beyond her. She had fought strenuously against being given this particular assignment for obvious reasons, but all to no avail. Apparently, she was the only person available who had Chinese experience at the Council. And there had been the fact that just weeks before she had been unceremoniously expelled from the People's Republic after that dreadful episode at the Shine School in Suzhou.

Luckily, or unluckily, depending on how you looked at it, the Foreign Office had managed to get that expulsion overturned and had even received an apology from the Chinese. It had all been an unfortunate misunderstanding, apparently.

She sighed and leant on a stack of rather natty leaflets which expounded the virtues of an education in the UK.

Just another four hours and she could retire to her room, have a nice hot bath and...

"Pssst," hissed someone, rather too near her left ear. Jane hopped like a startled rabbit.

"It's me," whispered the voice.

"I can see that," said a huffy Bobbin, as she looked into the eyes of her erstwhile colleague of so many years ago -Gilbert Grimm.

"Guess what?" said the clearly excited Grimm.

"You do not creep up on British Council employees and hiss in their ears," said Bobbin, hotly. "I am now at the apex of this grimy little industry and should be treated with all the decorum that I deserve. Don't forget, Gilbert, that the BC is the unofficial arm of the government out here. Now what is the matter?"

"Nice to see you too," murmured Grimm.

"I'm sorry," sighed Bobbin. "It's been a rather stressful time lately. Perhaps we can have a drink..."

"Look at this," interrupted Grimm, and pulled something out of his pocket. "It's his name badge."

"Whose name badge, for heaven's sake?" asked Bobbin, tiredly.

"Percy Gabbitt's," hissed Grimm, into her ear.

Jane Bobbin went rigid and a cold sweat broke out pretty much everywhere of note. She teetered slightly and sat down heavily on her chair. "And why have you got his badge?"

"I found it in the toilets. It's genuine," said Grimm, as he stared at his prize.

"In the toilets?" sniffed Bobbin, distastefully.

"I've got an idea," said Grimm. "Can I run it by you?"

"An idea? You? Am I going to regret this?"

"If I wear this badge and visit the Cambridge Universally stand, then I'll get all their commission and discounts sheets, which competitors don't normally see. They'll think I'm an agent, won't they? It could give us a small advantage when we sell our courses," said Grimm, hopefully.

"Of all the ridiculous schemes I've ever heard..." began Jane Bobbin.

"I've got to be a bit more pro-active, my boss says," interrupted Grimm, again. "Says I'm too much like an ex-teacher. He wants me to be more cut-throat and sales-orientated."

Jane Bobbin shuddered. Vocabulary like that had no place in her world and she turned to Gilbert Grimm with as stern an expression as she could muster. "Taking another delegate's name badge and pretending to be him is not only fraudulent, but also quite stupid. There aren't that many people in this hall who don't know that despicable person. Furthermore, what happens if you bump into him, while waltzing around the workshop wearing his badge?"

"I never thought of that," muttered Grimm.

Jane Bobbin sighed, closed her eyes and looked up at the ceiling. Just under four hours left of this nightmare, she thought and sighed again.

The Scrubs School of English table was devoid of life - both delegates had disappeared. A woman called Beppo Kim from 'Yummie Uhak' in Seoul was sitting at the table and looking impatient. Teddy Jensen appeared out of nowhere, beaming happiness and confidence.

"Everything OK here?" he asked, leaning into Beppo's eye-line.

"No, it not. They no here. I waste valuable time. Maybe they hate Koreans!" exclaimed the ruffled Beppo, who then folded her arms and puckered her top lip, sulkily.

"Ah, I think not," said Teddy, with a warm smile. He was on home ground again. "I'll make an announcement over the speaker system and I'm sure they'll come back here immediately.

"I no want see them now," said Beppo with a dismissive sniff. "They lose Yummie Uhak business! Maybe they like Japanese more," she exclaimed loudly and flounced off in the direction of the cake and coffee trolley on the balcony.

Teddy Jensen sighed. Agents could be so... fragile, he thought, hopelessly. He stared at the empty chairs on the other side of the table and frowned deeply. Where in god's teeth were those two delegates? Didn't they know the afternoon session had started?

"Excuse me," said a voice from behind him.

"And how can I be of..." began Teddy.

"I Singing Park from 'Top Uhak Uhak' in Korea. Where delegates?"

"Singing..." began Teddy.

"Singing Park. My name," said Singing.

"From..." tried Teddy again.

"Top Uhak Uhak," came the reply. "Where delegate? I had meeting this morning and they not here," persisted Miss Singing.

Teddy Jensen sighed and looked at her as seriously as he could. "I will sort this out immediately," he said and marched to his podium in the middle of the hall.

"So, we meet again," murmured Chief Inspector Pringle, with a small smile.

"Do we?" asked an innocent Percy Gabbitt. He was just getting his notepad and pencil out and preparing to look vaguely professional.

"Oh yes, indeed we do," said Pringle, quietly.

Gabbitt stopped his fidgeting and stared at the man on the other side of the table. He looked vaguely familiar in a not very nice way.

"I'm sorry," said Gabbitt slowly. "But I don't remember..."

"Oh, I think you do," said Pringle.

"I'm not sure..." began Gabbitt.

"Oh, I think you are."

Gabbitt scrutinised the man. No, he didn't...

"Box Hill," said Pringle, thickly and sat back in his chair. "Box Hill," he repeated, emphasising each syllable with as much hatred as he could pack into those two small words. "Box Hill," he said again.

"What about it?" squeaked Gabbitt.

"We have a long memory Mr Gabbitt. Mr Percy Raymond Gabbitt. Future resident of Wormwood Scrubs."

"We?"

"We."

"Ah," said Gabbitt, as the penny dropped. "The copper with the truncheon… and the panda."

Pringle's smile faded and became a pained expression. "The Force has a long memory for villains like you," he said, leaning forward on his elbows and looking into Gabbitt's eyes.

"I didn't do anything," said Gabbitt defensively. "It was all a sad case of..."

"Of course it was," interrupted Pringle. "But we both know that a leopard can't change its spots. Once a bad egg, always a bad egg."

"I'm not a leopard or an egg," said Gabbitt. "Just a someone who happened to be in the wrong place..."

"Of course, you were," interrupted Pringle again. "Just bear in mind that if you ever set foot in England again, I'll be waiting for you, Mr Percy Raymond Gabbitt."

"But I haven't..."

"Of course, you haven't," interrupted Pringle once again.

"But..." began Gabbitt.

"There is a way."

"What?"

"Only one way to clear your name completely."

"But my name is already clear."

"Not to me, it isn't."

Gabbitt sighed and sat back in his chair. Clearly, this man copper was the epitome of the dog at a bone.

"Ninety-three break-ins and sundry acts of vandalism," said Pringle, airily. He was actually beginning to enjoy this.

"But I haven't..."

"So, come back with me and clear your name," said the smiling Chief Inspector.

"Will I be arrested?"

"You bet your socks, you will," said Pringle, instantly. "So fast your feet won't touch the ground."

"So, why...?"

"And stay here forever?" asked Pringle.

"Well, not forever, but..."

"So, come back with me now and clear your name."

"It doesn't sound much of an incentive when I'm going to get arrested immediately for stuff I haven't done."

"Your choice."

"I'll have to think about that," said Gabbitt, slowly. "I just want you to know that I have never..."

"I think the bell has just rung, Mr Percy Raymond Gabbitt," said Pringle, standing up. "This meeting is now at an end. Just remember that we never forget, Mr Percy Raymond Gabbitt."

Gabbitt rose as well. As he turned to leave Pringle's table a man stood up three rows away and began punching the air, angrily.

"No, no, no! We don't have Green Diarrhoea Syndrome at my school!"

Chief Inspector Pringle heard nothing though. He was sitting back in his chair with a contented smile on his face. The meeting had gone quite well, he thought.

He then hit the Play button of a small tape recorder placed in a jacket pocket and inserted two small earphones into his ears. Strains of a song called

'Wondrous Stories' stated flowing through his happy mind.

"I should cocoa," he whispered to himself.

Just to one side of the central podium where Teddy Jensen was heading, were the four tables of the Cambridge Universally delegation. It was unashamedly the largest of the private language schools in the workshop and had eight full-time delegates all beavering greedily away at their tables.

The company had been created by a Swiss businessman called Ludwig Stein and had been deliberately named so as to cause confusion among less careful agents. Said quickly, Cambridge Universally could easily be mistaken for the 'big' place down the road, of course. This had opened a lot of doors and had been the cause of many an unexpected booking.

It should also be mentioned that their main school was not situated anywhere near Cambridge. It was based in Ramsgate and had spectacular views of the Sally Ferry Terminal.

The sales team was composed of bright young things, who had a hatful of e-marketing diplomas and from an assortment of red-brick universities. Of the eight CU delegates selling year-round and summer junior courses, none of them had taught a lesson in their lives or had even set foot in a school. Which was fine. After all, as Ludwig Stein had pointed out at a Board meeting: why expose your sales staff to the rubbish that they were selling?

Susie Hamilton was the main sales manager. She flitted from table to table, trying to find fault with the presentations of her inferiors.

Susie was about thirty-five years old, divorced twice, had short blonde hair, a pretty face, large blue eyes with rather too much green eye shadow. She was also wearing a dress which Hilda Fennell would have described as 'not leaving much to the imagination'.

She was the ultimate professional marketer and considered using absolutely every possible weapon in her extensive armoury to get the sale.

Susie was sitting next to a young and spotty, but well-brushed, junior executive called Jimmy Bunn, when a Chinese agent plumped down in the chair opposite them.

"The name's Gabbitt and I'm err, an agent from err..." said the delegate trying to look at his name badge. "Arapa...Arapacan... Arap... and I want to know your best prices... please."

"Right," said Susie brightly and offered the man her business card which had appeared in her hand with all the speed of an expert magician producing the Ace of Spades. Jimmy Bunn pulled his out and promptly dropped it on the floor.

Susie rolled her eyes and looked up at the heavens the way senior managers sometimes do when sitting with less experienced colleagues. She laughed softly and flashed a slightly lascivious smile at the agent.

Time to get down to the nitty-gritty, she thought. No sense in wasting a single second. She licked her top lip and leant forward in her chair so that the agent could get a better look at her plunging neckline.

"So very nice to meet you, Percy," she said after the merest of glances at his name badge. "We would love to work with you. Do you have a ... BIG business here in China?"

Gilbert Grimm was beginning to sweat. He thought that he could just slide in… and then out of the CU stand, with a bag bulging with confidential information. He did not imagine that he would have to answer difficult questions about a company he knew nothing about.

"Quite big," he mumbled. "And I'm English too. And am living here in China. Not Chinese at all. Very English. From top to bottom. English."

"I had spotted that, Percy," chuckled Susie, after another glittery smile. "How long have you been here?"

"Err, well..." began Grimm, worriedly.

"Scuse me," said a voice behind Grimm's head. He started. "Could we have a quick word with you, Mr Gabbitt?"

"I beg your pardon! It is our turn to have a meeting now, not yours," she said sharply to the interrupter, who wore the badge of a competitor.

"Only take a sec," said the voice and rested a large hand on Grimm's shoulder.

"I don't care how many secs it would take. You'll wait your turn," said Susie, standing up. She had not made it to sales manager without a few dust-ups with people.

"Get stuffed, missy," said the man and lifted Grimm out of his seat.

"How fucking dare you!" exclaimed Susie, all the glitter and warmth falling from her demeanour in one split second.

"Be back in a mo'," lied Mr Chipchase, through a toothy grin. "Nice dress."

"Put my agent down," bellowed Susie Hamilton loudly. Heads began to turn.

"Medical emergency," said an inspired Bibby to everyone within listening range and wormed his arm under Grimm's.

In just a few short moments, the unfortunate Gilbert Grimm had been frog-marched down several aisles and out of the main hall. He was gurgling and panting the way you do when absolutely terrified. How had they discovered his deception so quickly? Surely it would just be a friendly reprimand, not strong-arm stuff like this. If only he had listened to his friend, Jane Bobbin. If only...

"Nice and easy," said the man on his right. "We don't want no problems, do we Mr Bibby."

"Indeed not, Mr Chipchase.

"Nice and easy."

"But I'm not..." squeaked Grimm, now very worriedly.

"Best keep quiet, Mr Gabbitt, sir," said Chipchase under his breath. "Or it may get a little… unpleasant."

"Who? What? But I'm not..." tried Grimm again, his brain going into meltdown.

"…going to make any trouble," finished Chipchase, with a gleam in his eye. "Back to our room I think, Mr Bibby, to give Mr Gabbitt something to make him sleepy and then we'll get a cab to the airport."

"But I'm not..." attempted Grimm, again. He then tried a half-hearted struggle to get free.

"I'm sure you're not, sir," said Chipchase. "But best not wriggle too much, or Mr Bibby here might accidentally break something.

"What?" squawked a now desperate Grimm.

"He can be a little rough," whispered Chipchase, through an evil grin, which implied a lot of pain and suffering.

And with that, the three of them entered the elevator and an uncertain future, at least for one of them.

# NINETEEN

*"Further to our emails, please understand that we will take appropriate action should you continue your current marketing plan which involves selling Ramsgate as a suburb of Cambridge."*

**(Arapacana's first shot over the Cambridge Universally bows. Needless to say, nothing was done and, only then, did AA move in)**

"A boat trip on the river? Are you mad?"

"It's been planned for ages and is supposed to be the centrepiece of the workshop for us."

"But that's one of the busiest rivers in Asia. You can't just hire a pleasure boat and pootle all over it. Have you seen the size of some of those barges which crawl up and down the bastard? It's dangerous with a capital D."

"All taken care of... Teddy. No problems. You're welcome on board too. It should be a fun evening with lots to drink, heaps of food and even a bit of dancing."

"Thank you, but I rather think not. Got a lot on my mind."

Teddy Jensen and Susie Hamilton of Cambridge Universally were standing at the organizer's podium in the middle of the workshop hall. It was close to the end of the first day's meetings and Susie just informed Teddy of the school's proposed boat trip on the Huangpu River. She had had a pig of the day and was not in the mood for Teddy's procrastinations. She had already given him an earful after the abduction by competitors of one of her agents and was simply not going to stand for anymore messing about.

Cambridge Universally had decided long ago that they wanted to do something unforgettably spectacular at the end of the workshop – to show agents and competitors alike that they were top dogs at the event. A boat trip had seemed the perfect answer, followed by a firework display, of course. It would be a nice way to show CU as the biggest and best outfit in the business, especially since their firework display would take place a few minutes before Teddy's official one, which was not up to much, apparently.

Teddy Jensen was not thinking of the size of their fireworks though. It was the boat trip which was centre stage in his appalled mind. He had been to Shanghai enough times to know that you didn't mess with that river. It would be like planning a garden party on the central reservation of the M1 on a Monday morning. Things were always chugging up and down the swine - things which looked so heavy they defied description. It would be wrong to say that these bastards were boats or barges either, since they just resembled floating platforms weighed down with mountains of metal crates and boxes.

To have a pleasure cruise among this slow-moving traffic jam seemed insanity on a scale unimaginable to Teddy Jensen. He stared at his microphone and prepared himself for the official announcement inviting all agents to almost certain death the following evening.

Just two rows away a voice rose above the general groundswell of marketing noise.

"We don't fucking have any fucking diseases at the school. It's completely fucking safe. You can't catch fucking Guinea Worm or River Blindness at my fucking school. Fucking guaranteed, you sick fucking bastards!"

It was early morning in Wormwood Scrubs, but in the cell occupied by Nero Handsworth it was party time. He stood by his door and smiled broadly. Life was definitely on an upswing. He felt a bit like criminal mastermind in that film about Michael Caine and Benny Hill stealing gold bullion from right under the noses of the Italian police and the Mafia.

Nero took a deep breath. Percy Raymond Gabbitt was on his way to the airport and a flight home. It could not have been better. Job done.

Chipchase and Bibby had come up with the goods this time. For all their chronic uselessness, those two had managed the impossible. It was unbelievable. Unbelievable and wonderful! Wonderful and fantastic. Fantastic and... well, unbelievable! A tear began to well in Nero's eye.

He sniffed as he thought of the pleasure he would have in personally giving them a five thousand pound reward for their efforts. He smiled cruelly. That would be more than enough for them. After all, it was just a little kidnapping. They could not really hope to expect fifty grand for such a tiny job. And they'd had a holiday in China as well. This was the real world, after all. Five thousand would be more than enough.

Anyway, it did not really matter if it was five, fifty of five million. Fred the Throttler, the Shotgun Sisters and all those other nasty psychopaths would see to that.

And then it would be his turn. Three years in the nick, a ruined marriage, a blown-up school and his life in ruins all because of Percy Raymond Gabbitt. Revenge was a dish best served… Nero paused. Served with what? Custard? Chocolate sauce?

*"Tea anybody? I would rather recommend the Orange Pekoe. It has a decidedly woody aftertaste which lingers on the palate. And please take a scone. They were freshly baked this morning by Barnaby the balrog and are absolutely delicious."*

*The final encounter of the whole quest was not going the way Roger had envisaged. To be honest though, the whole adventure had not really gone the way he had intended. However, this was proving to be the last straw.*

*The heroes were arranged in a rough semi-circle around a central dais in a large cavern. What made things a little different was that the cavern itself had been extremely tastefully decorated in various shades of orange and luminous green. There were even a few Laura Ashley throw cushions and the odd bean bag on the floor. The place exuded a worrying sixties decadence.*

*The final incongruity was that the Dragon King himself seemed quite a jovial and thoroughly good-mannered host.*

*This was certainly not how it was supposed to be. The villain should have been casting fireballs and summoning minions as fast as he could. Instead, he was recommending Orange Pekoe tea with freshly-baked scones.*

*The Dragon King himself was of average height with short-cropped hair and was wearing a quilted maroon jacket and had a red smoking cap with a long golden tassel. On his feet were a pair of tartan-coloured slippers.*

*Roger hefted Dune Blade and thought about rushing up to the man and hewing his head off. Such an action, though rather excessive, would have been perfectly acceptable and certainly within the rules of the dungeon dimensions. Moreover, the swine had a pet balrog called Barnaby. That alone merited a bit of beheading. Roger grunted unhappily and stared at the king.*

*"So, have you enjoyed yourselves?" asked the Dragon King and lit a fat cigar. He then slowly sat down on a long, padded couch and picked up a chunky crystal glass containing a large brandy.*

*"Not sure what you mean. You are the Dragon King, aren't you?" asked Roger, hoping that the answer would be in the negative.*

*"Indeed I am for my sins, but you can call me DK."*

*"DK?" croaked Roger, in horror.*

*"Yes, that's what they call me here," sighed DK, taking a long puff on his cigar. "So, I hope you've all had a lot of fun? After all, that's what it's all about, isn't it? Fun, games and high jinx."*

*"It's been... enlightening, DK," said the Snark Maiden, chewing on a scone and arranging herself decorously on a beanbag.*

*"Ah, enlightening," repeated the Dragon King, with a smile. "Now that is a nice word."*

*"We've come for the goblinesse," said Endymion, a trifle bluntly.*

*"Of course, you have, my dear boy," said the DK. "Of course, you have."*

*"So, where is she?" asked Roger thickly.*

*"In the back room. Over there," said DK airily, waving a hand at a distant corner. "Doing her hair, I believe."*

*"Doing her hair?" squeaked Tammy, incredulously.*

*"Well, she may be doing her nails. I really don't know what female goblins get up to in their free time," said DK.*

*"Free time?" spluttered a bewildered Tammy.*

*"Just bring her out and we'll be going," said Roger, with his hand back on the handle of his blade.*

*The Dragon King frowned and took a small sip of his brandy. He then sighed deeply and got up. "I wish it were that simple," he said and walked slowly to a large lectern near the Snark Maiden's beanbag.*

*The heroes tensed. So, this was it. The moment of truth. The moment when all hell would be unleashed and they would be soon knee-deep in blood, gore and entrails. The moment when...*

*"She's writing my autobiography," said DK and flicked open a large tome which rested on the lectern.*

*"Writing your what?" asked Roger, uncomprehendingly.*

*"My autob… my life story," explained the DK.*

*"I know what it means," mumbled a wounded Roger.*

*"It's a tale of bravery, happiness, sadness and a little… romance," said the DK, winking at the Snark Maiden. "She thinks it could be a bestseller."*

*"A what?" asked Roger, now in totally unchartered waters.*

*"A book which everyone will be clammering to read," explained the Dragon King.*

*"I know what that means too," remonstrated Roger.*

*"So, she's not your prisoner?" asked the Snark Maiden.*

*"My prisoner?" queried the Dragon King. "I rather think not. More like I'm her prisoner," he said and chuckled through a cloud of blue smoke.*

*"What?" squawked Roger. "All this way and all these fights just to find out that she's here to write a book."*

*"Not just any book," said the Dragon King in a slightly wounded tone. "It's going to be the book of the century. A book which shows that we're not all uncouth animals. A book which takes the lid off the goblin warrens. A book which shows the softer side to the Dragon King. Its working title is rather good. DK OK sort of says it all and should appeal to the younger goblins too. A winner in every way."*

*"But... but..." tried Roger. His voice then became a series of strangulated grunts.*

*"Why did you fight us every inch of the way?" asked the Snark Maiden. "You could have just told us at the entrance what you were up to."*

*"Well, this is a dungeon," said the Dragon King. "And you were expecting a bit of fisticuffs. Seemed a shame to disappoint. I'm sure that the goblins on the higher levels would have obliged had you simply asked them to see me."*

*"Just asked them to see you?" squeaked Endymion. "And then what?"*

*"An early tea and probably a few beers, while listening to the first reading of Chapter One," said the Dragon King. "For example, did you know that my name was Garfield Rotter before all this Dragon King paraphernalia came along. Just a normal common-as-you-like beastman going about his daily business without so much as a by-your-leave."*

*"Just a moment," interrupted Roger. "So, there's no big fight now?"*

*"Well, I hadn't planned on one," said the Dragon King, slowly.*

*"There's always a fight at the end of the quest. You can't just let the whole thing just fizzle out over tea, buns and a book reading. We did and blow a whopping great hole in your dungeon," said Roger.*

*"Well, yes I know. I have to admit that I was a little put out by such radical interior design changes, but after the initial shock had worn off, I have to say that I rather like it. I might even put a nice new elevator in there."*

*"An elevator?" squeaked Roger. "You should be furious, frothing at the mouth and chucking everything you have at us."*

*"Well," said the Dragon King after a long sigh, "I could oblige if you like. There's a couple of pygmy Minotaurs and six pit snappers that wouldn't mind going a few rounds with you, if you want. It's really your choice. I would far prefer a cup of tea, another currant scone and a little chat about my book."*

*"That's not how it's supposed to be," said a very unhappy Roger.*

*"Sorry to disappoint," said the Dagon King. "But that's progress for you. Things have moved on a bit in the dungeon business. They're not all just great big badly-lit and leaky places crammed with nasty creatures out to bite your head off at every turn. This is the future, you know. Now please sit down and finish your tea."*

*"I haven't fucking come all this way to have fucking tea with a middle-class twat in a red dressing gown," mumbled Crystal Meth, provocatively.*

*"Ah, the entertainment has arrived," said DK, brightly. "There's always one. And all dressed up in retro-black to match her slightly off-piste tongue."*

*"What the f..."*

*"Wonderful," interrupted DK, clapping his hands enthusiastically.*

*"You're going the right way to get a fucking sword shoved..."*

*"Thank you," interrupted the Snark Maiden, quickly. "I think we should all take a deep breath and reconsider the situation before us."*

*"I want to see my sister," said a little voice just under Roger's elbow.*

*"Then just go in there and have a chat with her, my little friend," said the Dragon King. He motioned Tammy to the door behind the dais where Bunty was supposed to be arranging her hair or doing things with her nails.*

*There was a long pause as the heroes thought long and hard about the dilemma facing them. Should they get involved in a massive bloody fight or should they settle down on a bean bag or two and shoot the breeze with this rather genial senior citizen of the dungeons?*

*"Well, after much thought and consideration, I'm all for the tea and cake option," said Endymion, eagerly reaching towards the bun and scone trolley.*

*"Us too," agreed Julius and the two other black orcs. Neither really wanted a fight which would probably end up with them being scraped off the walls.*

*"Ah, Julius," said the Dragon King smoothly. "Pleased you've come back. Sorry about my harsh words concerning your portrait of me. I just don't see myself as an impressionist cherub with wings fluttering over some woodland pond. Not good for the image, Julius. Not good at all. Not that I want to be portrayed as a demon with red eyes and glossy whip either. Something more Fauvist perhaps?"*

*"What about artistic licence?" began a sulky Julius. "I don't see myself as a Fauvist or any of that modernist crap..."*

*"What about a compromise," interrupted DK, quickly. "I'm in a good mood today. How say you paint me in a pointillist style, or even something post-modernist with a few factory chimneys in the background and the odd cow which has been sawn in half."*

*"Well, all right then," said Julius, slowly. "But I get to choose the pose."*

*"Of course you do, my dear fellow," said DK, brightly. "Now what about a nice cup of tea, my orcy friends?"*

*"Just a minute," said Roger. "What about all the treasure?"*

*"Treasure? What treasure?" asked a suddenly bewildered DK.*

*"There's always a load of gold and jewels at the end of the quest. Sort of prize for getting through in one piece," sniffed Roger, feeling embarrassed for some reason.*

*"How very adolescent," said DK, through more cigar smoke. "But somehow charming in its way. Well, my friends, you can have a look in my treasury at the back there and choose anything you like. But please don't pick the mountain bike. I'm rather into that at the moment."*

*"Mountain bike?" groaned Roger and collapsed heavily onto a luminous green bean bag.*

*"Yes indeed," said DK, enthusiastically. "It's the future you know. I plan to equip all my goblins and beastmen with the things. Wonderful for getting around quickly and no excuses about being late for a battle."*

*"The BMX 7000 series," piped up a small voice which had hitherto been unusually silent.*

*"I beg your pardon," said DK.*

*"Top of the line and with excellent gear control, the latest all-weather tyre tread with multi-coloured seats and, most importantly... I know where you can get a couple of hundred at ten per cent wholesale discount," said Tubby the Goblin, in his best sales voice.*

*"I'm listening," said DK, moving closer to the sales goblin."*

*"This is not happening," groaned Roger and reached for a cup of tea.*

<Are you there?

<No>

<Don't be difficult>

<Sorry Caroline. Just had a pig of a morning>

<What? Standing in Piccadilly dressed up like panda constitutes having a pig of a morning>

<You don't know the half of it. There's a lot of panda haters out there, you know>

<Thank you for that. I'd rather I didn't know>

<So... what's all this about? Have we got a problem with this weirdo calling himself the Dragon King... or DK?>

<Not that, but it does seem a bit strange>

<Dungeons aren't the same any more. Too much political correctness around nowadays. I liked the old quests where there was blood everywhere and you didn't have to do much thinking. Now we have pet goblins, artistic orcs and a Dragon King who sounds like he should be on Channel Four>

<I have to agree with you for once, Dave. There are just too many geeks, nerds and general do-gooders messing with the game innards>

<Odd having a quest that ends in a picnic and not a fight>

<I thought that was rather nice. Don't know who designed that little denouement, but he or she gets my vote>

<Not sure about the mountain bike stuff though>

<Yes Dave. A Dragon King pedalling to a battle doesn't really seem that terrifying. I wonder if he rings his bell if orcs and goblins get in the way>

<Sigh>

<As long as we don't have to fight any more duckmen. They were the pits>

<Hello everyone>

<Hello Obby.... or should I say Mr Copper?>

<Obby will do>

<So, what's up?>

<Percy should be logging on any moment now>

<The big man himself. I thought he was at a conference somewhere in chinky land>

<He is and I wish you wouldn't call it that, Dave. It's offensive as well as being racist>

<Sorry Cas>

<It's Caroline as you well know>

<Sorry CAROLINE>

<Percy's still in Shanghai at that very nice hotel, to answer your question. And he's getting to a computer to have a quick chat. It's evening there and he's got an hour free apparently>

<Does he know about our Obby here?>

<No>

<Are we going to tell him?>

<Of course, Dave. We don't keep secrets from our friends>

<Naturally, Caroline>

<Hello>

<It's you?>

<I've only got a minute on this machine. I'm in my room using the Arapacana laptop and it costs about ten quid a second>

<Shit on a stick>

<That's already twenty and counting>

<Christ on a crutch>

<Forty>

<Have you two quite finished?>

<Hello Caroline. What's up?>

<Lots of things. How's it going there?>

<What? The Conference. It's a laugh a minute. The things we've done today would make your hair curl. And you never guess who I came across today?>

<Who?>

<That mad copper from Box Hill. The one with the panda. He's running a language school now. Odd how things work out, isn't it? Also said some weird things which sounded like threats, but I'm getting pretty used to that sort of thing>

<What... Pringle?>

<The very same>

<You never told us that he was out there, Obby>

<Top secret, Caroline>

<I thought we were being honest and open about everything>

<Sorry... forgot about that>

<What? About being honest?>

<No, about my guv being out there>

<What are you lot talking about?>

<Well Percy, we've got some news which may make your hair curl a little too>

<Don't tell me. Dave's been beamed up to an alien vessel and been experimented on for the last twenty-four hours>

<Nope>

<It's nothing to do with Nixon again, is it?"

Nope. Obby's a copper>

<???>

<Works for that panda bloke>

<??????>

<He's been undercover in our game to get you to come back to England>

<I would never have guessed>

<I know. He's a bit heavy-handed>

<But why?>

<All this stuff about school break-ins and your fingerprints everywhere>

<Ahh>

<They want you to give yourself up and get on the next plane>

<But I haven't done anything>

<DC Ford here, Mr Gabbitt. Or Obby, if you prefer. You're probably innocent of all charges, but we just need to ask a few questions, that's all>

<So, it's Mr Gabbitt now, is it?>

<Sorry Percy. I never meant any harm and the more I've got to know you, the less I think you're guilty of anything. Anyone with two goblin friends can't be all bad>

<Very funny. So... what now? I just come back to the UK and give myself up?>

<You do realise you're number two on the most wanted list in the UK>

<Who's Number One?>

<You don't want to know>

<So I'm in good company then. And if I come back, you can sort all this mess out and clear my name?>

<Yes Percy. But there is something else>

<What now?>

<We just had word that you're already on your way to London... right now>

<???????>

<???????>

<So now I really can be in two places at the same time?>

<It appears so, Percy>

<Just got a report from our men on the ground that several well-known villains were all seen boarding a flight back to the UK a few minutes ago. And we know they had gone to China with just one purpose on the evil little minds>

<To get me?>

<It would appear so>

<But why?>

<You tell me. Anyway, they're scuttling back home as we write this>

<With me?>

<Yes. With you>

<OK, I give up. I'm writing this on a jumbo at thirty-five thousand feet over Lesser Mongolia, while being held captive by sundry criminals unknown>

<You are?>

<Sarcasm, Mr Copper. Sarcasm>

<What does your panda man have to say?>

<He also said he'd drop by your room in a few minutes to verify your presence there>

<Fine by me>

<Sorry about this, Percy. I should say that I had a great time in the quest. Never had so much fun. Do you do this often?>

<Too often, Obby>

<Well I want in on any future adventures, Caroline>

<We'll have to see about that>

<Shit, I have to go. Someone's at the door>

<Probably my gaffer, Percy>

< Bye for now>

<Look after yourself>

Gabbitt snapped his laptop closed and went to the door. He had a quick look through the spy-hole and saw Bob Irwin's familiar form waiting impatiently in the corridor outside.

"What's up, Bob?" asked Gabbitt as he opened the door.

"Just need to run over a few things before tomorrow. I've had a few ideas to add some spice to Bob's phases."

"Isn't what we're doing more than enough?"

"Nothing like gilding the lily," chuckled Irwin and marched into the room. "Oh and Bob has asked me to remind you about that missing name badge."

"Shit, I'd forgotten all about that," said Gabbitt. "I'll pop downstairs and see if it's still in the toilets. You never know, miracles have been known to happen."

"Check Reception too. Some kind soul may have handed it in," said Irwin, as Gabbitt put the door on the latch and strode into the corridor. A few moments later he was in the lift going down.

Irwin looked around the room for something to play with and then sat down on Gabbitt's bed. He picked up the TV remote and was about to hit the 'On' button when there was a small but persistent knock at the door.

"It's open," he shouted, half-expecting to see another member of the Arapacana team.

The door slowly opened and a woman with short blonde hair, green eye-shadow and wearing a shimmering silver, very off-the-shoulder evening dress, slinked into the room. She was also carrying about ten brochures in one hand and a bottle of champagne and two glass flutes in the other. It was this that Irwin noticed first. He frowned and put down the remote. "Room Service?" he tried.

"You could say that... but you're not Mr Gabbitt," said Susie Hamilton of Cambridge Universally, twinkling outrageously. She then sat down on the bed next to Irwin, dropped the brochures into his lap and gave him the bottle to open.

"I'm a friend," said Irwin, wondering why Christmas had suddenly come early.

"What sort of friend?" asked Susie, leaning closer. "A work friend, a friend friend, or a ... special friend?"

"The first one," growled Irwin, not liking the connotations of the third choice. He was an Australian after all.

"Very nice," said Susie, licking her top lip. "And how does Mr Work Friend see the world?"

"Usually through rose-coloured testicles," murmured Irwin, as the first waft of Chloe perfume wrapped itself around him and hugged tightly.

"I like that," giggled Susie and began to pull her dress off.

Down in the toilet area and then a little later in Reception, Percy Gabbitt was predictably not having much luck with the missing name badge, which incidentally had just climbed to thirty-five thousand feet and was somewhere over Beijing heading towards the Himalayas extremely fast.

Gabbitt plodded back to the lift feeling slightly downhearted. He hated losing things, especially official stuff which could cause complications. He had always worried about mislaying his passport or accidentally dropping an airline ticket on the ground in Terminal Three at Heathrow. And now it had happened with his ICAS badge. He would have to go, cap in hand, to that Danish bloke tomorrow morning and plead his case for a replacement. He sighed and entered the elevator.

His thoughts turned to Obby. A copper. That certainly changed things. The police infiltrating the Bromley Gaming Society? Where would it all end, thought Gabbitt sadly?

He was thinking these dark thoughts when he entered his hotel room and had the slightly disturbing vision of Bob Irwin's naked and hairy bottom bobbing up and down on the prone form of a very shapely blonde woman, who was still holding a champagne glass in one hand, while gasping loudly.

Gabbitt's first thought was along the lines that he had accidentally wandered into the wrong room, but seeing Irwin's buttocks machine-pistoning up and down just rubber-stamped the fact Irwin was a total bastard capable of almost anything… and in someone else's room. His.

Gabbitt did what any self-respecting Englishman would do in the circumstances - he 'coughed' his presence.

"Oh" squeaked Susie happily, as she spotted him standing by the bed. "A threesome. Lovely. Get your pants off."

Before Gabbitt could respond to this slightly unusual request from a language school delegate, there was another knock at the door and Chief Inspector Pringle nosed into room. "Glory be," he croaked as he took in the scene. "I think we need to have a talk, Mr Gabbitt."

"Ooo," squeaked Susie happily. "A foursome?"

The door then opened again and a man in an official uniform marched into Gabbitt's room. "This not good," he said.

"A uniform too," gurgled Susie, dreamily.

Chief Inspector Zhang waved a DVD in Pringle's face. "It freeze just before best bits. I not happy."

"What?" squawked Gabbitt.

"I beg your pardon," said a frowning Pringle.

"Donkeyman about to see Pussycat in her cat-suit and picture freeze. I not happy."

"Oooo, a fivesome," squeaked Susie Hamilton, slightly worriedly. There was a limit as to what she could and would do for Cambridge Universally, no matter what the bonuses were at the end of the year, although she rather liked the idea of someone in the group wearing a cat-suit and someone else wearing a uniform. She rather hoped it would be her in the cat-suit.

"What going on here?" barked Zhang, pointing at the naked thrashings on the bed behind Gabbitt and Pringle.

"I wish I could answer that question," murmured Pringle.

"Take my copy, it's on the table by the telly," grunted Irwin from the bed.

"What happening here?" persisted Zhang, determined to get answers for this western debauchery.

"The Donkeyman goes live," moaned Irwin.

# TWENTY

*"Everybody knows that the world finds it far easier to punish the monkey than to have a go at the organ-grinder. Arapacana gives the chimp a banana and then gives the organ-grinder a damn good thrashing."*

**(A serious Bob Burley at a Monday morning marketing meeting at Arapacana Associates)**

Day Two of the first ICAS workshop at the Pudong Shangri-La Hotel started much like day one except that all the delegates were on maximum alert and very aware that something untoward was happening in the workshop hall.

Most had brought their own water bottles with them and there was an air of suspicious mistrust all about. The old saying that you could fool a marketing person once, but that it would take fifty per cent commission and a shedload of bonuses to fool him twice, had never been more appropriate. The delegates were treating day two the way they would tiptoe through a meeting with a Colombian businessman.

Teddy Jensen rang the first meeting bell and agents started sitting down for their scheduled twenty-minute meetings.

Rather predictably, just as the first agents had settled into their seats, a familiar voice rang out across the hall:

"For pity's sake! I don't even know what Green Jungle Rash is!"

The two Bobs, Pamela and Percy Gabbitt then sauntered into the hall. They looked well rested and relaxed, especially Bob Irwin, who gave a cheery wave to a blonde-haired woman on the Cambridge Universally table. She blew a kiss back.

"So, what are we up to this morning?" asked a frowning Pamela.

"Absolutely nothing," beamed Burley, happily.

"Nothing?" queried Gabbitt.

"Nothing at all," repeated Burley. "Nothing quite like a lot of nothing to increase the psychological warfare."

"Brilliant!" exclaimed Irwin, who was feeling a little tired and in need of lots of nothing.

"Just think," explained Burley. "A couple of hundred schools all apprehensively sitting there the whole day expecting something nasty to happen. The sword of Damocles hanging over the lot of them and then... nothing happens. It'll drive them all crazy."

"And then?"

"And then there's the river boat cruise tonight," said Burley, with a twinkle in his eye.

"Oh no," said Irwin, rolling his eyes.

"Oh yes," said Burley. "Phases eight to thirty will happen on that boat this evening."

"Jesus," said Irwin, gulping audibly.

"They will most definitely need him," said Burley.

"So... what are phases eight to thirty?" asked Gabbitt.

"Consult your manual," replied Burley, putting an arm around Gabbitt's shoulders. "But I would suggest that you sit down when you begin reading."

"Jesus," repeated Irwin.

"But now to the bread and butter of the day," said Burley. "We have to visit a few of these schools and generally grease the wheels a little before tonight."

"Grease the wheels?" asked Irwin.

"What I suggest is this," said Burley. "In our guise as bona-fide Chinese agents, we tell schools that we can send in the region of a hundred students to each institution, if given the right deal. Just watch them salivate over that offer."

"A hundred each!" gasped Pamela.

"To each and every one of them," responded Burley. "But only at say, forty per cent commission and a bonus of ten per cent extra if we meet that target at the end of the year."

"Forty per cent!" squawked Gabbitt. Even Nero Handsworth at his most brutally nasty would never have that.

"That'll make them sweat a bit," said Burley. "But greed will have its day and I bet the majority will go for it. And don't forget that these are all targeted schools which require taking down a notch or two."

"I've got the Deidre Bowater Organization now," said Gabbitt. "What did they do wrong?"

"The owner is a dragon. A large and very overweight dragon," said Burley, with a frown. "Not that I've anything against dragons or having an addiction to pies. Anyway, she's been in the business for years and mainly offers kiddy courses. The teachers and courses are fine, but it's Deidre herself, who we are after. The woman terrorises her staff and hires and fires like it was going out of fashion. She's driven five marketing people and two secretaries to nervous breakdowns and treats the rest like slaves. The woman is reviled by everyone and needs to be taught a lesson. You're the man to do it, Percy. Just be yourself," smiled Burley and reached for a cup of black coffee from the trolley near the door.

"So, no plan then?" asked Gabbitt, worriedly.

Both the Bobs laughed. Irwin then patted Gabbitt on the back. "Percy, old son, you don't need a plan."

Several thousand miles away and deep in the bowels of Terminal Three of London's Heathrow Airport, Gilbert Grimm was also in desperate need of a plan. He was severely jetlagged, in a state of shock and totally terrified.

"Wonderful," said Chipchase and pulled his green Samsonite suitcase from the baggage carousel. "That's both bags in the first batch. Can't say fairer than that. Must be our lucky day, Mr Bibby."

"Indeed," replied Bibby and put an arm through Grimm's. "Time to go I think," he said and urged Gilbert towards the Customs barrier.

"I don't know what you want," murmured Grimm slowly. "I'm just a teacher from the London Institute of Proper Spoken English."

"That's right, Mr Gabbitt," said Chipchase.

"But you saw my passport," tried Grimm again. "It said Gilbert Grimm, not that Gabbitt swine."

"Nice one that," said Chipchase, tapping a nostril in a knowing way.

"But it proves..." squeaked Grimm.

"...that you're a tricky little bugger," completed Chipchase, brightly.

"But I really am..."

"...not going to cause any problems," said Chipchase, as he steered their luggage trolley through the Customs barrier and into the bright lights of Terminal Three.

In just a few minutes they were standing outside the terminal and breathing cold, damp English air again.

"Good to be back, Mr Bibby," said Chipchase, happily.

"Indeed," agreed Bibby.

A moment later and a large black Renault with 'Snappy Taxies' written along back door pulled up and a portly man jumped from the driver's seat. "Pick-up for a Mr Chipchase," said the man loudly.

"Excellent," sighed Chipchase and pushed their cases into the car.

"No need to do that, sirs," said the driver. "Just you get in and settle down. I'll deal with the bags. Better service than Uber and friendlier than Addison Lee."

Thank you," said Chipchase and herded Grimm into the back seat, where he sat between the two kidnappers.

The driver jumped back into his seat and clunked his door shut. "Welcome to Snappy Taxies," he said, loudly. "I'll have you into town before you can say Jack Robinson. My name's Nigel and I'll be your driver. Help yourself to the bottled water on the back windowsill behind the seat, but try not to put your hands in the side compartments. They're still drying out. I had a bit of a problem with a pick-up in Acton Town last week. The gent in question had had a skinful and..."

Back at the terminal and a tired Fred the Throttler had just boarded a black cab and said the words he had always dreamt of uttering.

"Follow that car!"

Several yards away and Detective Constable Ford had just issued the same instruction to three unmarked white Ford Transit vans. The Grey Hippo and Wild Elephant squads then swung into action.

Teddy Jensen was having an attack of the trembles in most of his right arm. He was also feeling rather sick and considerably unhappy. Day two of his ground-breaking workshop had to be better than day one.

To be honest, it had begun reasonably quietly. No one had vomited on the floor and there had been no police raids... yet. Chief Inspector Zhang had appeared to be looking unusually cheerful at the breakfast buffet earlier.

But now there was a growing crowd of discontented delegates and agents besieging his podium with odd and worryingly unexpected problems.

Teddy had done a lot of homework prior to the workshop and had drawn up a list of about sixty possible problem areas, which he had imagined would raise their ugly heads at some time during the workshop.

These problems generally revolved around delegates missing appointments or complaining about noisy or small hotel rooms. Simple stuff to solve.

He had not been expecting problems which involved food poisoning, pornographic DVDs and controversial posters. He had also not expected to have to bribe a senior police official who had been vomited on from a great height, by a man dressed up as Elvis Presley.

As such, Teddy Jensen was counting off the hours till the end of the workshop. He could not wait until five-thirty came along and the thing could be officially closed.

He was currently sitting at his table and listening wearily to an incessant tirade of misery pouring forth from a large woman in a floral marquee, which she called a dress. Teddy stared at her in a distant way and sighed from the bottom of his boots.

"I want this man expelled!" exclaimed the woman angrily.

"Expelled?" repeated Teddy, wondering how he had suddenly metamorphosed into a headmaster of a school.

"The man is guilty of gross misconduct and should be barred from all events like this for life."

"What exactly did he do, Miss Bowater?" asked Teddy, with commensurate patience.

"He tried to turn my best agent against me. And he did it right under my nose. The cheek of it!"

"Who did?"

"That young man over there," said Deidre Bowater, jabbing a finger in the direction of the Arapacana people who were having a laugh by the coffee and cake trolley. "They're all laughing at me as well. It's a disgrace. I shall report them to the British Council, the British Embassy, the Foreign Office and the police. And I shall report you too, if you don't do something about it immediately!"

"What did he..." began Teddy, now with his head in his hands.

"He told my best agent in Taiwan not to touch me with a barge-pole! The cheek!"

"With a..."

"A barge-pole. How insulting is that?"

Someone sniggered behind Deidre. She swung round and looked at the stony-faced crowd behind her. Clearly the sniggerer had gone to ground, so she turned to a wispy-looking employee of hers and spat: "You're fired. Get out of my sight immediately."

"But it wasn't..." began the tearful employee.

Deidre Bowater turned to face Teddy again.

"A barge-pole," she repeated.

"And why did he do that?" asked Teddy.

"I don't know!" All I said to him was that we would never work with Arapa... whatever they are called, since Chinese agents never pay their bills, which is true. There's nothing wrong with that. All true. Every word!"

"Oh god," groaned Teddy.

"He then proceeded, without invitation, to criticise my brochure, which I designed myself and is perfect in all ways."

"What did he say?"

"That's not the point, Mr Jensen. I want an apology and I want it now."

"Well, it might help if I knew what he was supposed to be apologising for," tried Teddy, a little daringly.

"He said something insulting about my flags. It's so trivial. And then he told my best agent in Taipei not to touch me..."

"With a barge-pole," finished Teddy. "So, tell me about these flags?"

"It's so silly," said Deidre Bowater, dismissively. "Something on page two of our brochure," she said, laying the aforesaid document on Teddy's desk. "Ridiculous!" she squawked, again. "I want that apology now... and in writing too."

"But, you've coloured in a map of the whole of the British Isles with a Union Flag," said a frowning Teddy.

"What of it?" barked Deidre Bowater.

"Ireland is not a member of the United Kingdom."

"Well it should be," announced Deidre. "And I don't see why that is such a big problem. It's only a flag after all. And a damn decent flag too. The Irish should be pleased that I've given them the honour of our glorious flag covering their country!"

"Ahh," sighed Teddy.

"I still want an apology."

Teddy Jensen was not really listening any more. He had just flicked to pages four and five and noticed that Deidre Bowater had also decided to re-write the borders of a few Asian countries too, namely that a Chinese flag now stretched to cover the island of Taiwan and a Japanese flag covered the Korean peninsula.

"You may have a slightly bigger problem on your hands than you thought," he said slowly.

It was a bright and balmily day as Bob Brand and Jack Melligan made their way from the heliport and towards a row of houses.

"Nice place," said Melligan and took a deep breath of clean, unspoilt air.

"The perfect place to retire to," said Brand.

The two of them had just landed on St Mary's on the Scilly Isles and were making their way to somewhere called the Bell Rock Hotel and two nights on the Arapacana expense account.

"The hotel's got a swimming pool," murmured Brand, happily.

"Won't it be a bit fresh at this time of the year?"

"It's covered," said Brand.

"I could do with a drink," said Melligan. "Never like helicopter rides. Seems like an unnecessarily dangerous way of travelling."

"Cars are worse," muttered Brand, as the two reached a road and began their descent into the Old Town.

"Well I don't like them."

"Fair enough, Jack," said Brand, with a smirk. "We'll take the boat back. Half a day on a choppy swell to Penzance should change your mind, I think."

"Whatever," replied an unhappy Melligan. "So, when do we pay them a visit?"

"I rather thought we'd drop by the local pubs tonight. Have a bit of R and R. We'll go and see them bright and early tomorrow morning."

"The pubs?"

"We'll start at the Atlantic, then move onto the Bishop and the Wolf, before finishing at the Mermaid."

"How come you know all the pubs, when you've never been here before?" asked Melligan.

"The joys of the world-wide web and more specifically, a website called 'www.beerintheevening.com'. One of my favourites," said Brand.

"I don't suppose they get many visitors out here, off-season," said Melligan, as the two reached a few stone buildings with Bed and Breakfast signs in the front windows.

"That's probably true, Jack," agreed Brand. "The place is geared up for summer tourists, I imagine."

"I don't suppose Timothy and Fleur Gabbitt will be expecting visitors then."

Five-thirty came and went at the Shangri-La Hotel in downtown Shanghai and Teddy Jensen and his exhausted team of helpers all collapsed into the bar on the top floor of the hotel, intent on drinking the place dry. Just the firework display later that night and the whole bloody thing would be history.

Several of the more sycophantic English school delegates had turned up to pat him on the back in the hope that they might get a small discount at the next workshop. Fat chance of that, Teddy had thought.

"I'd like to propose a toast," said Deidre Bowater, lurching to her feet in a dark blue marquee with matching dolphin ear rings. "To Teddy Jensen for organising a quite memorable workshop. I think I speak for everyone at the event when I say that you did a wonderful job under extraordinary circumstances."

There were murmurs of agreement and the odd clap from the small crowd in the bar.

"To Teddy," said Deidre, raising her Margarita and Coke. "A truly great Dane."

A few hundred yards away and just outside the hotel near the waterfront it was the turn of Susie Hamilton, Jimmy Bunn, Stevie Talbot, Jason Barkworth and Dave Sanders to start feeling the heat a little.

The five employees of Cambridge Universally were all standing with hands on hips and staring in total disbelief at what looked like three small prefabricated portakabins on a wooden raft.

"I'm going to have a coronary," said Susie, reaching for a cigarette.

"I agree. It's not quite what I expected," said Dave Sanders slowly.

"Of course, it's not, you pillock," barked Susie, vitriolically.

"The boat company said it would be a party vessel big enough for over two hundred revellers," said Jimmy Bunn.

"And a band," added Dave, quietly.

"I know what the boat company told us," said Susie, puffing anxiously at her Marlborough Light.

"It looks a bit... manky," added Jimmy, rather unwisely.

"I know it fucking does," said Susie, becoming very angry. "I'm not standing for this!"

"Me neither," muttered Stevie Talbot, as he watched the raft bob up and down by the makeshift jetty beside the Shangri-La.

"We could rig up a few fairy lights," suggested Jimmy.

"I fucking don't believe this," said Susie and threw her cigarette at the vessel in question. "Time we had a word with these boat people. And bring that bag full of their daft currency. I know much they like brown envelopes here - so let's blow their tiny little Chinese minds."

Alfred and Hilda Fennell were in their hotel room and getting ready for the evening.

"It should be fun, Alfred," said Hilda brightly, as she brushed her grey hair.

"Last time I was on a boat it certainly wasn't fun," growled Alfred.

"But that was the war, dearest. Being shot at near Dunkirk doesn't really count," said Hilda, softly.

"I don't trust them," said Alfred, grumpily.

"Don't trust what?"

"Boats. You're at the mercy of a captain you don't know and on a boat which probably has holes in it."

"This one will be fine. It's only a river cruise, that's all. And Percy said there'd be a bit of dancing."

Alfred growled again. He disliked dancing and hated dressing up. "Do I really have to put my glad rags on," he asked, thickly.

"We're on holiday, Alf and if you want me to be in a good mood for the rest of the holiday, you'll put your suit and tie on - just for me."

Alfred retired to the bathroom for a bit more growling.

"And you'll enjoy it too, or you'll answer to me. And no more fights with the natives," added Hilda. "I don't think that watch salesman will have very good things to say about British people, from now on. Throwing his suitcases in the river was one thing, but getting him carted off to the police station was an entirely different cup of tea," muttered Hilda.

There then followed a long ten minutes during which both of them thought deeply about the evening before them. The toilet then flushed and the door opened. Alfred walked back into the bedroom and sat down heavily on his side of the bed.

"And I hope you washed your hands," said Hilda, scrutinising him.

Alfred sighed, stood up and returned to the bathroom. He knew when he was beaten.

"All aboard, me hearties. Oo ahh!" grunted Bob Irwin and slapped Susie Hamilton on the bottom in a totally unacceptable and instantly sackable way.

"Ouch," said a slightly dishevelled and thoroughly out-of-sorts Susie. She adjusted her shimmering silver evening dress and took a step away from Bob Irwin, muttering about sexual harassment.

"Nice dress," said Irwin, looking at the shimmering Susie. "Very nice."

Susie frowned hard at him.

"Nice boat," he added, as he surveyed the vessel bobbing up and down before them.

"Very funny," murmured Susie.

"What's that big blue box at the back for?"

"It's the passenger cabin," replied Susie, testily.

"And where does the wooden staircase go?" persisted Irwin, unwisely.

They both looked at a rotten set of steps which was attached to the side of the passenger cabin.

"To the dance floor."

"But that's just the top of the blue box."

"To the dance floor, as I said before," repeated Susie, irritably.

"But there's no railings around the edges. One twirl and you'll be in the drink."

"Then avoid the twirls," said Susie, reaching for a cigarette, nervously.

"It's a bit... basic," said Irwin, struggling for the right word.

"You should have seen the previous offering. This is positively luxurious compared to that."

"The previous one?" asked Irwin.

"It doesn't matter," said Susie. "This is the best I could do given the time-frame… and our reserve sack of emergency cash."

"Ahh," murmured Irwin, frowning hard at the vessel before them.

"Indeed," said Susie. "The bastards took every note they could and then came up with this load of junk. Bastards."

"Well, I like it," said Irwin, after a long think. "Reminds me of one of the cruisers we use down-under to go crocodile hunting. No frills, but lots of shooting access points."

"I think I'm going now," said Susie and flounced her way on board the vessel where Jimmy Bunn and Dave Sinclair were waiting in tuxedos and black bow ties.

Irwin chuckled to himself and then made his way along the promenade and away from the vessel. Time for a quick drink or two in the bar, before the thing kicked off.

He took one last look at the vessel, which had been described on the poster at the language show as a modern, well-equipped pleasure cruiser perfect for a night of fun, fun and fun.

Three funs, thought Irwin, thinking of Susie in that silver dress.

"Looks like someone's cobbled together two coal barges, then added the top of a blue caravan and screwed the lot to the back of an oversized Mini Metro," said Alfred Fennell, observantly.

"It does look a little strange," agreed Hilda, fingering her handbag, anxiously.

The two pensioners were sitting on a bench in a small grassy area adjacent to the hotel. They were staring at their proposed mode of conveyance later that evening.

"One thing I'm certain about," began Alfred.

"What's that, dearest?"

"It's not seaworthy. That thing couldn't survive a mild swell in the Channel. Probably wouldn't even manage the river Nene," he said and put both hands in his pockets.

"The river what?" asked a mystified Hilda.

"Runs from Northamptonshire to The Wash via Peterborough," explained Alfred.

"Really?" came the bewildered response from Hilda.

"That thing would go straight down if the smallest ripple hit it," said Alfred. "All hands lost in a few moments. Not a chance for anyone. Davy Jones Locker and no mistake, even on the Nene," he said and clapped his hands.

"Perhaps we should have a long walk along the promenade instead," said a genuinely worried Hilda.

Not a bit of it," said Alfred, thickly. "You said you wanted to dance and you're going to."

"Evening all," said a voice.

The two pensioners looked round at their visitor.

"Evening," said Alfred, suspiciously.

"Lovely evening, isn't it?" said the tall man.

"If you're selling watches or anything, then I'd move along sharpishly, if I were you," whispered Hilda, trying to get a look at the man's face in the shadows.

"Watches?" queried the man. "Oh no, not at all. Just taking in the evening air, after that ridiculous conference."

"What? The lavvy convention?" grunted Alfred.

"Err, probably," said the man, a little taken aback.

"Alfred and Hilda Fennell from Bromley Common, London," said Hilda.

"In England," added Alfred, loudly.

"Oh, I know where Bromley Common is," said the man, moving into the light. "Chief Inspector Pringle," he said, taking Hilda's hand. He bowed gently and said, "Charmed, I'm sure."

"Stone the crows!" exclaimed Alfred. "It's the man from the airport."

"The very same," smiled Pringle.

"Red Leicester cheese," said Alfred and gestured to him to join them on the seat.

"Mad country," said Pringle, quietly.

"Barking," agreed Alfred.

"But very friendly," added Hilda.

"So, what brings you to Shanghai?" asked Pringle.

"Our next-door neighbour invited us," said Alfred, flatly.

"Ah," said Pringle. "So, you're here on holiday."

"For a couple of weeks. Just to see young Percy and do a bit of shopping. They say it's quite cheap here, especially the silk. I want to get some silk pyjamas for Alfred," said Hilda.

Alfred grunted again and looked at the grass beneath his feet. He was not at all sure that his wife should be telling strangers about his bedware.

"Percy Raymond Gabbitt," said Pringle slowly, emphasising every single syllable.

"You know our Percy?" asked Hilda.

"Indeed, I do," said Pringle, quietly. "Indeed, I do."

"A very nice young gentleman," continued Hilda. "But he does get into some scrapes. Like my Alf here."

Alfred grunted again.

"Indeed, he does," said Pringle, quietly. "So, is he out here long?"

"He said he might stay for a year or two, but that depends on Nixon."

"Ah, the cat," said Pringle, sitting back, deep in thought.

"Yes, his cat. He misses him a lot."

"Someone tried to catnap him last month," said Alfred, suddenly. "Bastard Teletubbies and Frisbees."

"Be quiet, Alf," said Hilda. "The Chief Inspector doesn't want to hear your feelings on modern-day society."

Alfred grunted and resumed staring at the grass.

There was a long silence, after which Hilda took a deep breath and turned to the inspector, looking serious. "He helped Alf put a new layer of felt on the garden shed last autumn and sometimes does our lawn, if Alf has his tummy problem."

Alfred growled.

"Sounds like a very nice young man," said Pringle, through pursed lips.

"The best," said Hilda. "Just wish he'd settle down with a nice young lady. Someone like that Catherine what's-her-name who visits now and then."

"The one that looks like our Susan," added Alfred.

"Caroline Geraldine Williams," said Pringle, through his teeth.

"You know her too?" asked a surprised Hilda. "My goodness, the police are good nowadays."

"Indeed," said Pringle. "It is a shame that such a nice man doesn't come back to England. What he sees in China, I can never guess," he said, slowly shaking his head.

"That's what I keep saying," said Alfred. "It might do some nice noodles and creditable prawn crackers, but it's no substitute for a full English."

"Indeed," repeated Pringle. "Well, I should be going. Got to get ready for a party on a boat tonight."

"You're invited too?" asked Hilda, with a pleasant smile.

"Yes, though I can't imagine why," said Pringle. "Thought they only wanted Chinese business contacts on the boat, not the police."

"I'm damn sure they won't get any business from me," said Alfred.

"Well, I'm pleased you're coming as well, Chief Inspector," said Hilda. "It'll be nice to have someone of our generation to chat to."

Pringle smiled stonily and got up. "Then I shall see you later," he said and walked back to the hotel.

"What a nice man," said Hilda, after he had disappeared back into the shadows.

"Coppers are always after something," muttered Alfred, with a frown.

"Well, I like him," said Hilda. "And he kissed my hand like a true gentleman."

Alfred grunted again and resumed staring at the grass beneath his feet.

Eight o'clock arrived and guests for the Cambridge Universally boat cruise began arriving at the boat. Susie Hamilton and Jimmy Bunn stood on either side of a makeshift gang plank, each holding a silver tray of champagne flutes.

"Welcome to the CU cruise," gushed Susie to a woman with a pinched expression, wearing a faded blue dress which looked as if it had been machine-washed fifty times too many.

"Do you have any mineral water?" asked the woman.

"On board," beamed Susie, attempting to read the damn woman's name badge in the half-light.

"Jane Bobbin," sniffed Bobbin, aloofly.

"Welcome to our cruise, Ms Bobbin," glittered Susie, insincerely.

Jane Bobbin moved a little unsurely onto the gang plank and then onto the boat. When she had disappeared into the blue box at the back, Susie turned to Jimmy and said, "British Council cow."

More guests arrived. Twenty minutes later and about fifty delegates and agents had boarded the SS CU, intent on getting through the next two hours without drowning.

"The boat can't take any more," said Dave Sanders. "We're only three inches above the waterline," he added, rolling his eyes melodramatically.

Susie Hamilton sighed. The boat should have been able to take upwards of a hundred, not fifty, according to the man who had rented the thing out to her earlier. He was probably counting small, anorexic Chinese children, not large overweight foreigners. She reluctantly gave the signal to two Chinese boatmen in drab brown jackets to withdraw the plank and set sail.

"Ho!" shouted a voice loudly from the gloom of the path beyond. "Just a minute!"

Susie squinted into the darkness. Five people then appeared, half-running and half-staggering towards the boat.

Susie was about to shout that they had missed their chance of the cruise of a lifetime, when she spotted that they were Chinese, which meant business possibilities. The gang plank was swung back into place.

Susie Hamilton bit her tongue and decided that five more bodies on the boat would not matter that much.

Then she spotted one last person bowling along the path to the boat. It was Deidre Bowater. Shit, thought Susie. She was a whole inch all to herself.

Everyone boarded. She smiled pleasantly at Ms Bowater and directed her to the bar in the blue cabin at the back of the boat, saying a silent prayer.

# TWENTY-ONE

*"Greed is a two-headed dog, with a head at either end. It has no tail because the head at the back ate it. It is also a very confused dog, because both heads are always fighting."*
**(Suzhou student trying to explain a complicated Chinese saying to a drunk Bob Irwin)**

Seen from the top-floor balcony bar of the Pudong Shangri-La Hotel, the maiden voyage of the SS Cambridge Universally was enough to send the observer scuttling off for a double-brandy.

The strange-looking boat lurched out into the murky waters and attempted to traverse the Huangpu River in a straight line to the other bank, through two crowded shipping lanes.

The captain was a young man of about twenty-two years of age from a city called Ningbo, which was just south of Shanghai. He had been paid nine pounds for the evening and was determined to give all the foreign delegates a voyage they would long remember.

It should be added that this was his maiden voyage as well, his day job being a burger flipper at Mr Huang's Premium Socialist Burgers in the old town.

Finally, it should be further noted that he was not at all au-fait with the various moods of the Huangpu River and somewhat naively considered the best route between points A and B to be the most direct and extremely straight one. Such a route might seem sensible to the inexperienced river pilot, but given that rivers with such a mixture of currents as the Huangpu generally need points C, D and even E to get to point B in one dry piece, the most direct route was often the most treacherous.

Captain Zhang had been assigned the job of piloting the vessel mainly because he had an elementary standard of English, which meant he could probably hold his own in a with the foreign tourists on board.

His English classes had sadly not covered any aspects of nautical English and he was still many lessons away from phrases like: man overboard; oh shit, we're sinking and every man and woman for him or herself!

Captain Zhang squeezed the throttle and a massive belch of oily black smoke plumed from the small engine at the back of the boat. The craft began chugging uncertainly to a point roughly in the middle of the river, currently occupied by a massive barge with about two hundred industrial containers stacked on its caste-iron decks.

"Wonderful," said Susie Hamilton, happily. "Feel that sea breeze in your lungs," she added and had another puff at her third Marlborough Light of the hour.

"I'll circulate what's left of the champagne and then you can officially welcome everyone on board, Susie. Then we can have the toast," said Jimmy Bunn excitedly. He was enjoying being first mate.

"Very good, Mr Bunn," said Susie, getting into the role of captain, just as nicely. "Steady as she goes," she added, as the boat listed slightly, as it attempted to negotiate the first of many small waves which emanated from the enormous barge lying in front of them.

"Can you contact the firework boat to follow us? I don't want to lose contact with the thing," said Susie, staring into the gloom.

"Already done," said Jimmy Bunn. "It'll be ready when called upon. I've made sure of that."

"There'll be bonuses all round if this comes off," said Susie, puffing nervously.

"It's bonus enough just to be able to work with you," murmured Jimmy, adoringly.

Down in the passenger cabin it was a tight huddle as delegates and agents attempted to retrieve a drink and some nibbles from various well-positioned silver platters, while trying to look calm, contented and, above all, ready for business.

The whole effect was similar to having a business drinks party on a Japanese commuter train in the rush hour, while the carriage was rocked from side-to-side by a strong wind.

"Got any salt and vinegar crisps over there?" shouted Bob Irwin, over a sea of Chinese heads.

"Only the spicy Thai ones," replied Gabbitt, as he trawled through the nibbles trays. "But they do have cream cakes covered in shaving foam and cherry tomatoes."

"Great," said Irwin, unenthusiastically. He wanted crisps with his lager, not frothy cakes and tomatoes.

"Fresh air, I think," said Bob Burley and started pushing towards the open sky.

On the roof of the pleasure boat, Jane Bobbin and four intrepid agents were attempting an impromptu 'salsa', after Jimmy Bunn had inserted a CD into the boat's 'entertainment' system. Jane Bobbin reluctantly threw a few moves, much to the delight of Ribena Ping and Eustace Kim, who both clapped her enthusiastically. Tomoko Nakajima and Britney Kim joined in with a very Asian version of a salsa.

Chief Inspector Pringle was also outside. He was standing at the stern of the boat, leaning gingerly against one of the few rails which ran along the back of the boat near the distinctly Mini-Metro bit. He was attempting small-talk with Sweetie Chao of 'Come Quickly Travel'.

"Nice city."

"Too many people," said Sweetie. "Taipei much better. More civilised."

"Ah," said Pringle, having a sip of something which might have been warm lager.

"Mainland Chinese people all from countryside," added Sweetie as she popped a small, pickled cucumber into her mouth. "Not polite."

"They don't seem that bad," said Pringle, as an agent from Beijing leant over the side and spat voluminously into the river swell. "But I do see what you mean," he added with a frown.

"You from a school?" asked Sweetie, putting her professional hat on, as she pulled a business card from her fake Gucci handbag.

"No, well yes, I suppose so," said Pringle. "We're quite new to the game. You probably would not be interested," he said, trying hard to back-peddle the school stuff.

"A top up?" asked Susie Hamilton to the two as she swept past with a half-full bottle of bubbly in one hand and a cigarette in the other.

"Thanks very much," said Pringle and held out his glass. But he never received the top-up, since the SS CU seemed to hiccough loudly and jump two feet to the right.

There were screams and shouts from inside the passenger cabin as glasses emptied down people's fronts and nibbles got thrown skywards. In just one small second, three quarters of all the food and drink were on the floor of the small boat, but that was not of prime concern to most of the passengers.

Even Captain Zhang did not seem to register that his own glass of champagne had toppled over the side and into the swirling waters of the Huangpu. He had bigger fish to fry. In fact, the size of his fish might have resembled Moby Dick proportions as the SS CU bucked again, creaked horribly and then started listing badly to starboard.

"Tell Deidre to stop moving around," shouted an unkind voice from near the bow of the vessel. There were isolated pockets of nervous laughter.

The boat then did a complete revolution and, for a moment, pointed in the right direction again. There were multiple sighs all round. However, the relief was only for a brief moment. The SS CU skipped forward suddenly and attempted to tackle the formidable wake of the departing cargo barge, now a hundred yards down river. A large wave hit the vessel hard, the boat rocked violently to starboard and two feet of dirty river water sloshed over the side and into the passenger cabin.

"So, you send three hundred students to the UK a year?" asked Susie, already up to her ankles in cold, dirty river water.

"What?" screamed a Korean called Darius Park from 'Uhak Yoohak Uhak' in Seoul.

"We offer outstanding commission and a whole raft of bonuses," squeaked Susie, as the boat started to spin gently and let in more water.

"Aaaaagh!" screamed Darius, as he fell into the rising waters.

"We can also offer lucrative and very bespoke targets," continued Susie doggedly, kneeling next to him. "CU has answers to most questions,' she shouted above the screams.

"Good," shouted Darius in terror. "Where's the fucking lifeboat?"

"Ah," said Susie.

It was this moment that Captain Zhang made what was probably the worst decision of his short nautical life. He attempted to turn the boat one hundred and eighty degrees and return to the Shangri-La jetty. In normal circumstances this might have been a laudable action, but on a dark night on a crowded river it was the final straw that broke the camel's back.

The SS CU chugged jettywards and sideways onto the current of the river for about ten seconds before the engine made a loud clanking noise and then seized up completely as river water sloshed into the engine compartment, leaving the craft drifting rather dangerously back into the busy shipping lanes. It was like breaking down in the fast lane of the M25 in the dead of night without any lights on.

What made matters worse was the fact that unlike cars, massive coal barges take quite a long time to come to a complete standstill or even change direction. Something sudden happening directly in front of these barges would inevitably lead to catastrophic results.

As bad luck would have it, a particularly large brute, covered in a mountain of massive cardboard boxes which had been hastily-lashed down by an overworked loading crew back in the city of Nanjing, happened to be steaming down the Huangpu and past the Shangri-La at that exact moment.

The captain of that vessel, also a Captain Zhang, quickly spotted the wallowing pleasure boat, but could do little more than implore Buddha and then wait for the inevitable crunch of impact.

Any thoughts of trying to steer around the small vessel were quickly discarded, as he looked at the oncoming lane of coal barges chugging heavily towards him. Any attempt to play games with that lot would only lead to an even larger mess than just steaming over the little boat directly in his path.

This did not really seem like the best course of action to the passengers on the ill-fated SS CU. It was the salsa group on the disco roof who raised the alarm with loud ear-piercing screams.

"Sounds like they're having a ball up top," said Jimmy Bunn, happily. "I'll get up there in a minute with what's left of the nibbles."

An agent fell full-length next to him and tried to swim out of the passenger cabin as the water level rose again.

"Please do not be alarmed!" shouted Susie Hamilton, from the rear of the boat where the captain should have been sitting. He had already decided that enough was enough and was swimming hard for the jetty.

"Start the fireworks!" shouted Susie to Dave Sinclair. "Maybe we can save the day yet?" she cried, as two agents dived into the river from the disco roof and disappeared into the swell.

"Right," said Dave and barked loudly into a mobile phone.

Unfortunately for all concerned, the firework boat, which was little bigger than the pleasure boat, was also experiencing a few problems of its own with the heavy barge wakes which were enveloping the SS CU.

The two Chinese 'firework-lighters' on board stood at the back and tried to steady the craft as it bucked in the high waves. A phone beeped and was answered.

Now it has been said before that when a Chinese person is given an order, he always carries it out to the letter, no matter what the circumstances. This was the case on the firework barge. The two firework technicians started hurrying about the boat with glowing spatulas, lighting numerous blue touch-papers.

The boat then rose high on a final wave and quickly descended into a trough. This was appallingly unlucky, since it was at that exact moment that a massive salvo of rockets which had been earmarked for the heavens, shot horizontally away from the listing firework barge at a height of three feet.

It was like watching one of those movies of the high seas when the pirate's galleon lets loose a cannon volley at the French frigate... with predictable results.

However, where a French frigate should have been, sat the luckless SS CU. It took the full brunt of the rockets from bow to stern and for a few insane moments was lit up with a million red, blue, green, gold and silver starbursts.

To an observer on the river bank it would have actually looked quite pretty from some angles. From an observer on the SS CU though, it was hell on earth and then a lot worse.

What had seemed like a fairly nasty disaster involving lots of drowning, now became a much nastier disaster involving being burnt alive… and then drowned. Most delegates and agents instinctively ducked into the knee-deep water on the deck.

Percy Gabbitt patted out something hot and uncomfortable which had dropped into a trouser turn-up. He turned to a smiling Bob Irwin and put a small fire out which had broken out on his back.

"Quite a show," said Irwin, as a rocket the size of a large ferret shot between them and exploded in a wall of sheet silver against the side of the passenger cabin. "Reminds me of Sydney on Millennium Eve. Only this is a lot more... hands on. Anyone fancy a drink?" he shouted, as a burning marketing man abandoned ship and began to strike out for the Shangri-La jetty.

"I think the bar just closed," said Burley with a frown as the roof of the passenger cabin gave way and half-collapsed into the cabin below. There were several screams from the few agents left inside.

"Time to say goodbye to this little cruise, I think," said a breathless Pamela Henderson, who had just joined the group.

The four ducked as three rockets whooshed over the sinking craft and hit something dark and large not fifty yards away.

"Looks like trouble ahead for the SS CU," said Burley, as the black outline of Captain Zhang's massive coal barge reared into view.

"Time for a swim?" queried Gabbitt, looking at the oily brown waters, uncertainly.

"Not quite," said Burley, looking at Irwin and Gabbitt. "You two, see if you can drag what's left of that wooden roof away from the passenger cabin. Maybe we can use it as a raft."

"What about phases eight to thirty?" asked a crest-fallen Irwin.

"Yes, I'm sorry about that too," tutted Burley, sadly. "A lot of work went into planning those."

"Next time," sympathised Pamela, patting her boss on the back.

"Shame really," said Burley ruefully. "But I have to say that setting fire to the boat would have made a very nice Phase Thirty-One."

"It's always a bit of a letdown when things happen that you didn't actually engineer yourself," said Irwin, as a rocket hit a boat cable and then zigzagged about the deck spraying agents and delegates with golden and silver stars. Five more leapt riverwards.

"Indeed," agreed Burley, having a last sup of his champagne flute, which he then tossed into the river. "But now I think it's time to leave the SS CU and get back to terra-firma and a indulge in a nice double Scotch. Get busy with that roof, while I look for something unsinkable we can hold onto should it prove not to be very buoyant."

Gabbitt and Irwin trotted down the length of the boat, passing a hysterical Jimmy Bunn and an extremely angry Susie Hamilton. Susie now had the bullhorn in her hands and was attempting to placate her guests. "Please do not panic," she tried, as another two splashes next to her signified the exit of two more possible clients.

"On the left bank, you can see the hotel where Scott Joplin stayed," she barked doggedly into the bullhorn. "He wrote 'The Sting' there," she said, as the boat dipped again and another wave poured over the starboard side.

Irwin and Gabbitt reached the passenger cabin just in time to pull Ribena Ping and Britney Kim clear. Both were still attempting to get their salsa rhythms correct and seemed oblivious of the impending doom. Jane Bobbin had already completely disappeared in the gathering maelstrom.

"Pull the roof off," shouted Irwin. "On three. One, two..."

Irwin never got to 'three'. A massive splash rather like someone dropping a ten-ton weight into the water next to the boat rocked the craft savagely from bow to stern. Everything fell first to starboard and then hard to port.

Deidre Bowater had hit the water from a great height.

Irwin got to his feet and was about to shout three again when he noticed that the space on the other side of the broken roof, previously occupied by Percy Gabbitt, was conspicuously empty. Irwin said two choice four-letter words and pulled part of the roof clear. He then pushed it overboard and gestured to Pamela and Burley to join him on the makeshift raft.

"No sign of Percy," said Irwin, as he helped Pamela aboard.

"Probably saving a few people," said Burley, getting onto the roof section, while clutching six bright red party balloons in one hand. "He's like that, as we all know."

"Nice balloons," said Irwin, admiringly.

"Buoyancy aids as well as being nice markers for anyone daft enough to come out here attempting a rescue. Now all we need is a couple of paddles."

"No problems," said Pamela, producing a several stout, glossy Cambridge Universally brochures. "Not just great at selling courses but also waterproof," she said, waving them in the air.

"Excellent," said Burley. "Time to get clear of all this, I think," and they began paddling away as quickly as they could.

Percy Gabbitt was indeed rescuing other people, more by accident though than by any true heroism. Ms Bowater's tidal wave had sent him tumbling into the back of the passenger cabin with six other luckless people. There was a lot of gasping, swearing and a few coughs. A voice then spoke in the gathering gloom.

"We can also offer tailor-made exclusivity, if we can agree on an annual student target." Susie Hamilton was still selling furiously.

"We're all going to die," said a strangulated voice. "Drowned on a boat in China. What a way to go," it continued ruefully."

"Didn't two of your students die at your school recently of amoebic dysentery?" asked a Chinese voice.

"Who told you that? I've had enough of all this. My school has not got any diseases and, if I ever get my hands on the swine who started spreading these rumours, there'll be blood spilt," frothed the voice in the darkness.

No one dies at Cambridge Universally," said Susie smugly, as the water level reached her chin. "We have a very proud record."

"Well, that record goes tonight," said another voice.

"Bloody Teletubbies," said another English voice.

"No need for us all to panic," added yet another voice - a very English voice. "Just help me with this plank. It seems rotten right through and should give way if we hit it a little."

"And then what?" asked the man with the sickness problems at his school.

"Then we swim clear, using these planks as lifebuoys."

"I wish I had my hammer," said Alfred Fennell. "I can do pretty much anything with a lump hammer."

"Yes, dear," said Hilda patiently, as the water lapped up to neck level. "Just help the inspector with that plank, will you?"

"We're all going to die," whimpered the sick school man.

"Chin up," said Alfred, loudly. "Takes more than a little water to finish off an Englishman!"

"That's the spirit," said Pringle and began punching at the plank next to him.

"The back panel looks loose," said Percy Gabbitt, as another wave lapped into the back section taking the water level up a few more inches. "Maybe we could ease the thing off and use it as a raft or something?"

"Oh, hello young Percy," said Hilda. "Nice to see you. Are you having a nice time?"

"Well, I've had better, I have to say," said Gabbitt, as the water level pushed up around his nose.

*Roger the Norse Fighter strode up a narrow passage and into bright sunlight. He took a deep breath and blinked a few times, as his eyes became accustomed to normal daylight again. He then walked slowly into a small glade sided by banks of small yellow buttercups and Michaelmas daisies. It was good to be out of that dungeon. He sat down on the grass.*

*A few moments later and an elf, a wizard, a warrior, a dwarf shaman, two goblins, three black orcs and finally, a strange human woman dressed in black, padded into the glade and sat down around him.*

*Roger stared up at the heavens. In the good old days it would just have been him staggering out, bloodied but unbowed. He sighed. How times change, he thought for the millionth time, as he looked up at a few mashed potato clouds skudding across the deep blue sky. A shape filled his skyline. A distinctly goblin shape. He sighed again and sat up.*

*"You did all this for me?" asked the shape in a small voice.*

*"Yes," said Roger and arranged himself so that he sat cross-legged.*

*"And all because you thought I had been kidnapped," continued Bunty.*

*"Yes," said Roger again.*

*"How sweet. II would have expected my Tammy to get all silly about me disappearing, but not a great Norse Fighter like you."*

*Roger shifted uncomfortably. He was not sure about being called sweet by a goblin, in front of black orcs and and goblins, no matter how friendly. "Just another rescue quest, that's all," he mumbled, quietly.*

*"Well, I think you're a very nice man," said Bunty and leant down and gave him a small kiss on the cheek.*

*"Right, I have to get back down there," said Bunty with a sigh. "DK expects chapter two to be put to bed, before the end of the day."*

*She got up and slowly made her way back to the dungeon entrance where a couple of beastmasters and a hellhound, which was happily wagging its tail, were awaiting to escort her underground. Bunty turned round just before entering the complex again.*

*"Thank you," she said and blew a kiss in Roger's direction.*

*There were sniggers from the two goblins present and then a small silence.*

*"So, what now?" asked Obby, seriously.*

*"Back to Waendelsburgh," said Roger, after a thoughtful pause.*

*"Really?" croaked Crystal Meth. "You're coming home? Dad will be pleased. I mean..."*

*"It's all right. I know what you mean," interrupted Roger, wearily." And yes, I am," said Roger, standing up and sheathing Dune Blade.*

*"But you hate towns," said Obby.*

*"Time to face the music, I think," said Roger and began marching out of the glade. As he reached the tree-line, he stopped and turned round.*

*"What music?" asked Tammy the goblin.*

*"There's always music to answer for in towns," said the Snark Maiden, standing up.*

*"Oh," said Tammy.*

*"You've all done me proud," said Roger gruffly. "But this next battle is mine and mine alone. You don't have to come with me, you know."*

*And with that Roger the Norse Fighter disappeared into the shadows.*

*There was a moment of quiet reflection and then the rest of the party all stood up and followed him.*

It was total mayhem on the Huangpu River in central Shanghai. People were being pulled out of the water on both sides of the river by the police and helpful passers-by. It was a scene of utter chaos.

Inspector Zhang stood, with hands on hips. by the Shangri-La jetty and stared into the darkness before him. He was feeling a little confused. What were these strange foreigners thinking of, taking a boat out onto the river at night? Didn't they realise that you don't mess with China like that?

He looked on in disbelief as an extremely large woman in a soggy blue dress was pulled clear of the water and rolled onto the concrete jetty. She looked like a beached whale coughing water from its lungs. What on earth were they thinking, thought Zhang again?

Three helicopters made a low pass over the Inspector and began hosing the waters with bright white spotlights. Zhang looked on, hoping that there would not be too big a body count when dawn broke in a few hours. That would not look good on his CV and, worse still, he would lose a lot of face even though it was hardly his fault. What on earth were these mad foreigners thinking?

Zhang sighed and watched a makeshift raft being pulled ashore by three bystanders and a policeman. The extremely wet occupants staggered onto the jetty and walked past him.

"Well, that was fun," said Bob Irwin, brightly.

"A tall drink, I think," said Bob Burley.

"A hot bath and a new set of clothes for me. And can I keep the balloons?" asked Pamela Henderson.

Inspector Zhang let them walk back to the hotel. Fun? A tall drink? A hot bath? Balloons? Totally mad, all of them. And they think we're the developing country.

He frowned deeply and came to a decision. It was not a hard decision to make, but it was a moment of clarity for the inspector. He decided that the next person who stepped out of the water and onto the jetty, would be arrested and charged with as many things that he could think of relating to taking small boats out onto the Huangpu River in central Shanghai in the dead of night.

He did not care if the man or woman was not really responsible for the debacle unfolding in front of him. These foreigners would have to learn that while they were in China they would have to be responsible citizens and not insane lunatics intent on disrupting the normal ebb and flow of Chinese society, let alone police time and energy. He noticed two fire appliances drawing up by the hotel and a cluster of firemen begin busying themselves with ladders and hoses for some reason. And firemen's time too, he thought grimly.

Out on the river things were quietening down a little. The SS CU had almost completely sunk, although one could still see the a small part of the stern bobbing in the waves.

The massive coal barge had been and gone, neatly slicing the pleasure boat into two and dragging a large portion of the bow section along with it for the ride to Manila in the Philippines. Unknown to most people at the time, a terrified Jane Bobbin lay clutching a stray plank within the bow, as it motored towards the high seas.

Jane Bobbin was not the only unfortunate one. The impact with the small pleasure boat, albeit a small vibration to such a mighty vessel, had been enough though to send ten badly-lashed cardboard boxes into the river far below. They bobbed away in the barge's wake like overweight square seals. The barge captain, a Captain Zhang from Hubei province, frowned and wondered if the loss of the boxes would cost him his bonus.

They say that one man's loss is another man's gain and this was certainly the case for a few other occupants of the river. Take Ribena Ping and Eustace

Kim, for example. They both gratefully grabbed hold of one of the boxes and began shouting for help.

They were quickly pulled onto a passing police boat. Ironically, the incident formed a bond between the two agents and six months later Ribena Ping became Mrs Ribena Kim after a lavish wedding in Seoul, where the wedding cake was shaped into a mock-up of the SS CU.

Further down the river and what looked like a sinking Mini Metro bobbed gently towards the river bank with a cluster of delegates, agents and guests holding tightly onto the bumpers. It eventually made landfall near to where Inspector Zhang was standing. The two fire crews helped pull the six wet survivors onto the jetty, where they sat breathing heavily for a few moments.

Zhang smiled to himself and approached the group. He was about to carry out his plan of arresting the first person he came across – in this case a belligerent-looking Alfred Fennell, when he spotted the man from the DVD shop and the wrecked school in Suzhou – the same man who had vandalised his car.

There was not even a moment's hesitation. He signalled to two constables to assist him and then proceeded to manhandle the villain to his feet, where he was formally charged with ninety-two different misdemeanours. Zhang was beginning to feel quite pleased with himself.

"Steady on," said Chief Inspector Pringle, standing up. "You can't arrest him. He was just a guest like all of us. He wasn't responsible..."

"Move aside," said Zhang, as dangerously as he could.

"I am a police inspector, as well," tried Pringle.

"Stand aside, or you will be arrested too," announced Zhang, loudly.

"This man is also wanted by the British police force," said Pringle, a little desperately. "We have first dibs on him, sunshine."

"Dibs? Sunshine?" queried a perplexed Zhang, staring up at the odd foreigner.

"He's ours," emphasised Pringle and squared up to Zhang.

Inspector Zhang roughly pushed Pringle to one side and walked after his constables.

"How dare you!" said Alfred Fennell, standing up. 'He's an English gentleman and an officer of the law, I'll have you know."

"Alfred, not now," said Hilda, quickly.

Alfred Fennell hesitated and then sat back down. Even in his world, it was not a wise course of action to have a dust-up with a Chinese policeman in his own country, especially when his wife disapproved. He probably hated cheese as well. Barbarians – every man-jack of them.

Inspector Zhang produced a small whistle and blew a piercing blast. Immediately, twenty policemen appeared from nowhere and began herding the wet foreigners away from the arrested man.

"We also do English for Law Enforcement," said a member of the group of survivors. She then produced a sodden business card and thrust it into Zhang's hands. "I can get you thirty per cent discount and... other extras," she said and winked lasciviously at him through a garland of river weed.

Totally insane, thought Inspector Zhang, as he tossed the business card into a puddle and marched off after the policemen trundling Mr Percy Gabbitt to the back of a white squad car.

"Thirty-five per cent and free accommodation for the first two weeks," cried the voice, again.

As the police car departed with lights flashing and sirens wailing, more agents and delegates sloshed ashore. It had certainly been an evening that none of them would forget in a hurry.

A short fifty yards away and amid a large crowd of amazed and horrified onlookers, Teddy Jensen smiled. It was a small smile, but rather a cruel one. That'll teach the bastards, he thought a little unkindly. He then nodded towards a crew of ten Chinese helpers for his own firework display to begin.

A few moments later and under a bright gold, silver, red and green twinkling canopy of starbursts, about three hundred English school marketing people started networking feverishly with the remaining agents who had not been invited on the Cambridge Universally cruise and were now feeling extremely smug.

The disaster, which they had all witnessed, was quickly forgotten as thoughts of getting that extra group of teenagers to summer centres in Margate and Paignton dominated their sales horizons.

Back in the Shangri-La Hotel Bob Burley was doing a lot of very quick thinking too, following the arrest of his hero and inspiration.

"Bastards!" exclaimed Irwin, passionately. "Typical Percy though. He does a hatful of stuff which breaks the law and then gets arrested for something he had nothing to do with."

Bob Burley frowned and reached for his cell phone. He knew that something important had just happened and he also knew that he would have to act fast.

The riverboat disaster, Percy's arrest and probably all the other unplanned events at the ICAS workshop, may have changed Arapacana's stance in the delicate framework of things that constituted their careful relationship with the local police force in Suzhou.

Questions were bound to be asked at higher levels. And no amount of dinners or fat parcels of rubber-banded bank notes in brown envelopes, would appease a system where 'loss of face' was everything.

A moment later and he whispered just two words into his mobile phone, before snapping it shut and reaching for a second double Scotch.

Further down the bar and tucked into a dark alcove, sat Chief Inspector Pringle. He had his feet up on a neighbouring chair and was feeling rather stunned. After all, he'd just survived a holocaust. He was also thinking hard and fast, as he sipped at a large Suntory Snow Beer. The Universe had somehow altered over the last few hours for him too. And to complicate matters further, his daughter had just phoned him and had blubbed about falling in love with some blighter called Roger. It was most out of character for a neo-cyber Goth.

Then there was this Gabbitt fellow - the perpetrator of so many crimes back in the UK and an international terrorist. The swine had actually helped save those people on the boat. Villains were not like that. Pringle thought hard.

Then there was the Chinese police. They had nabbed Gabbitt for something that clearly was not his fault. It was just not right. Not fair. Not cricket. Not English.

Something would have to be done, decided Pringle and reached for his small tape recorder. On a silly whim, he pushed the Fast Forward button so that he could pick a song at random. He hit the Play button. A moment later and Jon Anderson and Chris Squire were screaming into his ears that 'yours in no disgrace'.

"I should cocoa," said Pringle and supped hard at his beer.

Several thousand miles away in Wormwood Scrubs prison, Nero Handsworth was enjoying a fat cigar with two other elderly inmates.

"Best day of my life," said Nero, honestly.

"You must have had a sad life,' said a bald man with a twitch under his left eye.

"So, you've met my wife then," chortled Nero happily through a cloud of blue smoke.

"How can anyone have their best day in a place like this?" asked the third member of the group, a large man with a moustache and a sweaty face.

"How indeed?' responded a smug Nero. "You will never know."

"You getting out of here soon?" asked the first man.

"Much better than that," replied Nero, through more cigar smoke.

"Better?" queried the fat man in total bewilderment. "Britney Spears is coming for conjugal rights... even though she's not married to you?"

"Much better," said Nero in a far-off voice.

"Amanda Holden?"

"No."

"Not Kate flippin' Beckinsale. Please not her."

"Oh, much, much better," murmured Nero.

"Nothing can be better than that, surely," sighed the large man with the sweat. "Oh god," he said suddenly. "Not all three at the same time."

"No."

"So, what is it then, Nassington, you bastard?" asked the bald man with the twitch.

"What comes on a dish served cold?" asked Nero.

"Blancmange," said the fat man after a thoughtful pause.

"No, I'm being metaphoric," said Nero, quietly.

"Meta what?" asked the fat man, thickly.

"Quiche?" tried the bald man. "Cream caramel?"

Nero Handsworth sighed and put his cigar down. He then leant forward and whispered slowly: "Revenge."

"Ah," sighed both of the other men, as they instantly understood their companion's glee. That was infinitely better than Britney, Amanda, Kate, blancmange, quiche and crème caramel.

The object of Nero's revenge sat tied to a chair in a small locked room somewhere on the Isle of Dogs. Gilbert Grimm was wide-eyed and almost beyond help. He had been sitting in this dark and silent room and was beginning to feel extremely desperate.

It all seemed somewhat over-the-top to punish him like this, when his only transgression had been to imitate an agent at a workshop in Shanghai. He would never have guessed that such a crime could carry such a heavy penalty.

The journey back from Heathrow had not improved his mood either. To be truthful, his captors had seemed similarly uncomfortable, as that appalling taxi driver droned on for what seemed like hours on end. The driver had only finally stopped talking after Chipchase had thrown up over the passenger head rest after a harrowing story involving 'number twos' in Waitrose shopping bags.

What was he to do? He was back in England without any of his treasured possessions and sitting in a locked room somewhere in London. Gilbert Grimm trembled from head to toe, whimpered slightly and wet himself for the ninth time since his abduction.

He would probably have wet himself for the tenth, eleventh and twelfth time had he known that not a hundred yards away in various hidden locations were Fred the Throttler, the Shotgun Sisters, Slicing Sammy, Barry the Bagman, Stabbing Sid, Three-Knives-Nigel and 'The Bear'.

And unknown to all of them was the fact that DC Ford was sitting in an unmarked white Ford Transit with three distinctly civilian companions.

"Percy's in that warehouse?" asked Caroline, in disbelief.

"Taken in there ten minutes ago by a couple of known villains," replied Ford, knowledgeably.

"But I thought he was in China," said a man in a panda suit, with its head on his lap.

"Got whisked back here by these two for reasons unknown," replied Ford. "A least that's what we think. Difficult to tell though given the confusing reports from over there in China. My guv' says Gabbitt's still over there, but we can't be sure. He could have a body-double, you know, like Hitler or Stalin. But we'll find out soon enough what's going down."

"Percy's got a body-double like Hitler or Stalin?" asked Dave Springett, in awe.

"It's been known," replied Ford.

"Pardon me for asking, but why did you have us brought here?" asked Joe Slimm, still in his faded corduroy teacher's jacket. "Gave everyone a very nasty shock at the school, when one of your cars showed up for me, with the lights and sirens on. My kudos with 5C will have soared, I reckon," he finished with a wry smile.

"Thought it was the least I could do after my deception in Dark Dawn Three. Can't tell you how sorry I am about the whole thing. Just not good to try to fool fell quest members like that. I thought you three might like to be around when we rescue Roger... I mean Gabbitt...Percy."

"Or his body-double."

"Indeed."

"We're not expected to do anything though, are we?" asked Springett, hopefully.

"Goodness me no," replied Ford. The last thing he wanted was a man dressed as a headless panda wandering around his crime scene. He sighed and stared at the floor of the van. "Just can't tell you how sorry I am," he repeated, overplaying his apology a little.

"Oh, don't worry about that," said Springett. "Stuff like that happens all the time in fantasy land."

"But I'm usually a pretty straight-down-the-line man," continued Ford, seriously. "I've never tried to fox comrades in arms before."

"I think you're taking it a bit too seriously," said Slimm. "It's just a bit of fun."

"Not to me," persisted Ford. "Reminded me that honour and companionship are more important than anything."

"Oh dear," said Caroline. "It's really bitten you, hasn't it?"

"What do you mean?" asked a bewildered Ford.

"It happens quite often to new games players. Once in, it becomes an obsession for a few months. Drives you potty and generally takes over your life."

"That won't happen to me," said Ford firmly. "But," he added after a pause. "Can Obby join you on your next quest?"

Caroline smiled and was about to answer when Ford's radio crackled into life. It appeared that something was about to happen.

Ford picked up his radio and whispered last instructions to the occupants of five other unmarked vans dotted around the warehouse. The Grey Hippo and Wild Elephant squads were about to be unleashed.

It promised to be an interesting afternoon on the Isle of Dogs, east London.

A few hundred miles away as the crow flies, Bob Brand and Jack Melligan were stepping onto a helicopter and preparing themselves for the short ride back to the mainland from a particularly sunny Scilly Isles.

"That shocked him," said a chuckling Melligan. "Never seen a man more shocked in my life. Thought he was going to have a heart attack."

"He did seem a little... amazed," agreed Brand.

"A little amazed? The man had to sit down for a few minutes with his head between his legs," chuckled Melligan.

"Well, it would shock most people, I think."

"His wife seemed happy."

"I think they both will be, after the shock has worn off."

"So," said Melligan, after a short pause as the helicopter began cranking up its rotors. "What now?"

"The difficult bit," said Brand, rubbing his hands together. "Should be fun. I've never done anything like this before."

"Beats me what we are expected to do with fifty-six oil paintings, which we have just purchased for eighty thousand pounds of Arapacana's money," said Melligan, shaking his head slowly.

"I think that life is going to get extremely interesting for the two of us," said Brand with a twinkle in his eye.

Inspector Zhang sat in the front passenger seat of the lead squad car as it wailed through the early morning suburbs of Suzhou. He was both happy and angry at the same time. True, he had the main culprit of the riverboat fiasco securely trussed up the back seat of his car and true, he had also arrested the porn DVD purveyor. Sort of nice and unexpected way of killing two birds with one stone, he had initially thought.

But, it was not all peaches and cream for Zhang as he stared out at the empty streets of his city. The early morning raid on the headquarters of this villain's empire, had been a singular failure. Reports just coming in were sketchy, but what was undeniably true was that the large warehouse offices of the Arapacana agency had simply disappeared.

First officers on the scene had found that the place had been stripped bare with not even a scrap of paper left behind. It was all extremely vexing and odd.

And the remaining three delegates attending this workshop – those same three who had nonchalantly walked past him airily chatting about hot baths, balloons and such-like, had checked out of the hotel and disappeared as well. It was all distinctly annoying.

But, sighed Zhang, as he looked round to check the back seat, he did have an ace in his hand. He had their ring leader in his hands. He smiled slowly. Perhaps life was not that bad after all.

Percy Gabbitt thought it was though. Sitting in handcuffs and racing towards Suzhou in a siren-wailing police car was not how he had intended to spend his last evening at the workshop in Shanghai.

He frowned and looked out of the window as the police car sped over a bridge and into central Suzhou. Ahead of him in the early morning light, Gabbitt could just make out a high wall and a guard turret manned by a man in a peaked hat and holding an extremely large gun.

# The End

## of

# Friend of China

### (The Marketeer: Three)

# EPILOGUE

And that's about it.

The spit clock registers that it's four in the afternoon and from my window I can see that the rain clouds are starting to gather.
A small tear forms in my eye.
I bite my bottom lip which starts to tremble.

It's then that I hear a voice.

**The Marketeer Series continues with:**

# The Long Road Home

(The Marketeer: Four)

www.ingramcontent.com/pod-product-compliance
Lightning Source LLC
Chambersburg PA
CBHW070539030726
47505CB00001B/89

*9780244864446*